The Dreamless

Other books by Jen Williams

The Sleepless

Published 2026 by First Ink,
an imprint of Pan Macmillan
The Smithson, 6 Briset Street, London EC1M 5NR
EU representative: Macmillan Publishers Ireland Ltd, 1st Floor,
The Liffey Trust Centre, 117–126 Sheriff Street Upper, Dublin 1 D01 YC43
Associated companies throughout the world

ISBN 978-1-0350-5808-2 Hardback
ISBN 978-1-0350-5809-9 Paperback

Text copyright © Jen Williams 2026

The right of Jen Williams to be identified as the author of this work has been
asserted in accordance with the Copyright, Designs and Patents Act 1988.

All rights reserved. No part of this publication may be reproduced,
stored in a retrieval system, or transmitted, in any form, or by any means
(including, without limitation, electronic, mechanical, photocopying, recording
or otherwise) without the prior written permission of the publisher.

Pan Macmillan does not have any control over, or any responsibility for,
any author or third-party websites (including, without limitation, URLs,
emails and QR codes) referred to in or on this book.

1 3 5 7 9 8 6 4 2

A CIP catalogue record for this book is available from the British Library.

Printed and bound in the UK using 100% Renewable Electricity by CPI Group (UK) Ltd

This book is sold subject to the condition that it shall not, by way of trade or otherwise,
be lent, hired out, or otherwise circulated without the publisher's prior consent in any
form of binding or cover other than that in which it is published and without a similar
condition including this condition being imposed on the subsequent purchaser.
The publisher does not authorize the use or reproduction of any part of this book in
any manner for the purpose of training artificial intelligence technologies or systems.
The publisher expressly reserves this book from the Text and Data Mining exception in
accordance with Article 4(3) of the European Union Digital Single Market Directive 2019/790.

Visit **www.panmacmillan.com** to read more about all our books and to buy them.

For Jenni, ever a shining star in my personal constellation

PROLOGUE

At the beginning of all things

The crows kept up their rusty clatter, only growing louder and more insistent the deeper the two of them ventured into the sea of hawthorns.

It didn't bother the child. Very little did. Brishta, god of the dawn, balance and all things that shone, paused to hold a branch out of the way for him as they made their way down the narrow, twisting path. He had picked something up off the ground and wasn't looking where he was going, so intent was he on examining it. She smiled fondly.

'What have you got there, Tython?'

'I don't know, Mama.' He held it up for her to see: a small glossy brown object spotted with leaf litter. 'Isn't it fine, though?'

'Ah, it's a horse chestnut. Or a conker.' She looked around, but could see no such tree, just the twisted shapes of the trees that flooded *his* domain. A shadow threatened to pass over her heart, so she plucked the conker from her son's hand as they walked. Overhead, the clouds were dark and low, and she pictured the two of them as the crows might see them: a woman of golden hair and golden armour, and a boy with skin like polished marble – two points of light in a gloomy landscape. 'I wonder how it got here. They're the seeds of the horse chestnut tree, and, I agree, they are very fine.' The conker shone extra brightly in the palm of her hand, seemingly the only thing in that landscape with any light to it. 'There's a game you can play. Perhaps your father can show it to you. Or I could. You pass a thread through the middle, and then you strike your conker against another's, until one breaks.'

'Wouldn't that spoil it, Mama?' He looked up at her, concern on his face, and in an instant the shadow in Brishta's heart was back. For a horrible, razor-sharp moment, she teetered on the edge of tears. He was perfect. Such a beautiful, kind-hearted, perfect child. He was everything they had hoped he would be, everything the child of two gods should be, and yet . . .

Brishta squeezed the conker tight in the palm of her hand, focusing on the little knot of pain it produced, and forced herself to smile. As she did so, the sun briefly appeared from between the clouds.

'It's just a game, Tython. If we find a conker tree, you'll see, there will be hundreds of conkers to play with.'

'But this one feels precious,' he said, taking it back as she held it out to him. Brishta slid a hand over his golden head, his hair as cool as silk between her fingers.

'Yes,' she agreed, looking at him. 'It does.'

They continued in silence for a little way. It was possible now to see the dark towers they were heading towards, their needle-fine points disappearing into the cloud overhead. It was so different from her domain. Where Brishta lived, the sun soaked all things, and the sky was thick with birds of all colours. Here, there were only crows, and hawthorn trees, and a growing sense of dread.

'What is this place, Mama?'

'I told you, darling, remember? This is the domain of one of our brother gods. We're going to pay him a visit. And ask him for a favour.'

'Oh.' He opened his mouth to say something else, but instead a cough ambushed him, deep and rattling and too big for his small frame. The boy bent double with the violence of it, and she held him until it passed, her own heart thudding sickeningly in her chest.

No, she thought fiercely for the thousandth time. *He is a child of gods! I will not stand for it.*

When they reached the threshold of the first and largest tower, they paused. The lintel was hung with dried herbs, giving the air a spicy, medicinal scent that set Brishta's nerves on edge. Up close, it was possible to see that each giant block of black stone that formed the towers was covered in fossils: bones of things long dead pressed into an eternal stillness. Tython ran his fingers over them. The skin around the boy's eyes was dark with exertion, and tiny beads of sweat marked his forehead.

'What are these things, Mama?'

'Don't worry about them. These are just how my brother chooses to decorate his domain.' She took a deep breath. 'Now then, Tython, I want you to be brave for me. Can you do that? Remember, even when there's darkness all around, the light is still with us.'

The boy nodded. Brishta went to knock on the door, but it swung open before her knuckles could make contact. Inside, there was a vast chamber of grey stone. The walls were lined with tall figures carved from yellowed bone, their arms crossed over their chests and their eyes shut. Each head brushed the ceiling. In the centre of this open space, there was a simple red chair and on it sat a hooded figure. A long bone-coloured beak protruded from its cowl.

'Sister,' said the figure. The Hooded Crow's voice was warm. This, Brishta knew, was the last thing mortals expected from the god of death, medicine and herbs. 'I receive so few visitors. How good it is to see you, and young Tython there.'

The boy was pressed against her legs, terrified.

'I want you to look at him.' Brishta had intended to sweet-talk the crow, to exchange the usual godly pleasantries of the Twelve, but all at once she couldn't stand to wait any more. This had been hanging over them all for too long. 'He's not himself and I . . . I want you to look at him.'

She propelled the boy forward, too aware of how the pair of them stuck out in this strange, silent room. She was wearing her gold plate, so bright and glittering even in the gloom, and the boy, even diminished as he was, shone like a freshly minted coin. The Hooded Crow was a thing of dust and shadows, and when he stood to meet them – looming much too tall – Brishta felt some of her own courage falter.

'Mama . . .'

'Just be still, Tython. For me.'

A long bony hand emerged from the Hooded Crow's sleeve, and although he didn't touch the boy, his fingers drifted through the air directly over his head. Within the hood, Brishta could see the faintest suggestion of two black eyes, wet and lidless.

'Well?'

The Hooded Crow hesitated.

'Perhaps you should send the boy away for a moment . . .'

'No. Speak it. Tell me.'

There was a beat of silence, and in it Brishta could hear the crows calling again.

'He is dying,' said the Hooded Crow. 'But you knew this, sister.'

'Then take it back. Make it stop.' Tython pressed himself to her legs again, making a small noise of anguish, but she had no time for it. 'This is your domain, isn't it? This is your power, isn't it? He's a god. A child of gods. How can he be dying? How can he even be ill?'

The Hooded Crow shook what passed for his head. 'Some things are bigger even than us. You are the god of light, Brishta, but you can't knock the sun from the sky.'

'What does that even mean?' She was raising her voice and

frightening Tython, but she couldn't stop herself. 'He is perfect. How can he be dying? *Why?*'

The Hooded Crow looked again at the child. To her growing fury, she sensed he was trying to be kind.

'It is in the nature of some things,' he said eventually. 'It is his fate, you might say. Even the gods don't stand outside the realm of fate, sister.'

She swore loudly then, the forbidden word bouncing around the walls of the Hooded Crow's sanctum like a trapped bird. Tython was very still; she could tell that she'd briefly startled him out of his fright.

'It is his nature,' the Hooded Crow repeated. 'I cannot change it.'

'Then I will.'

Brishta knelt and wrapped her arms round her boy, burying her nose in his hair and breathing in the scent of him. He was so thin, so fragile, and it made her want to squeeze him all the tighter. It had to be possible, she thought, to squeeze this fate out of him, like poison from a snake bite. The Hooded Crow was watching her carefully.

'What do you mean?' he asked warily.

'I am a god,' she said tersely. 'I will change him.'

'That's not within your power, Brishta. Your realm is that of light, the dawn, of beginnings and hope.'

'*Beginnings* and *hope*,' Brishta spat. 'What use are those things if they cannot save him? No. I can change him.'

'Change him?' For the first time, the Hooded Crow sounded irritated. 'How much will you have to change him to save him, sister? At what point will he stop being Tython?'

The boy shivered in her arms, as though rousing himself from a deep sleep.

'Mama,' he said, 'can we go home now? Don't be upset, please. I feel quite well—'

'Quiet, Tython.' Her arms coiled round him tighter, holding him still. She lifted her head to address the Hooded Crow. 'If you won't help him, you useless old bird, I will do what I have to do.'

'And what of your husband? Do you think that the god of purity will approve of what you plan to do to his son?'

'Trilot will do anything to save Tython.' As she spoke the words, Brishta realized she didn't really believe that – there was a coldness to her husband, a shard of clear glass deep inside that would cut before it would break. And what she planned to do would strike against everything Trilot stood for.

'Brishta—'

'Enough. We are leaving.'

She shunted Tython towards the doors, which were still standing open, looking out onto the dense landscape of thorns and cloud. As they left, the giant bone figures by the walls turned their heads to follow their progress, and behind them she felt the regard of the Hooded Crow, those lidless black eyes judging her. She vowed then that she would cause trouble for him one day, somehow – a little shard of gratitude for his refusal to help, and his judgement. It was an easy promise to make to herself.

When they were outside again and the doors had closed behind them, Brishta took her son's hand and squeezed it, giving him her brightest smile. The boy regarded her warily.

'Mama, what is happening?'

'Never you mind. Come on. Let's see if we can find another conker to match your first. Then we can play.'

CHAPTER 1

The moon was as bright as Elver had ever seen it, a perfect silver coin in the night sky. She felt the back of her neck prickle as they skirted the path to Sunay's cottage; anyone could see them if they cared to look. She imagined Maura's acolytes hiding behind the tall forms of the chestnut trees, and her poison blood teemed in response.

'There aren't any lights on,' Lucian said quietly. 'I don't imagine Sunay to have the sense to sit in the dark.'

'She's more sensible than she looks.' She glanced at him, picked out as he was in tones of silver and grey. He wore Artair's face – handsome and serious, with a long straight nose and the slash of a scar through his eyebrow – and Artair's body – tall and lean and broad-shouldered – but, as ever when Lucian was home, he moved and spoke like a different person. *Because he is a different person*, she reminded herself. He was sharper somehow, his movements more precise. He'd taken to wearing his hair pulled back in a tail too, making him look sleek and contained.

When they reached the door she rapped on it with her knuckles, wincing at even this soft noise. Somewhere in the trees behind the cottage – where the real temple of Tisk the trickster god waited – an owl hooted as if in response.

Nothing happened. There was no sound from inside, and no lights blossomed into being beyond the windows. Elver eyed the sign on the door. It said: *Sorry, Tisk is closed for business! See you soon!* A fox had been painted under the words in gold.

She knocked again, a touch louder. When Sunay failed to

materialize for a second time, Lucian sighed – a little dramatically, in Elver's opinion. She slipped her hand into her pocket and found the conker she had picked up the first time they had visited Sunay's little cottage. Then, she and Artair had been desperately seeking help from a mage in the hope that an illusion spell could outwit Maura, and the shiny chestnut had reminded her of home. It still gave her that warm feeling of comfort.

'She said she'd be here. She said she had something to tell us.'

'She is a mage dedicated to the god of lies,' said Lucian. 'I'd take everything she says with a pinch of salt.' His tone was sarcastic, but she saw him look over his shoulder at the dark behind them. He was worried too.

'Whether she's here or not, we need to get inside.' Elver put her shoulder to the door, and gave it a sharp shove. The cottage was old and she suspected the lock wasn't in the best shape, but she still felt a little shiver of mingled fright and satisfaction at how easily it gave way. Since the Queen of Serpents had replaced Elver's heart – giving her, technically, her third attempt at life – she was stronger than she had once been.

They stepped inside, the shop bell jingling into the dark. Around them, the various wares of Tisk's temple glinted in the moonlight coming in through the windows. Moving quietly, they searched the cottage – the cosy little room where she and Artair had once drunk tea with Sunay, the chaotic kitchen, the upstairs rooms. One of these had a number of god-tithes hanging from the ceiling, and she noticed Lucian thinning his lips in recognition; of course, he had been bound and locked in this room, once, before the three of them had formed their uneasy truce.

'The magpie isn't here,' he said needlessly.

'There must be something wrong. Or she was delayed.' Elver thought of the mage and the young keltraxia cub, out in the night somewhere. 'Still, we know this place is safe, right? We can at least sleep here, and wait for her a little while.'

Lucian gave a sceptical snort at the idea of sleep, but otherwise didn't comment.

Elver made tea in the cramped kitchen, then brought it up to the bedroom that looked out over the path. Lucian was standing by the window.

'I could use magic to find out where they are.'

Now it was Elver's turn to snort. 'That has worked well for you so far.'

He gave her a sharp look. 'It will work eventually, monster girl. I can feel it, burning under my skin.' He held up his hands, and in the darkness she could see a faint red glow around them, like the embers of a dying fire. The colour of it – red as blood – made her think of Prideful Leap, where she had been forced to stand in a pool of blood to be sacrificed to a god. Mother Maura had intended to take that power for herself, to knock the Bloody Claw from his place amongst the Twelve, but the power had been split, part of it siphoned instead into Lucian. Now, the Bloody Claw's essence coiled within him, hot and unstable. And unusable, it seemed. 'I just need to . . . I just need to figure out how to use what my lord gave me.'

Elver shrugged and sat cross-legged on the bed, a cup of tea cradled in her hands. 'Sure. Knock yourself out. But draw the curtain first. You'll light this place up like a beacon.'

He drew the curtain – a little more tersely than was necessary – and sat on the other side of Sunay's wide, plush bed. He cupped his hands in front of him, and the red light that moved restlessly over them grew brighter, bathing his face in a ruby glow.

'How do you know what to do?'

'I don't,' he snapped. 'That's the problem. When I was a mage, before I was trapped in this idiot monk's body, I asked my god for boons, and provided the tithes he required. Then the power would be mine.'

Elver narrowed her eyes at him, but he was too busy looking at the ruby light. Once, *she* had been a tithe for the Bloody Claw, and it had been Lucian who had delivered her to that fate.

'Now, though,' he continued, 'the power is already here, inside me, but it is . . . unwilling to do what I wish. It's like it doesn't recognize my right to use it.'

'That power is used to being inside a giant lion made of stolen flesh,' said Elver. She took a sip of her tea. 'It's probably wondering how it ended up inside a stringy teenage boy.'

'Stringy?' Lucian looked up at her, one eyebrow raised, and she felt her cheeks turn pink. 'I've seen how you look at this body, Elver. I don't think stringy is the word you'd really use.'

She turned away, glad that her face was hidden in shadows. What would Artair say if he heard that?

Lucian continued talking. 'I suspect you're not far off, though. I need the power to know that it is rightfully mine, and it should obey my commands. Without the tithe granting me validation . . .'

'What? Do you need to sacrifice things to yourself now?'

He ignored that. Instead, he brought his hands slowly apart, pulling the red light between them like raw wool on a spindle. Threads of magic began to circle in the gap he'd created, a tiny whirlpool, and shadows coalesced between them. Shapes almost like figures began to appear.

'It's working.' He spoke through gritted teeth.

Elver shuffled closer, her tea forgotten. It was like looking into the surface of a dark pond, where the reflections were painted in blood. She almost believed she recognized the shapes that moved there – surely that lithe shape was Fleet – but it was confusing, stormy. Lucian, meanwhile, was shaking with the effort. Tiny beads of sweat had popped into being on his forehead.

'Be careful,' she said. When he didn't respond, she reached out and touched his knee. 'You know what happened last time.'

'No. It's *working*. Look. Can you see?' He grimaced with the effort. 'Can you see where they are?'

'I can't even tell if it's really them. It's too messy, Lucian.'

'Wait! No, gods damn it . . .'

The whirlpool of magic blinked out of existence, plunging them into the dark, and Lucian pitched forward, all the strength gone from him. Elver, slopping her remaining tea over the bedspread, grabbed him with her free arm and shook him by the shoulder. For a dangerous moment, his eyes were unfocused.

'Lucian! Are you alright?'

He placed his hand over hers and held it there. Since he had recovered his memories, her poisonous touch no longer revealed the ones Maura had taken from Lucian before casting him out of his own body. It meant that this kind of casual touch from him was more common, a fact that quietly pleased her.

'I'm fine,' he said. His voice was hoarse, as though he'd been shouting for hours.

'Every time you try to use the Bloody Claw's power, it wipes you out.' She realized she sounded angry. 'It's dangerous.'

'Better I try it, then, when I have you here to look after me, monster girl.' He dropped her hand and stretched out on the bed, his feet sticking out over the end. Sunay was a good foot shorter than Artair. 'I don't understand it. When we were in Prideful Leap, I summoned that portal as easy as breathing. But now when I reach for the power it's slippery. Like trying to mould water into a shape with your hands.'

'What was different then?' Thinking about that time gave Elver a slightly cold feeling. When Lucian and Artair had passed through the portal, they had been carrying her body.

'I don't know. We were all about to die? I only know that I had a control that I don't seem to have now.'

'Maybe humans aren't meant to have this power,' said Elver. 'And if you're struggling with it maybe that means Maura is too.'

Lucian raised his eyebrows.

'Gods, let's hope so. We need every advantage we can get.' He sighed. 'If I had my own body, my old body, perhaps the magic would respond better. The monk is no mage. Perhaps the Bloody Claw's power knows it, and is insulted to find itself in such a place. I know I am.' He yawned hugely. 'Gods, I'm knackered. I need to sleep.' He gave a bitter laugh at that. 'What passes for sleep for me, anyway. You should rest too. We've been walking for hours.'

'I will in a bit.'

He lifted his head. 'You'll force yourself to stay awake. For *him*.'

'Artair needs to know what's going on.' It was too dark to see the expression on his face, but she could feel Lucian's disapproval like brushing her hand against the thorns of a blackberry bush. 'Go to sleep. We'll keep watch.'

For a second, it looked as though he might say something more, but in the end he let his head drop to the pillow.

A few moments after that, Artair opened his eyes and sat up carefully. All Artair's movements were careful, considered: the movements of a person who had spent much of his life training his body with exercise and meditation. It was one of the ways she told them apart.

'We're at Tisk's place? Where is Sunay?'

'That's the question, isn't it?' She put her tea down on the bedside table and shuffled a little closer to him. 'No sign of her or Tisk. It could be she's just been delayed somewhere, or Fleet has caused trouble. That's what he's good at, after all.'

'She said she had news.' Artair's hand drifted to the cord holding his hair back, and he tugged it free with a little flicker of irritation. His dark brown hair fell loose to his shoulders.

'Lucian tried to find her using the magic, but . . .' She lifted her hands and then dropped them. 'It almost looked like it was going to work for a second.'

Artair stood up from the bed and moved over to the window, his movements as graceful as ever. Elver tried to ignore the little shard of sorrow that blossomed in her chest. When she had returned to them from the sea at the edge of the shadow realm, she and Artair had kissed under the trees. The memory of it was still incredibly vivid to her – the softness of his lips, the scent of his body, the sheer warmth of him – but to Artair it almost seemed to have never happened at all. She wondered now if he'd only kissed her because moments before he'd believed her dead, and if, now that they were back in the world, travelling together, he realized he'd made a mistake. And who could blame him? She thought of her new strength, her new powers. She grew stranger by the day.

'I wonder what it was she wanted to tell us.' Artair used one finger to pull the curtain back a few inches and a slice of moonlight touched Elver where she sat on the bed. He stood up a little straighter. 'Elver, there's a light by the trees opposite. It's moving.'

She joined him at the window. Sure enough, almost dwarfed by the glow of the moon, there was a small yellow light moving at around the height someone would carry an oil lamp. Her new senses prickled: an awareness of danger, sharper than a hunch and less familiar – this was how a monster in the Jih Forest felt when they caught scent of a human. She shivered, trying to ignore the sensation.

'It's them,' she said, already backing away from the window. 'Shit, how did they find us again so quickly?'

'You're sure?'

'As sure as I need to be to say we have to get out of here now.'

But he was already gathering his things up from where Lucian had left them. Elver grabbed a pencil from Sunay's desk and wrote a few words on a scrap of paper – where they might go next, where Sunay might meet them.

'If you leave that here, they'll just find us again. You could hide it, but . . .' He looked around at the shelves full of junk that lined every wall. 'She might never find it.'

'I'm not a complete fool, Artair.' She pursed her lips. The truth was, she'd had an idea, and the moment it had formed in her head it had become irresistible. And that sudden need to act frightened her.

On one of the shelves there was a small plant growing out of a pot, a slightly sickly-looking thing with tiny green leaves. Elver slid the rolled-up scrap of paper into the soil from which it was growing.

'What are you doing?'

Elver hesitated. She had used this strange new ability a couple of times now; every time, it was exhilarating, frightening, and slightly out of her control.

She touched a finger to the dying plant. 'Grow,' she told it. 'Change.'

At once, the plant did as she commanded. The tiny leaves grew long and glossy, and fresh buds burst into life, opening fleshy pink and purple blooms; each flower had a spiky green tongue. Elver knew from looking at it that no plant exactly like this had existed before. This was perhaps the strangest of the Queen of Serpents' gifts, and the most alarming. It was like flexing a new muscle; it felt satisfying, yet the sight of the newly jih plant frightened her deeply. Her god had told her that she would be less human than ever, but she hadn't thought to mention that she'd be changing the world around her too.

What did the Queen of Serpents do to me? What has this new heart got to do with it all?

Artair's hand brushed her arm.

'Are you okay?'

She forced herself to smile past the fright. 'I'm fine. Although I think it was easier when my touch just poisoned things.'

'It's a good idea. Sunay will certainly know you've been here when she sees it.' He looked back towards the window, and the moment passed. 'We should hurry.'

CHAPTER 2

It was almost exactly the same as it had been back then. Almost. This was the thought that had haunted Maura since she had arrived in her own godly realm.

The little brick house sat at the back of the field, ringed by the wonky fenceposts Maura's husband had made, the crooked chimney pointing towards the mountain that loomed behind it – this was before the mountain had been shattered in a magical war, pulverizing the little brick house into a pile of rubble and horror. When her home had been real, they had planted all kinds of things in the field – beans, peas, carrots, daffodils, even corn – joking that eventually they wouldn't have to go to the village for food at all. Now, in this strange, broken domain, the field grew only grass. When she woke in their old bed – because she still needed to sleep, despite her supposed god status – the space next to her was always warm, as though her husband had just slipped out of it. Sometimes, she found herself lying there with one hand resting on that faint, warm patch, watching the door. *Any moment,* she would tell herself, *he'll come back in. And he'll be holding them in his arms.*

She stood by the front door, looking out across the grass. The other clue that this wasn't the home she had lived in thirty years ago was the way the world faded to nothing beyond the field. A mist began at the fenceposts and then grew thicker and thicker until there was simply a wall of white. The only thing that existed beyond her home was the mountain, a fact that caused her to smile bitterly – of course the mountain would be here. There was never any escaping it. Not for her.

The high merry sound of children's laughter floated over the fenceposts and Maura felt her whole body go tense. The laughter of children should have been a sweet sound, it should have been a treasured memory, but somehow it felt like a threat.

She turned away and headed back inside, closing the door firmly behind her.

When she had been a mage dedicated to that charlatan Tisk the Trickster, she had done much of her work in a small room just off the kitchen, and that was still there, her ratty old desk taking up most of the space, bunches of dried herbs hanging from the windowsill so that she could always smell mint and sage while she worked. And now she was a god, this was still where she spent much of her time.

She sat down at the desk, running her fingers over its scratched surface, and sighed. They were waiting for her. She could feel it.

'Speak.'

At once, a tiny human figure appeared on the desktop, no taller than the span of her hand. It wore practical travelling clothes and a red hood, on the back of which had been embroidered two white circles, one sitting within the other – this was the sigil her followers had chosen for her. It meant 'Mother'.

The tiny figure offered up his tithe: a scrap of paper, childish words written upon it in thick crayon. It appeared briefly in front of her – the child who had written the note had scrawled: 'The Mother blesses us all with her love' – and then shivered out of existence. She gestured to him to continue. A woman in his village was worried about her son, he told her, who had married a girl who wasn't, in her opinion, good enough for him – was there anything the Mother could do?

Maura nodded, and reached out a hand to the figure, touching the top of his hooded head with the tip of her finger. There was a faint glow as the magic he'd requested passed to him, and an answering shard of pain blossomed in her chest.

When that mage disappeared, satisfied, another appeared in his place, and again she accepted the tithe, listened, nodded and granted the power. Again, her heart seemed to try to pull itself apart when she did so.

By the fifth mage, she felt a thin layer of sweat break out across her brow and back, and a dark little smile visited her lips. She was a *god*, one of the Twelve, and all this power cost her was agony and exhaustion. She had always thought that the tithes were what the gods fed on, a kind of spiritual food, yet when she consumed the offerings her mages brought her, she felt nothing at all – they certainly did nothing to cancel out the pain of giving away her power.

When her hands started to shake, she stood up from the desk, breathing hard. There were still supplicants waiting, their fierce need grasping at her like the small, sweaty hands of children, but she had nothing left to give – not without a rest, at least. Instead of retreating to her old bedroom, though – with that faint, ghostly warmth on the mattress – she went to another door. This one had never existed in their old house, and when she stepped through it, she found herself standing on a bleak shore, under a bone-coloured sun. This was the space between the mortal realm and the shadowed lands, the place where the gods could be summoned.

'I want an audience.' When the wind snatched the words away from her mouth, she raised her voice. 'I demand you speak to me! Any of you. Or are you afraid?'

The twelve totems poking out of the surf glistened in the pale light, the silver sea surging around them. The axe that had once represented the Bloody Claw had finally fallen into the water, lost to view, but the others were still there: the shining trident for Trilot the Faceless; the mirror of black glass for the Queen of Serpents; a clay heart for the Threshold; a smiling wooden mask for Tisk the Trickster, painted all over with autumn leaves. Her own totem, the toy bear that had once belonged to her youngest, was still missing its pearl button eyes.

'Well? Are any of you brave enough to face me?'

The wind surged, blowing her long white hair across her face. When she'd impatiently pushed it back out of her eyes, several strange figures had appeared on the shoreline. One of them at least was unmistakable to her, his orange beard and sharp eyes spoke too strongly of the fox for him to be anyone else.

'Mother,' said Tisk, granting her a quick grin that promised both merriment and violence. 'Struggling with godhood, are we?'

The others just stood watching her, and Maura had to fight against the feeling of superstitious awe that threatened to overwhelm her. These were them, the other gods. Not all of them; no Hooded Crow, she could tell that at a glance, and no Queen of Serpents, but a handful of the others. Here was a figure that had to be Lady Dusk, the god of divination, endings and secrets; she was a tall, willowy woman dressed in owl feathers, a beaked cap on her head covering her long dark hair. Next to her stood a woman with blue skin and three heads, all facing different directions, and beneath her voluminous skirts the toes of six feet poked out – Enos, the god of sleep and dreams. Standing slightly apart from those two was a broad, handsome man with a beard of fire, which had to be Barleycorn, god of the hearth. Strangest of all was a floating cloud of wolf heads, every set of glowing yellow eyes trained on her. This, she assumed, was the Pack. Maura cleared her throat.

'I am one of you now. There's no denying it. I have my own domain, and I can gift my power to the mages dedicated to me, just as the Bloody Claw did to me, once. Just as Tisk did, once.' She threw him a barbed glance. 'I see so much. I know so much. And I feel it.' She pressed a hand to her chest, where the boiling heat of the Bloody Claw's stolen power waited, just under the surface. She wanted nothing from the gods, after they'd failed her for so long. Yet she had to ask. 'But using this power pains me. It exhausts me. Why?'

'You know why,' said Tisk.

'That boy has the tiniest fraction of my power,' she snapped. It was infuriating that Lucian continued to vex her, years after she had cast his soul from his body. 'A pathetic little scrap, thrown to him by a dying idiot. *I* am a god. *He* is a mistake. I must be doing it wrong.'

'You misunderstand.' Lady Dusk's voice was soft and not without kindness. 'You are no true god. Not while you're incomplete. In this moment, you are a broken vessel. The tithes do not feed you as they feed us, so every boon you grant saps your strength.'

Maura closed her hands into fists. 'What do you mean, *I am no god*? I'm here, aren't I?' She pointed to her totem in the surf. 'The Mother stands as one of the Twelve. The people know it. The people worship me. They love me.'

'Ah, the people. Whoever thought it was a good idea to listen to them?' Barleycorn laughed. 'Even the good ones are fools at heart. Show them a new, shiny thing and they'll flock after it, thinking it will solve all their problems, even when their problems are things they've created for themselves.' He chuckled fondly, shaking his head, then fixed her with a look that wasn't remotely friendly. 'You're a fad, woman. You won't last.'

'This is all beside the point,' said Tisk. He walked out of the surf, slipping into his fox form as he did so with a flash of orange light. 'I tried to tell you before, Mother, but listening was never your strong suit. While Lucian has that piece of the Bloody Claw's power, however small it is, you are a half-formed joke of a creature. You are just a vessel for the power, not a thing wrought from the power itself. So you can use it, you can pour it out of yourself, that power, but it is *not you*. Do you understand?'

Maura said nothing.

'You can feel yourself dying.' This was Enos, her three mouths speaking as one. 'I see it in your dreams, Mother. Every time you use your power, you're pouring a little piece of yourself away with it. It terrifies you.'

'Nonsense.' Maura took a step away from the shoreline. It was growing colder, the wind at her back picking up. 'You lie!'

'You feel nothing when you consume the tithes, am I right?' Barleycorn asked, then grinned when she didn't respond. 'I'm right.'

'Take the power back from the boy and you will be complete,' continued Enos, 'and you will be one of us. As much as that may sting us.' All three pairs of eyes glanced at Barleycorn, who was no longer smiling.

'There is another path,' said Tisk, his tail twitching.

'And what is that?'

'Renounce this nonsense. Give up your godhood. Return to being human and live out the rest of your life. You already know that this power can't give you what you want. Give it up.'

'She won't,' said Lady Dusk quietly.

Tisk continued as though the other god hadn't spoken. 'If you continue down this path, Mother, blithely passing out your power to every mage that asks, you will fritter away your godhood and eventually become nothing. Less than nothing. You'll die. Are you listening to me?'

Maura looked away from the fox to the silver horizon. Sometimes, when she was in the field outside her little house, she saw the ghostly shapes of children beyond the fence, running and laughing, chasing after each other. They looked to be made of the white mist that lay beyond her domain, and she couldn't see their faces, but she knew what they were. They were her madness given shape, and every day they drew a little closer to the house.

'I shouldn't be surprised that you won't help me,' she said. 'I'll always be an upstart to you, an interloper. But I *will* have what I want. Think of all that I have done already . . .' She looked at each of the gods in turn. From the unsettled looks on their faces, she knew that they were thinking of how their brother the Bloody Claw had died, choking on a poison sacrifice she had fed him. 'Ask yourselves if you'd rather have me as a friend, or an enemy.'

With that, she turned and walked away from the shoreline, heading towards the door to her kitchen, which still stood on the sand, a window onto another world.

Back at her workworn desk, she summoned Dalesh. The woman appeared, her red hood thrown back and her shoulders squared. Of all Mother's mages, Dalesh was the bravest, still able to face her without flinching, perhaps because she had known Maura the longest.

'They got away again, Mother,' she said. 'We tracked them to the Temple of Tisk, but they were already gone.'

Maura curled her lip at the mention of the fox's name.

'Never mind that now. Dalesh, my firstborn: from now on, you will be my chief mage. You are the only one I will grant my power to. Through you, I will enact my will. All other mages must stand aside.'

Although the figure was tiny, Maura could see the woman raise her eyebrows.

'It'll be my honour, Mother.'

'Instruct the priests to continue with the production of the tithes – it could be that they will still come in handy.' She took a deep breath. 'But for now I will gift you my power directly, from my heart to yours. You, Dalesh, will be my right hand. And, daughter, we have a lot of work to do.'

CHAPTER 3

Artair and Elver reached the Temple of Milik the Small the next morning and were relieved to find it deserted. Here, they could wait for Sunay in relative safety, and once they had her news they could decide what to do.

The building sat on the edge of a small lake, looking a little like a beehive with its squat shape and rounded walls, and through its many small round windows tiny birds flitted. Where its stones touched the green lake water, fish of all colours teemed, and on its roof sat a little statue of a mouse-like being in a robe. Artair looked at it for a moment, remembering the little figurines of Milik they had kept in the monastery kitchens – supposedly they kept the mice away from the food stores.

Elver sat herself at the edge of the water, some of the tension leaving her shoulders, and they waited, listening to the quiet chirps of the birds that seemed to be the only inhabitants of the temple. They did not speak much.

Artair found that his eyes were drawn to her as she looked out at the water. There was something different about Elver these days. Since she had returned to them from the shadow realm – *since she died*, he thought, *again* – she seemed both stranger and more changeable than she had been before, and he hadn't failed to notice that she was stronger and almost supernaturally alert to the dangers that surrounded them. He didn't know what had passed between her and the Queen of Serpents, but he suspected that was the source of these new changes.

'This lake is deep,' she said, her eyes unfocused.

Artair looked at the dark green water. All he could see was the sunlight dancing across the surface.

'You can tell?'

She shrugged. 'I can tell.'

They had both fallen into a state of lazy quiet when they heard Sunay, her voice full of its usual good cheer and at least three times louder than it needed to be. Elver stood up, smiling, and a moment later the mage emerged from the treeline.

'There you are!' Sunay grinned at them both, her dark eyes full of sunlight. She still had the fox tail the trickster god had given her, and she swished it from side to side as she trotted towards them. 'I found your note, Elver, very clever. Bit weird too, if I'm honest, but then I never could get that plant to thrive.' She embraced Artair, squeezing him round the middle in a way that made him laugh. 'Which of you is it?' she said, peering up at him. 'Well, I've hugged you, and you don't look like a cat that needs a shit, so I'm guessing . . . Artair?'

He laughed again. 'It's me, Sunay. I mean, yes, I'm Artair.'

Rather than hugging Elver, Sunay carefully took hold of her forearms, where they were covered by her sleeves, and gave them a little shake.

'I can't tell you how glad I am to see you both.'

'Likewise,' said Elver. 'But where is—'

A blue-and-red blur shot from the treeline and bounded up to them, yipping, before launching itself into Elver's arms. Despite her new-found strength, Elver nearly toppled backwards into the lake – Fleet looked to be almost twice as big as when they'd last seen him, his shoulders more muscular and his paws more in proportion to his body. The little keltraxia cub was growing up.

'Oof, you are too big!' Elver put him back on the ground, and for a few moments Fleet danced around her like a puppy, his green eyes flashing. 'He says he's a hunter now,' she said, translating for them the words only she could hear. 'He's hunted lots, apparently. Better than everyone else, he says.'

'Yes, Bawric tells me that the wolves were rather taken with the little tyke. Eventually.' Sunay reached down to brush an errant red feather from her skirts. 'I think they would have kept him there if they could.'

Fleet paused to sniff at Artair's boots, rub his head briefly against his knee, then trotted off to investigate the temple.

'I'm sorry to have missed you at home,' said Sunay. 'Here, let's rest and chat for a bit, shall we? Keeping up with Fleet has made my feet sore.'

Elver drew them back to the edge of the water – she did that often these days – and they sat.

'Maura's lot almost caught us at your cottage,' said Elver, her tone growing serious. It was a bright wintery day, and her white hair shone like polished silver. 'I suspect all the places we've been before aren't safe any more. Maura knows about you, Sunay, so she guessed we'd head back there.'

Artair thought of the monastery. He longed to go back, to see the other novices and check that they were all right, even to move them somewhere else, if they could. But he had no doubt Maura would have thought of this too. They had to keep moving; they had to keep safe. The power that Lucian carried within him – *within me*, he thought, feeling faintly queasy – meant that Maura would stop at nothing to kill them and take it back.

He pressed a hand to his chest. Sometimes he thought he could feel it, a banked heat that didn't belong. It felt dangerous. Not for the first time, he thought of how much easier his life would be if he could throw Lucian's spirit out.

'They can't have guessed we'd come here,' he said, nodding

towards the Temple of Milik the Small.

'Not many people come to her temples,' said Sunay. 'Her blessing isn't as vital as Barleycorn's, not as thrilling as the Threshold's.' She also nodded to the squat little building. 'No offence, Madam Mouse.'

'In your last message you said you had news?' asked Elver. 'I'm hoping it's something that'll help us figure out what to do about Maura.' She looked uneasily around the lake. 'We can't keep running forever.'

'Yes, and that was why I failed to meet you. I had work to do.' Sunay leaned forward and shrugged the pack off her back. 'And I have *fantastic* news. My lord has agreed to speak with us.'

Artair could tell that Sunay expected this pronouncement to be met with relief, possibly even cheering, but it was all he could do to keep from frowning. After all, Tisk had been the one to side with Lucian, freeing him so that he could escape across Tlevrae on his own dark mission while Artair had been kept bound in a closet. It seemed to him that the god of lies and deception was an uneasy ally.

'He has?' Elver also looked uncertain.

'Yes! Although of course I had to find the appropriate tithe for this particular boon, and that wasn't easy, let me tell you.' Sunay began pawing through her pack, delving past thick jumpers, packages of cheese, a hairbrush, little paper parcels marked 'kopi', and other things Artair could only guess at. Eventually, she pulled something white from the general mess and held it up. It was an elbow-length white glove.

Elver laughed. 'You took that from a Faceless priest?'

'It's true that my lord will take anything that rightfully belongs to another god, but I personally believe he especially likes it when I steal from Trilot, that pompous streak of bird shit.' She ran the silk garment between her fingers. 'Since we can't return to my beloved little cottage, we'll have to take this to one of my lord's sacred places and offer it to him there. I can't tell you for certain whether he will help us or not, but I think it's worth a try. Mother Maura's history with him means he'll certainly be interested, at least.'

'A place sacred to Tisk?' Elver frowned. 'You mean we'll have to go to another of his mages?'

'Oh no, we needn't concern ourselves with *those* charlatans,' said Sunay, cheerfully enough. 'Tisk has many sacred places, all of them secret, and I happen to know of one nearby. But that's not where we're going first.' Sunay stood up, stuffing the white glove back in her bag.

'It's not?' asked Artair.

'Nope. Before we do that, I have something absolutely horrifying to show you.' She reached a hand down to him, grinning. 'Won't that be fun?'

'Are we sure this is safe?'

They stood at the edge of the trees, looking up at the simple wooden building that sat at the top of the hill. It was so new that the wooden planks looked raw, the scent of sap still sharp in the air, and nearby there were men loading axes and hammers and other building materials into a cart. Over the lintel of the temple someone had painted, in a faintly unsteady hand, two white circles, one within the other.

When Sunay answered Artair, much of the cheeriness had gone from her voice. 'I believe so, yes. None of her mages are here. I passed it on the way to meet you both and gave it the once-over. These people . . .' She shrugged. 'These are just the people who worship her. Each of the temples functions as an orphanage too. You bring her your lost and abandoned children, and the Mother will care for them. Or so they believe.'

Elver felt that old anger beginning to build, coiling in her chest like the Queen herself. There were a number of people here, ordinary people with children in their arms, with carefully patched clothes and the lean physiques of farmers, and they were streaming in and out of the temple. Because that was what it was: a temple to the Mother, Maura's new godly form.

'Why are people such fools?' she hissed. She thought of Maura's hand gripping her shirt, the pitiless look in her green eyes as she threw her to her death. The knife she had held to her throat at Prideful Leap. It felt obscene that there would be orphanages built in her name.

'And this isn't the only one I've seen, I'm afraid.' When Elver looked sharply at Sunay, the mage sighed. 'They're cropping up all over. You know what people are like – it's new, they're excited. And she looks like them – or, at least, she looks more like them than the other gods do. It makes her more approachable, I suspect. Here, worship the embodiment of motherhood, a human woman who has ascended to godhood through her virtuous nature . . .' Elver snorted loudly. 'Or worship this giant crow in a cowl. People care about their children more than anything, Elver. And that is what she claims to be a god of – maternal instinct. Bringing new lives into the world, and looking after them.'

'Maura doesn't care about them. She certainly doesn't care about their children.' Elver stepped out of the treeline. 'I'm going up there. I want to see.'

'Elver.' Artair's hand brushed her arm. 'We shouldn't . . .'

'You can stay here.' Feeling how harsh her words were, she made herself turn back to him and briefly grasp his hand. 'It's most dangerous for you and Lucian, so you should stay. But I want to have a look. I won't be long.'

Without waiting to hear his or Sunay's objections, she strode away from them, joining the muddy path up the hill and slipping into the stream of people entering the temple. There was a man to one side of the door, selling something from a cart that she couldn't see.

Inside, it was bare, with just a few wooden pews for people to sit and, at the far end, a wide altar with a number of small white objects on it. To one side, there was a doorway that led into another chamber, and in there she saw rows and rows of children, none more than ten years old, sitting on the floor with their legs crossed. They wore simple clothes, and each of them had a white circle painted on their foreheads, and in their laps they each had a board with a sheet of paper pinned to it. A man with a similar circle on his head and the robes of a priest was talking to them in a low voice while they slowly scratched words onto the paper, their heads bent in concentration. These must be the children of the temple's orphanage, each of them being cared for and educated in the name of the Mother.

She wondered what they were writing, and who it was for.

When she got to the front, she saw that the white objects on the altar were tiny clay figures of children, all of them more or less identical. Someone had lit candles behind them, and a large square of gold cloth had been hung above the altar, the two white circles embroidered in the centre.

Elver glared at it all, seething, as other pilgrims came and went, their voices low. For the first time in a while, she felt a surge of disgust for humans; they were so fickle, so easily led. She reached out with one hand and picked up one of the clay figures, rubbing her thumb over its blunt face. She would take it, she decided. A little gift for Tisk. Who knew when they might need another boon?

'This isn't over, Mother,' she said quietly. 'You want to hunt us? We're not the prey creatures you think we are.'

Next to her, a young woman with bloodshot eyes stepped up to the altar, placing a figurine in the gap that Elver had left. Her voice, when she spoke, was hoarse from crying.

'My wife,' she said, 'please help her, Mother. The baby was supposed to come over a week ago, and the pain – it's too much . . .' She cast her eyes up at the white circles, an expression of sorrow on her face, then shuffled away. The man outside had to be selling these little statuettes of children, Elver realized. So that people could offer their prayers to Tlevrae's newest god.

Elver watched the young woman leave, then placed the figurine of the child back on the altar.

'It's not over,' she said again, before turning to go. 'You'll see.'

CHAPTER 4

It took time to reach the place where they could make the offering to Tisk, long enough that they had to stop to sleep, which meant that Lucian got to stretch his legs for a while. He didn't care particularly for Sunay, and, he suspected, she wasn't especially fond of him either. But he was pleased to see her anyway; the little packets of kopi she habitually carried had been a boon for him, and as they walked into the dawn light he took frequent sips from a cup of the hot, black liquid. Kopi was a stimulant, keeping him awake long after he should have slept, and he didn't want to perpetually be a creature of the night. As Sunay led them down a stony path out of the wood, he found himself appreciating the way the mauve light of dawn made everything seem half real. Gradually, he became aware that Elver was watching him closely.

'You're quiet this morning.'

'Am I?' He glanced at her. Fleet, the monster creature she had gone to so much trouble to rescue from Mother Maura, had scampered on ahead with Sunay. For the moment, they were alone. 'I'm being hunted by a god and I have magic burning inside me that I can't control. I have a lot on my mind, monster girl.'

'We're all being hunted, Lucian. You're not alone.' When he looked up at that, she turned her head away slightly. He thought again, as he frequently did, of the way she had kissed him in the Jih Forest. In his previous life as one of Maura's acolytes, there had been the odd fellow student who had shown an interest in him, which had led to a few stolen kisses in the quieter corners of Prideful Leap, but none of those kisses had felt like that one – there was a wildness to Elver that seemed to simmer just under the surface, threatening to spill over. To his own chagrin he found that he very much wanted to experience that feeling again, but, of course, Elver was still under the impression it had been Artair she had kissed.

If I had my own body, this wouldn't be a problem.

Except, of course, that his own body was long lost, and he knew of no way to create a new one, even with the power of the Bloody Claw simmering inside him. Despite their cosy new alliance, his secret hope was still to oust Artair, somehow. But would Elver ever forgive him for such an act?

'You're right,' he said. 'And I'm glad of the company. Your company, at least.'

To his surprise, she smirked at him. 'Yeah, you like me so much you had me thrown into the sea.'

'Ouch.' They had not talked about this directly before, and he found it difficult to tell exactly how Elver felt about it. Certainly, at the moment she was smiling at him, but there was a sharp edge to her expression that threatened to turn deadly. 'I had hoped you might have forgiven me.'

'Why would I have done that?'

Much to his annoyance, Lucian felt his face grow warm.

'I've helped you,' he said, hating the slightly affronted tone in his own voice. 'I helped you free the monsters at the circus. And I came back to the shattered mountain when I knew you were in danger. I worked with the idiot monk to save you.'

'Actually, you came back to Prideful Leap because you found out that Maura was the one who cast you out of your body, and you wanted to give her a good kick up the arse.' Lucian winced, but Elver's tone, he noted, was light. 'As soon as you had your memories back, you scrambled back to the Bloody Claw.'

'I had to know who I was.' A flicker of that old anger returned, the one that used to fill him every night when he woke up in the monastery. 'Everything had been taken from me. I had to get something back.'

Elver nodded. 'I suppose I can understand that. I know what it's like to have everything taken from you, after all.' Her voice was still light, but he felt the weight of her words anyway.

The anger left him as quickly as it had arrived.

'Elver . . .'

Ahead of them, Sunay called over her shoulder. 'This is the place!'

She had led them down into what appeared to be the ruins of a village. Once, it seemed, there had been around fifty cottages grouped around a communal well, but now they were all in pieces, rubble strewn across the overgrown paths and ruined walls standing like broken teeth against the sky. Orange and yellow poppies were growing everywhere, and the only sound was the wind through the weeds.

Lucian frowned. '*This* is one of Tisk's sacred places? I suppose this is what I should expect from one of the lesser gods.'

'Don't let him hear you say that, or no one will ever believe another word from you – he'll make sure of it,' said Sunay brightly. She picked her way carefully through the weeds.

'Those poppies shouldn't be blooming at this time of the year,' said Elver. 'There's something weird about this place.'

Fleet was sniffing around the old well, which had a small tree growing out one side of it. The sun had risen above the horizon, banishing the dawn.

'Yes,' said Sunay, stifling a yawn. 'Like me, the poppies should still be in bed. But, like I said, this place is sacred to Tisk, and so it is a little magical. This village, you see, is the site of one of history's most impressive lies, would you believe? My lord treasures it. Such an extraordinary and ridiculous lie, the likes of which you have never heard.'

'I have a terrible feeling,' said Lucian, 'that you wish to tell us the story of this lie, Miss Tiskertalia.'

'Why yes, Lucian "stick up his arse" Prideson, I do.' The mage made a face at him. 'It won't take but a moment, I promise. I do not wish to interrupt his godliness's schedule.' She made an elaborate bow.

Lucian sighed. 'Just get on with it.'

'Once, this picturesque pile of rubble was the village of Scribton. A man came here once, claiming to be a mage of the Hooded Crow – a healer, in other words, and a dealer with the dead. He had with him on his cart a fresh corpse, and in full view of the people of this place he roused it to speak and dance a jig.'

Lucian snorted. 'What is the use of that sort of magic, I ask you?' Although his mind unhelpfully conjured an image of his own yellowed bones, presumably scattered somewhere across the shattered mountain.

'News of the mage spread. If he could bring the dead back from the shadowed lands, he had to be the greatest of all healers! Soon, this mage was making a reasonable amount of coin, selling his penny ointments and salves, setting the occasional broken bone and pulling the odd bad tooth. Every now and then, one of the villagers might die – of old age, usually; this was a quiet place – but the tithe price set by the magpie was always much, much too high for these poor villagers, so he never had to perform that magic again. Until word reached the ear of a warlord, one who had recently lost a portion of his army in a skirmish. He rode into Scribton and demanded the mage bring back his men – he was rich enough to pay the tithe, after all. The mage, at knifepoint, was forced to reveal that not only could he not bring the dead back to life but he wasn't in fact a mage at all. And the corpse he had claimed to reanimate was actually his brother, who was quite well and hiding out in a nearby abandoned farm. They had simply painted him a greenish colour.'

Elver kicked at a broken piece of stone on the path. 'I think I can sense where this is going.'

'The warlord was displeased,' said Sunay, 'and he set fire to the whole place. A number of people escaped, but Scribton was no more. And the so-called mage was definitely no more.'

With that, she pulled the white glove from her pack and stepped up to the well. She dangled it over the opening, murmuring something to herself as she did so. Lucian recognized the act of tithing, the necessary words that opened the connection between a mage and a god. Now that he carried a portion of the Bloody Claw's power, he would never have to do that again. *Assuming I can get it to work.*

Sunay dropped the glove into the well.

'When you said impressive, I thought you meant really clever, or useful,' said Elver. 'That man's lies were just impressively stupid.'

'My lord appreciates it when people go for broke, you see,' said Sunay, and then she stepped back from the well. 'Ah. My lord. Are you there?'

A fox with fur the colour of flames scampered over the lip of the well. Fleet gave a surprised yip and tried to hide behind Elver's legs, something he wasn't quite small enough to manage any more.

Lucian straightened up, eying the fox warily. It was true that Tisk had proved to be a valuable ally in the past, but that didn't mean he was trustworthy. This god was the very definition of slippery.

'My friends,' said Tisk. 'The last time I saw the two of you, things were not going so well.' He sniffed in Elver's direction. 'You were dead, for a start.'

'I got better,' replied Elver. 'Can you help us?'

'I'll be clear with you, for once. Maura has taken her place amongst the Twelve, but it is not smooth sailing. That hot little slice of power the idiot cat slipped you before he died, Lucian, is the last piece in her godly jigsaw puzzle. Without it, she cannot function as she should.' The fox paused, as if he were about to say something else, and then he transformed into the more human-looking version of himself. He brushed his velvet jacket down and smoothed his moustache. 'Ah, that's better. Speaking through fox teeth is a little distracting.'

'Well?' snapped Lucian. 'You've not told us anything we don't already know, or haven't guessed. She's got people hunting for me all the time. What are we supposed to do about it? Are you going to help me or not?'

'I see you are as charming as ever – no wonder you were Maura's favourite little mageling. As for helping you, there is only so much I can do. Gods can only act through their chosen mages, such as Sunay here, who I am happy to see is already doing good work. What I can offer you, however, are the beginnings of a plan, and something potentially even more valuable: allies.'

'What do you mean, allies?'

The temperature dropped abruptly, and the shadows around them grew deeper despite the blue sky overhead. Fleet whined.

'My lord?' Sunay looked abruptly as if she wanted to be elsewhere.

'Maura, or the Mother, as she styles herself these days, murdered a god,' Tisk continued. 'In her eagerness to throw her weight around, I believe she hasn't stopped to consider the consequences of that. Who she might have alarmed, or angered.'

Although moments ago the skies had been quiet, suddenly they were full of black wings and the harsh calls of crows. A shadow appeared next to Tisk, tall and dark, and as they watched, it grew darker and more solid, until standing in front of them was a hooded figure around eight feet tall, a long bone-coloured beak protruding from a cowl.

'The Mother makes mock of my domain,' said the Hooded Crow. 'Gods should not die. And mortals do not get to make themselves immortal.'

Despite himself, Lucian found that he had stepped away from Tisk and now stood with his arm pressed to Elver's. Her cold fingers found his hand and squeezed it.

'It's an insult, is what it is.' A broad, handsome man with a flaming beard stepped out of one of the ruined cottages. He grinned at their surprise, then winked at Elver. 'I'm Barleycorn, my love. Believe me, I'm very fond of you mortals – too fond, it's been said – but we can't have you getting ideas above your station. Where would that end?'

Next to him, Lucian felt Elver bristle.

Another, smaller figure was climbing out of the well. It was about the size of a small child, but it had the head of a mouse, with soft brown fur and large rounded ears that were pink at the edges. The creature wore a finely embroidered blue robe, and it blinked large glossy black eyes at them.

'Milik the Small!' exclaimed Sunay, who had pressed both hands together in apparent delight. 'It's an honour, my lady.'

'Greetings, child.' Milik sketched a quick bow. 'Now, I am not so concerned that one of our number has been replaced.' Her voice was soft, barely more than a whisper. 'Change has happened before.' The mouse god glanced at the Hooded Crow and away again. 'But the Mother is unwell. Her thoughts are poison. Her heart has been burned to pieces with rage. She should not have the powers of a god.'

'Not all of the Twelve feel this way, unfortunately,' said Tisk. 'After all, if there's one thing the Twelve could always agree on, it's that we should disagree. Contrariness is in our nature. But, you see,' he gestured to the three gods standing next to him, 'you have a great deal of might on your side.'

'This is all very well,' said Lucian, 'but if you can't move directly against Maura, what use are any of you?'

Sunay shot him a warning glance, which he ignored.

'We can act in subtle ways,' said Barleycorn. 'And we can instruct our mages. Do not throw away our assistance so casually, Prideson.'

'And I told you of a plan, did I not?' Tisk produced his silver fox-headed cane from thin air and twirled it lazily in one hand, making Milik the Small twitch. 'Maura refuses to put aside her godhood, so, in truth, there is only one thing you can do: kill her.'

'Thanks,' said Elver. 'It's such a relief you're here, because we never would have thought of that.'

Lucian felt a bubble of laughter rise in his throat. He bit it down before it could escape.

'There is a weapon,' Tisk continued as though Elver hadn't spoken, 'a weapon capable of killing a half-god like Maura. It is the very first Jih ever created.'

There was a moment of silence. Elver's golden eyes were very wide.

'What are you talking about? A monster that could kill Maura? I'd know about it.'

'For reasons that should be obvious, hardly anyone knows about its existence,' said Barleycorn.

'The First of Monsters has been hidden for a long, long time,' said the Hooded Crow. 'There is only one being who might know where it is now, and she will not want to tell you.' Deep within the hood, lidless black eyes glistened wetly. 'She certainly won't tell us.'

'If *we* knew,' Barleycorn added, 'the creature would have been killed thousands of years ago. A monster that can kill the gods is too dangerous, if you ask me.'

'Who? Who knows where this jih spirit is?' asked Elver, although Lucian could see from the look on her face that she already knew.

CHAPTER 5

'I'm not a mage – I can't just demand an audience. Usually, the Queen of Serpents calls me to her. Or just turns up in the lake.' Elver paused. 'But I think there's a way.'

The three of them were watching her, Fleet's eyes eerie green lamps in the dark. Once the gods had vanished again, they had moved away from the ruined village without having to discuss it – sleeping overnight in that haunted place felt like inviting trouble. Eventually, they had made camp on a small hill that looked down over a wooded valley, scavenging together a dinner from what Sunay had in her pack and what Elver had been able to forage on the way there.

'I've always wondered about the Queen of Serpents' aversion to making mages,' said Lucian. 'It's damned inefficient, if you ask me. And it shows a lack of ambition. How can she enforce her will on the world if . . .' He caught the look she gave him and waved a hand at her. 'Forgive me. Please carry on, monster girl.'

'Since I . . . came back, I've felt this particular connection to water. I don't mean rain, or water in a glass in a tavern—'

'Not much water in taverns generally,' Sunay remarked.

'I mean rivers, ponds, lakes. Even the sea. I can feel them.' She raised a hand and held it out to the west. 'I know the sea is over there.'

'Well, so do I,' commented Lucian. 'Because I have seen a map.'

'Will you shut up? I know the sea is over there, because I can *feel* it. Waiting . . .' How to explain this feeling? It was as if something huge, and cold, and teeming with life was looming just over the horizon. She was aware of it, and it was aware of her. The feeling had been growing since she had returned from the shadowed lands, and she had been doing her best to ignore it. Until now. 'The queen is connected to the dark, cold places. I think if I can get to a deep enough body of water, I'll be able to send her a message.'

'There was a river we passed this afternoon,' said Sunay. 'Would that work?'

'No, it has to be deeper than that. It needs to have places where light can't reach the bottom.' She wasn't sure how she knew that was true. 'There's something not far from here. A lake, I think. Inside a cave.'

Both of them looked sceptical, but Sunay shrugged and took a sip of her tea.

'Until we get this sorted, none of us will see any peace from Maura's goons or those faceless bastards, so the sooner the better, I say. We can head there tomorrow.'

Let's go now! Fleet pressed himself to her legs, his feathery tail swishing back and forth. *I want to run, want to hunt. I can find this lake. It'll have fish. I can hunt them.*

'The wolves taught you to hunt fish?' Elver knelt to rub Fleet's ears. 'That's very useful.'

Well, they didn't really, but I bet I could do it. I can hunt anything. Let's go now!

'Fleet, everyone else needs to rest.' She turned to the others. 'I think I'm going to take Fleet into the woods for a bit, let him run around. He's had to follow at our heels all day and I think he needs to stretch his legs. He has too much energy.'

'Are you sure?' Sunay blinked. 'It's very dark.'

'I can see in the dark.' Elver glanced at Lucian to see if he would offer to come with her, but he had a thin thread of red fire cradled in his hands – another attempt to use the power of the Bloody Claw – and his attention was focused entirely on that. Ignoring the pang of disappointment in her chest, Elver stood. 'I won't be long.'

The pair of them walked down into the wooded valley, Fleet running off ahead a little before circling back to tell her what he had seen and smelled. It was a far cry from the journey they had made to Prideful Leap, when she and Artair had to hide the cub in a sack for his own safety, but he was still far from safe, Elver reminded herself. They were out in the wilds here, but jih were still hated and feared by humans, and if they came across anyone in the valley – travellers or hunters, perhaps – trouble would quickly follow. Outside of the Jih Forest, Fleet wasn't safe. Neither of them were.

'We'll take you back soon,' she told him when he returned to her with a pine cone held between his teeth.

Where?

'Home. To the Jih Forest.'

Oh. He crunched the pine cone between his jaws, then spent some time spitting bits of it into the undergrowth. A low mist was growing up around the bottoms of the trees, and Fleet's feathers were dotted with thousands of water droplets. *Why would we do that?*

'To see your mother, and your brother and sister. You're old enough now to leave the nest. You could explore by yourself. There are lots of things to see in the Jih Forest.'

There are lots of things to see here, replied Fleet. He was sniffing madly at a cluster of mushrooms growing around the roots of a tree.

'It's dangerous for us here,' said Elver. 'Out in the world, people don't like to see jih spirits. It scares them.'

I don't know why they're scared of me – I've never even eaten a human. Do you want to go back to the Jih Forest?

The question took her by surprise. Did she? She realized that she hadn't thought much beyond survival for the last few weeks. The question of what the future looked like was a troubling one. She missed the Jih Forest, still carried it with her in her heart – her hand closed around the conker in her pocket – but now she knew there was so much to see beyond it. She had mocked Artair's monastery once, but was going back to the Jih Forest so different?

'I don't know,' she said, startled to find that was the truth of it. 'A lot of things have changed. If you truly don't want to return to the forest, Fleet, you don't have to. But you might want to one day.'

Not today I don't, said Fleet. *I'm the lord of my domain, whichever domain I choose. That's what the Pack said.*

'You spoke to them? The Pack?' The god of the hunt had not appeared with Tisk in the ruined village, which presumably meant that it was not siding with Lucian. She could only hope it wasn't in that case siding with Mother Maura. It made her think of the Queen of Serpents too. The god who had given Elver her life back rarely seemed to take an interest in human affairs, or the affairs of other gods, but these were strange times. They had no idea of her motives, or whose side she was really on. 'What was that like?'

They spoke through the wolves, or sometimes through the wind when it moved in the trees. The Pack taught me to listen all the time, and think about what I'm hearing. I . . . Fleet stopped in his tracks. They had come to a space where the trees weren't so close, and the moonlight glimmered against his scales, turning them silver. *Can you hear that? It's one of us, Elver, and it's in danger!*

'What? You mean Artair and Lucian?' She cast a glance back over her shoulder, but Fleet was already running into the trees ahead, away from their small camp. 'Wait!'

Elver was good at moving quickly through thick foliage, and the darkness itself was no problem, but Fleet was much too fast and it wasn't long before he was little more than a flash of movement ahead of her amongst the trees. Reluctantly, she cast her own awareness forward, questing with that new sense that seemed to be able to tell her when something was awry, and she caught a flicker of something – fright and anger in the night, a loud spot where it should be quiet. She stopped trying to follow Fleet and headed towards where her senses pointed her instead. Hopefully, they would lead to the same place.

A terrible screeching cry shattered the quiet of the forest, and Elver felt all the hairs on the back of her neck stand on end; abruptly, her sense that something was wrong doubled, and she picked up the pace. Ahead of her, a ruddy glow was peeking through the trees, and she started to worry that this was one of Maura's acolytes coming at the group from a different angle —

Fleet collided with her leg, almost dancing up and down with agitation.

There are dangerous humans here, he told her. *Shall I go and bite them?*

She put her hand on his head. 'No, I need you to stay here, Fleet, and keep watch. Just in case there's anything else behind us. Okay? Stay out of sight if you can.'

It was difficult to tell with his feathers and scales, but she thought he looked a little relieved at that.

Beyond the press of pine and fir trees, there was a cottage built of logs, with a single candle burning in the window. Outside it stood a pair of humans, who were shouting and shaking their fists at the sky – one of them had a spear, which she was jabbing upwards violently.

The source of their anger and fear was easy enough to see. A large creature hung in the air above them; to Elver it looked like a giant bat with dark grey fur and glowing red eyes the size of dinner plates, although its wings were marked with whorls and dots of colour – blue, orange, light grey. A pair of thickly furred antennae grew from the top of its head, and when it opened its mouth to shriek, she could see rows and rows of sharp little teeth. It had something clutched in one of its back legs, although everything was moving too much for her to make it out.

A jih spirit. That was what Fleet had meant by 'one of us'.

The woman with the spear had climbed up onto the lower portion of a fence, trying to poke at the creature; the rusted tip passed inches away from the jih spirit's furred stomach. Elver stepped out of the trees.

'What are you doing? What's going on?'

Both humans turned to look at her, startled, and the giant bat-moth gave another piercing shriek before flapping its wings and lifting up into the night sky. It seemed confused by her presence, even frightened.

'Who are you?' demanded the man. He was thin and balding, with salt-and-pepper stubble on his chin.

Above them, the bat-moth seemed to hesitate, and then it moved away, dropping behind the trees into the dark.

'Bastard thing!' shouted the woman, who was climbing down from the fence. She was much stockier than her partner, and there was a fine layer of sweat on her forehead. She threw the spear into the dirt with both frustration and relief. 'That's the third duck this month that thing has made off with.'

'The jih spirit has been stealing your ducks?'

'Who are you?' the man asked again. 'It's the middle of the bloody night.'

'My name is Elver. I'm just a traveller.' She moved closer to the faint light coming from their cottage, wondering if they would see her golden eyes in the dark. 'I heard all the noise and—'

'We need those ducks,' the woman said shortly, wiping her hands on her shirt. 'Especially as winter is all but here. Those eggs keep us going, see. Three ducks we're missing now. Twelve curse us.'

'Jih spirits don't normally attack without reason,' said Elver.

'*Jih spirits*,' jeered the man. 'Bloody monsters, you mean. What if it decides a few scrawny ducks isn't enough? What if it comes back for our children?'

'We sent for a priest of Trilot to clear the thing out, and he was supposed to be here by tonight.' The stocky woman sighed. 'Course he didn't turn up in time to save our second best layer. Just our luck, really.'

At the mention of Trilot, Elver stood up a little straighter. A priest of that god would bring a purifying lamp, something that would burn the jih spirit down to nothing, causing agony all the while. The creature that would be left behind after that wouldn't be jih any more, and it wouldn't be breathing, either. She couldn't let that happen. The memory of the temple in Ashingdown was suddenly very close: how the light had burned her, trying to remove the parts of her that were special, unique.

'I'll go and find your ducks,' she said quickly. There would be time. She would *make* time.

The human couple boggled at her.

'Find them? It'll have eaten them!' cried the man. 'What are you, some wandering idiot? And what good will that do, anyway? It'll just come back.'

'Nah, best leave it to Trilot, love,' said the woman. 'He'll be here shortly, I'm sure. Kind of you to offer, though. Do you want to come in for a cup of tea? Something warming? You're hardly dressed for a walk in this weather.'

'Turn the priest of Trilot away when he gets here,' said Elver, already walking away in the direction the bat had taken. 'I'll find the jih creature for you and tell it to leave you alone.'

She was in the trees again, Fleet shadowing her steps, when she heard the man turn to the woman and say, 'Did she just say she was going to bloody *talk* to it?'

CHAPTER 6

'Don't go too far ahead. There's a priest of Trilot on his way here, and the last thing we need is for him to see you.'

Fleet gave Elver a sharp yip in response, and disappeared into the gulch ahead of them. As she ran on behind him, her feet easily finding spots clear of vines and brambles, Elver remembered.

Her first years in the Jih Forest had been hard ones. Thanks to growing up in the orphanage, she had been a little more self-sufficient than the average twelve-year-old, but, even so, there had been things she had to learn, and learn quickly: like how to build a fire safely, how to find clean water to drink, what plants and mushrooms she could eat without poisoning herself – the irony of that – and how to keep warm through the night when ice crept across the lake and snow powdered the tops of the trees.

Luckily for her, the jih spirits that were her kin had shown her all this, and more. On that first day, when she'd climbed up the sea cliffs into the forest itself, her hair still full of salt water and the wounds the Queen of Serpents had left her with still leaking black blood, it had been a group of keltraxia who had gathered around her. They had pressed their warm bodies against her until she was dry, and they had carefully licked the poison blood from her face. A friendly slowjorn had shown Elver where to find dry kindling for fires, and the froudians had brought her foraged food until she had learned how to find her own. When winter fell in that first year, when the previously colourful and welcoming Jih Forest had seemed endlessly dark and dangerously cold, she had spent much of it curled up in a kartesh den, her head resting on the furry tummies of kartesh pups that were twice her size. The jih spirits were her brothers and sisters, they were her kin, and they had saved her. In return, she had become the guardian of their forest, keeping out curious humans and helping them in any way she could – if a cub got lost, she found it; if a creature broke a bone, she mended it.

And if a jih spirit was in danger – from humans or from themselves – she saved it.

Fleet had slowed down. *It's up there*, he cried. *Can you see it? I can, because I am a natural-born hunter.*

They had come to a portion of the valley wall that was significantly steeper and rockier, the raw earth orange and brown where parts of it had fallen away. Into this softer section many animals had made their homes; Elver could see rabbit holes at the base, and untidy birds' nests at the top. In the middle, something large had dug a much wider hole, still shallow enough that she could see the shadowy shape crouched within it. A pair of giant red eyes glowed in the night.

'Hello,' Elver called up to it. She remembered what Bawric, the mage of the Pack, had told her about names. It was respectful to know them and use them, he had said. 'Who are you?'

The bat-moth did not reply, although in the dark she could see it retreat a little further into its cave.

'I'm not an enemy,' she continued. 'I am jih, just like you. If you look at me closely, you can tell.' She shrugged. 'You can probably smell what I am.'

Into the silence that followed there came a single, plaintive duck's quack.

'Listen, I'm here to help you. I know that you can understand me. What's your name?'

I am called Fire Eyes, said the bat-moth. His voice was soft and sad in her head.

Not as good as my name, put in Fleet.

'It's good to meet you, Fire Eyes.'

What are you? asked the bat-moth. *You do not smell human, but you have their shape.*

'I am a child of the Queen of Serpents, just like you.' Elver peered at the ragged wall of clay. Gnarled roots were growing through and across it like shaggy braids. 'Can I climb up there to speak to you, Fire Eyes?'

If you must.

The wall was easy enough to climb, with the odd jagged rock or loop of roots providing good handholds, and very quickly Elver was making herself comfortable on the edge of Fire Eyes' cave. Fleet sat below them looking up, his ears twitching to pick up their conversation.

'Now then,' said Elver. 'Why are you stealing those ducks? There must be loads of things you can hunt in this forest that don't belong to humans.'

I'm not hunting them! said Fire Eyes, sounding appalled. *I am caring for them. They are mine.*

Two of the ducks were crouched close to the cave wall, their bills pressed to their chests and their eyes like tiny beads of black. The third was held cupped in the long-fingered hand that sprouted from the end of Fire Eyes' left wing; it was peaceably running its beak over its feathers.

'Oh, I see. Unfortunately, the humans need them. They eat their eggs, you see. So I have to take them back. And you need to stop taking them. Humans aren't reasonable – they'd have you killed for less.' She paused. 'They've summoned someone to come and hurt you, Fire Eyes.'

You can't take them. The bat-moth pressed the duck to his chest and stroked the top of its head with one long finger. *The humans don't look after them. They leave them out in all weathers. They do not hold or talk to them. Why do humans not care for their young properly? I will care for them. They are mine now.*

Elver felt a flicker of frustration. Didn't she have enough to deal with without brokering ducks?

'The ducks aren't human young,' she said. 'They're more like . . . pets.'

Under the last eye-moon, my den was filled with my young, the bat-moth continued quietly. *I had three kits of my own. This cave I dug for them. I hunted for them. I kept them warm. But they were weak, and did not make it to the claw-moon.* He lifted the duck and pressed his furry face into its feathers.

'These ducks are not your kits,' said Elver, swallowing past a ball of sadness in her throat. She remembered the keltraxia cub who hadn't been able to hatch from its egg. 'They'll never grow to be like you, Fire Eyes. They will always just be ducks. Probably quite confused ducks, living in a cave in the wood. You'll have to watch them all the time, because they'll wander off.' Although, she noted, the one that the bat-moth was cradling looked happy enough. She sighed. 'Let me take these other two back to the humans, and you can keep one. Alright?'

Fire Eyes turned his huge red eyes on her. *I can keep this kit?*

'Just leave the humans alone from now on.' She thought of the plant in Sunay's cottage, and the urge to change something came over her again, stronger this time. It frightened her, that feeling, because she was barely in control of it. 'Can I see it a moment? Your kit?'

Elver took the duck from his outstretched hands and gathered it carefully to her own chest, feeling the rapid patter of its heartbeat. The duck was brown and grey with a white breast, its beak a sunny yellow. Could she change a living creature? She didn't know if this was the right thing to do or not – she couldn't ask the duck its opinion – but the urge to make a difference here was overwhelming, a tide that was rising within her and threatening to sweep her away.

It was a wild power, a frightening one. But she was right about the duck. It wasn't suited to living in a cave with a bat-moth. She could make it into something that was.

Screwing her eyes shut, she pictured Fire Eyes' young in their den, how they might look, with their big eyes and oversized ears. *Become this*, she thought at the duck, *and have a better life: one that isn't an endless production of eggs followed by a cleaver and a cooking pot. Become what you want to be.*

Elver felt a surge of power within her, a rising tide of silvery black, so much stronger than when she had changed the plant.

The shape of the duck shifted in her hands, and when she opened her eyes, she was looking down at a rangy little creature that certainly was not a duck. Its downy fur was still brown and grey, and there were a few stray feathers sprouting from its wings, but otherwise it rather resembled Fire Eyes. *I've changed its nature*, she thought. *It'll never be part of the human world again.* There was power here, a terrible power she had never asked for. A cold feeling flooded her chest.

When she passed the newly created bat-moth-duck back to Fire Eyes, the larger creature looked stunned.

My kit! Where did you find him? How did you do this?

'Just promise me you won't go back to that cottage,' said Elver. Shakily, she gathered up one duck and stuck it in the top of her pack, and then tucked the other under one arm. 'Do you promise, Fire Eyes?'

I do. I swear it. The bat-moth was looking down at his new kit in amazement. *I'll never go back.*

CHAPTER 7

Elver and Fleet picked their way back through the forest carefully, the silence occasionally broken by a disgruntled quack. As well as the ducks, Elver found that she was carrying an uncomfortable mixture of exhilaration and horror. Before, she had only changed small, quiet things – the plant in Sunay's room, a sapling, a cluster of mushrooms to make them edible. The duck hadn't seemed too concerned by what had happened to it, but it was still a thinking, feeling creature that had once been a part of the natural world, and was now a part of the unnatural one. She had essentially given it more problems than it had before. If a human saw its new shape, they might try to kill it; perhaps it would find eating with a mouth rather than a beak too strange. Yet, despite all that, changing the duck had felt *good*. It had felt like making something new, and on a deeper level it felt as though she were fulfilling a purpose. She had wanted to change the animal – more than that, she'd felt as if she *had* to. Changing the animal had given it a better life.

The cabin appeared through the trees, lights still on in its windows, but as they approached, Elver realized she couldn't see the human couple. Likely they had gone inside away from the cold, to wait for the priest of Trilot. She could just put the ducks in their yard and go, and certainly that was what she would have done once, but now she wanted to talk to them, explain to them, perhaps, why the jih spirit had been taking their animals. It seemed to her there was something important there, a point that needed to be made.

With those thoughts on her mind, Elver made her way towards

the cabin, only to be surprised by another figure lurching round the corner. They wore a white robe over travel clothes, and a silver half mask that left their mouth exposed. When they spotted Elver, that mouth creased into an expression of fury.

Elver cast a hand behind her, waving Fleet back.

'Run!' she told him. 'Go back to Sunay and Artair.'

'You!' The priest of Trilot squared their shoulders. Now that they were closer, Elver could see that it was a woman, dark hair pulled into a bun at the back of her head. 'We were warned about you.'

'What?' Elver put the duck she was carrying down on the ground and it waddled rapidly away towards the cabin.

'A girl with white hair, yellow eyes, scars.' The silver mask flashed in the moonlight. 'You are the jih creature that wounded Kantor Witt and befouled the temple in Ashingdown. We were all warned you were still out in the world.'

'I'm flattered. Good to know I made such an impression on Trilot's order of turds.' Elver grinned. 'How is Witt? Last time I saw him, he was being dragged to jail by a load of pissed-off humans.'

'And you have that!' The priest leaned out, pointing past her at Fleet, who had failed to retreat into the woods like she'd told him to. 'A monster at your heels! Father of purity, father of justice, let us not be tainted by those with ill blood . . .'

When the woman began chanting, Elver turned to Fleet again, her heart sinking at the sight of his bright green eyes, the feathers across his brow bristling with distress.

'GO!'

But when she turned back, it was too late. The priest had brought the lamp out from inside her robes, and they were hit with a blast of light so bright it lit up the cabin and the surrounding woods like a summer's day.

'Send your light, to burn the monsters away!'

Elver jumped in front of Fleet, her arms out to either side to shield him as much as possible. The keltraxia cub yowled with pain and surprise, and Elver braced herself for what was to come – the terrible burning, the feeling that her skin was being exposed to an open flame, and worse, the sensation that something essential about her was being boiled away.

And yet . . . it didn't come.

The light still felt uncomfortably hot, but, rather than shrinking away, her core monstrousness seemed to be growing

She felt angry. She felt powerful. She opened her eyes and saw the priest staring at her with her mouth open; behind the mask, her eyes widened, and she gave a strangled shriek at the sight of Elver.

Confused, Elver glanced behind her, thinking something must have come out of the woods – the bat-moth perhaps, come to retrieve the rest of his kits – but instead she saw her own shadow cast out across the ground by Trilot's light . . . Except it wasn't hers.

The shadow was strange, full of impossible movements and shapes, suggesting something much bigger, something in flux, something very definitely not human. She caught a glimpse of snake-like coils, a bristle of horns and spines . . .

When she turned back, the priest of Trilot had dropped the lamp and was running. As Elver watched, the woman flew past the cabin itself and ran straight into the woods, the sound of her body crashing through the undergrowth very loud.

Elver stepped up to the lamp, now darkened, and trod on it firmly with her boot. The tin flower that held the light of Trilot snapped easily under her weight. A moment later, the door to the cabin opened and the two humans poked their heads out.

'What's all that screaming?' said the woman, while the man said: 'Where's the Trilot priest?'

'I don't know,' said Elver. The human couple just looked mildly baffled. Whatever it was that had terrified the priest of Trilot and turned her shadow monstrous, it was gone now. 'Here.' Elver put her pack down on the ground so that the final duck could waddle out, then stood up. She had intended to give them a speech, about how they shouldn't judge the jih spirits, that the bat-moth was a creature trying to live in the wood, just like them, but somehow the words wouldn't come. The image of her shadow was too clear in her mind. Her human shape felt flimsy all of a sudden, as though it were a thin shell covering something else entirely. 'I've brought two of your ducks back. I couldn't find the third.'

'Well . . . thank you?'

Elver turned away, her sharp eyes seeking out the dark shape of Fleet, who had slunk away to the edge of the property now the danger had passed.

'You're welcome,' she said as she walked away, and then added, over her shoulder, 'you should talk to them, the ducks. Keep them warm in winter, that sort of thing.'

She disappeared back under the trees, glad to be out of their sight.

'You've been gone hours. Are you alright?'

It was clear it was Artair from the way he stood, concern in every angle in his body. Once, his concern would have irritated her; now it gave her a feeling of longing that was almost as frightening as her new monstrous powers. Sunay was curled up by the fire, her dark hair hidden under both a woollen hat and the hood of her winter cloak. Her snores sounded like the plaintive cries of something small and furry.

'I'm fine.' Elver came over to the fire, not quite meeting his eyes. It had never been in her mind to conceal what had happened with the bat-moth and the cabin in the wood, but as she stood there, in the warm circle of orange light, it was as though all her words had fled. She had changed an animal into a jih spirit. A hot prickle of guilt moved down her back and settled in her stomach. And then there was what the light of Trilot had hinted at.

'Fleet got away from me a couple of times, that's all.' She glanced at the keltraxia cub, who had slunk over to sniff at Sunay's bags, where most of the food was kept. 'I was running after him half the time – he's faster than he used to be.'

Artair watched her for a moment, and she had the distinct sense he hadn't believed her. The urge to tell him everything rose up in her chest – surely, of anyone, Artair would understand? He had carried something unknown around for years, and, more than that, he was the person she cared about more than anyone. He had kissed her – he was the only person who had *ever* kissed her.

Or she could wait for him to go to sleep and speak to Lucian instead; Lucian knew what it was to be changed by a god and, even if he didn't have kind words for her, he'd certainly be interested in her problem. If this was a new kind of power, possibly too interested.

The moment passed. Artair went back to his bedroll, and Elver sat up alone, keeping watch. After a while, Fleet came and laid his head near her feet.

'Did the light hurt you, Fleet?'

You stopped it, he said. *So it didn't get me.* He shifted on the ground, feathery tail lashing back and forth. He was agitated. *You looked different. In the light.*

'Yes,' she agreed, keeping her voice soft. 'Did you see what I . . . what I was?'

The tail lashed faster. His eyes were very wide, and she realized with a sinking in the pit of her stomach that he was frightened. Frightened of *her*.

No. You were difficult to look at, though. I thought that if you wanted to, you could hunt me. What's happening?

Elver reached down and stroked his ear. 'I wish I knew, Fleet.'

CHAPTER 8

Artair woke up and lay still, waiting for the wave of disorientation to pass.

Since he and Lucian had come to a kind of agreement, the place where he laid his head down to sleep was usually not the place where he woke up, and this had taken some getting used to. Today, he was at the bank of a narrow river, and it was late afternoon, when his last memory was of a ruined hut where they'd decided to rest the night before. Elver and Sunay were on their feet, and no fire had been built; this wasn't a place for them to rest. They were waiting for him to get up.

'He was basically a dead man walking,' said Sunay as Artair got to his feet. 'So bloody stubborn, your counterpart! I said to him, several times, you need to have a rest or you'll just keel over into the mud. Kopi only gets you so far, I told him, but he wouldn't listen.'

'So he did indeed keel over into the mud,' said Elver drily. 'Are you alright? Must be weird to wake up with bruises when you don't remember the knocks.'

'I'm fine.' He got up, stretched and tugged out the band holding back his hair. Once, when he and Elver had gone to the Temple of Threshold, he had been pleased with how his hair looked brushed back from his face, but now he associated it with the times that Lucian inhabited his body. 'Where are we?'

'We're close,' said Elver. She pointed beyond the stream to a place where green hills folded the land into a series of peaks. 'I can feel the water, just beyond these green places.'

She sounded distant, as though her mind were a long way from them, as though she were already ankle-deep in the water she could sense.

'Then let's keep going,' he said.

When eventually they reached the bottom of those hills, they were all surprised to find what looked like a rough stone doorway leading into the base of the nearest one. Elver walked up to it and rested her hand on the grey lintel, which was on a level with her head.

'It's in here,' she said. 'The lake. Here, I should be able to ask the Queen of Serpents where the First of Monsters is. One step closer to killing Maura.'

'This place is *old*,' said Sunay. She seemed reluctant to step beyond the doorway. 'It's a place dedicated to one of the most ancient gods, I think. Can you feel it?'

'You don't have to go in if you don't want to,' said Elver. Fleet had already found a patch of grass to roll around in and seemed to be paying them no attention at all.

'No, it's fine,' said Sunay, running her hand across the stone. 'I just wonder who it was, is all. There's a sadness to this place, an emptiness. Or I'm being overly dramatic, one of the two.'

'You, overly dramatic?' asked Elver. 'Surely not.'

Sunay laughed.

'Look, there's writing here.' Artair, taller than the pair of them, ran his fingers over the top of the grey stone, wiping away some clumps of moss. 'It says, "Even in darkness, light". I wonder what that means.'

Sunay frowned. 'It doesn't point to any of the Twelve in particular.'

'It doesn't matter,' said Elver. 'Come on.'

The three of them entered the hill, picking their way carefully down a path cluttered with stones and old, dead leaves. It grew perilously dark very quickly, but Elver led the way, her golden eyes piercing the deepest of shadows. And then, strangely, it grew light again. Artair realized he could make out the shape of Sunay's hat, and his own fingers as they trailed along the wall. The light was shifting and almost felt alive.

After a few minutes, the passage ended in a wide cavern, the floor of which was covered in water like a vast mirror. Somewhere, high above them in the cavern ceiling, there was a circular hole. Artair could see late-evening light spilling through it, and it was this that filled the cavern, a shivering watery glow that painted everything with movement.

'Wow,' said Sunay, and Artair had to agree. It might be disorientating, waking up in a new place each day, but it was a vast improvement on the same four walls of his cell in the monastery. If the Order of the Perpetual Morning had had their way, he'd never have seen any of this.

Elver was busily unlacing her boots.

'What are you doing?'

'I have to get in there.' She nodded to the lake. 'To call the Queen of Serpents. And I have to get in deep.'

'Rather you than me,' said Sunay. 'Didn't you say that there had to be places the light didn't reach for this business to work? There's light everywhere in here, somehow.'

'Not everywhere.' Elver grimaced. 'Like I said, I'll have to go in deep. It might take me a while.'

'Is that safe?' asked Artair. A memory of Chessun rose up in his mind, the blond novice whose cavorting in the waterfall had led to his death – the end of an arrow abruptly sprouting from his throat.

Elver gave him an impatient look. 'These places are . . . well, they are my places now. Water can't harm me.' She shrugged off her cloak and, without pausing to explain how she knew that, began walking down into the pool. Quickly, the water came up to her knees, her thighs, her waist.

Sunay, standing next to Artair, hugged herself. 'It looks bloody freezing,' she said, her voice partly muffled by her own scarf. 'I don't see how she can stand it.'

'She doesn't feel the cold. Not like we do.'

When the water closed over Elver's head, Artair took half a step forward, unable to stop himself. They could see her shape in the water, distorted and difficult to make out, but the further she walked, the less it looked like her. He blinked and rubbed his eyes, and looked again. Now she was just a smudge of colour; the next moment, he couldn't be sure where she was at all, and a rising anxiety gripped him.

Here and now, in this moment, I am safe. The words of his old mantra felt mildly foolish.

Yes, but is Elver safe?

She's stronger than you'll ever be, he reminded himself. *She's come back from the dead twice, has lived in a forest full of monsters and faced down priests that wanted to kill her. Holding her breath for a while isn't going to be a problem.*

Even so, she was gone for a very long time, and when Artair glanced at Sunay he saw that her face was a shade greyer than it had been. The silence of the cavern felt ominous, as though it had been a tomb all along.

'You should tell her,' she said, her eyes still trained on the surface of the lake. It had returned to its mirror-like stillness.

'Tell her what?'

The mage glanced at him, the quick grin on her face reminding him briefly of Tisk. 'That you love her, idiot.'

'I . . . What?' Artair swallowed hard. 'I don't know what you're talking about.'

'*Psh*. Please remember that I'm very good at spotting when people are lying, Artair. I don't know, it's just that when I see people doing extremely risky things, like walking into a freezing-cold lake to speak to an unpredictable god, it makes me think that we need to grasp all the opportunities for happiness that we can, right?' Her fox tail swished back and forth. 'Do you know what I mean?'

'Not really, no.' There was a prickling sensation on the back of his neck. He wanted to leave the lake, go back outside and be alone, but that would mean leaving Elver to her fate.

'Sure you do,' said Sunay brightly. 'So why not? Why don't you tell her, Artair? What could you possibly lose?'

'Her friendship,' he said promptly, surprising himself. 'What we have is fragile. And it should be enough for me. And . . .' He swallowed hard. '*He* has more in common with her. He's smart, like she is, and sharp.' The words felt like shards of glass in his throat.

'He's also a little shit,' said Sunay. 'I just think—'

'I don't want to talk about this,' said Artair, a little louder than necessary. 'Please.'

Sunay shrugged, and for a while they lapsed into silence again. Eventually, when the light streaming in through the roof of the cave had dimmed considerably, Sunay opened her mouth again, clearly about to exclaim that all this was madness, that their friend had just wandered into a lake and drowned herself, what, by all the Twelve, were they doing just standing there – when the surface of the water broke, and Elver emerged with a wet crash, gasping. Artair and Sunay both jumped.

'It took ages to find the right place,' said Elver, wading out of the pool with water streaming from her hair and clothes, utterly sodden. 'And that was cold, even for me.' She shivered violently.

'Did it work?' asked Sunay. 'How will we know if it does?'

Artair pulled off his own fur-lined cloak and wrapped it round Elver's shoulders. He thought she might protest, but the grateful look she shot him made him feel warm. He deliberately did not look at Sunay.

'I don't know,' said Elver, 'I've never tried this before. When

I'm in the Jih Forest—'

She was cut off by the sound of bells ringing, and the light dancing over the walls of the cave took on a golden hue, as though it were reflecting off thousands of shining coins. The surface of the lake broke again, although silently this time, and the enormous head and flexible neck of the Queen of Serpents rose to tower over them. Artair had seen the god twice before: once, when he had followed Elver to a frozen lake and witnessed the serpent strike the girl with the lash of her tail, and finally when the queen had burst out of the dying body of the Bloody Claw. Both times, he had been some distance away; now he was close enough to see each yellow scale, and the lights like stars that scattered across the god's black, lidless eyes.

Poison child. He felt the voice enter his head without troubling to go through his ears. The great horned head turned slightly to regard them all. *And others. What do you want?*

Elver stepped forward. She looked swamped in Artair's cloak, but she lifted her head up and spoke clearly.

'The First of Monsters. What is it? Where is it?'

For a time, the Queen of Serpents didn't speak. Beneath the water, the golden coils of her body shifted and seethed, but her head simply hung above them, unmoving.

Who has told you of him?

'Other gods,' said Elver. 'Mother Maura is out to kill us, and we need something capable of killing a god. According to Tisk, the First of Monsters can do it.' She paused, and when she spoke again her voice was quieter. 'I've never heard of anything like this in the Jih Forest.'

Such things are not for mortal ears.

'Well, I'm not really mortal, am I? You made sure of that.'

Artair felt something tighten in his chest. He knew that Elver had changed, but it was hard to hear it spoken out loud.

The Queen of Serpents raised her head and looked at him and

Sunay – the inference was clear.

'And these two are my friends. They've cared for me more than any other humans, so what you tell me you can tell them. Right?' Elver's tone was forthright – the dynamic between her and the god had changed significantly since he'd seen them together at the frozen lake. 'Maura tried to kill me – did kill me, in fact. Don't you want to have revenge?'

Very well. It is not a small thing you ask of me, poison child. This is a wound I have kept hidden for thousands of mortal years, and it is a great agony to expose it. However . . . The god lifted part of her body out of the water, causing the sunlight to roll across her scales, casting golden light against the wall. Images began to form there, figures made of light. *Once, I had an ungainly form like yours . . .*

A shape like a tall woman with golden hair moved across the wall – Artair heard Sunay gasp with wonder.

At the very beginning of time, I was Brishta, god of light and all shining things.

'Even in darkness, light,' murmured Elver.

I was married, and we had a child, called Tython, continued the serpent. *Tython was perfect.*

On the cave wall, another figure appeared, smaller and brighter than the first. It danced across the rock, happy and carefree, tugging at his mother's hand.

But Tython carried within him a seed of death, and despite his godly nature he began to fade, and grow sickly. His father and I did everything we could – even beseeched our brother, the Hooded Crow, to close his realm to our child, but that cowardly bird would not help. He told me instead that it was in Tython's very nature to die.

The bright figure of the child grew dimmer, flickering and guttering like a candle in too stiff a breeze. Artair looked at the Queen of Serpents' long snout, but it was impossible to guess what she might be feeling.

'What did you do?' asked Sunay, swept up in the story.

I changed his nature, said the queen. *I was a god, was I not? I reached into the very core of my child and I moulded and twisted and changed every part of him until that seed of death had become something else entirely – it became the ability to give death where none should exist. He was new, and strange, and his heart was formed of poison, but he was no longer dying.*

The dim figure of the child fell away into strands of light, then re-formed over and over again, a different shape each time.

Artair glanced at Elver; she looked uncertain, a frown creasing her brow as she watched Tython be twisted into a myriad of inhuman forms.

When I had finished, Tython was . . . not as he had been. And neither was I. This magic, this power, had re-formed me as it had re-formed him.

The woman of golden light changed too, becoming long and slender, arms and legs forming into one sinuous being, her head lengthening and splitting open, growing sharp teeth.

We had both become something else, continued the Queen of Serpents. *I was no longer the god of bright things – I was the god of change. My husband, Trilot, was displeased.*

Elver jumped as if she'd been pinched. 'Your husband was Trilot? The god of purity? That bastard?'

The queen's coils moved sinuously, rubbing scale against scale – the sound it produced was like a wet finger running round the edge of a glass goblet.

That's not quite who he was then. Then, he was a god of balance, and peace, but he also changed, although not in the same way Tython and I did. He could not accept that our son was no longer perfect – not perfect, but alive! The great serpent slashed her tail through the water. *No, he became obsessed with perfection and purity, praising it where he found it and burning difference and flaws from everyone else. And he called* me *the monster.*

'This is a lot to take in,' said Sunay. 'I had never heard of Brishta, or of Trilot having a form before the one we all know and love.'

'Tython is the First of Monsters,' said Artair quietly. 'Isn't he? What happened to him?'

The Queen of Serpents lowered her body back into the lake, and the golden shapes on the wall swirled and died.

Tython could not understand what he had become, or why his father hated him so. And the other gods, they were terrified of what I had created, because Tython could kill that which should not die. The great serpent snorted. *Because they were weak.*

'So he can do it? The First of Monsters kill a god?' asked Artair.

It is why I had to hide him, somewhere deep and dark, where only the fish can see. Just like humans, the gods cannot tolerate what is different. That was the end of my family, she added.

'Where is he?' asked Elver.

I cannot tell you. I swore that I would never reveal his location, not to anyone. And if I tell you now, what's to say the other gods will not find out? They would kill him, if they got the chance. Trilot would . . . Trilot would be very glad to see Tython finally purified. As she spoke, her snout turned towards Sunay, who took a couple of steps back. *And the reek of other gods is strong on your companions, poison child.*

'If you trust me, you can trust them,' said Elver shortly. 'Tell us where he is.'

I cannot, and I will not, said the Queen of Serpents. Her voice was like a door slamming shut. *Do not ask me again.*

'Is he like me?' asked Elver, apparently ignoring the god's tone. 'Somewhere out there is another poison heart, right? A heart like mine?'

The Queen of Serpents did not answer. Instead, she began to sink back into the black water. Elver watched her go.

'Fine,' she said, as the water closed over the last of the serpent's shining horns. 'Fine! Do you hear me? I'll find him myself.'

CHAPTER 9

They stood for a long moment, all of them, watching the water where the Queen of Serpents had vanished.

'Trilot,' said Elver into the silence. Of everything they had just heard, this seemed to her the hardest bit to take. 'Trilot? She married *him*? And then never thought to mention it?'

'Ah, well, sometimes old relationships are too painful to talk about,' said Sunay in a world-weary tone. 'I think if I'd been daft enough to end up shackled to that self-righteous weirdo, I'd also keep it quiet.'

'And to think she was human-shaped once,' said Artair quietly. 'To go from being the god of light to a giant serpent, with all the teeth, and horns . . .'

Elver glanced at him as her stomach turned over. What would Artair think if he'd seen her shadow? Would he run screaming, like the priest of Trilot had? She had once thought him weak, but Artair had a quiet strength, and wasn't easily frightened. He might not run, but he might be horrified, and somehow that was worse.

'I don't imagine that was easy,' he continued. 'Perhaps that was another reason she never spoke about it.'

'I wonder what *he* looks like,' said Sunay. 'The first ever jih spirit! The first being to ever step outside the bounds of the natural!'

'Whatever he looks like, we need to find him.' Elver went and crouched down by the water, letting the tips of her fingers dangle in it. 'I have an idea how to do it. I don't know if it will work.'

When her head had slipped under the surface of the lake, she'd had a brief moment of panic. She had felt strongly that the water couldn't do her any harm – water was the queen's element, and it was loyal to her and her children – but drowning still felt like a distinct possibility. Yet, when that fleeting bubble of panic had passed, she found the water that seeped up her nose and into her mouth was friendly, and around her the bottom of the lake shimmered into a bright and oddly colourful life: bright green water grasses and the blue frogs; tiny silver fish and bubbles like glass. She knew, looking at them, that beneath the lake was a series of waterlogged tunnels – the fish were very familiar with them, these hollow fingers pressing deep into the earth. And, sensing that, she felt an echo of other, nearby watery places. They were all connected.

'What do you need us to do?' asked Artair.

'Leave me be for a while,' she said. Realizing that her words had an edge she didn't mean, she turned and looked at the pair of them. 'I mean, go and check on Fleet, will you? I need to concentrate in here and he might be getting in trouble.'

'What will you do?' asked Sunay. Elver could tell from the look on her friend's face that she was worried she'd be going back into the freezing lake.

'The Queen of Serpents has hidden the First of Monsters in a watery place – she said that only fish could see him. And I think I can find those – the watery places, I mean. Whatever the First of Monsters is, he must be at least a little like me. Neither of us are normal jih – we are both her children.' Her hand drifted up to touch her breastbone. 'He also has a poison heart.'

Neither of them looked convinced. In fact, both Artair and Sunay looked concerned, as though she had started to lose her mind, and it was annoying.

She waved them off. 'Go on. Go check on Fleet. I'll tell you if I figure it out.'

When she'd heard their footsteps diminish, she bent back down and slipped her hand into the water again. Her awareness of the lake blossomed, closer and faster now that she had already walked across the bottom of it, and from there she let her water-sense spread further, trickling out across the dark earth. There were tiny rivulets of lake water splitting off from the larger tunnels, too deep and dark and narrow to carry even the smallest fish. Somewhere to the east, there was a trio of fast-flowing rivers, joining up with each other and then splitting, only to mingle their waters again even further east, like children skipping a rope. Northwest of them, there was a spring, the water as pure as sunlight, and then to the west a whole series of lakes. With her new awareness of the queen's element, she sensed how they were linked to each other, green waters moving deep, deep underground.

It was the furthest of these, almost beyond her range, that she felt something . . . new.

In all the watery places, she had been aware of the teeming little lives that depended on the lakes and ponds and rivers. The fish, the frogs, the toads, the eels, the water spiders, the otters, the voles, the bright blue birds that made their nests in the slippery mud of riverbanks. She even came across the odd jih spirit, wanderers who had left the forest behind. But this was something else.

This felt like . . . her.

She threw her awareness towards it, seeking out a greater darkness in the midst of the watery murk. There, deep below the surface, under water filled with the flitting golden movements of thousands of fish, another poison heart was beating. She felt her own tremble in response to it.

There you are.

She could not see what he looked like, his size or shape, but she felt the First of Monsters become aware of her presence. There was a flash of surprise, then fear, then anger, and the lake full of golden fish that her mind was touching suddenly became a place of thorns and jagged edges. Instinctively, she recoiled, pulling her awareness away, but not before she heard a ragged hiss, in the very centre of her head.

Stay away, the First of Monsters said. *Or I will hurt you.*

Elver stood up, shivering violently. The voice had been filled with a kind of blind fury and shock, turning the water black, and the remnants of it felt chilly in her head, making the backs of her eyes throb. She drew a sleeve over her mouth, tasting the brackish lake water on her lips.

'I can't do that,' she said aloud. 'So you'd better get ready for company.'

CHAPTER 10

They had left the hill behind and were walking under a bright, wintery moon, all of them too awake to consider camping just yet. There was something about standing and talking with a god, Artair mused, that made everything too sharp to sleep. Elver particularly seemed filled with energy. She had told them that she had managed to locate the First of Monsters through her sense of the water, and although Artair was fairly sure he had no idea what that meant, he trusted that she knew what she was talking about. Now she was leading them steadily east. All of them were keeping their eyes open for signs of Maura's acolytes, but so far they had seen nothing.

'We should pass the very edge of the Jih Forest on our way,' said Elver. She nodded at Fleet. 'So if you want to go back, Fleet, now is the time to say so.'

The keltraxia cub looked back at her, ears pricked, and Artair watched Elver react to something he said. Despite Artair's own jih nature, Elver was the only one who could understand Fleet. She was smiling.

'What did he say?' asked Artair.

'He wants to stay with us,' she said. 'Even though you smell too human, he's got used to it, apparently. And he still has designs on the last of Sunay's socks.'

'Here, look at that!' broke in Sunay. 'That's not something I wanted to see in the dark. Or in the daylight either, to be fair.'

Poking up over the low brow of a hill was the vast stony profile of a lion, its jaws agape. Artair felt a shiver of something like fear go through him, and also, very briefly, a deep familiarity – since Tisk had pushed them together at Prideful Leap, he occasionally experienced echoes of Lucian, as though the mage were standing just behind him, whispering into his ear.

In the moonlight, the lion was a thing made of crisp shadows, and he realized he wouldn't have been surprised if it turned its head to look at them. It was large enough to be too close to the real Bloody Claw, the god made of blood and flesh that had eaten Elver in one bite.

'What is it? A temple?' asked Artair.

'I should think so, yes,' said Sunay. 'We're passing that way. Shall we go and have a look at it?'

'Lucian would want to, I think,' said Elver.

'We're going to find the First of Monsters,' said Artair. 'Not doing a tour of temples.' Elver talking about what Lucian might want gave him a tight, hot feeling in his chest. It seemed that she trusted him too readily these days.

'I'd have thought you'd want to see all the sights,' Sunay commented mildly. 'Given how long you were locked up in that monastery.'

As they made their way round the base of the hill, the stone lion emerged fully into the night. It stood crouched on its back legs, sitting as a human might, with its front paws held in front of its chest. Although they weren't lit, Artair could see braziers inside its enormous gaping mouth, and there were steps leading up to a wide doorway in its belly. The double doors stood open, darkness yawning within. There were no lights anywhere that they could see, and no movement either. A bird had nested in the nook between one great ear and its head.

'It's abandoned,' said Sunay. 'I wonder what it felt like, to his mages, when the Bloody Claw died. Lucian doesn't talk about it.'

'Good riddance.' Elver kicked a stone down the path towards the temple. 'I'm still glad to see the back of that mangy old cat, even if it means Maura is throwing her weight around. I wonder if there's anything useful inside?'

Sunay's eyebrows pricked up. 'Items stolen from a temple of the Bloody Claw might still have value to my lord . . .'

Artair followed them up the path, a mixture of emotions weighing heavy in his chest. Picking over the remains of the Bloody Claw's temple felt wrong somehow, although he couldn't put his finger on why – which made him suspect that this was Lucian's sentiment bleeding through. Did that mean that Lucian experienced echoes of his emotions too? He watched Elver moving lightly up the path, the moonlight making her white hair shine like a beacon. Did it mean that Lucian knew how he felt about Elver? There was something awful about the idea. He and Lucian might be on the same side, but he still felt like an enemy; the thought that his enemy might know, or even suspect, his true feelings . . .

Red light washed over the stone face of the lion, and for a brief second Artair thought the old god was back, appearing here in the middle of nowhere to finish the meal that killed him – and then he realized he could hear rapid footsteps crunching on the gravel behind him. He turned in time to see a fiery red portal wink out of existence and a figure running directly, furiously towards them.

She wore a white tunic with Maura's two circles embroidered on the chest, and a red silk mask – only her eyes were visible, and they were fixed on him.

'Give back what you stole, Lucian!'

She raised one gloved hand and above them several new stars sprang into being, hovering just above their heads. When he looked closer, he saw that they were all hands made of a glittering white light, their fingers hooked into claws. Beams of light flew from their palms, coalescing into one wider beam, which was aimed at him.

'Move!'

He leapt out of the way just as the beam hit the ground, sending up a hot sizzle of sparks, and then Elver was barging past him, hands outstretched.

The mage, though, was faster. She raised her other arm, and a ghostly hand the size of a person scooped her up, moving her rapidly away from Elver's poison touch. Behind him, Artair could hear Sunay swearing colourfully.

'Which of you is it? The turncoat or the monk?'

Artair realized that he recognized the voice the second before Dalesh leapt down from the ghostly hand. She had pulled a curving dagger from her belt, just like the ones he'd seen in the hands of Maura's acolytes at the monastery – daggers that had slit the throats of every brother and sister of the order. She leapt at him, blade flashing, but she wasn't fast enough and he brought his arm up in a sweeping motion and easily knocked the dagger from her hand, sending it spinning away into the dark. Dalesh hissed and scrambled backwards.

'I knew we should never have trusted you.' Elver rammed into the woman, knocking her flying, but before she even touched the ground, a chorus of glowing hands had righted her and were already forming another beam of magic.

'Look out!' cried Sunay.

The beam of energy struck Elver in the shoulder and she flew back, arms pinwheeling before she struck the back foot of the giant stone lion. Artair's heart leapt into his mouth, but Elver was already picking herself up, albeit slowly.

'How is she doing this?' Sunay had run to Elver to help her to her feet. 'This is spell after spell after spell. It shouldn't be possible!'

'I am more powerful than you can imagine!' bellowed Dalesh,

followed by a sharp exclamation of pain: Fleet had his jaws clamped round her ankle. 'Get away from me, you little freak!' She struck at the keltraxia cub with her fist, and abruptly Artair found that he was running towards the mage, with no idea what he'd do when he got there. The ground under his feet, however, had other ideas; white light rose out of the grass, pooling and forming a wide palm framed with giant fingers. He had a moment to glance up at the twin hand that had appeared directly above him, before it crashed down in an almighty clap.

Lucian awoke into confusion: noise and lights everywhere, the smell of damp grass in his nose and his ears ringing as though someone had struck him about the head. He scrambled to his feet, trying to take in what was going on around him. They were in the hills, outside a temple of the Bloody Claw, and Elver and Sunay appeared to be in the middle of a fight with a masked mage – although, truth be told, it was really only Elver who was doing the fighting. Sunay, her fox's brush bristling with alarm, had scampered to the top of the stone steps to be out of the way. The enemy mage was summoning hands of pearly white light to swipe at Elver, who was doing a good job of dodging, right up until the moment that she wasn't; as he watched, one of them caught her in the centre of the chest and she flew back into the dark, yelling with pain and fury.

The mage turned to look at him, triumphant, and he realized it was Dalesh. She saw the recognition in his own eyes, and snatched her mask away, grinning.

'There you are,' she said. 'It's time to give back what you took, Lucian. Mother is waiting.'

He raised his hands, excitement making them tremble. This was it. The power of the Bloody Claw would work now. It had to.

'Be careful!' called Sunay. 'She's pissing through spells like water.'

'Mother has blessed me,' said Dalesh. She drew a complicated shape in the air and a halo of hands appeared around her, the fingers long and tapered into wickedly sharp nails of light.

'Maura wouldn't know a blessing if it bit her on the arse, Dalesh,' said Lucian. He reached for the power, letting it pool in glowing red threads in his own hands, but it was too slow, and still reluctant to behave how he wanted.

The white hands surrounding Dalesh glowed brighter and brighter, the fingers stretching and weaving like snakes, and then they were flying towards him, nails like wolf's fangs diving for his throat.

'Lucian, look out!' This was Elver, who had pulled herself out of the mud.

With no idea what else to do, Lucian threw up his threads of power, briefly casting a net of glowing red lines around himself; where they struck it, the white hands faltered and vanished, and as he glanced through the net, he saw something unexpected – standing behind Dalesh was a tall figure with long white hair, her eyes as green as emeralds and her hand resting on Dalesh's shoulder. When the threads fell, she vanished, but he knew what he had seen. Maura was here somehow, passing her power directly through Dalesh.

Moving on some instinct he didn't understand, Lucian grabbed hold of one of the remaining hands of light as it spun in the air and yanked it towards him. There was a shriek from Dalesh, and again he had the briefest glimpse of Maura – ghostlike, this time, but still there, and he distinctly saw the look of surprise that passed over her face.

'If you had any sense, Mother, you'd give what remains of His power to *me*. I was always His favourite.'

He clasped the hand to his chest, where it dissolved into red light and sank through his clothes into his skin. There was a rushing sensation, as though the world were suddenly spinning under his feet, and he felt the power that had been banked inside him grow – a tiny amount, but enough to make him dizzy. Maura screamed as though she felt it too, and then she winked out of existence, along with all the burning white lights.

Dalesh stumbled, almost going onto her knees in the mud. 'Mother?'

There was an answering silence, broken only by the sound of Elver breathing hard.

'She's gone, Dalesh. Left you to die in the dirt, and are you even surprised?' Lucian took a step towards the mage, murder at the forefront of his mind, but then another feeling made him hesitate: mercy. It was the monk, he realized, breathing down his neck somehow. 'I should . . . I should kill you now, in front of His temple, just for old times' sake.' A wave of tiredness moved through him, turning the edges of his vision dark. 'Your blood belongs on my knife, Dalesh.'

But he didn't move, and when the mage got up and ran away into the dark, he didn't follow.

CHAPTER 11

Maura lurched back from her desk violently enough to upend the chair and send herself sprawling onto the hardwood floor, smacking the back of her head. In seconds, catlike, she was back on her feet, but the terrible sensation had left an echo behind – the power being drawn out of her, spun away into someone else like a fine line of silk on a spindle. She had felt her strength fading, her godhood shrinking.

'Lucian, you duplicitous little shit. I will shred your life between my fingers. I will pull your guts out through your eyes. I will . . .' Maura pressed her hand to her chest as though she could hold the power there. Her fingers were trembling. She didn't know how he'd done it, but he had taken what was hers. *Again.* 'Dalesh!'

The doll-sized image of the mage appeared on her desk. The woman was bent over at the waist, her hands on her knees, apparently breathing hard.

'All you had to do was kill him, Dalesh. That was all. I gave you access to the power of a god and you failed. You failed!'

'Mother.' Dalesh lifted her head. 'He wasn't alone.'

Maura held her hand over the figure of Dalesh, fingers curled into claws. 'I should kill you. I raised you above all of my followers, Dalesh, because I foolishly thought you were the best of them. And you failed me. I should kill you now, just for the insult of it.' Slowly, she lowered her hand back to her side. 'But Mother is merciful to her children. That is what a mother does. Get out of my sight.'

'I'm sorry I failed you, Mother,' Dalesh said quickly. 'Please, if you gave me the power again . . .'

Maura made a curt gesture and the figure of Dalesh vanished.

She sat for some time at her desk, lost in her own thoughts, when she realized that the shadows around her had grown deep and black, and when she tugged the curtain to one side she saw that for the first time night had come to her domain. A crescent moon sat in the sky like a silver sickle, although she could see no stars.

Warily, she left her little room and stepped out the front door. In the grass to one side of the vegetable patch, a woman with three heads was waiting.

'You had better have a good reason for exerting power over my domain, Enos,' said Maura. 'Or for being here at all.'

One of Enos's three heads glanced up at the moon as though she had no idea it was hanging there.

'She follows me, sometimes,' she said fondly, as though speaking about a beloved pet. 'Apologies. I came to offer you advice, actually.'

Enos's blue-black hair was braided into multiple plaits, two of which hung between each head, and her lips were painted black too – striking against her blue skin.

'Mother, I can feel what you are doing back there.' One of her many arms gestured to the house. 'You have created a direct link with a mortal that requires no tithes.' She turned slightly, allowing her second head to speak. 'Do you know how dangerous that is, my friend?'

'I need to act quickly to get what I need from Prideson. I don't have time to play it safe. The tithes are simply greed and vanity.'

'Not so.' This came from the third head, who, to Maura's eye, had a slyer look about her. 'They don't just give us sustenance – they are the barrier between mortal and god. Take away that barrier and anything may happen. We need to keep our distance from them, Mother. You are simply too recently mortal yourself to see why.'

'Dalesh has always been half terrified of me – she would never turn,' Maura replied dismissively, one hand rubbing absently at her breastbone. The pain was nearly constant now. 'Is that all you have come here to say? I am busy.'

Enos lifted one of her hands above her head and gestured to the moon, turning her fingers delicately as though she were beckoning a child. The moon, which up until a moment ago had appeared as distant and as solid as it always did, shifted and trembled as though it were made of paper, and then it fell, as slowly and as gently as an autumn leaf. It shrank as it fell, until by the time it drifted into Enos's hand it was no bigger than her palm. The moon glowed there for a moment, and then she closed her hand, and it was gone. All three heads smiled.

A demonstration of power, thought Maura.

'There are creatures out in the world called the sleepless,' Enos said eventually. 'I know that you are familiar with them.'

'Obviously I am. Lucian hides within a monk in this fashion. I intend to kill them both.'

'The Sleepless are creatures that never know true sleep, or dreams. They exist outside my reach.' For the first time, Enos frowned, each blue brow furrowing in an identical manner. 'It pleases the Queen of Serpents to hide displaced souls inside the bodies of the living, to vex our brother the Hooded Crow. When I reach out, I can feel all those who sleep, sleepers unending, all across our world. Little blue lights in the dark, under my care.' Her voice had grown soft, but now it sharpened again, her lips thin with anger. 'But there are numb places too, places where I can see and feel nothing, and these are the hateful sleepless, always absent from my realm.'

Maura sighed. 'What is your point?'

'My point, charmless one, is that I hate them, and I will enjoy helping you strike down the sleepless you seek. I can't act directly, but a mage of mine can.'

'Can you kill them?'

'My power is not the power of blood and death, like your old master,' said Enos. 'I have other talents. But I can certainly make things difficult for them.' She raised all six of her arms, and around them the inky darkness of the sky began to lighten at the edges. 'If you wish.'

Maura swallowed hard. It had always been her way – since her family had been killed, at least – to strike out on her own, to be the tip of the spear. There had been acolytes and mages below her, of course, fuel for her to burn, but accepting the help of someone equally powerful? It felt slippery to her, like a loss of control. Yet she remembered the sensation of her own power being pulled from her, the pain as she blessed each mage, and knew that her opportunities to kill Lucian were shrinking fast. She needed all the help she could get.

'You would have my thanks,' she said, forcing each word through her teeth like sharp little pieces of gravel.

Enos nodded with all three heads, black braids bobbing. 'We shall have some fun, Mother. And I'm sure I am not the only one who will help. Just you wait.'

CHAPTER 12

That night, when they paused to rest – all of them still rattled by Dalesh's attack – Elver found herself falling asleep almost as her head touched her bedroll. She dreamed of searching watery places, following a thin line of gold from pond to river to lake and back again, her feet always wet, the mineral taste of silt on her tongue. In the dream, she crested a hill and spotted a tiny boat in the middle of a vast lake – a lake so big it was almost the ocean. The golden thread led to it and seemed to end there. A hard stone of excitement in her chest, she began to run down the hill, but, as she did so, she felt her body change; abruptly, she wasn't running on legs – she had hooves like a horse, talons like an eagle, paws like a bear, claws like a lizard. The sense of excitement became a hot flare of panic, and she woke with a gasp, heart hammering in her chest.

Lucian, who was sitting on the far side of the fire, looked up at her with a raised eyebrow. He had been whittling something with Artair's knife, too small to see.

'A bad dream, monster girl?'

'Something like that.' Around them, the world was still dark, although there was a softness to the night sky that suggested dawn wasn't too far away. Sunay and Fleet were curled up together, their twin snores making a sound that was almost musical. The mage's fox tail was draped over the jih spirit's flank.

'Do you want to talk about it?'

Elver shook her head. 'It was just a dream.' Although moments ago she had felt completely awake, she realized that sleep was claiming her again, making her eyelids and her limbs too heavy to lift. She lay back down. 'I think I need to . . .'

'Go back to sleep.' Lucian gave her a sad smile. 'It's okay. I'm used to it by now.'

The look on his face made her feel strange, and she wanted to look more closely at it, talk to him about it, but the urge to sleep was just too strong. She closed her eyes, and was gone.

It was the next morning, and they had come down out of the hills into a place bursting with lakes, like a puddle-strewn pavement after a heavy storm. Elver could feel all of them: cold, dark presences filled with their own quiet secrets. The brackish taste of still water seemed to lurk at the back of her throat. Somewhere, out there, was the First of Monsters. She could feel him now, certain in the way that you knew the moon was in the sky even when it was hidden behind a thick layer of cloud. *Stay away, or I'll hurt you,* he'd said. The water had turned black with his anger. But they had no choice.

'Did he talk about Dalesh last night?' asked Artair. 'Lucian, I mean.'

The monk had been in a bad mood since he woke up, or at least, his version of a bad mood, which mainly seemed to mean staring sadly at his own boots and not saying very much. When Elver was in a bad mood, she sought out humans to poison – it always made her feel better.

'Little that was coherent, if I am honest with you and, while I am taking the unusual approach of being honest, I'll tell you I can't entirely blame him,' said Sunay. Despite the mage's initial aversion to travelling on foot, she seemed to be growing more used to it, and in the bright morning sunshine had even dared to take off her woolly hat. 'He seemed to think he had drawn Maura's power out of her through the magic that your old pal Dalesh was using.' The three of them had explained their complicated histories with Dalesh already: how the woman had once thrown Elver into the sea, then trained alongside Lucian before his banishment and eventually dragged Artair across the shattered mountain. Sunay's only comment was that Dalesh was clearly a very busy woman. 'I've no idea how that works, given I am not at all familiar with mortals being given the powers of gods directly.' She sniffed. 'But certainly it appears Dalesh was using magic without paying the tithe, which suggests that dear old Mother was pushing it through her somehow. And where there's push, there's pull.'

'And, after that, Dalesh ran away?'

'She looked scared half to death,' said Elver, smiling.

'And I was no use at all.' Artair frowned. His dark hair, released from its braid, had fallen forward to frame the line of his jaw. Elver found it distractingly pleasing to look at – it brought to mind the kiss they had shared in the Jih Forest, how she had pushed her fingers into his hair. Yet that moment now felt a million miles away. How had so much changed, so quickly? 'The last thing I knew about it was those giant magical hands closing around me.'

'Don't be so hard on yourself,' said Sunay. Fleet was trotting along next to the mage, and as they walked, she leaned down to tug her fingers through the red feathers on his ears. 'Magical battles are not for everyone. They certainly aren't for me! I very nearly ruined my britches.'

I bit the bad mage, Fleet exclaimed happily. *With my teeth! I am a brave warrior.*

Artair, though, did not seem reassured by this. As Sunay walked ahead with Fleet, Elver reached over and briefly squeezed his hand.

'We were all in trouble,' she said. 'Even Lucian. It was just luck that got us out of it. It's like the magic that Maura is hoarding wants to return to him.' She cleared her throat, glancing at Artair's hand. It felt good to touch him. 'Artair, I need to ask you something.'

He finally looked up from his boots, his brown eyes full of curiosity, and she felt the question die on her lips. It felt so strange that they had kissed, and then never spoken of it: if she asked him about it now, would he be ashamed? Clearly, he now thought it had been a mistake. Was it worth humiliating them both?

'You do?'

'Hey, what's that over there?' Sunay's voice cut across them both, and Elver turned gladly away, ignoring how her cheeks were burning. 'What's a kid doing out here in the middle of nowhere?'

They were skirting the edge of a deep, green lake, and on the bank nearest to them was a ramshackle little shed covered in moss, its door hanging open on one hinge. Two long narrowboats were pulled up onto the white sand of the shore, and curled up in one of them was a small shape that initially looked to Elver to be a dense pile of odd clothes. And then, as they drew closer, she saw that it was a round-faced child of around eight or nine years old, apparently asleep. He wore a hood pulled tightly round his head, but a few little curls of red hair poked up from his forehead.

'Weird,' said Elver. 'Humans need to watch their cubs more closely. Oh well.' But when she began walking on past, she saw that Sunay and Artair had both stopped by the boat. 'What are you doing? We've got places to be, living weapons to find, to avoid being murdered by an insane demigod. Remember that?'

'Where are his parents?' Sunay looked around, her eyes narrowed. 'Since we started following Elver's route of watery places we've barely seen anyone, save for that charming woman who tried to kill us, and I can't see any sign of anyone else, can you?'

'It certainly is a mystery,' said Elver. 'There's a lake with a lot of edible fish in it just over this next hill. If we hurry up, we can make it before sundown and do some fishing.'

'We can't just leave him here alone, Elver,' said Artair. He was climbing down the sandy bank towards the boat. 'We should at least wake him up and make sure he's alright.'

'I don't know if that's a good idea.' Elver watched as Sunay joined the monk. 'It's probably like baby animals, right? If we touch it, the mother might not like the smell of it when she comes back, and then she'll stop feeding it.'

Sunay made a tutting sound. 'Really, Elver, anyone would think you were raised in the woods. Hello? Hello! Sorry to startle you, little one. We're friendly, I promise.'

The boy in the boat opened his eyes slowly, like a toad, and sat up. He looked around at them all as though he didn't have a clear idea where he was.

'What's your name?' asked Artair.

'Plinko,' said the boy.

'Well, Plinko, are you aware that you are asleep in a boat and there's no one else here?' asked Sunay. 'Where have your parents got to?'

'Plinko doesn't have parents,' he said in a tiny, scratchy voice, as though he'd been asleep for days. His eyes were large and blue.

'Oh. Someone who looks after you, then? The owner of these boats, perhaps?'

The boy stood up and climbed awkwardly out of the narrowboat, dropping down onto the sand with a soft thump. His hood and cloak were patched with many different colours, which Elver realized was why she'd taken him for a pile of clothes.

'Plinko is an orphan,' continued Plinko. 'He lived in a temple of the Bloody Claw.'

Elver and Artair exchanged a glance.

'Were you a mage of the Bloody Claw, Plinko?' asked Artair. 'Or a . . . a priest?'

'No magic for Plinko,' the boy replied. 'Plinko was a servant. He served the head priest his meals, he cleaned the head priest's robes and sometimes he did tricks for the head priest, to make him smile.'

'So why are you in a boat out here, my good fellow?' asked Sunay, her hands on her hips.

'New people came to the temple, and Plinko's master was driven out. All of the priests and novices, all of the servants, scattered in the dark. Plinko was lost.' The boy paused. 'The new people wore circles on their heads, or on their chests. The other servants, they said they would go to Micelle, a nearby town. They said they could find work there.' He performed an elaborate shrug. 'Plinko is lost. He doesn't know where Micelle is.'

'Does anyone else,' asked Elver, 'find the way he is speaking incredibly annoying?'

'Micelle is not that far from here,' said Sunay.

'We can take you, Plinko,' agreed Artair. 'Someone will be able to look after you there.' He turned to Elver. 'Maura's followers have made this child homeless. Don't you think we should help?'

Elver looked at the boy, and then at the boat. Some vestige of her dream floated into her mind – there had been something important in the boat, something she had to reach. And, more to the point, once again Maura was spreading her misery, making the life of an orphan worse than it needed to be. To her annoyance, she felt a pang of sympathy for Plinko.

'We've got better things to do than herd some human child into a human town,' she said, but without any real heat.

'We can hardly leave the little mite out here under the elements,' said Sunay. 'What do you say, Plinko? Fancy some company on the road?'

The boy with the round face tipped his head to one side, blinking. 'Is that a monster with you? Plinko has never seen a monster.'

Elver winced. Fleet had been dragging his paws, sniffing every new smell he could find as they made their winding way through the lakes, but now he came trotting over to the edge of the lake, bold as brass.

Is this our dinner?

'No, Fleet. This kid is going to be travelling with us for a while.' She gave Plinko a hard look. 'As long as he can keep his mouth shut about anything he sees during the journey?'

The boy nodded, his eyes very wide, and Sunay put an arm round him, steering him away from the lake.

'That's good enough for me. You must be hungry, my friend. Would you like some dinner? Shall we share some tricks? Juggling? Sleight of hand? I'm sure you have much to teach me . . .'

Elver watched them walk back up towards the shed, a worried crease in her brow.

Artair smiled. 'It's fine. He's just a kid. We'd get kids that young turning up at the monastery every now and then, scared and lost. They just need a little help.'

'I don't know.' She thought of the dream again. 'If Maura attacks us again, we could get this kid killed.'

'Maura won't attack us in a town. It's too public,' said Artair, although he didn't sound sure.

'I hope you're right.'

That night, after they had spent some time catching fish at the lake beyond the hill, Elver set up her own bedroll some distance from Sunay's, who had taken it upon herself to look after Plinko. The boy had been fed as much baked fish as he could handle, and then wrapped in enough blankets to suffocate him; his cheeks had turned quite pink.

One by one, they settled down for the night, and Elver once again found herself barely able to keep her eyes open. It had been a long day of travelling, after all, and often over the last week she had stayed up late, chatting to whichever of the boys happened to be awake at that time.

Even so, she felt mildly unnerved as sleep eased its heaviness into her limbs and her eyelids. She wanted to keep an eye on Plinko, if she could.

But sleep was too persistent. She was watching the embers of the fire burn down as her eyes drifted shut. The last thing she saw before she dropped off was the sight of Plinko slipping from his blankets, his small form oddly graceful as he moved around the fire.

CHAPTER 13

When Elver awoke, it was still night-time, or else very early in the morning. A faint lilac light was dancing across the surface of the lake, and her sharp ears picked up the soft noises of the world waking up: birds beginning their dawn announcements, smaller creatures emerging from their burrows. To her surprise, Sunay and Fleet and the boy Plinko were nowhere to be seen. There was just Lucian, sitting by the embers of their fire, his head down as though studying something. When she stretched, her shoulders making a sound like a knot of wood popping in the fire, he looked up.

'Monster girl,' he said. 'Come and look at this.'

'Where's everyone else?' She stood up and looked around. The unease she had gone to sleep with blossomed anew in her chest.

Lucian snorted. 'That little brat needed the toilet, and Sunay, thankfully, was happy to take him. With a bit of luck, they'll both get lost in the trees. Elver, how have we picked up a snotty child? I might expect this of the monk, but you have more sense.'

She half smiled at that. 'You should be more sympathetic. He used to be a servant at a temple of the Bloody Claw, but Maura's people threw them all out. We're taking him to a town nearby, so soon he'll be someone else's problem.' She paused. 'Something about him gives me the creeps, though. Maybe because he used to belong to your old god.'

'Hey.' Lucian looked at her from under his eyelashes. '*I* don't give you the creeps, do I? In fact, I'd started to hope you'd grown rather fond of me.'

'You are more appealing than a snotty little kid – I'll give you that.'

He raised an eyebrow at this, a sly smile creeping across his mouth in a way that was annoyingly attractive.

She dragged her eyes away from his. 'Anyway. What was it you wanted me to look at?'

'Oh yes,' said Lucian lightly. 'Here it is, see. What is it?'

As she drew closer, she saw that he had created a little paddock on the ground with his bedroll and bags. Within it, there was a tiny creature, no larger than the palm of her hand. She saw immediately that it was a jih spirit – one of the froudians, in fact. It looked somewhat like an oversized mouse with the head of a robin, and it had a little sack made of green leaves slung over its back. The froudian was darting back and forth, trying to find a way out, but when it tried to climb over the bedroll, Lucian reached over and gently pushed it back down. The creature squeaked with indignation.

'I found it poking around our bags,' said Lucian. 'I've never seen anything like it, so I assume you will know what it is.'

'Let him go,' said Elver mildly. 'He's a froudian. A jih spirit. They're foragers.'

'I didn't know jih spirits could be so small,' said Lucian, not moving to free the creature. 'Did the Queen of Serpents make these too?'

Elver knelt to address the froudian directly.

'Hello. You're some distance from the Jih Forest, you know. Do you need some help getting back?' If they had to herd Plinko to a human town, it seemed that the least they could do was carry a lost monster back to the forest.

But at the sound of her voice, the froudian visibly jumped. It turned eyes on her like tiny red bubbles of ink, and then it made several loud squeaks, clearly upset or frightened. She could not understand what it said.

'Hold on,' she said, frowning. 'Slow down, speak normally . . .'

The froudian shrieked again and threw itself to the far side of Lucian's little paddock, hard enough that the bag moved an inch or so. It scrambled up, tiny limbs flailing, and then it leapt down the other side. Lucian laughed.

'What's it saying?'

'I can't tell – it's just making noises, which is weird. Normally, they're very chatty.'

Curious, Elver followed the creature. The sky was getting lighter all the time, although she didn't need the sun to see the froudian. To her, the jih spirit seemed brighter and crisper than anything around it.

'Are we chasing it down? This reminds me of the time we snuck into that circus and I got punched in the face for you. Remember that?' Lucian's voice came from just behind her.

Elver let her eyes track the froudian as it scampered through the undergrowth. It had to be heading back to more of its kind. Froudians always moved in groups – they were incredibly sociable creatures – and perhaps she'd be able to get some sense out of the others. It could be that this particular froudian wasn't able to speak, or had been injured in some way.

'I remember it,' she said. Back then, she had barely known Lucian, but he had agreed to help her where Artair couldn't. 'Hopefully Booster Barnham is out of business now. I should think—'

Suddenly, the ground under her foot slipped away and she pitched forward. Too late, she realized that the jih spirit had scurried down a sharp incline, hidden by a thicket of blackberry bushes, and she was about to follow it down there at speed. Before she could fall, a strong arm looped round her waist and pulled her back. She and Lucian stumbled together, trying to keep on their feet and only just succeeding. Somehow, she had ended up in his arms, looking up at him.

'Nearly lost you there, monster girl,' he said, too brightly, before letting her go. For a few seconds they stood close, just inches apart.

'Thanks.' She cleared her throat. The sense of his arms round her, warm and solid, did not quite want to leave her; more than that, she wanted to feel it again.

'I've missed that, you know,' he said quietly. 'Uh. Touching you, I mean.' He glanced around, as though expecting Sunay and Plinko to suddenly stumble on them. 'There was a time when it was all I could think about. Because you were giving me back pieces of my life.'

'You don't think about it any more?'

He grinned and leaned in closer to her again. 'Oh no, monster girl, I think about it all the time. It seems that even with all my memories restored, your poison touch is something I crave.'

Around them, the lilac light was fading, edging towards the clear blue of an early winter morning. There was a look in Lucian's eyes that she was half certain she had not seen there before: there was the usual cunning watchfulness, ready at any time to tip over into mockery, but underneath it was something close to nerves. It was remarkable to see, like finding a pearl amongst waterlogged pebbles.

'Here. How does this feel?' She took hold of his wrists gently, sweeping the pads of her thumbs over the delicate skin there, her fingers resting on the backs of his hands. His eyes widened, and she laughed, delighted. There was something especially delicious about surprising Lucian.

'It feels wonderful,' he said.

And she thought she might try to surprise him again, but he beat her to it, lowering his head and catching her mouth with a kiss. She stepped into the circle of his arms and he pulled her close in one fierce movement, as though worried she might slip away again. When his tongue touched hers, it was as though every part of her lit up, like a paper lantern aflame, rising into the night.

Lucian.

They moved together naturally, almost . . .

Almost as if they had done this before.

She pulled back, suddenly certain that it hadn't been Artair she had kissed in the Jih Forest after all. Lucian smiled at her, and she found that she was almost . . . glad? She reached up to stroke his cheek, as she had done in the woods that time, but what came into view wasn't her hand – it was a hooked appendage with three clawed fingers, a section of greenish web between each of them, thick and slimy. As she watched, the jagged claws tore into his cheek, opening his flesh as easily as a hot knife through butter.

'Why, Elver,' said Lucian, grinning all the wider, 'you're beautiful.'

She woke with a yelp, her heart hammering in her chest. They were still in the camp, they were *all* in the camp, and they were all staring at her in surprise. Ignoring them, she looked down at her hands, half expecting them to have changed – but they were as they had always been. Pale. Human-looking. Normal.

It was a dream, she told herself. *Just a dream. It doesn't mean anything.*

'Are you alright, Elver?' In her confusion, she couldn't tell if it was Artair or Lucian speaking.

'I'm fine,' she said shortly, before standing up. It was late morning, and she had slept later than normal. Plinko was awake too, playing solitaire with a deck of cards he had produced from one ragged pocket. The boy looked up at her with his round, expressionless face. He looked, somehow, younger than he had the day before, as though a year had fallen away from him overnight. Holding her eyes, he placed a single card in front of him. It was the card of Beginnings, illustrated by a spider spinning a web. Elver frowned at him. 'Let's just get out of here.'

CHAPTER 14

The hills and lakes ended, the water becoming less and less contained until it had sunk into the earth, and they found themselves picking their way through the beginnings of a wide, open swamp. The water was still and green, covered in a skin of lurid algae, while odd, fat-bottomed trees broke the surface, none of them growing any taller than Artair himself. There were ridges of firmer land, and these were what they followed, taking a snaking route deeper into the swamp. The place had a very particular smell Artair had not come across before, a kind of thick, vegetable rot, and he thought that of all the places he'd seen since leaving the monastery, this might be his least favourite. At least the shattered mountain had had a decent view.

As they walked, Elver and Sunay argued about the route.

'There has to be a more picturesque way to our destination,' said Sunay, her usually bright tone significantly dimmed.

'This is the quickest,' snapped Elver. 'And it goes through Micelle. You want to get that kid to someone who can look after him as soon as possible, right?' She lowered her voice. 'Listen, Maura has messed up his life, so I want to help him too, but it's worth remembering that *our situation* isn't exactly safe.'

'Think of my boots, Elver,' said Sunay wistfully. 'Think of my socks. I only have a few good pairs left since Fleet stayed with me.'

Artair glanced at Plinko. The boy was watching his own feet as he walked, taking care to step on the driest bits of grass. He didn't talk much and when he did, it was, Artair had to admit, mildly unnerving. It felt like Plinko spent most of his time in his own private world.

'Once,' Artair said, 'Brother Benzin lost a box of laundry in one of the storerooms. It stayed there for the whole summer, hidden behind sacks of flour. When we found it again, it smelled quite a bit like this place.'

'You should both be glad we're here at the beginning of winter,' said Elver, who was walking in ankle-deep swamp water and didn't seem to mind. 'If this were summer, we'd be eaten alive by bugs.'

The landscape around them was mostly flat, and shrouded in a shifting mist that made everything feel cold and damp, but Artair thought he could see something else, something in the distance coming closer. For a time, he did not mention it, thinking that Elver's eyes were sharper than his, and it had to be an illusion created by the water and the fog. But Elver, he gradually realized, was out of sorts, and not paying attention to the world around them as she usually did. He cleared his throat, and pointed.

'What are those tall structures? Are there buildings here?'

The two women lifted their heads. Plinko kept his eyes on his boots.

'Ah!' Sunay straightened up. 'I think I know what those are.'

'You do?' asked Elver. She had cupped her hands around her eyes, her mouth turned down at the corners. Her white hair was spangled with beads of moisture, making the ends curl up wetly. He imagined for a moment pushing his fingers through her hair, chasing the water from it; he thought of her leaning into his touch.

'Priests of Vilon the Many Limbed,' said Sunay. 'Weirdoes, even by my standards.'

'The gods of the arts?' Artair dragged his mind back to the present moment. 'Why would their priests be weird?'

'Just keep your eyes on those towers,' said Sunay.

They continued picking their way forward, and gradually the shapes did indeed resolve into towers: tall, thin and simple, they were built mainly from grey, moss-covered stones, although some appeared to have been augmented with other possibly scavenged materials – an old wooden crate, the metal frame of a bed, rusted iron chains. On top of each was a small platform of wooden planks, and, on that, a single figure. Most were sitting; a few were standing. Just from where they were, Artair could see around twenty of the towers.

'I don't like that,' said Elver. 'What if one of them spots Fleet? Perhaps we should go the other way, after all.'

Sunay threw her arms up. 'When you've already ruined my boots? It'll be fine. You'll soon see why.'

As the sun began to dip towards the horizon, a deep orange light flooded the swamp, burning away much of the mist and revealing the gaunt figures on the tops of the towers. The closest was a short figure in ragged clothes, his arms bare to the shoulders, his fingers clutching a long brush. Over his head he wore what Artair initially took to be a warrior's helmet, until he saw that it had no eye holes – no holes at all, in fact. It was made of metal and had flourishes where the parts of a face should be, but no way for the man to look out. When Artair glanced at the other figures nearby, he saw that they were all wearing similar things.

'Trilot's withered arse. How do they not fall off?' asked Elver.

'And why do they do it?' asked Artair. 'What are they doing up there?'

'I told you, didn't I?' said Sunay, sounding pleased with herself. 'Most of the god-touched are strange – and, yes, I include myself in that – but the artist priests of Vilon are a particularly dedicated bunch.' She gestured to the nearest platform. 'In order to receive Vilon's purest inspiration, their priests hide themselves away from the world – in boggy little shitholes like this one – and then they tune out all things so that they can receive Vilon's messages more clearly. They can't see anything with those helmets on, and there's nothing much to listen to out here, either.'

'For what?' demanded Elver, who sounded unusually outraged.

'Inspiration, like I said! Supposedly the priests of Vilon produce some of the most important works of art Tlevrae has ever seen. Surely you have heard of Priana's Michael? Or Flotella's great painted ceiling in the shrine at Addersport?'

Elver looked blank. Artair felt for a moment that Lucian was close – in fact, he had the sense that Lucian knew of both works of art, and had strong opinions on them. Then it was gone.

'Neither of you?' Sunay looked scandalized. 'Priana spent seven years at the top of her tower, only coming down at night to eat and drink, and at the end of it she had the sketches for one of the most acclaimed statues in the world. I bet she never had to work again.' Sunay's voice took on a musing tone. 'In a way, these priests are almost mages. They offer up their deprivation and solitude to Vilon almost like tithes, and in exchange they are granted a glimpse of their greatest work.'

'Or maybe they're out here so long their heads cook inside their helmets, and their *inspiration* is a fever dream,' said Elver hotly.

'This upsets you,' said Sunay. It wasn't quite a question.

'It's stupid! There's all of the world to take inspiration from, and these lot are spending their lives looking at the inside of their own eyelids.'

'The inside of their helmets,' said Plinko, and for a dangerous second Artair thought Elver was going to kick the child into the water.

Sunay slid a little on the damp grass, her fox tail swishing back and forth. 'Well, I quite agree, Elver. It is rather stupid. But the good news is they are very unlikely to spot our friend here and cause any trouble. So there's no need to turn back – as much as that pains me to admit.' Fleet didn't seem concerned at all, and had taken himself off to cock a leg against one of the towers. Artair held in a laugh, and glanced at Elver to see if she'd seen what the keltraxia cub was up to, but she had her head down, an expression of weariness on her face. She had been changeable since coming back from the shadowed lands, but today even her usual spark seemed dampened.

'Fine,' she said. 'Let's keep going. Perhaps we can get out of this swamp before it gets too dark.'

That, however, proved to be optimistic. The five of them continued to pick their meandering way through the boggy water as the sun set and a thin layer of ice began to scud the edges of the solid land. The swamp – with its priest towers – seemed to stretch on and on. Once, as they passed under a tower, the figure on top of it sprang to her feet and cried out, her voice as shrill as a night bird's. She had a bundle of parchment in one hand.

'Vilon, I thank you!' she called. 'I see it now! What this story is missing is a transformation, a terrible creature lurking beneath the surface. I will make notes right away . . .' The artist priest yanked off her helmet and sat down on the platform, but she never even glanced over the side. They carried on away from her, being especially quiet, until the shadows were so deep Artair found that he kept nearly treading on Plinko – the boy had slowed down drastically, and had pulled his deck of cards out of his pocket. Rather than looking at the makeshift path, he was shuffling them slowly.

'We should stop for the night,' said Artair. He hated to admit it, but he suddenly felt incredibly tired. Traipsing through the mist and icy ankle-deep water had worn him out more than he realized.

'Where?' said Elver sharply. 'Unless you feel like drowning in five inches of bog water.'

'Here, look.' Sunay broke away from the path, sploshing through the swamp. Ahead of her were two towers, each with empty platforms at their tops. 'Me and Plinko can take this one, you and Artair take the other. Fleet can join who he pleases. I imagine you'll have to carry him up, though. Those paws don't look much good for climbing. That way, we're out of the water, and Maura's acolytes will find it much harder to sneak up on us.'

'He says he doesn't want to go up the stupid tower,' said Elver, looking doubtfully at the structure nearest them. 'He will hunt instead. Listen. Won't these have priests coming back to use them?'

'If they do, just stick a bag over your head and pretend you're one of them,' said Sunay, who was already climbing. Plinko made his way up behind her, apparently unconcerned by the rickety tower.

The tower Artair and Elver were standing under was one of the sturdier ones, the whole thing built from grey stone that had been shaped and placed by someone with a skilled hand. There were large wooden pegs sticking out of the gaps at regular intervals, and Artair supposed that was what passed for a ladder. The platform above them looked just about big enough for them both to sit on, if they sat close.

'I can go and look for another empty one,' he said quietly. 'If you want more room . . .' It seemed important to give Elver some space – whatever it was she was going through, it appeared she didn't want to share it. Yet the thought of traipsing off to find another empty tower filled Artair with disappointment. He wanted to be close to her.

Elver gave him a tired look. 'Come on. Let's just get up there.'

When they reached the top, Artair was struck by how different the swamp appeared from above. The mist had cleared out, leaving a raw, star-strewn sky behind, and milky starlight painted the water white and grey. There was more movement than he'd been expecting. The surface rippled with glimmering circles as the tiny frogs and fish that made the swamp their home went about their lives. The towers of Vilon stretched in all directions, figures with lumpy, misshapen heads standing or sitting in silence.

'The world certainly is stranger than I was expecting,' he said aloud.

Elver grunted. She had already pulled out her bedroll and was trying to get comfortable on it. Awkwardly, Artair sat next to her. If he stretched out fully, his legs would stick off the end.

'You'd think that they'd at least build a little fence round the edge of this thing,' said Elver, pausing to yawn. 'If I roll over in my sleep, I'll break my neck.'

'I could hold you, if you like.'

'What?'

Artair felt his cheeks burn. 'I mean, I could hold on to the back of your coat, so you don't fall.'

'You can hardly do that all night.'

'I don't really sleep, remember?' The thought of going to sleep, then having Lucian wake up to share this tiny space with Elver was an uncomfortable one. He suddenly wished that he'd asked Sunay for some kopi before she climbed the tower.

For a moment, the weariness that had hung over Elver all day seemed to lift, and she smiled a little.

'That's kind of you, Artair. If you need a break from stopping me from plummeting to my death, do wake me up. It might be good to talk without Fleet trying to eat my boots.' She paused and yawned hugely. 'Right now, though, I need to sleep. Gods, I'm tired.'

With that, she curled up on her side, facing away from him. After a moment, Artair laid down behind her, and lightly placed one hand on her shoulder; there was a good portion of her coat to grip there. But after a few minutes her cold hand reached up to take his, and pulled it round so that his arm looped her waist, their fingers intertwined. She seemed to relax then, a warm form curled just in front of him. From where they lay, it was possible to see the tower that Sunay and Plinko had climbed. The pair of them were still setting up for the night.

'I'll be glad to be rid of that kid,' said Elver softly. She sounded half-asleep already. 'Something about him tires me out.'

'Sunay seems quite taken with him,' said Artair, only half listening. His mind was abruptly occupied with the idea of staying awake as long as possible. If he went to sleep now, he'd be delivering Elver literally into Lucian's arms. The thought filled him with quiet alarm. He shifted, trying to find a less comfortable position, but Elver made a noise of complaint, so he stopped.

'Sunay is . . . a fool,' said Elver, her words muffled. 'She thinks trouble . . . is fun.'

On the other platform, the mage had apparently made her bed, but Plinko was still up. Artair watched the child walk back and forth on the platform, his hands moving. He thought perhaps he was shuffling his cards still.

'What's he doing?' whispered Artair, but the only answer was Elver's soft, fluting snore. Plinko, meanwhile, had stopped and appeared to be looking across at their platform. He was holding up a card. Artair frowned, and then lowered his head back to the bedroll. *Let Plinko do what Plinko wants*, he thought. *I have to stay awake.*

CHAPTER 15

Artair lay listening to the sounds of the night swamp.

Curled just in front of him, Elver was a warm presence, her side rising and falling in the slow rhythm of someone deeply asleep.

He wondered what that was like; what it felt like. The sensation felt long lost to him. Once, before the Golden Tower of the Perpetual Morning, he had slept long and deep. He'd had vivid dreams and even remembered some of them on waking. There hadn't been many lazy mornings – his people woke with the sunrise, and there were always ponies to be tended, dogs to be fed – but he dimly remembered that sense of slowly climbing out of a dream into waking, the world taking on a solidity again. Now, though – no sleep, and no dreams. Not for him. His eyes moved back to Elver again. He could smell the scent of her hair. It seemed there were a number of things that were out of reach, but at least he had this small moment with her.

On the other platform, Plinko had settled down, but there was still movement over there. Curious, Artair propped himself up on one elbow.

Sunay was awake. He saw her stand up, lit by the milky starlight, and scamper over to the edge of the platform, her fox tail bobbing. All around them, the towers of Vilon stood silent, like accusing fingers pointing at the inky sky, and the figures that sat on them were unmoving – caught, he supposed, in contemplation of Vilon's vision. The shrill *reep reeps* of tiny frogs floated up from the waters below.

Sunay sat down on the edge of the platform, her legs dangling off the sides, swinging her feet back and forth. It seemed she couldn't sleep, and it occurred to Artair that he might go and see if she wanted company – she always had interesting stories to tell, and, of course, there was the kopi in her pack . . . But then Elver shifted in her sleep, pressing her back more firmly to his chest, and he abandoned all thoughts of that.

Sunay, still kicking her legs back and forth, raised a hand, and to Artair's surprise the night seemed to grow a little lighter. It was true that he had lost track of time, but it couldn't be anywhere close to dawn. Yet there was a soft orange glow reflected in the still waters, and Elver's hair was soaking up the light, turning each strand into something fire-touched. And then he saw that the light was coalescing in front of Sunay, a soft ball of light as orange as pumpkins, and he knew what it was. Or *who* it was. Lying next to Elver, Artair frowned.

Tisk appeared out of the light, stepping into thin air as casually as a man stepping in his own front door. He was in his human form, a dapper man with a gingery moustache and a fine velvet frock coat. The god gestured at the space in front of him and the orange light pooled there, creating a second platform in midair. After a moment of obvious indecision, Sunay stepped over onto it.

'My lord,' she said. In the hush of the swamp, her voice was unusually clear, even though she was evidently speaking quietly. 'I'm not sure you should be here.'

Artair felt the hairs on the back of his neck prickle. Yes, Tisk was technically an ally. He had told them of the First of Monsters, a weapon that could stop Maura, and he'd promised the assistance of other gods too. But he had also sided with Lucian, helping him to escape and going as far as locking Artair in a cupboard. Even at Prideful Leap, his actions had felt slippery with motives that Artair could hardly guess at. And here he was, consulting in secret with his mage.

'I go where I want, Sunay. You know that.' Tisk held out one hand to her, and when she took it he lifted her arm, making her twirl on the spot. 'How are you getting on with the tail?'

'Oh, you know, it's fantastic. I had to cut holes in all my trousers, skirts, my underwear. I keep forgetting it's there and sitting on it, so that when I stand up it's all flat and I have to brush it out. I've been passing it off as the latest fashion accessory in town.' Sunay ended the twirl with an elaborate bow. 'Any chance you've come here to take it away?'

'I'm afraid it's still amusing me greatly, so, no.' Tisk looked around the swamp. Even from atop the other tower, Artair could see the unimpressed expression that passed over the god's face. 'Well, this is an interesting little armpit you've found yourself in. How goes our scheme, Sunay?'

The mage glanced over at their platform. Artair held himself very still. If Sunay didn't want them to hear her conversation with her god, then he definitely wanted to hear it. The sense that Lucian was close abruptly returned, as though the mage were sitting just behind him, watching Sunay just as closely – he almost thought he could feel Lucian's anger building, a red shadow of his own.

'I'm doing everything you told me to, lord,' said Sunay, slightly plaintively. 'I watch. I report back. I make them think I'm on their side.' She paused. 'I *am* on their side, in truth. They're good kids, my lord. Yes, Elver is a little spiky and Lucian is undoubtedly a self-important little oik, but Artair is good and kind. And I suppose I just don't see why we should make their lives even more difficult than they are.' The fox tail swished in agitation.

'Trickery, deception, lies and stories, those are the things we dedicate ourselves to, Sunay,' said Tisk. 'Or have you forgotten? Did you think your role was plucky friend, good-hearted mage, confidante?'

Sunay turned her face from the orange light so that it was cast into shadows. Artair couldn't see the expression on it.

'No,' she said. Her voice was so flat he almost didn't recognize it. 'I haven't forgotten.'

'That's my girl. Well, the smell of this place is displeasing, so I shall leave you, but don't forget – Mother and I will be watching.'

Artair swallowed hard. He found he was squeezing Elver's hand in his, so he forced himself to relax. On the other tower, Sunay stepped back onto the platform, and Tisk vanished in a swirl of autumnal light.

For a heartbeat, Artair didn't know what to do.

Sunay, their friend, wasn't their friend at all, and the god of lies had, perhaps predictably, lied to them – he was working with Maura after all. Beings like Tisk thrived on chaos; he had proven that when he'd helped Lucian to escape his bonds. All at once, Artair knew that he had to confront the mage. He had to do it right this moment, so that she would know he had heard it all.

He let go of Elver and began to clamber to his feet, but it was as though something were holding him in place – shaking him, even. Assuming this was more of Tisk's magic, he tried to throw the weight off, coming perilously close to the edge of the platform, but the sensation only grew more intense: someone had hold of him by the shoulders and was briskly shaking him back and forth. He blinked, and the light around him changed; starlight became daylight, a white and unforgiving pressure on his eyes that made him wince.

'Lucian? Can you hear me?'

It was Elver, leaning over him, her face cast into shadow by bright sunlight. Sunay was there too, and she had hold of his arm, tugging it urgently as though he were late for something.

'He's never done this before,' she said, her brow creased with worry. 'Do you think it's the swamp?'

'Lucian?' Elver pushed his hair back from his eyes. 'Look, he's waking up now, I think.'

'I'm not Lucian,' he said gruffly, sitting up so the two of them had to draw back slightly. They were all on the one platform so they were squashed in close together. The sound of Fleet's frantic barks floated up from below.

'What do you mean?' Elver exchanged a glance with Sunay. 'You've been asleep for hours. We couldn't wake you. And you were Artair before you went to sleep, so . . .'

'Asleep for hours? If that's a joke, it's not funny.' He looked around. On the tops of the other towers, he could see that some of the artist priests had taken their helmets off and were looking their way, no doubt drawn by the sound of raised voices and Fleet's barking. One at least was starting to climb down from their platform. Artair shook Sunay's hand off his sleeve. 'Why did you do it, Sunay?'

She looked at him blankly. 'Do what?'

'Betray us! I don't know what Tisk has asked you to do, but you could have said no. We trusted you.'

'Maybe it *is* the swamp,' said Sunay, turning to Elver. 'You get strange gases in swamps. Something to do with air trapped under the water for ages – I don't know.'

'Artair,' Elver said firmly. 'You've been unconscious for hours. What's going on?'

'I saw Tisk last night. He turned up, and he talked to Sunay about his scheme. He told her to keep watching us, keep reporting back. And he said he was working with Mother Maura!'

Sunay laughed. 'You just had a very vivid dream, Artair. I've had no visit from my lord. And he certainly would never work with that monster.'

'I don't dream,' he said. They all got to their feet, and Artair moved to the edge of the platform. He brought the words of his old mantra to mind: *In this moment, in this place, I am safe.* 'Everyone knows the Sleepless don't dream.'

'They don't lie unconscious for hours, either,' said Elver. 'And where is Lucian?'

'Why are you so worried about him?' He threw his hands up. He couldn't keep this particular awful truth to himself. 'The point is, Sunay is working with Maura!'

The mage shook her head slowly, her hands on her hips. She looked as though she were trying to solve a particularly hard puzzle; her hair, normally so sleek and black, had worked itself into a tangle overnight and the skin under her eyes looked grey. 'I swear to you, I have not betrayed you, Artair, my friend . . .'

'So says a mage of lies.'

Sunay flinched.

'I suppose I should have expected that,' she said. 'And it certainly does feel like some kind of trickery is afoot. Just not *my* trickery.' She made her way to the edge of the platform. 'Come on. Let's get down from here and I'll throw some magic around, see if I can't uncover a few hidden things.'

The three of them climbed down in a simmering silence. Plinko was waiting at the bottom, and to Artair's eyes he looked oddly smaller, and younger, his patched clothes hanging too loosely on him. Fleet danced around them in circles, quiet now but still clearly agitated. Sunay led them over to a hillock of green grass rising out of the shallow water, then rolled up her sleeves.

'Here, I was saving this in case we had dire need of it, but perhaps now is as good a time as any. Barleycorn left it behind, so I nabbed it.' From her pocket, Sunay produced a simple doll made of corn stalks, no more than two inches long. She twirled it between her fingers and it vanished in a wink of orange light, which then sank into the fingers of her right hand. 'Lord Tisk,' she said. 'Things have been hidden from us, I feel, and we are the masters of hidden things. Show me what I haven't spotted.'

With the fingers of her right hand, she drew a wide square in the air in front of her; the edges of it glowing faintly.

'What are you doing?' asked Elver.

'Through this magical frame, I will be able to see things that are usually hidden from us. My lord is the master of all hidden things, you see.' She swiped the orange square of light towards Artair, and her eyes widened.

'Lucian!'

Artair frowned. 'I'm getting pretty tired of being called that this morning.'

'You can see him?' asked Elver. 'What does he look like?'

'I can, just faintly. Better-looking than I was expecting, if I'm honest.' Sunay's eyes flickered to where Elver stood, framed by the square of light, and abruptly all the colour dropped from the mage's face. She stumbled backwards, her arms coming up as if to ward off a blow.

'Sunay?'

'Tisk save us . . .' The mage's back foot found the edge of the hillock and flailed into space, and Elver shot forward, grabbing her friend's hand to balance her. There was a scream, and Elver let go. The skin on the mage's hand and wrist was instantly a livid red.

'Shit, sorry. Sorry!'

But the mage, crashing back through the fetid water, turned tail and ran, splashing awkwardly through the stinking swamp until she was lost in the mists.

CHAPTER 16

Elver watched her friend disappear into the murk. Very quickly, even the splashing of her footsteps was lost, muffled by the heavy air of the swamp.

'Sunay, come back!'

A cold tide of misery washed through her heart. Sunay had looked at her just as the priest of Trilot had, as though she were looking at something terrifying, something that made her fear for her life. And when Elver had tried to help her, to take her hand as a friend would, she had burned the mage. If she had held her hand just a few seconds longer, she would have killed her. Elver thought of what the Queen of Serpents had told her when she had brought her back to life a second time: that she would be even more monstrous. That humans would not accept her.

She ran forward, boots slipping in the silty mud even as she searched for signs to show where Sunay had gone – a shadow, a footprint. But the water and the mist had erased everything.

'If she doesn't want to be found, you won't find her,' said Artair. He appeared at her side, looking dishevelled and tired. 'She's a mage of illusion, remember. What made her run like that?'

'I don't . . . I don't know.' Elver bit her lip. He would see it sooner or later, her true monstrousness.

'I say!' They both turned round to see a gangly man with a long, raggedy beard looming out of the mist. He was strikingly pale, and was blinking wetly, as though he'd just crawled out of a dark hole. Under one arm he carried a helmet with no eye holes in it. 'I say, what's all this racket? Can't you see where you are?' He gestured with one skinny arm at the towers that rose around them. 'We are creating *art* here. For the glory of Vilon!'

There was a murmur of agreement from the other artist priests in the vicinity. Plinko, Elver noted with a shred of gratitude, was standing just in front of Fleet, shielding him from view.

'I'm sorry,' said Artair. 'We'll just be on our way . . .'

'How are we supposed to concentrate?' The man's voice was gaining in volume. 'It is essential that we maintain a pure link with Vilon, untainted by sight or sound. We cannot possibly do this when our ears are assaulted by the raving of random wandering ragamuffins! The likes of you couldn't possibly understand, of course, the importance of our work, but I would at least expect the basic respect due an artist from those untouched by greatness. Furthermore . . .'

Even Elver didn't know she could move so fast. One moment she was standing with her boots wedged in thick mud, the next she was snatching the helmet from the artist's arms – it was as easy as plucking a flower from a meadow. As he watched in horror, she held it up in front of him and slowly tore it in two. The metal screeched in protest, but, again, this was easy. When it was done, she threw it down into the shallow water by his feet and pointed at the pieces.

'Here is my artwork,' she said. 'I call it, "Talk to Me Like That Again and I will Pull Your Arms Off".' She turned to Artair. 'Let's get out of this stinking swamp.'

It took them all morning and most of the afternoon to leave the swamp behind, with none of them in good spirits. Even Fleet spent most of the journey with his side pressed to Elver's shin. She suspected that the argument between Artair and Sunay had unnerved the cub, and, of course, Fleet had grown quite fond of Sunay. Plinko was quiet too, and somehow diminished. Occasionally, she would glance at the child and try to remember how he had looked asleep in the boat. Hadn't he been more robust? Taller?

The land beneath their feet dried out and became much more barren: there were rocks, and grass, and frost, and not much else. The lack of watery spaces tugged at her heart, a faint discomfort, like wearing a scratchy jumper. The presence of the First of Monsters had faded again, as though he were muffled by all the dry land. And all the while, out there somewhere, Maura was conspiring against them. Elver tried to stay alert, but being constantly on guard was exhausting, spreading her awareness too thin. The temperature dropped too, the wind biting with sharp teeth at any exposed skin. It didn't concern Elver particularly, but Plinko pulled his hood down over his face, and Artair's nose turned quite pink. She gave him her fur-lined cloak to put over his, although he tried to refuse it.

'I don't feel the cold, honestly. It's just an extra thing for me to carry.' When he'd pulled it over his shoulders, he thanked her, and some of the tension that had been hanging between them eased slightly. 'What happened with Sunay. It was just a dream. You know that, right?'

'I can't dream,' he said, although he didn't sound as sure as he had before. 'I haven't had a dream since I was twelve.'

'But you were asleep,' said Elver. 'For hours. We couldn't wake you. I bet that hasn't happened since you were twelve, either. And do you really believe Sunay would betray us? Come on, Artair. She helped us steal the frozen heart. She went all the way to Prideful Leap with me. She even used her magic to pretend to be you. All so that we could save the novices and keep Fleet out of Maura's clutches. All I'm saying is that's a lot of work to go to just to stab us in the back.'

'Her god is the god of lies. He's the god of back-stabbing, Elver.'

He sighed. 'I guess I just don't know. It all felt so real. And I don't remember falling asleep at all. In fact, I was trying especially hard to stay awake, because . . .' He trailed off.

'Because why?'

'It doesn't matter. Elver, it's been a long time since I've had a dream, but I don't remember them feeling like this one did.'

'What about Lucian? Where is he?'

Speaking his name made her think of her own dream. That had felt real too; certainly, what she had felt when Lucian had pulled her close had been real. And then she had torn his face to pieces with her claws. The idea that she might somehow have killed him in her own dream floated across her mind and she brusquely pushed it away. Artair, meanwhile, just shook his head. The dark clouds overhead had taken on a yellowish tinge, and a light snow was starting to fall. Elver could see tiny snow crystals settling on Artair's hair and eyelashes.

'It's funny. I can feel Lucian around more often,' he said quietly. 'When you tore up that helmet, I could feel him laughing. He enjoyed that a lot.'

'Ha. Well, at least he's having a good time, I suppose.' It was odd to think of Lucian lurking there, just under the surface. She remembered Sunay saying that she could see him with Tisk's spell. She wondered what Lucian's own face looked like. 'Listen. I don't believe Sunay betrayed us. I can't,' she said firmly. 'And it might be that we can't find her if she doesn't want to be found, but that doesn't stop her finding us. Hopefully. We just have to get this kid to Micelle, and we can get on with finding the First of Monsters.'

At this, Plinko looked up. 'Plinko heard the magpie talk to the foxy man. Plinko was there. He saw what happened.'

'What?' Elver glared down at him. 'You didn't think to mention this before?'

The boy shrugged. 'Plinko doesn't deal well with shouting.'

'I'm sorry, Elver,' said Artair. The look he was giving her was genuinely regretful, which only made her angrier. 'I know she was your friend. *Our* friend. We were too quick to trust her.' He paused. 'She ran away, Elver. She couldn't face us in the end.'

'Sunay ran because I burned her,' Elver said firmly. It hurt to say it, and even as she did, she wondered if it were completely true: perhaps she had given Sunay the perfect excuse to run.

She put her head down and focused on the ground. It was growing crisp underfoot with a light layer of snow, and in the distance there were shapes close to the horizon that had to be buildings of some kind. They were getting close to Micelle.

'Come on,' she said, not looking at either of them. 'We're nearly there.'

Yet Micelle remained slightly out of reach, and eventually they did stop briefly to eat something. Elver built a fire, around which Artair, Plinko and Fleet crowded gratefully, and they shared some of the dried meat from their packs. Sunay, Elver remembered with some regret, had the good tea leaves in her bag, as well as some well-wrapped slices of seed cake. Plinko got his cards out and shuffled them slowly. His hands, Elver realized, looked smaller than they had. She was sure of it. Either that or the cards had got bigger.

'Plinko, where did you say you were from?'

'Plinko is from nowhere. He lived in the temple, until he didn't any more.'

'And what did you say you did at the temple? You said you didn't do any magic?'

The boy flipped a card from the pack, letting it land face up in front of him. It was the Card of Control, illustrated by a woman in a broad hat herding cats with a broom.

'No magic,' said Plinko. 'But some magic tricks. Plinko does tricks with cards.'

There was a loud, musical snort. Fleet, who had curled up at Elver's feet, had gone to sleep and was snoring. Elver nudged him gently with her foot.

'We're not staying here, Fleet. We've got to get to Micelle before it gets dark. You'll all freeze if we're sleeping out here in the open.'

The cub rolled over, his paws twitching. Somewhere behind the darkening clouds the sun was setting, and in the direction of the town, warm yellow and white lights were blossoming into life.

Artair stood, gathering things back into his pack.

'A final push and we'll make it, I think,' he said. 'I can't say I'm not looking forward to a night under a roof. Possibly with some hot food. What do you say to that, Plinko? You look like you could do with a few hot meals.'

'There's still the question of what to do with this little scamp. We'll have to hide him in the town.' Elver bent down to ruffle Fleet's feathers and wake him, but as she did so he jumped up, feather's all sticking up, and he lunged forward and bit her hand.

'Ow!' Elver snatched her hand away. 'Fleet! What did you do that for?'

The keltraxia cub leapt away like a scalded cat, his legs stiff and his green eyes flashing with light.

You poked me with a stick! A stick with a hook on the end! And you said that I was useless and small, no good at hunting, with little baby's teeth! He snapped his jaws in her direction again. *See how big my teeth are! I can bite anyone! Even the poison child!*

'Elver, are you alright? What's going on?'

'I'm fine.' Her hand was weeping black blood, but it wasn't a particularly bad bite. She knelt and rubbed at the wound with a handful of snow, cleaning it and soothing the pain. 'Fleet, you had a bad dream – that's all. I would never poke you with a stick. You know that.'

Fleet's eyes flashed again, and she realized he was more frightened than angry. The black misery that had threatened to overwhelm her when Sunay had run away returned, deeper and darker than before. She swallowed it down, trying to make it a part of herself.

'Elver . . .' Artair reached for her hand, but she held it away from him.

'I'm fine,' she said shortly. Perhaps this was the life of a jih spirit, after all. Feared by all, loved by none. Deep in her chest, the poison heart throbbed, and she felt a powerful urge to run away – away from her feelings for Artair and Lucian, from her responsibility to Fleet, from her damaged friendship with Sunay – she could run away from all human concerns, and find a deep, dark lake to hide in. She imagined the black water closing over her head, her bare feet sinking into black mud. 'Fleet just needs to learn the difference between dreams and reality.' She turned to look at the distant lights, putting the thoughts of a watery rest to one side. 'Let's get under cover.'

CHAPTER 17

The town of Micelle was unlike any Elver had seen before. It was a place of large, conical tents, crowded together in bunches. They all had thick walls made of leather and felt, and even in the dark, it was possible to see that some of them had been painted with bright colours. Artair seemed to brighten a little at the sight of them; he said they reminded him a little of the way his own people lived, before he was carted off to the monastery. Most of them had oil lamps posted just outside, but as they skirted the edges they could see very few people. Towards the centre, it looked as though there were tents as big as some of the biggest buildings in Addersport.

'This yurt looks abandoned,' said Artair, who had crouched by one of the tents that stood apart from the others. He was peering in through the fabric door. 'We could shelter here for the night. Then, in the morning, we can look for a place for Plinko to find help.'

Inside, there was a strong smell of animal fat – Artair cheerfully pointed out that this would have been used to thicken the felt. There was an old hearth in the centre covered in fine, grey ash, so Elver cleared it out and built a new fire. Above them, there was a small hole revealing a portion of the night sky, and the smoke from the fire spiralled neatly up and through it. With the tent flap pulled closed behind them, it very quickly became cosy in the tent, and Elver felt some of the tension drain from her limbs.

'Plinko is hungry,' said Plinko.

Elver sighed, but Artair was already moving, taking out some of the last dried meat and cheese and passing it around. Fleet lay on the far side of the hearth from Elver, his nose on his paws.

'I don't suppose Plinko has any of his own money to buy food, does he?' Artair gave her a look, so she shrugged. 'All I'm saying is we set out on this journey thinking we'd need to feed three people plus a ravenous monster. I did not factor in a ravenous child.'

'How's your hand?' he asked.

Elver glanced down at it, then hid it in her sleeve. It had almost healed over already; all that remained were a few faint dark spots where Fleet's teeth had punctured her skin. It no longer hurt, but it was also a reminder that she was still changing.

'I told you, it's fine. We're not all that far from the First of Monsters now,' she said, deciding to change the subject. She glanced at Plinko, but the boy was munching steadily through his food and not paying her much attention at all. 'I can feel the place where he's hidden. It's deep. I don't think it's going to be easy to get to him.'

Artair yawned, and Fleet yawned back, exposing his bright pink tongue.

'You should both get some sleep.'

'What? So you can have Lucian back?'

Elver blinked, surprised by the venom in Artair's voice. He sighed and pushed a hand through his hair, and she was struck by how exhausted he looked. He might have just had the most sleep he'd had since he was twelve, but he looked like a man who had been awake for years.

'Lucian is . . .' She glanced again at Plinko. 'He's not the monster you make him out to be, Artair. And I'll admit, I'm worried. What if Maura got to him somehow without us realizing?'

'If that was the case, then we'd be free, right?' He was looking at her very directly, his brown eyes almost angry. 'Once Maura has what she wants, she has no reason to come after us any more.'

'Except that she'd be a god! Do you really want someone as cruel and bloodthirsty as her as one of the Twelve?'

'Sounds like a regular god to me,' said Artair. 'I mean it, Elver. We could . . .' His expression softened. 'We could go wherever we wanted to go. We wouldn't have to be running from Dalesh all the time, or looking over our shoulders. Don't you want to just be able to explore Tlevrae? Don't you just want to be free?'

'There's no freedom for me in a human world,' she said coldly.

'Elver . . .'

Images filled her head: the expression of terror on the Trilot priest's face; Sunay's cry of pain; her own clawed hand, opening Lucian's face like a bloody flower.

'I'm not like you,' she said tersely. 'And I know you can see that. Since the queen brought me back, it's been worse. I'm stronger than I should be, I can change things, I heal too fast, I can breathe under the water . . . I can feel watery places like they are my own limbs. And you haven't been the same with me since . . . since all this happened. Once I was exciting to you – I was your strange, wild friend. Now I frighten you.'

For a long moment, he just looked at her. His face was very serious.

'Of course you don't frighten me,' he said eventually. 'Elver, I—'

'Enough.' A small bubble of bitter laughter rose in her throat. She shook her head. 'Don't. That pause was enough.'

After that, Artair grew quiet again, and an uneasy silence filled the tent. When he'd finished eating, he lay down on his bedroll, staring up at the hole that was letting the smoke escape. She wondered if he was thinking about his life before he had been Sleepless, and she realized she wanted to ask him about it, but there was no way back into that conversation that didn't feel painful. Plinko had finished his own meal and pulled out his deck of cards. Elver began to feel sleepy herself: the warmth of the tent, the fullness in her belly, the long trek through the swamp. She rubbed her hands over her face, trying to wake up. Fleet, though, did not look sleepy. He was watching her carefully, as though he expected her to suddenly grab a big stick and poke him with it.

'Fleet,' she said quietly. 'You must have had dreams before. Can't you see that's what this was? You are my kin. I'd never hurt you.'

Dreams are funny, said Fleet. *Funny like sometimes I can fly in them, or all humans are small enough to eat in one bite. This wasn't funny.*

'Alright, but you understand that dreams can feel very real when they're not? Which can be confusing, but—'

Artair sat up jerkily, and a moment later she realized, as he scrambled to his feet, that it wasn't Artair – it was Lucian. It was clear from the fury on his face.

'Lucian?'

He didn't look at her. Instead, he launched himself across the small space of the tent and picked up Plinko, one hand round the boy's throat. Plinko gave a strangled squeak.

'Hey!' Elver stood up too. 'What are you doing? Lucian!'

'This little shit,' he spat, 'has been playing us all for fools!'

'What are you talking about?' She went to them, taking hold of Lucian's arm. Plinko's face was turning an alarming shade of pink. 'He's just a kid. Let him go.'

'Absolutely not. My only regret is that when I kill him there's no Bloody Claw to reward me.'

Elver shoved him, letting a shadow of her real strength through for a moment, and Lucian nearly lost his footing. Plinko dropped to the floor, gasping.

'Idiot!' snapped Lucian. 'He's no child. He's a mage of Enos, Elver. Mages of Enos tithe away their age every time they use a spell.'

'What?'

But it was too late. Plinko had snatched up his cards, and

brandished several of them at once. Elver felt her legs grow abruptly heavy, as though they'd been filled with lead, and she sank to the ground, pitching over onto her side. As she fell, she saw Lucian go down too, his eyes rolling up to the whites, and even Fleet keeled over, his legs sticking up in the air.

The last thing she saw before her eyes slammed shut was Plinko, standing over Lucian's prone body, an expression of absolute malevolence on his chubby, round face.

CHAPTER 18

Artair knew immediately that he was in trouble.

He was in a dark place of red stone. A low ceiling held up by hundreds of roughly hewn pillars glowered overhead, somehow promising that he was deep underground, miles of earth hanging above him, ready to drop. Guttering candles of red wax sprouted from the pillars, splashing an ever-shifting light over the vast statue that stood at the centre of it all. It was the Bloody Claw, of course – what other god would be in a place like this? – huge and terrible, his jaws open in a frozen roar. There were people here too: children, by the looks of them, all wearing black and red robes, and when he drew closer he saw that wasn't the only thing they shared. They were all boys, and they all wore the same face: pale, sharply handsome, with tawny hazel eyes. They had hair as black as a raven's wing, and they paid him no attention. Each of them carried a bucket of blood and, as he watched, they carried them to the statue and poured the blood into a trench that ran around the Bloody Claw's giant feet. When they'd performed this function, they would run off into the dark, and then return with another full bucket. Very quickly, he lost track of how many children there were, and how much blood was being fed to the god. But it wasn't the blood that interested him.

'I know that face.'

'Yes. You've never seen it, but I suppose I must have haunted your dreams before.'

He turned to see a young man standing behind him. Like the children, he was pale, and although his face was older it carried the same handsomeness, only grown harder, and crueller. His eyes were a wolf's eyes, almost yellow in this light, and his hair was black, cut brutally short at the sides. He was bare-chested, and there were long, thin scars across his chest. Lucian grinned, although there wasn't a shred of humour in it.

'I know your face all too well, monk.' He moved, and Artair held himself ready, sure that his old enemy would attack him, but instead Lucian just walked past him towards the statue. He casually pushed a few of the children aside and knelt in front of the Bloody Claw. He pulled a dagger from his belt. His hands, Artair noticed, were pale, his fingers long and clever.

'What are you doing? Lucian, we have to get out of here.' The sense that they were somewhere they shouldn't be grew stronger. 'Elver is . . . I don't know where Elver is. Do you?'

'There's no time for that. Can't you see my lord is hungry?' Lucian drew the dagger across his own chest, following the direction of his old scars, and a long thin wound began to weep blood. But instead of running down his body, the blood curled itself into a thread and slid through the air towards the trench. Lucian shivered. 'He is always hungry.'

'Stop it.' Artair went to the trench, glancing at the child-Lucians with their buckets of blood. 'Your lord is dead, Lucian. Maura killed him. I think . . . I think this is a dream.'

The wound had healed up. As Artair watched, Lucian drew the dagger across his body again, and again the blood found its way into the trench. There was sweat in Lucian's hair, plastering it to his brow, and an expression on his face that Artair found difficult to look at; frightened, and desperate. All of them did, he realized. It might be a dream, but the compulsion that had Lucian in its grip was very real. The Bloody Claw loomed over them all, and they poured away their lives to him, hoping to satisfy a creature that was all appetite. Artair had a sudden image of the trench going down and down, deep into the earth, and crouched beneath it the real Bloody Claw, a creature of raw flesh drinking the blood of his disciples, forever and ever.

When Lucian went to cut himself a third time, Artair knocked the dagger away. It clattered onto the floor and vanished.

'How dare you!' Lucian stood up. 'Who are you to interfere with the rites of the Bloody Claw? Just some idiot monk from the plains who still stinks of horse, all these years later. I will kill you and feed your soul to my lord.'

'Lucian, listen to me. This is a *dream*. Don't you feel it? You have to help me figure out what's happening.'

'He *must* be fed, monk, or he'll kill us all . . .'

The ground under their feet began to shake. The child-Lucians cried out, stumbling into each other, and a terrible screeching filled the air, the sound of a mountain splitting in two, perhaps, or a hungry god crying out for more blood.

'Do you see what you've done?'

The statue of the Bloody Claw suddenly shattered down the middle, pieces of red rock flying across the cavern. Several of the child-Lucians were scattered by them, to lie broken and bleeding on the floor.

'Lucian.'

The voice was coming from within the statue, but it didn't sound like the Bloody Claw. There was a dark hole in the stone now and, inside it, something pale was moving. The remaining child-Lucians had all fled, leaving Artair alone with their adult counterpart, and around them the candles were snuffing themselves out, one by one.

'Artair.' Lucian grabbed his wrist with one hand, not taking his eyes from the busy dark within the statue. 'It's coming for me. It will kill me. Promise me you'll look after Elver?'

'What's coming for you? I told you already, the Bloody Claw is dead.' The circle of light around them grew smaller and smaller, pushing them towards the statue.

'It's not him. Gods save me, it's not him.'

'*Lucian*,' came the voice again. '*Come to Mother.*'

A long white limb slid out of the hole in the statue, followed by another, and another. They all had a clawed hook instead of a foot, and too many joints. More limbs followed, and then the head of the creature appeared, closely followed by its bulbous white body. It had eight red eyes, and a set of distended jaws that dripped with ichor. There were two red circles on its fat belly, one inside the other. The spider pulled itself through the narrow opening, scattering more pieces of red stone.

Artair stumbled backwards, a tide of revulsion pushing at the back of his throat, but Lucian didn't move. He seemed transfixed by the sight of the creature.

'Lucian, get up!'

The spider skittered easily over the trench of blood and descended on the young mage, multiple legs closing over him and drawing him close, as if to embrace him. But the jaws of the creature were opening wide and closing over Lucian's head. Lucian himself cowered on his knees. One clawed foot slid across his bare back, tearing the skin open. Blood soaked into the fabric of his trousers.

Artair stood, frozen. For much of his life, he had been tortured by the presence of Lucian. Whenever he gave into sleep, this dark spirit would steal his body and use it for its own dark purposes. He had been locked away because of Lucian. He had lost his family, and any sense of a real life, because of Lucian. Before he ever knew the spirit's name, he knew he was a monster. And perhaps this end was what he deserved.

Except, he realized, he didn't really believe that. Lucian might be a monster, but he was a monster who had been made by others, and maybe that did make a difference.

He darted forward and took hold of one of the spider's legs. It was about the thickness of one of Elver's arms, and it was terribly strong. When he tried to prise it away from Lucian, the thing ripped itself out of his grip, the tiny white hairs on its skin tearing at his hands.

'Lucian! You have to fight it!'

A memory surfaced of the monastery: standing out on the grass under the bleak mountain sunshine, circling through a sequence of punches and kicks. It was important, the brothers and sisters had told them, to keep their bodies occupied. Artair let the memory move his body, delivering several lightning-fast punches to the fat body of the spider, and at first it seemed to work. The swollen abdomen of the creature crumpled under his fists, and it made a high-pitched keening sound. But then it simply reinflated to its original size.

'Shit.'

He stepped away, uncertain what to do. The spider's mandibles were entangled in Lucian's hair now, almost as though it were caressing him, and blood ran in a sheet down his bare back. A tide of anger and frustration rose through Artair, and another memory resurfaced: Chessun, the expression of resignation on his face before the arrow passed through his throat.

No, thought Artair. *Lucian might be my enemy, but he's also the closest thing I have to a brother. I won't let him die.*

He looked down. Lying on the floor at his feet was the bow he had taken from the monastery, the bow that he and Elver had sold to Lorian Owllight. Next to it was a single arrow, the fletching feathers the same yellow as his old tunic. Artair picked up the bow and nocked the arrow. He aimed at the spider's distended belly.

'You'll have to do better than this, Maura,' he said quietly. 'We're stronger than you think.'

He loosed the arrow, and the spider burst like a balloon made of old skin. The legs curled in on themselves, shrivelling up into a wad of diseased flesh, and with her diminishing the darkness fled, the smell of blood vanishing. Lucian picked himself up carefully, looking around at the cavern as though he'd only just opened his eyes.

'What are you looking at me like that for?' he snapped. 'Haven't you ever been drooled on by a spider-version of your old mistress?'

Artair smiled. This was Lucian's version of a joke, which meant he was back to himself.

'Lucian, we need to get out of here. I think we're—'

'In a dream, yes, and we've been put here by that little turd Plinko. Enos is apparently working with Maura, which isn't the best news.' He pushed his hands through his hair, making it look as though he'd had a shock. Something about the gesture reminded Artair of Elver. He pushed away the confusion this summoned. 'I could feel the magic around us while you were awake, but couldn't figure out the source of it. And then you had that ridiculous dream about Sunay, and suddenly it was as clear as day. But because you weren't in a true sleep, I couldn't come through and kick him off the top of that tower.'

Artair winced. Sunay hadn't betrayed them after all, which meant he had accused her for nothing.

'So what do we do? How do we get out of here?'

'I need time to think. But, yes, we do need to get out of this temple. It's not safe. These dreams have been designed to hurt us. Maybe even kill us. I am sure there are other horrors just waiting to arrive.'

He was right. Soft noises were echoing up from the dark space in the centre of the Bloody Claw statue: the soft, skittering noises of something with too many legs. Together, they walked away from it, exploring the spaces between the pillars, but no obvious way out presented itself. It was only when they stopped looking that they found it.

Lucian sat on a boulder, complaining about the boredom of searching and his lack of a shirt, and it moved half an inch or so. A beam of soft golden light pierced the shadowy space, glittering with motes of dust.

'Well?' snapped Lucian. 'That's clearly what we're looking for. Use your overly muscled arms to move that rock and we'll be on our way.'

Artair prickled a little at being ordered around, but it was clear Lucian wasn't going to be able to move the boulder alone. He bent and braced himself against it, and when it did move, slowly but surely across the stony floor, he felt a small measure of satisfaction.

'Huh,' said Lucian. 'I will admit, that's not exactly what I was expecting.'

Around ten feet below them was an unremarkable patch of grass, dotted here and there with white daisies. It looked so cheerfully normal after the dark horrors of the cavern that it took Artair a moment to understand what he was looking at.

Lucian, however, had no such qualms. He sat down on the edge of the hole and dropped down onto the grass, landing with an unexpected cat-like grace.

'Come on,' he called up impatiently. 'I suspect you'll like this, monk.'

Artair climbed down, emerging into a bright, sunny day. The stone he expected to see above him was not there; instead, he was standing in part of the monastery garden. To his right, there was the yellow brick wall of the kitchens, and to his left, the narrow stone markers of the Sleepless who had died under the care of the brothers and sisters. Chessun's was there, and Reah's daisies were still there too, looking as fresh as the day she had picked them.

'I'm home,' he said. 'I'm *home.*'

'If you want to call it that,' said Lucian, who was looking around with his eyes narrowed. 'Although I will say that this is a lot nicer than your cell, which is, of course, the only part I ever got to see.'

Artair opened his mouth and then closed it, not sure what to say to that. It was strange to see Lucian here, his narrow form too pale, too sharp. The mage started to walk round the corner, and then stopped. He laughed.

'Ah. You should come and have a look at this, monk. We have another problem.'

CHAPTER 19

Maura stood on the shore that lay between the shadowed lands and the mortal realm, quietly fuming.

She had been summoned from her own realm quite gently, really – the sweep of velvet night consuming the nothingness, the silvery glow of a full moon producing a beam of light that waited by her garden gate. An invitation. She knew she was supposed to walk through it, and could even guess who had sent it, but it was still irksome to be directed in this way. She had assumed her godhood would finally make it so that no one had power over her.

Yet although she had waited for a time, glaring at the moon, eventually her need to know what Enos wanted was too great, and she had walked into the portal, and arrived on the beach. Now, infuriatingly, Enos wasn't even here.

They treat me like this because I was a mortal once, she thought. *To them, I'll always carry the stink of human about me.*

Standing in the surf were the twelve avatars of the gods. One of them was a harp made of mother-of-pearl, its strings the colour of moonlight, and, as Maura watched, the strings shivered, producing a soft, eerie music. The sound made her think of the silence of the deep night, when it felt as if all the world was asleep. A wave of drowsiness moved through her, so she pinched her own arm briskly.

'Don't use your magic on me,' she said loudly. 'You'll regret it.'

'I am sorry – that just happens sometimes.' Enos stepped out of the surf, all her six feet and the hem of her robe wet. 'Sleep is one of the most powerful forces in the world. Did you know that? You would have been familiar with it as a mortal, but did you ever try to keep it at bay for as long as you could? It's impossible to resist.'

Maura snorted. She had experienced sleepless nights with each of her babies. 'I was – I *am*, a mother,' she said. 'I know what it's like to exist outside of sleep's embrace, believe me. Your child cries, and you wake. *That* is impossible to resist. That is truly powerful.'

Enos did not look pleased by that answer, but she shrugged – a complicated manoeuvre with three heads.

'I have good news for you, Mother. I have caught your thief, along with the serpent's child, and I have them held securely in nightmares. I would suggest you send your mage to collect them. I have done all I can, which –' she curtsied, two arms holding the hem of her robe, the other four gesturing dramatically – 'I think you'll agree was more than enough. I will enjoy the moment when you slit the throat of the Sleepless one.'

'Where are they?' Maura felt her heart beating faster. It infuriated her that she had reason to be grateful to another god, but she could be angry about that later. The chance to kill Lucian and take back what was hers had landed in her lap, and there was no time to hesitate.

'On the edge of a town called Micelle. Asleep, unmoving and trapped. Under the care of a mage of mine.' Enos sighed. 'If you could instruct your mage to help mine, I would be most grateful. He has performed a great deal of magic in a small amount of time, and I suspect it will have left him a little . . . short.'

But Maura had already turned, was already summoning her own path back to her realm.

In the small room where she had once dried herbs and replied to the letters of those seeking help from Tisk, she summoned the tiny bright shape that was Dalesh. Even in miniature, the mage looked wary. She was carrying a stack of papers in her arms.

'Mother,' she said. 'I've collected the tithes from your temples. The priests have the children working all hours, and I thought that, with this many, our connection will be stronger than ever, and you won't have to stay so close to me. It'll be safer.'

Maura leaned back from her desk. She remembered speaking to the other gods, how they had pointed out that the tithes did not feed her as they were supposed to – because she wasn't quite a god. They had barely been able to conceal the glee on their faces.

'Dalesh,' she said, her voice soft, 'is that truly what you think?'

'What do you mean, Mother?' She lowered the stack of papers in her arms, and a few of the sheets on the top slipped away, sliding out of view.

'You truly think you know better than your Mother?' When Dalesh began to rapidly shake her head, opening her mouth to reply, Maura spoke over her. 'Tithes, I have decided, are for the lesser, needier gods. The gods who want to distance themselves from real work. But I am a mother, Dalesh, and there is no shirking work for us.' She leaned forward. 'Go to Micelle. Another mage, belonging to another god, has done your work for you. They have managed what you could not, even with all my power at your disposal.' Maura curled her lip. 'Lucian and the others are there, and they are currently in a magical sleep. Take some acolytes with you, and kill him. I imagine even you can manage that?'

'Your will is my own, Mother.' Dalesh cleared her throat. 'May I ask . . . will you be with me? Will you grant me the honour of your power again?'

Maura remembered the sickening sensation of her godhood leaving her, drawn through the connection she had opened with Dalesh. It had been like opening her own veins, and Lucian had been all too eager to drink. It was clear that giving Dalesh her power directly was much too dangerous. Yet, if the woman did manage to kill Lucian, she had to be there to absorb the last of the Bloody Claw's power.

'I will be with you,' she replied, 'but there will be no magic, Dalesh. Perhaps you do not quite grasp how badly you failed me . . . Until you have earned your place again as my most favoured mage, there will be no magic. Take a sharp blade. Slit Lucian's throat. Do you understand?'

Dalesh bowed her head.

'Good. Go. Kill him. And, daughter, this time, don't let me down.'

CHAPTER 20

Lucian watched a flurry of emotions pass over the monk's face with some small amount of pleasure. When he'd been trapped in the cell night after night, with nothing to look at but a tiny window or a cloudy mirror that showed the wrong reflection, he had dreamed of Artair's suffering as if it were an extravagant feast, a meal that could sustain him for a lifetime. Now, though, he just felt mild amusement and even a few crumbs of pity.

'I don't understand,' said Artair. 'Why is it like this?'

'It's *your* dream, monk. I thought you'd have some devastating insights yourself.' Lucian peered at him. 'Although, perhaps it doesn't take a genius to figure this one out.'

They were in the monastery, yes, but only a piece of it, and that piece was floating high above the ground. The garden ended in a ragged drop, and the yellow wall that ran alongside it crumbled into brickwork that looked as though a giant had taken a great bite out of it. The piece of monastery hung in a cheerful blue sky dotted with tufts of white cloud, and it was tethered to the ground by a huge iron chain, each link as long as Artair himself. There was a bolt holding it in place, sunk into the crumbling earth at the edge of the garden.

'We're trapped up here,' said Artair.

'We were always trapped here, monk,' said Lucian. 'You just chose to see it as your solemn duty, or some nonsense like that.'

Artair ignored him. He went walking off to the edge of the garden, and then followed it round, clearly looking to chart the boundary of the monastery. Lucian let him. He took a moment to look down at his own hands – his own hands! His own body. He had, he realized, almost forgotten it. He reached up to touch his face, marvelling at the shapes there, so dimly familiar. It was only a shame there was no mirror, or even a window to catch a reflection.

'I can't see any other way down.' Artair had returned. His hair, which he insisted on wearing loose, had fallen forward over his brow in a way that darkened his eyes. 'Explain this to me again. What are we supposed to do?'

'That delightful little urchin you picked up on the road is in fact a mage of Enos, and he has placed several unpleasant enchantments on us.'

Artair shook his head. 'Plinko is just a kid.'

'Ah, but he isn't. Not truly. Mages of Enos tend to be rare, because the tithe they pay to Enos is high. Those that use her gifts are often . . . people of dubious morals.'

'I suppose you would know all about that.'

'Careful, Artair, you'll hurt my feelings. Each time a mage of Enos uses her magic, she takes from them a year or so of their life. In that, they grow younger each time.'

'That doesn't sound so bad.'

'Doesn't it? No, I suppose to a simple mind that sounds like an attractive deal. Young forever, with magical talents to boot.' Lucian grinned. 'Except deals with the gods are never simple. The more magic a mage uses, the more years she takes. What if you need to do a great deal of magic in a short space of time? What if you need to perform a spell more than once a year? You'd never catch up. Plinko already appeared to be, what, ten years old when you met him? By now, I imagine he must be no more than five, or even younger. Tell me, Artair, would you want to be five years old again, and alone in the world? Your small body prone to tantrums, and not able to reach the middle shelf, let alone the high one.'

Around them, the wind picked up, and Lucian shivered. He wished he had a shirt.

'And, however you look, the reality is that your body knows, on some level, that you are *old*. And it behaves accordingly. It's possible that Plinko is actually our age, or much, much older. It's possible he has never grown hairs on his chest, but in his heart he is an old man.' Lucian shook his head. 'No, it's a strange bargain that Enos strikes with her magpies, and as far as I'm concerned she can keep it.'

For a long moment, Artair didn't say anything. Instead, he looked at Lucian, a considering gaze that went on so long that Lucian felt a spark of anger.

'What?'

'It's just strange. To actually see you. And speak to you. You're exactly how I imagined you'd be, but, also, you're not.'

'What's that supposed to mean?'

'You're funnier than I expected. And smarter.'

For some reason, this only made Lucian angrier.

'It's not hard to be smarter than you, monk. The point is, Plinko has trapped us in dreams and, because we are tethered to each other like this rock to the ground, we are dreaming together. We escaped my portion of the dream when we killed the spider—'

'When *I* killed the spider.'

'Yes, when you flexed your imposing biceps and killed the spider. The question is, what needs to be vanquished here? How do we wrest the dreamworld into our control?'

Artair crouched and ran his hand through the grass. He dug his fingers into the soil. Lucian looked again at his own hands, his arms, his feet. To be separate from the monk: this was all he had wanted for so long. Yet a dream was all it could ever be. This body was – he forced himself to think it – *dead*.

'Brother Benzin loved this garden. He tended it every day, and when he could he'd get us to tend it as well. Because it kept us occupied, but I think it was also because it gave us some peace to be out here.'

'What's your point?'

'My point is, Lucian, it's peaceful. There's nothing to vanquish, or kill. We're just stuck.'

'Well, we'll have to figure it out quickly,' said Lucian. 'While we're in here, our body is vulnerable. Maura will be on her way even now, I imagine, to cut our throat in our sleep. And there's Elver.' Artair looked up. It was strange, Lucian thought, to see that face moving with someone else's emotions. In his alarm, Artair looked younger. 'When Plinko cast this spell, he sent Elver to sleep too, and the monster pup. As far as I know, we're all in that old tent right now, unconscious, ripe pickings for Dalesh's dagger.' He snorted. 'Trust Maura to do it this way. She knows I'm too dangerous to face directly.'

Artair stood up. 'This is just a dream, right? Can't we wake ourselves up? I remember doing that sometimes, when I was a kid. If I was having a nightmare, I could force myself to wake up.'

'It's not that simple. We're not dealing with a normal dream here, monk. This is magic. If we die here, we *die*. And if we manage to avoid that for the time being, Dalesh will turn up and cut our throats in the waking world.'

'Then do some magic!' Since he'd mentioned Elver, Artair seemed much more agitated. 'You're the mage. In fact, aren't you supposed to be some sort of half-god now? Use what the Bloody Claw gave you and magic us out of here.'

Annoyingly, that was a reasonable suggestion, yet the power still lay dormant inside him, a line of embers where there should be fire. It had worked briefly, when he had pulled Maura's magic through

Dalesh, but that had felt instinctual. When Lucian reached for it now, he felt only a distant heat. It frustrated him, so he decided to change the subject.

'You're in love with the monster girl, aren't you?'

'What?'

'You're in love with Elver.' He had said it to embarrass the monk, to wound him, but to Lucian's surprise, he felt an answering pain in his own heart. He grinned to cover it up. 'It's pathetic, really. We finally escape the monastery and you fall in love with the first girl who talks to you.'

The monk looked properly angry, and it occurred to Lucian that if they got into a real fight, with no magic involved, he would be in real trouble.

'Can you do the magic or not, Lucian?'

He sighed and looked away. 'She's too good for you, you know. Too interesting. She'd be bored of you in a week.'

'Lucian . . .'

'No, I can't. The power is hidden deep, and it won't answer my commands, monk. We have to think of something else.'

A cloud passed overhead, briefly throwing them into shadow. Lucian found himself doing what Artair had done, tracing the edge of the piece of monastery on which they stood, looking. He skirted the place where the earth and grass fell away into space, and peered carefully down at the chain. It looked solid enough, and even a little rusty in places.

'Perhaps we just have to climb down,' said Artair. 'The spider had to be defeated in your dream. Maybe the drop needs to be defeated in mine.'

'Climbing down that chain?'

'Yes.'

'I don't fancy that much.'

'No. In truth, neither do I.'

Lucian let his gaze drift to the ground. Below was a flat landscape covered in tall yellow-white grass, and just beneath them there appeared to be a small settlement. At first glance he had taken it to be a dream version of Micelle; there were tents down there, clusters of circles from this high up. But there were also paddocks full of ponies, and the landscape itself was different, he realized. And, now that he looked properly, it was also vaguely familiar. A dark hand closed round his heart, and he opened his mouth to tell Artair not to look, but it was too late. This time, he watched the emotions play out across the monk's face with a deep sense of dread.

'No,' said Artair. 'It can't be.'

'It's a dream, remember,' said Lucian miserably. 'It can be anything.'

'I can see my family's yurt,' said Artair. 'I'd know it anywhere, because my father got it in his head one year that he wanted to paint the top sky blue. We visited three markets trying to find the exact shade. And there are the caravans. Ours had a little wagon on the back that my mother made for me when I was small. Look, you can see it.' He pointed. 'They're all here still. All the ponies, still alive. Nothing has happened to them yet.'

'The grass is dead,' said Lucian. 'Did you spot that?'

Artair rounded on him. 'This is what it is. We have to stop it before it happens! This is what we have to do!'

'It already happened, idiot. There's no stopping—'

Artair grabbed him by the tops of his arms, his hands like vices. Lucian expected to see anger in his face – expected, truthfully, to be thrown over the edge – but instead there was a kind of frantic terror.

'Lucian, please! I can't see it happen again. I can't live through that. We have to get down there somehow, right now, and stop it from ever happening. Don't you want to stop it? Don't you regret it at all?'

Lucian shook his head, not bothering to fight. 'Even if I did, Artair, how do we get down there?'

Artair turned back. 'The chain. We'll just have to be careful, and slow. I'm good at climbing, I can help you—'

As he spoke, the ground under their feet began to dip and shake, throwing them both to their knees. Big chunks of grassy earth crumbled from the edge of the monastery garden, and the yellow wall began to slide away from them, scattering bricks into the bright blue sky.

'Shit,' they both said together.

CHAPTER 21

Elver stood with her bare feet on the seabed, looking up. Far above her was a shifting caul of blue and green light, puddles of luminescence forming and re-forming across it constantly. It took her a moment to realize she was looking at the surface of the ocean, as seen from underneath. Around her, the sand was largely bare; there was the odd seashell, fish bones poking up through the grey-green sand like traps and, all around, a deeper indigo darkness that promised all manner of hidden things. The taste of salt was in her mouth, and she was alone.

'This doesn't seem right.'

It was hard to think. The shifting light of the sea made her remember falling from the Tumble Stone, striking the hard bodies of the serpents and sinking into the Queen of Serpents' realm. When the god had filled her with poison, the world around her had flickered with new life, full of colour and strangeness. That had been the beginning of her jih life, and it had only got stranger since.

'Hello?'

There should be other people here, she was fairly sure of that, but for the moment she couldn't picture their faces or think of their names. When she spoke, silver bubbles trailed from her mouth like coins and spun away above her head.

'Is there anyone there?'

I am here.

The words seemed to come from all around, a deeper echo from within the water, and at the very same moment a vast network of twisting black vines flickered into existence over her head, covered in thorns. She was dwarfed by the shape, a tiny figure under a cloud of sharp edges. Elver took a wary step backwards; the black thorns brought with them a sense of anger, fear, and simmering violence. They hung above her unmoving, yet it felt as though they could strike her at any moment.

'What . . . what are you?'

You know me.

Elver realized that there was something hanging in the centre of the great cloud of thorns. It looked, initially, like a large lump of black flesh, around the size of a grown man, riddled with faint lines of blue light like fat marbled through meat. And then it pulsed. A moment later, it pulsed again. A heartbeat.

'You have a poison heart, just like me,' Elver said. It was strange to see it; she had to assume that she had something very similar inside her own chest. 'You are the First of Monsters.'

I am poison. I am death. I will crush you and your friends. I am the end of gods, little one.

Elver lifted her chin. 'Less of that. We just need your help.'

You dare to ask me for a favour? I am not a god, and you cannot bring me a tithe to coax me into doing your will. I am a monster, child.

'Yeah, yeah, so am I. We're kin. Can't you feel it?' She reached out as she had done when she had attempted to find him before, but her questing mind found only a sense of emptiness. She frowned. Although she could see the heart, there was no presence behind it. 'That's weird. I found you before, when you were far away, and I could feel your mind, but now there's nothing.'

Do that again and I will kill you, continued the voice. *It would take little more than a moment – the tiniest scratch from the smallest of my thorns would stop your heart in an instant.*

Elver ignored him.

'Something isn't right here.' She reached out again, brushing aside the strangeness of the ocean, the taste of salt in her mouth and the threats of the pulsing flesh hanging in front of her. This time, when she reached out, she felt the faintest brush of another presence, and when she grasped it, they were startled. She felt its attention turn to her, and the sprawling tangle of black thorns shimmered, as though it were a reflection in a puddle. The connection felt very faint, as though the presence were a long way away.

No, stop that! I told you I would kill you! I am the bane of gods, the poison that can end worlds . . .

The vines curled in on themselves and turned white, as did the poison heart at the centre of it. A second voice spoke and, although there was still anger and fear in the air, the sense of simmering violence faded.

Who are you? What do you want?

'*There* you are,' said Elver, putting her hands on her hips. 'I'm Elver. I have to talk to you about' – except that she couldn't remember what she had to talk to the First of Monsters about – 'something. There was definitely something. Shit. Look, we're coming to see you. We need your help.'

No. Immediately, the presence that was the First of Monsters began to recede, and the poisonous heart at the centre of the tangle of thorns stopped pulsing. *Stay away. I'm warning you. Don't come here.*

'Wait!'

Leave me alone.

And with that, the presence vanished.

'How did you do that?'

The voice came from behind her. Elver whirled round to see a tall, blue-skinned woman with three heads standing on the sand, her silvery robes tugged this way and that by the currents of the sea.

The god raised an eyebrow.

'And you shouldn't be able to do that, either,' said the woman. 'See me, I mean. I am Enos, god of dreams and sleep, and when I spin a dream for a mortal I am always hidden. You didn't spot me the first time, but I think you were much too caught up with kissing that boy – and who could blame you? But now you just look, and you see. How curious.'

'What are you talking about?' Elver scowled. 'What's going on?'

'You must truly be god-touched,' Enos said in a musing tone. 'Still. It doesn't matter.' The god raised three of her arms, and the vines that had been hanging above them whipped through the water to wrap themselves round Elver, holding her tightly in place.

'Ow! Let me go!' Even as she thrashed against them, the grip of the vines grew more solid, pinning her arms to her sides. Inside her, a dark tide of fury rose up, looking to *change*, to become something else, but the bonds of the god of sleep were too tight.

'If it helps at all,' said Enos, 'you won't have long to wait. Your adventures are coming to an end, Elver of the Jih Forest.'

CHAPTER 22

Lucian clung to the chain, not daring to look up, or down. Instead, he focused on the surface of the metal, which had proven to be much rustier than he'd expected; on the one hand, this gave him firmer places to grip – on the other, it rather suggested that the chain might disintegrate at any moment. Sweat ran from his forehead into his eyes, stinging them.

'Keep moving,' called Artair from just below him. 'You're doing great.'

The wind picked up, and the chain swung a little with it, creaking in a worrying manner. Every muscle in his body screaming with tension, Lucian reached out with his foot, seeking the next piece of the chain. Incredibly, Artair had insisted they remove their boots before the climb, claiming that the flexibility of bare feet would be of more use than the rigidity of hard leather, so it was his toes that found the edge of the crevice. He couldn't see where it was, and for a moment his foot quested around until Artair's hand took hold of it and guided him to the right place. Lucian's outrage grew. How was it they were in Artair's dream, and he was the one being humiliated? He grunted with bitter amusement – of course, if Artair were truly in charge of the dream, he was sure he'd be experiencing much worse.

'All in all,' he shouted into the wind, 'I think I'd rather shoot an arrow through a giant spider.'

'We're nearly there,' said Artair. 'Not much further now.'

Instinctively, Lucian glanced down and instantly regretted it.

While it was true that they were more than halfway down the chain, the ground was still undoubtedly a short scream and a long drop away.

Artair looked up at him and, for reasons beyond Lucian, grinned.

'Being cooped up all those years has made you strange,' Lucian said, gradually inching his body across one link to the other. 'Did you know that?'

'What? I just never expected to be climbing down a giant dream chain, suspended between two different pieces of my past. Life is full of unexpected things. Isn't it great?'

'Hooray,' said Lucian. Tiny flakes of rust had smeared across his sweaty chest, and that was worrying him too. It was such a tiny, precise detail. He didn't know the rules that governed magical dreams, but if they were realistic enough to include tiny flakes of rust, he suspected they were realistic enough that a fall from this height would kill him.

Artair, meanwhile, did not seem to be worried. He was moving steadily, the muscles of his shoulders and stomach bunched with the effort, creeping ever downwards. He had stopped grinning, and a more familiar expression of concentration had returned; there was a task to do, and he would focus on it until it was done. Periodically, he would pause to check on Lucian, to offer him a hand across a difficult gap or, to Lucian's disgust, words of encouragement. It was strange to see Artair as Elver must see him, a tall young man with broad shoulders who moved with grace and a quiet kind of strength. Despite the terror of the drop, Lucian found himself thinking of the kiss he had shared with Elver – of course she had happily kissed him when he looked like this. The thought was a thorn pushed into his heart.

Eventually, they were no more than ten feet from the ground, and for the first time Lucian felt his heart slow. They would make it, after all. He watched Artair wriggle down and jump off, landing in the tall white grass. Facing away from him, the monk bent over at the waist, breathing hard. With slightly less grace, Lucian jumped down too, almost dizzy with relief to be on solid ground. With that thought, he looked up to the piece of monastery far above them and saw that there was barely anything left of it – a few last bricks floating in space, a small cloud of earth.

'It's a good thing the chain stayed up by itself,' he said, looking around. Just in front of them were the crowds of yurts that made up Artair's old settlement. They couldn't see the paddocks from where they were. 'Otherwise we'd have got down a lot faster than we'd like.'

Artair turned and looked at him. He took a piece of cord from within his shirt and used it to tie back his hair. Something about the gesture slid a needle of ice into Lucian's heart.

'Wait . . .'

Artair grinned again, except this time it wasn't him, not really. Lucian knew his own expressions, and found that he could easily guess the emotions that were churning inside the taller young man – terror, fury, desperation. The sense that spilling blood – death – could bring him power and send the terror away.

'You know what comes next, Lucian,' said Artair.

'You don't have to do this, monk.'

'A big enough sacrifice, and he will hear me,' said Artair, and Lucian knew the monk wasn't really listening to him any more. He was lost in the dream, caught in the events that had destroyed the little settlement and sent Artair to the Golden Tower of the Perpetual Morning. Had sent them both there. 'I don't know what has happened to me, but I know what can fix it.'

With that, Artair ran, disappearing round one of the yurts.

'Wait!'

Lucian followed after him, walking slowly. Beyond the yurt, he could see people milling about, living their lives. Some of them were gathered around a hole in the ground, a temporary well they had dug, searching for water during this driest of seasons; some of them were scraping leather, or weaving wool. There were dogs loping about, chased by children, and although a lot of work was happening, there was a lot of chatter and laughter too. It was all very different from the childhood Lucian had known, where he had studied more than laughed, and where much of his time was spent in dark rooms, filled with the smell of blood. Of Artair, there was no sign. In the way of dreams, he had vanished, although Lucian thought he knew where he might find him.

'Young man, do you need a shirt?'

An older woman with arms full of laundry winked at him, then threw him something, which he caught. It was a loose vest that looked as though it had once been red, but had been washed and washed until it was soft and pink.

'Put that on,' she continued. 'Do you want to be driving all the young ladies wild?'

He thanked her and put the shirt on, and she turned back to her work.

He remembered this place, dimly. Little details flashed up as he passed them: the biggest tent in the centre, which had colourful hand-woven flags flying from the top; the powerful smell of horse hair; the sound of the wind moving through dead grass.

And very soon there would be smoke, and fire, and screaming. The horses would scream, and the people would scream, and in his heart he would cry out for help . . . And nothing would answer. It had all happened before, and it would happen again.

'This is ridiculous. There's nothing I can do about it,' he said aloud. An older man carrying a child glanced at him curiously. Lucian paid him no mind. 'And why would I want to? The monk kept me prisoner all that time, just as much as the Order of the Perpetual Morning did. I don't owe him anything.'

But the hate that had always sustained him before wasn't there any more, he realized. Something had changed since Artair had walked away from the monastery, carrying them both out into the world. Where once there had been fury and hate, making everything simple – *do anything to regain your power* – now there were more complicated feelings, like guilt, responsibility, shame. Lucian stumbled, and fell onto the dry ground.

In his own dream, he had been caught by the spider, too terrified to move, and he felt an echo of that feeling again. The hot, feverish breath of the Maura spider had warmed his face, and he'd felt its drool drip down his neck . . . and Artair had saved him. Despite the burning of the ponies, and the fact that Lucian had ruined his life, Artair had decided that he wouldn't let him die in that awful place.

A dog trotted over, sniffed at his hand, then trotted away again.

He couldn't save Artair's old home. It was already long gone. But was he really going to let Artair live through the burning all over again, when he had the power to stop it?

Pushing away the terror and the pain, Lucian shakily got to his feet. He brushed himself off. He knew where the paddocks were.

'The monk isn't the only one who can do stupidly heroic things, after all.'

He found Artair, as he knew he would, sitting on the paddock fence, looking out across a shifting, snorting sea of ponies. There were around three hundred of the animals, all mildly agitated at being fenced in – these were animals used to roaming – and no doubt mildly anxious about the young man watching them, a torch burning brightly in one hand. It wasn't quite as Lucian remembered it. In reality, it had been night-time when he had burned the animals, and there hadn't been any other people around. It had been dark, because Artair's people had banned the lighting of fires during that dry season.

'Artair,' he said. 'You don't have to do this.'

The young man didn't turn his head. His eyes were fixed on the ponies, an expression of wild misery on his face that was difficult to look at.

'That's not my name.'

Lucian came and leaned on the fence next to him. He could feel the heat of the torch, fierce and dangerous, and he felt painfully aware of the dry grass under his feet.

'Yes. That's one of the few things you do know. You might not know where you are, what's happening or why you don't recognize your own face, but you do know your own name. And you know that, somehow, blood is your path to power. Death is the key to wielding control.' He gestured to the ponies. 'This won't work, though. That power – you won't have it again until you know who you are. All this will do is cause pain and suffering.' He paused, the memory of that night as hot and as close as the torch Artair was holding. Hundreds of beasts aflame, mad with pain and fear. They had crashed through the fences and streamed off into the night, setting other things alight as they went, and he had watched, waiting desperately for something to change inside him. It hadn't. 'Are you listening to me? It's stupid, and pointless, and will only make things worse for you.'

'What else can I do?' Artair lifted the torch, turning his face into a mask of orange light. 'I have to do something. I don't know these people. They're nothing to me.'

'Which doesn't mean they're worthless.' For some reason Lucian thought of Elver, of leading her to the Tumble Stone to be thrown to her death. He had thought her worthless too, once, only valuable as a tithe for his god. And now, he suspected, she was more important to him than anyone else in Tlevrae. He sighed. 'Artair, I know you're in there somewhere. Are you listening to this? Can you get control? I could try to wrestle you for the torch, but I think we both know who would win if we start rolling around in the dirt. Besides, if that torch drops, it's all over anyway.'

'There is no Artair,' the young man on the fence said tersely. 'He's gone. I don't know who you're talking about.'

'Oh, he's in there, believe me. Trapped, and this time he'll be forced to watch as you destroy his home and his family, all because you're scared and confused. Artair, do you remember that Tisk told us that we didn't have to be separate beings? That we were potentially capable of extraordinary things, together? We moved together once, and we saved Elver.'

Artair lowered the torch a few inches. There was sweat on his brow, and his hand was shaking.

'You can do this,' continued Lucian, watching the torch. 'You're stronger than this version of me – I promise you that. Strong enough to change things for both of us.' He laughed bitterly. 'It's something I admire about you, actually. Save yourself. Save us. Give me the torch, brother.'

Around them, the sun blazed and the ponies whickered. The moment seemed to stretch on into eternity, so long that Lucian began to wonder if this was the real nightmare: the two of them trapped forever on the precipice of disaster. And then Artair's shoulders relaxed, and he passed Lucian the torch without another word. He was back to himself, all the fear and cruelty washed from his features. Lucian held the torch, considering the red flame. There were no handy buckets of water to douse it in, and if he tried to extinguish it in the soil, the chances were he'd set the grass alight anyway. There was only really one thing to do with it.

He pressed the torch to his own chest. There was a moment of brilliant, terrible pain, the sense of burning passing over him in a flash, and then the fire sank inside him, back where it belonged.

'How did you do that?' asked Artair. He sounded genuinely interested.

'Magic,' Lucian replied. He climbed up onto the fence to sit next to him. In front of them, the ponies had calmed down and gone back to grazing. The grass had turned from white to green. For the first time, Lucian noticed all the colours of the animals: brown, white, black, tan, yellow, grey and red. He noticed their bright eyes, their shaggy hooves, the way their ears twitched and how they tossed their heads. 'They're beautiful,' he said. 'I didn't see them properly in the dark. It was a terrible thing I did, Artair. I see that now. No, actually, that's not quite right. I always knew it was a terrible thing – I just pretended that I had no choice, and I suppose that I'm ready to say that I chose to do this unforgivable thing, and I'm sorry for it.'

Artair nodded. He briefly clasped one hand to Lucian's shoulder, then let go.

'I think that's good,' he said in a musing tone. 'I'm not sure if it's everything, but it's something.'

To Lucian's surprise, he felt something loosen in his chest. He was afraid for a moment that he was going to cry, like some sort of pathetic child, but then he realized what it was: the banked embers of power inside him had flared into life, growing hot again. It was still buried deep, and it was still a fraction of what it was supposed to be, but, as Artair had said, it was something.

'What is it?' asked Artair. 'You look as though Fleet just bit you.'

'The power!' Lucian shook his head. 'I can't believe I didn't see it before. It's linked to both of us! And since we're always at odds it can't work properly. *You* are holding me back.'

Artair looked infuriatingly calm about this. He shrugged. 'That makes a lot of sense. When you think about it, I spent all my time in the monastery learning how to keep you from getting out. Holding you back from the world.'

Lucian hopped down from the fence. He felt as though the fire he'd consumed had given him too much energy, like a large cup of Sunay's kopi.

'Well, stop it! Let those barriers down, and we can work together to get out of here. We're on the same side here, Artair. *This* is the key.'

'You're asking me to trust you.' Artair looked out across the ponies. 'I don't know, Lucian. I don't know if I can.'

Lucian pushed his hands back through his hair. 'There's no time to dither, monk. Maura will have sent Dalesh after us, and our body is in the waking world, defenceless. Elver is up there too, in an enchanted sleep. She's in danger. Work *with* me, Artair.'

The mention of Elver had changed something in Artair's demeanour. He jumped down from the fence, and nodded, once.

'Very well.' He put his hand on Lucian's shoulder again, and Lucian felt the lines of power glow with new life. He drew a door in the air in front of them, sketching it out with a red fire that was heatless, sparkless. When it was complete, the dreamworld around them shivered as though it were a reflection on a lake, and then the portal opened. The pair of them stepped through it together.

CHAPTER 23

Artair awoke, and realized several things at once.

Firstly, that he had been tied up and was lying on his side in damp, cold grass. Elver was around ten feet away from him, her arms and legs bound with rope. Fleet, too, had been trussed up, as if they expected to cook him for dinner. They weren't inside the yurt any more; Dalesh and her assistants had moved them away from Micelle – there was no sign of the tent town – and instead they were beneath an old, dead tree, the only one that he could see for some distance. As well as Dalesh and several people wearing the white circle of Maura's order, there was Plinko. The boy now appeared to be a fat-cheeked toddler, sitting with his pudgy legs sticking out in front of him as though he'd been placed on the ground by an absent-minded adult. His colourful cards were spread in front of him. Dalesh was talking to her fellow acolytes.

'We're far away enough from that town to conduct our business in peace.' She sniffed. 'There are at least three temples to the Lady Dusk in Micelle, and not a single temple to our Mother. I'm sure that will change in time, but for now we need to avoid the attention that cutting a few throats will bring.'

The second and more pressing realization was that Artair could sense Lucian much more closely than he ever had before. The mage was a shadow in the back of his head, a muffled voice that he couldn't quite make out. And, for the first time in his life, Artair felt the presence of magic. It was coiled inside him, a heated wire of energy waiting to be unleashed into the world. He knew that if he chose to he could let it out, but that it couldn't act without his say-so. Almost immediately, he felt Lucian's impatience.

Let me through!

Artair lifted his head. At the same moment, facing him across the grass, Elver opened her eyes. He saw them widen with surprise, and then fury. Dalesh, who had been talking to one of her followers, noted the change too and drew a dagger from her belt.

LET ME THROUGH, ARTAIR!

Always, he had held Lucian back. The dark spirit that had been his responsibility for the last six years, that he had been told must never, ever be released – now it was time to let him out.

Artair felt something loosen in his chest, and instantly the magic surged through. The ropes that had been binding his wrists together flared with circles of red light and fell apart. Meanwhile, Elver had broken the ropes holding her together and was struggling to her feet.

'Shit.' Dalesh gestured to her acolytes. There were at least ten of them that Artair could see. 'Stop them! Plinko, we were told they'd stay asleep indefinitely!'

The mage of Enos blinked owlishly and then drooled a little. Dalesh hissed with annoyance.

'You should have killed us when you had the chance.' Elver looked wild, her yellow eyes almost seeming to glow in the dim light of dawn. She ran at one of the acolytes, faster than Artair thought it was possible to move, and she slammed into the young man, sending him flying backwards into the scrub. A moment later and she had hold of another by the collar of their robe, before punching them firmly in the stomach. The acolyte wheezed and fell over.

'Use magic, mistress!' cried one of them, who was attempting to hide behind the tree.

Dalesh shook her head, the expression on her face stricken.

'Subdue them, idiots.'

Artair stood up, the magic flowing around his body in a way that felt chaotic, uncontrolled. He could sense Lucian trying to direct it, to conduct it as a man in front of an orchestra might conduct music, but it was still reluctant to obey: it made him think of fireflies in a jar, bouncing madly against the glass.

Several of the acolytes rushed Elver at once, one tackling her round the waist and using their weight to drag her to the ground. Artair thought once again of the old physical training he had done every morning and every afternoon in the monastery, and then he was in the fray too, letting his body move through those familiar patterns – the palm of one hand struck the jaw of the biggest of the acolytes, sending him to his knees, and suddenly his fists lit up with ruby-red light. The magic was in play, finally, and when he struck the next assailant, a portal formed in the air around them and they vanished.

'Plinko!' Dalesh was backing off, the dagger held out in front of her. 'What is the point of you, you little bastard!'

The boy reached out and gathered his cards into one fat little fist, clearly meaning to summon another spell to send them to sleep. But then the cards shimmered with orange light, and the pictures on them changed: the spiders, cats and owls changed into foxes, all of them leaping happily through autumn leaves. One of the acolytes, one who had been hanging back from the fight, made a curt gesture in the air and suddenly Sunay was standing there, an uncharacteristically stern look on her face. Artair's heart lifted at the sight of her.

'That's quite enough of your mischief, Plinko.' She reached down and snatched up the cards. 'It's the height of rudeness, you know, not to introduce yourself when in the presence of another mage. Shame on you. Oh, and try anything else and I will personally feed you to Fleet. He deserves a treat.'

Plinko's round face pinched with fury and he threw himself into the dust, kicking his arms and legs in a tantrum.

Meanwhile, Elver had grabbed one of the acolytes and yanked their hood away before pressing her hand to their neck. There was a high-pitched scream that echoed eerily across the empty plain, and then she was rounding on Dalesh herself. Artair sent another two through portals with his fiery fists, and then quite abruptly it was just the four of them: Artair, Elver, Sunay and Dalesh. Mother Maura's chief mage had backed away against the tree, the dagger held out in front of her.

'Stay back!'

'What's the matter, Dalesh? Did Maura take away your teeth?' Elver held up her hands. Her hair was wild, as though she'd had a shock. 'I only gave your little friends a light poisoning, but somehow I don't feel like holding back for you.'

Artair bent and untied Fleet, who began bouncing around, barking in agitation. He could still feel Lucian nearby, although the magic seemed to have ebbed away again.

'You wouldn't dare,' spat Dalesh. 'Touch me, and the Mother will strike you down.'

'I wouldn't bet on that,' said Artair quietly. 'If you could use her magic, you'd have done that the second you saw us wake up.'

'Shows what you know, monk.'

Elver advanced, and Dalesh snarled, dropping the dagger and raising her arms. As they had during the fight in the hills, glowing white hands of magic appeared in a halo around her head, their fingertips as sharp as the blade she had discarded. Artair became aware that the light of the magic seemed to reveal another figure standing behind Dalesh – it was Maura, her long white hair falling over her shoulders. She looked startled, and somewhere inside his head, Lucian laughed.

Dalesh is taking without asking, said Lucian. *Unwise.*

The glowing halo of hands flew outwards from Dalesh towards Elver, fingers hooked into claws. But, before they could reach her, Artair felt his arm fly up of its own accord, and instead Dalesh's magic veered away from Elver and twisted towards him. When it met his fingers, it poured inside him, a churning river of power – instinctively, he took hold of it and, sensing Lucian next to him, they both began pulling the magic out of Dalesh. There was a pair of twin screams, from both mage and god, and Maura looked more solid for a moment, as though the act of dragging the power out of her had forced her to appear.

'Dalesh!' she bellowed. 'You will stop, or I will kill you!'

'Mother, please.' Dalesh was shaking, either with fear or the violence of the magic, Artair couldn't tell. 'They will kill me! I am your faithful servant—'

'*Fool.*' Maura reached forward and curled her hand round Dalesh's forehead as if to bless her. 'You leave me no choice.'

Abruptly, the magic pouring into them stopped. Maura vanished, and Dalesh dropped to her knees. She was bleeding from her nose and ears, and when she opened her mouth, more blood ran over her chin. For a second, Artair was held on the spot with shock, and then he ran over to the woman, catching her just before she collapsed to the ground.

'Don't move,' he said, lowering her gently onto the grass. 'Don't try to speak. We can get you back to the town . . .' He glanced up and across the bleak landscape. He had no idea where they were.

'She was always . . . hard.' Dalesh shuddered in his arms. 'Becoming the Mother . . . made her worse.' The woman opened her mouth, as though to say something else, but her next breath never came. Dalesh was dead.

CHAPTER 24

The acolytes who were still conscious did not wait to retrieve Dalesh's body. They picked up their fallen friends between them and limped off without another word, although Elver caught them throwing unfriendly looks over their shoulders as they left. Two or three of them had livid red marks on their arms and faces where she had touched them, and she suspected they wouldn't be forgetting that in a hurry.

Good, she thought. Perhaps they'd think twice about obeying Maura in the future.

'We should bury the body,' said Artair. He looked pale, and she could tell that Dalesh's death had unsettled him deeply.

'I want to talk about that magic you were doing,' said Sunay. 'You were, what? Punching people into oblivion? Exciting! Also, how did that work?'

'I'm not sure I understand it myself,' he said, looking down at his own hands. 'We sent them through portals. Somehow.'

'Sunay, I'm glad you're back. Really glad.' Elver carefully patted the mage on the shoulder where her jacket was thickest. She was enormously relieved that there was no trace of fright on Sunay's face now. Whatever she had glimpsed through the magical frame, it was gone. 'There's a lot to talk about, but I don't think we should do so here. It's too open.' The sun had risen during their desperate fight, and the frost on the plain was melting, covering everything in a chilly glimmer. 'Anyone can see us. We should move.'

'I quite agree, and for now I will just say how pleased I am to see your lovely faces. What should we do about him?' Sunay pointed at Plinko, who was lying face down in the mud. Elver had the sense he had been hoping they'd forget about him if he was quiet.

She shrugged.

'I suppose we can't leave him out here in the middle of nowhere, as much as I'd like to. We take him, I guess. And find somewhere to leave him.'

I could eat him! put in Fleet happily. *He's not as juicy-looking as he used to be, but I am hungry. I could manage it.*

'No, Fleet.' She raised her voice slightly to be sure that Plinko took the point. 'No eating Plinko. Not unless Plinko decides to be difficult. Come on, let's get moving.'

'First, the body,' said Artair, in a tone that suggested he wasn't going to be persuaded otherwise. 'We have to bury it. I don't want it . . . eaten by animals.' He glanced at Fleet and then away.

In the end, the ground was too hard and they had nothing to dig with – although the keltraxia cub gave it a good try. Instead, they collected rocks and found a shallow dip in the earth in which to lay Dalesh. Artair covered the woman's face with her own cloak, and then carefully they covered her body with the stones. When it was done, they all stood awkwardly for a moment, not sure what to do next.

'Dalesh wasn't a good person,' said Artair. 'She only helped us escape the Temple of Trilot because she needed Elver to get to Prideful Leap. But I don't know. It still doesn't feel right that she died here, in the middle of nowhere, and her own people left her body behind.'

Elver knelt and picked up a smaller stone. It was black and shiny, and stood out a little from the others. She placed it on the largest rock at the head of the grave.

'Dalesh helped to set my life on this path when she took me to the Tumble Stone,' she said. 'It was a terrible thing to do to a kid, but I don't regret my life, or who I am. I think probably Dalesh had some regrets, and maybe she was as badly used by Maura as I was. Or nearly as badly, anyway. She at least deserved the loyalty of her god.'

When that was done, they made a rough harness for Plinko out of Artair's old ropes, and Sunay slung him onto her back as if he were just a particularly hefty baby. They didn't know where they were exactly, but Elver could still sense the First of Monsters somewhere to the east, so they headed that way, hoping to find shelter.

Before long, Elver saw a light winking in the distance. Sunay saw it at the same time, and pointed it out.

'What do you think? A settlement? A campfire?'

'Too soon to say,' said Elver. 'Hopefully, a place big enough to get some food and rest.'

The light soon resolved into a pair of lamps on the front of a tall building. The closer they got, the stranger it became: it looked like the kind of slumped old tavern that lined many of the streets of Addersport, but it stood alone in the middle of the plain, with no neighbouring houses and no road leading to it. And the closer they got, the more excited Sunay seemed to grow.

'*Oh*,' she said eventually. 'I think I know what this is.'

'What is it?' asked Elver, a shade impatiently.

'You'll see,' said Sunay. 'I don't want to spoil the surprise.'

When they eventually stood outside it, it seemed even stranger and more incongruous than when they'd seen it from a distance. It was a loud, raucous tavern, set in the middle of a desolate plain, clearly crammed with rowdy customers despite the early hour of the morning. The lintel above the front door was carved with great bushels of wheat and a huge tankard, which was pouring foaming ale all over the crop. The sign that hung from one of the outer beams read: The Inn at the End of All Worlds.

'What an extraordinary place,' said Artair. 'Sunay, have you been here before?'

'No, but I've heard of it. This is powerful magic – the most powerful spell, in fact, afforded to the mages of Barleycorn. It's a tavern that is unmoored in space and time, and only Barleycorn's most esteemed mages – who call themselves the Lords and Ladies of Hospitality – are able to summon it. I've always wanted to get a drink here.'

'Sunay, none of what you just said made any sense,' said Elver. 'Will Fleet be in trouble here?'

'No, no,' said Sunay, stepping eagerly up to the door. The iron knocker was in the shape of a horseshoe. 'If anything, he'll be the least strange of the sights in here.'

Before she could reach it, the door swung open to reveal a short older man dressed in a jacket of crushed yellow velvet and a pale green waistcoat, both of which looked as if they'd seen better days. His eyes lit up at the sight of them.

'There you are!' he said brightly. 'We've been waiting. Come in, come in. The room is all ready for you.'

'You were expecting us?' asked Artair.

'Yes, yes, of course.'

The little man began waving them in. The top of his head was a shining pink, and his eyes were very blue. Sunay was the first through the door, taking the man's outstretched hand and shaking it enthusiastically.

'Are you a Lord of Hospitality?' she asked.

'Why, yes,' said the little old man. 'But you can call me Bob, my dear. Come along.'

Bob led them into the Inn at the End of All Worlds. Inside, there was a confusing set of rooms, all of them decorated differently, and filled with people who looked as though they might have been snatched up from every corner of Tlevrae. Elver saw men and women with white powdered wigs as big as baskets balanced on their heads; people with oiled chests and braids, great swords strapped to their backs; men and women dressed in white suits with their faces painted to resemble animals; people in extravagant silk gowns, kneeling in front of tea sets. The one thing this remarkable collection of people had in common was that they all appeared to be having a good time. There were plates of food and bottles of drink on almost every surface.

They were marched up a set of winding stairs – despite his apparent age, Bob moved very quickly and they had to scamper to keep up – and along another corridor. Here they passed rooms that contained sights even stranger. In one, Elver was sure she spotted a group of people about the same size as Bob, but they looked like giant rodents, with big soft ears and large red eyes. All of them wore gaudy little crowns. In the next, what looked like a giant lizard reclined on a plush sofa while a small woman with horns polished the scales on one of its giant feet. Elver drew to a stop at this, sure she must be looking at another jih spirit, but Bob waved her on.

'No time for gawking, I'm afraid,' he said cheerfully. 'My lord has instructed you have this room for a single day and night, and I'm sure you'll want to make the most of it.'

'You mean Barleycorn has arranged this?' asked Artair.

'Yes, yes, special instructions from on high,' said Bob. 'Here you go. This is your room. In this place, you can eat and drink and rest, safe in the knowledge that no one untoward can find you. You have the safety of Barleycorn's hearth and hospitality. Quite a blessing, I think you'll agree!'

He swung a door open. Inside, there was a pleasant room with wide windows looking out across the plains, and a jumble of well-made furniture, including beds, desks, tables, chairs and elaborate standing lamps. On the biggest table, there was more food than Elver had ever seen in her life; she was amazed the table hadn't collapsed from the weight of it.

Bob nodded them inside, then bowed once. 'Enjoy! If you need anything, just bang on this door and I will be here.'

With that, he left them.

Fleet made a beeline for the table. To stop him from crashing through all the food, Elver took a leg of lamb and placed it on the floor for him. Sunay took Plinko out of his harness and placed him on a sofa.

'A blessing from Barleycorn, who'd have thought? You know, they say that this place can exist in all worlds, at all times. Which is why the clientele are so varied.'

'Yeah,' said Elver. 'I thought I saw . . . well, I thought I saw some strange stuff.'

'Sunay.' Artair cleared his throat. 'I'm so sorry. I accused you of terrible things. I should have trusted you.'

The mage waved away his apology. 'Don't tie yourself in knots, Artair dear. We were all under a sticky little enchantment, thanks to this little scamp.' She patted Plinko on the head and he scowled. 'Making us believe things, and see things, that just weren't true.' She glanced at Elver. 'He had us all at sixes and sevens, which I'm sure was the point.'

'What happened?' asked Elver. She took an apple from the table and sat on the edge of one of the beds. 'Last we saw of you, you were heading into the swamp.'

'Ha, well.' Sunay poured herself a hot drink from a tall silver pot. A spicy scent filled the room. 'Oh, chai, my favourite. I wish I had a more exciting story for you both, but the truth is I got a decent night's sleep and the dream magic Plinko had woven around me fell away. It seems he can't maintain it over a long distance.' She shook her head in a wry fashion. 'It's slippery, though. To think I believed you to be some sort of terrifying beast, Elver!'

'You think . . . what you saw with Tisk's magic when you looked at me was part of Plinko's spell?' Elver watched the mage carefully.

'Why, of course! I'll admit, I thought the magic of Enos had to be mired firmly in dreams, but perhaps she can cause a kind of waking dream.' Sunay shook her head as though she'd been foolish to ever believe such a thing, and Elver wondered if she was lying. 'And when I realized what had happened,' Sunay continued, 'I started to head back towards you, except I spotted Dalesh and Mummy's little acolytes, and of course I knew they would be heading straight to you anyway. A little illusion spell, and I slipped in amongst their ranks. Easy really. I'm more interested in what is going on with you two.' She pointed at Artair with her spoon.

Artair glanced at Elver. 'Us? Nothing's going on with us . . .'

Sunay rolled her eyes dramatically. 'I know *that*, more's the pity.' Elver looked away with a sinking feeling in her chest. Now that she was fairly sure it had been Lucian she'd kissed in the Jih Forest, she was even less sure how Artair felt about her – but this seemed to make it clear. 'I'm talking about you and Lucian,' continued Sunay. 'Something's changed, hasn't it?'

'I . . . Yes.'

A few moments of near silence passed, filled with the sound of Fleet chewing loudly.

'Well?' Elver crossed her arms over her chest. Artair's presence had been a comfort – she remembered his arms around her on the platform, holding her close – but it hadn't stopped her worrying about Lucian. 'What happened? Is he alright?'

'We dreamed together,' said Artair. 'It was the strangest thing. He was there as himself – he wasn't wearing my body – and we had to . . . we had to work together to escape the dream. To break the spell. And I think working together like that, it's changed the way the Sleepless magic works. When we were fighting Dalesh, he was there with me – like he was at Prideful Leap, only more so, somehow. He's been struggling to use the magic because I was holding him back.'

'And now you're not?' asked Sunay.

'I'm trying not to,' said Artair. He picked up a cup from off the table, turning it over in his hands. He looked troubled. 'It's difficult to trust him, even now. But, when I let him through, the magic worked. You saw it.'

'What is it?' asked Elver. 'You look like you're unhappy about something.'

'I sent those people through portals with the magic, but I don't know where they went. I asked him, but he's quiet now. I think that the connection wears him out as much as it does me.' He looked up, meeting her gaze with his own. 'What if I killed Maura's acolytes, Elver? What if I sent them to the bottom of the ocean, or somewhere worse?'

Hesitantly, Elver went to him and took his hand, ignoring the smirk on Sunay's face.

'They were trying to kill us, Artair. They chose to do that, and we chose to defend ourselves.' She squeezed his hand, and then dropped it. 'Let's eat and talk. When we've all caught up, we can try to find someone in this inn who wants a baby that can do card tricks.'

CHAPTER 25

The laughter of the children was louder.

Maura stood at the door to her cottage, listening to them. They seemed less playful and more mocking than they had done, and it was easy to guess why. In her mind's eye, she saw Dalesh fall again, she heard her plead for help and she felt the brittle snap as she'd broken the mage's neck. Dalesh had been the best of them, and yet even she had let her down in the end. To save her own life, she had used the connection between them to draw on the magic without permission, and in doing so had allowed Lucian to steal it.

'If I hadn't killed her, he would have taken all of it,' she said aloud. The ghostly presences at the edge of her field kept laughing, paying her no mind. 'He would have sucked me dry until my godhood was nothing but a shadow, a husk. I had to sever the connection. Besides which, Dalesh *disobeyed*. She was an ungrateful daughter.'

She'd had no choice. That was what she had to remember. Dalesh's death had been forced on her, and in truth it was the fault of the god who had not kept her promise.

'Enos! Enos, where are you? I know you can hear me, moonwitch.' She raised her voice, shouting over the laughing children. 'Enos! You will explain your failure!'

'I beg your pardon?'

There was a rustle of silk, and, when she turned, Enos the god of sleep and dreams was standing in her kitchen. She gave off a faint blue light that turned the shadows into an inky midnight darkness.

'You told me you had them,' spat Maura, stepping back inside and slamming the door behind her. 'That your magic had them subdued. But what should I find when I send my people to kill them? A trio of very wakeful troublemakers, more than able to deal with your pathetic mage. Clearly, I should have dealt with one of the more powerful gods – you must be a lesser part of this pantheon.'

Enos trembled with rage. She grew taller, so that her three heads nearly brushed the ceiling, and more arms sprouted from her sides. The shadows grew darker, and longer, and in the window the moon appeared, sickle-sharp.

'You would dare to speak to me like that, you upstart? After I offered my help to you in the spirit of friendship?' She advanced a step. Maura held her ground. 'It was your mage who failed you, not mine. She failed to kill them when my mage had offered them up on a silver plate.'

'Dalesh had to deal with the failings of your magic. It wasn't her fault.' As soon as the words were out of her mouth, she knew it was the wrong thing to say.

Enos grinned, exposing long, sharp teeth.

'Then why is she dead, Mother? Why is your mage mouldering under a paltry pile of stones? Her flesh turning to liquid, her soul in the hands of the Hooded Crow?'

'Enough,' said Maura. 'Get out. Leave my realm at once.'

'You have insulted me, Mother. And you will pay for it.'

'An empty threat. This is my realm, moon-witch. You can't do anything to me here.'

'That is true.' Enos swept across the floor towards her, bending down to whisper into her ear with three mouths. 'But perhaps you will dream. And in your dream, the ghost children will not stay at the gate. Perhaps they will come into your home, and slip into your bed, their cold hands grasping at your sleeve. They will be hungry, and only Mother can feed them.'

She gave Maura one last grin, and then she vanished, along with the moon and her shadows.

Later, Maura stood ankle-deep in the surf, the hem of her dress heavy with seawater. In front of her was the avatar of the Lady Dusk. It was an owl feather as long as her arm, hanging suspended above the ocean. The tip of the feather was a deep purple, which shaded to a shining gold at the quill. She bent and reached out a single finger to touch it.

'Lady Dusk,' she said. 'Will you speak to me? I sensed kindness from you when we spoke before.'

At first, nothing happened. And then the sea grew as still as a lake, and when she stood up she was in an entirely different place. There was a dark forest all around her, and the sky overhead was mauve, and streaked with orange clouds. Looming over the forest, larger than the tallest buildings of Addersport, was a great grey owl. Its eyes were vast and dark, and scattered with tiny points of light, like stars. In a small clearing in front of Maura, there stood an ivory throne, carved all over with hundreds of lifelike moths. Sitting on the throne was the Lady Dusk, a veil drawn down over her eyes.

'You have my gratitude,' Maura said, a little stiffly. She had been struck by the eerie grandeur of the Lady Dusk's realm, and was wondering why her own was so, well, homely.

'I am an old god,' said Lady Dusk. 'So my realm more closely reflects my nature. If you live, Mother, your realm will gradually change too. Not even I could say what it will become.'

'You can hear my thoughts?' asked Maura.

'Sometimes.' The Lady Dusk lifted her chin. 'I am the god of the hidden, of mysteries, and secrets. Nothing is ever entirely clear.'

'I need your help, Lady Dusk.' Maura lifted her chin. 'My attempts to reclaim the rest of my power have failed. But you can see what will happen, yes? You could tell me what course of action will give me the results I need.'

For a long moment, the Lady Dusk was quiet. Maura sensed that she was being judged in some way. She curled her hands into fists, letting her fingernails dig into her flesh. *Hold your temper*, she told herself.

'There are, perhaps, some things you should know,' Lady Dusk said eventually. 'I cannot promise that you will enjoy this knowledge, or that it will help you in the way that you seek. Divination can be like grasping a blade with a bare hand – you may have gained a weapon, but it might also make you bleed.'

'Tell me what you can,' said Maura.

'Very well.'

The Lady Dusk reached up and pulled back her veil. The eyes she revealed were white from lid to lid, but above her the great owl blinked once, twice, and its eyes filled with a shifting violet and green light – it made Maura think of the lights in the sky she had seen in the far north, when she had been very young.

'Mother Maura. Born a mage of Tisk and reborn as a mage of the Bloody Claw. Godkiller and widow. Vessel of power, vessel of ambition.' The Lady Dusk's voice sounded distant now, and Maura imagined her looking through the eyes of the giant owl, staring off at the unimaginable distances of the future. 'The ones you seek are also seeking. They look for the kin of gods, one who has been hidden since time out of mind . . .' A crease appeared between her brows, as though this knowledge made her uneasy. 'They will find him. And it will be the kin of a god who is your downfall, Mother.'

'What?' snapped Maura. 'What do you mean, my downfall?'

'Find the child, and it will place you on the path to find them. But my vision of this is clouded, for the child they seek is hidden in the darkest place and with the deepest magicks.' The Lady Dusk shook her head. 'No. Here, everything becomes obscured. I can tell you nothing more.'

'Wait. What about my own children? Do I ever get them back?' Maura knew, even as she spoke the words, that she did not want the answer to this question. If the Lady Dusk told her no, then it would have all been for nothing – and still she would not be able to stop.

'I can tell you no more,' repeated the god, her tone final.

Above them, the giant owl closed its eyes and appeared to go to sleep.

'You have . . . my gratitude,' said Maura. 'It's hardly enough, but it's better than nothing.'

Abruptly, the Lady Dusk stood up, the feathers on her cloak standing on end like a startled bird, and Maura thought that she had angered the god. But, instead, the Lady Dusk raised an arm and pointed over her shoulder. Her voice, when she spoke, quivered with rage.

'Not you,' she said. 'Get out. I will not have you here.'

Maura turned. Behind her was a being of shining white cloth, a shifting white glow where its body should be. Instead of a face, a simple silver mask etched with gold hung in the air. Empty eye holes regarded her without emotion.

Peace, Dusk, said the figure. **I only come where my own business is discussed.**

'Leave, Trilot,' she said again. 'Your presence taints my realm.'

The god, who Maura supposed was Trilot, placed a hand on her shoulder. In an instant, they were back on the shoreline between the realm of mortals and the realm of shadows. Where the god had touched her with his gloved hand, Maura's flesh had turned numb. She stepped away from him sharply.

'Touch me again and you will suffer,' she said. 'I don't care who you are.'

Trilot only nodded.

Mother, I think that we can help each other. My faceless priests already seek one of those you chase, and now your quarry head towards the place where my child is hidden.

'Your child?'

Yes. He was hidden from me, at the beginning of all things, and I think perhaps you can understand the pain of that, Mother.

'Why was he hidden from you?'

It doesn't matter. I offer you my assistance, Mother, in the capture of the filthy jih spirits.

'You'll be more use than Enos, I hope.'

Trilot's tone did not change.

I will send my best hunter after your enemies. I will burn the jih who has wronged me, and extract from her the location of my child. I will keep your old acolyte weak. I will make him fear for his life, until you are ready to take back what is yours. And in return I ask only that Tython, my child, be turned over to me. The mask tilted in the subdued light, and Maura had the strangest sense that somehow it was smiling. **I will have Tython, and finally he will be cleansed.**

CHAPTER 26

'What is happening? What is this place?'

Lucian snorted at the monk's questions. It was obvious to him, at least, that they were dreaming together again. They were both sitting on a cliff edge, legs dangling. The land far below them was green and heavily forested, and off to the east it grew darker, as though it were always caught in shadow. Lucian was in his own body, and Artair was in his.

'My guess,' he said, 'is that you have just gone to sleep. And I am about to wake up.'

'Is this Plinko again?' asked Artair. 'Is this more of his magic?'

Lucian shook his head. 'No. I can smell no magic about this. I suspect the truth is that since we formed our connection, or whatever you want to call it, we're not quite as separate as we used to be. I wonder if we'll have this short dream together every time I take over your body? Wouldn't that be wonderful?'

Artair nodded slowly. 'You're talking to me like I'm an idiot, but actually I understand what you mean. It makes sense. How long will it last? This dream?'

'Too long, I expect,' Lucian replied drily.

'Then I want to ask you some things, quickly. When we did magic together – were you aware of what was happening? It felt like you were there.'

'I think technically *I* was the one controlling the magic. It's not like you've had any training, or studied even the first thing about it.' Lucian sniffed. 'But I will admit that you provided a certain amount of brute force. Using the force of your strikes to form a portal is a good idea – I'll give you that.'

'How gracious of you,' said Artair. Somewhere below them, an eagle floated past on an air current. 'What was it like, being in my head?'

'Stifling. It was like . . . a restless night's sleep. Sometimes I would wake, and become aware of you, and what was going on, and then I would sink back into nothing. It was strange.' As they were talking, snatches of memory were returning to Lucian, not all of them pleasant. He remembered Dalesh, blood pouring from her mouth. He cleared his throat. 'Thank you. For burying Dalesh. Or trying to.'

Artair looked surprised. 'I didn't think you'd care about something like that.'

'I'm not a monster, monk. I thought we'd established that.' Lucian paused. 'I've known Dalesh since I was a child. My whole life, really. It feels strange that she's dead.'

'Do you want to talk about it?'

Lucian scowled at him, furious to find that he did. 'She was a few years ahead of me at the temple, and I won't try to tell you that we cared for each other, or anything wholesome like that, but we worked together, and sometimes looked out for each other. I suppose she was the only family I had, apart from *Mother*.' A sour smile twisted his lips. 'You might say it's no surprise I turned out the way I did.'

'Did you never have anyone else that cared for you?' The look of pity on Artair's face made Lucian want to push him off the edge of the cliff. He doubted it would do the monk any harm, but it wouldn't be pleasant, at least. Still, there were other ways to hurt him.

'No,' he said lightly. 'But now I suppose I have Elver to care for me.' He turned to Artair to see how these words landed and was pleased to see a tightening of his jaw. 'She's fierce, and wild, and I certainly wouldn't want to be her enemy, but when I kissed her I could tell—'

'*When you what?*'

Out of nowhere, Artair was on his feet. Lucian grinned up at him.

'I could tell that she has a tender heart, underneath it all,' he said. 'Didn't she tell you, monk?'

The light around them was changing, the sky in the west brightening dramatically, and Lucian felt his grip on the dream slipping.

'You're lying,' said Artair. 'When did this happen?'

'Oh no, Artair, I'd love to tell you all about it, but I . . . I think I'm waking up . . .'

Lucian woke up laughing. He was in a room crammed with an eclectic mixture of furniture. The place thrummed with magic. Curious, he sat up just as Elver came back into the room. Her hair was wet and her cheeks were flushed, and the room she left billowed with steam. She was wearing an old silk vest of Sunay's with a pair of trousers, and he could see scars like blue slashes across her bare shoulder and arm.

'Lucian, is that you?' When he just grinned, she smiled back. 'What are you laughing at?' she asked.

'Oh, nothing much.'

'Well, there's hot water,' she said happily. 'It's like a hot spring, with soap, and oils, and a big scrubbing brush. You should make the most of it, Lucian. We've only got the morning left here. And . . . it's good to have you back.'

This day is just getting better and better, he thought.

'What is this place? I can feel another god's magic all over it.' He climbed off the bed. There was a fireplace in the room; this and the long table covered in food felt particularly thick with magic.

'Sunay said it was the Inn at the End of All Worlds.' Elver picked up a towel and rubbed her hair briskly. 'If that means anything to you.'

'It does. How extraordinary.' He watched her drop the towel and stretch like a cat, her hair a mess of damp curls. There was no sense of Artair being with him, and the conversation he had just had with the monk felt close; it made him bold. He went over to her and peeked into the room beyond. There was a large ceramic bath in the centre of a tiled floor, and the humid air was thick with the scent of rose oil and orange blossom. 'Where is our fox-tailed mage?'

'She's taking Plinko around the inn, trying to find someone to take him, I think. Fleet has gone with her. Apparently, no one will bat an eyelid at him in this place.' She looked up at him curiously, her golden eyes narrowed. 'You're staring at me. What is it?'

'Your scars,' he said, and she flinched, just a little. 'That is where the Queen of Serpents bit you?'

'Yeah.' One hand rose to cover the largest scar on her shoulder, and she looked away from him. 'It didn't take me long to heal, but they hung around.'

He sensed he had made her self-conscious, and all at once he was filled with the need to chase that feeling away.

'May I?' he said, holding his hand out to her.

For a long moment she looked at him like he was mad, and then she shrugged.

'Knock yourself out. Which is what would happen if you weren't jih, I suppose.'

Lightly, Lucian touched a finger to the ragged blue shape of her scar, and traced the line of it over her shoulder and across her collarbone. Then he traced another, one that circled the base of her neck.

'I have scars too,' he said quietly. 'Not this body, of course, but on my own.' The next scar wound its way down her arm, so he followed that too. 'Yours are prettier. I like the shape of them.' He went back to the scar that flowed across her collarbone. 'They make me think of the sea.'

'How did you get yours?' asked Elver. She had leaned into his touch, just slightly.

'They were punishments, mostly,' he said, smiling. 'They had a long, thin cane at the temple they called the Penitence, and when I got caught stealing food from the kitchens, or teasing a fellow acolyte, or not studying diligently enough, I would earn a few lashes. And sometimes the blood was drawn for the Bloody Claw himself. They weren't pretty, those scars. But I'd give anything to have them back, because that would mean I was in my own body again.'

'If you have the powers of a god now, couldn't you, I don't know, make it again?'

The question surprised him, mainly because he hadn't thought of it himself.

'I don't know. We've barely managed to use the magic at all. And, even if I could, how would I transfer my spirit out of Artair's body into mine?' He frowned. It was something to think about, though. 'Elver, if I had my own body, would you . . . I mean, if I was my own person again . . .'

'What?'

'Once, you wouldn't even speak to me. Remember that? You threatened me with a knife, kept me tied up. But now . . .' He let his eyes trace the shape of her scars again, and he was pleased to see the pink in her cheeks deepen. 'We seem much closer, you and I. And I like it. I *really* like it. I think maybe you do too.'

'Lucian . . .'

Another door to the room opened and Sunay burst in carrying Plinko, who was struggling in her arms. She was followed in by a woman Lucian had never seen before. She was around ten years older than all of them, and was wearing an extravagant gown, sewn all over with opals. There was a thin circlet of gold on her head, and she looked around the room with an expectant expression. Elver took a step away, her hand finally rising to cover the scar on her shoulder.

'Elver, Artair . . . Lucian?' asked Sunay. Lucian nodded. 'Elver and Lucian, meet Princess Cariloco, heir of the third house of Starrymorn, queen-to-be and guiding light of her people.'

'Er, hello,' said Elver.

The woman curtsied deeply. 'It is my honour,' she said.

'Princess Cariloco has agreed to take Plinko off our hands,' continued Sunay, 'but she insisted on meeting you both first, so she could be sure that you agreed.'

'Oh, we agree,' said Lucian. 'By all means. I can't wait to get him out of my sight.'

'You're very welcome to him,' said Elver in a slightly more agreeable tone. 'But, um, why would you want him?'

'I cannot have children of my own,' said Princess Cariloco. 'But there was a prophecy that I would come across a foundling child in the house of a strange god.' She gestured around the room grandly. 'This is it, and that is he.'

Elver pulled her fingers through her hair, straightening out the wet curls.

'Sunay, did you let the princess know about some of Plinko's more, uh, unique gifts?'

'Ah, well, that's the best bit about all this.' Sunay passed the struggling baby to the princess, who gathered him up in her arms and rained noisy kisses on his head. 'The world where Princess Cariloco rules is very different from ours. There are no gods, and therefore no mages. Isn't that marvellous?'

Lucian laughed. 'Did you hear that, Plinko? You'll just have to grow up like everyone does, and, eventually, die like everyone does.'

The princess didn't appear to be listening. She kissed the child on his cheek. 'We'll likely change the name,' she murmured. 'I'm not sure about Plinko at all. It isn't very regal.'

With that, she swept from the room. Lucian just caught Plinko's fat little face peeking over her shoulder, an expression of absolute boiling rage making him look much, much older.

When they came to leave, Bob met them at the front door, smiling affably.

'Now, do you have everything you need?' he asked. 'While you stand on this side of the door, I am at your complete disposal.'

'Thank you, Bob,' said Elver. 'But we should go now.'

'It's been an absolute pleasure,' added Sunay. 'Really, just fabulous. Everything I've heard about this place was true, and more!'

'Very well.' Bob put his hand on the door handle. 'We've moved the inn somewhere more convenient for you. You may find it a little bit disorientating, but the good news is that it's far away from your last location, so anyone seeking you will have to seek just that little bit harder.'

Lucian was expecting the desolate plains they had left behind. But when Bob opened the door it was onto a field of lush green grass, a line of tall trees in the distance.

'This is closer,' Elver said, the surprise clear in her voice. 'I mean, it's closer to where we need to get to.'

'Naturally,' said Bob, before giving them a little bow. 'Best of luck to you, friends, and remember to keep Barleycorn close to your heart. He sends his warmest regards.'

The three of them walked out into the sunny morning, Fleet at their heels, and when Lucian turned back for a last look at the Inn at the End of All Worlds, it had vanished. They were suddenly very much alone again.

'Barleycorn was as good as his word,' said Sunay in a considering tone. 'It never occurred to me that his help would come in the form of the inn. I feel very fortunate to have seen it.'

'I'd feel more fortunate if his help had come in the form of a weapon, or men to fight Maura's minions,' said Lucian.

'Those trees are very old,' said Elver. The closer they got, the more Lucian realized that they were bigger and taller than any trees he had seen before, and there was something unwelcoming about them. They stood close together, the canopy casting a thick darkness onto the wood below, and there were no obvious paths that he could see. He found it difficult to imagine any people travelling through this forest.

'Can we go around it?' he asked. Sunay twitched her tail in amusement, and he scowled at her.

'What? No.' Elver was marching towards the wood with purpose. 'The First of Monsters is in there somewhere. Not close yet, but the place we have to get to is in this forest somewhere. I can feel him.'

When they passed into the wood, the shadowy canopy closing over their heads, Lucian felt an uncomfortable shiver of dread. It felt for a moment as if Artair was standing behind him, and Lucian sensed the monk's own uncertainty.

Yet, for some time, nothing happened at all. The forest was uncommonly quiet, with only the occasional bird call breaking the silence, and they passed no other travellers, and saw no animals. Fleet scampered off ahead a few times, scouting for an easier way through the trees, while the rest of them concentrated on climbing through the thick bracken and the knots of gorse that covered the ground. The brief wintery day passed quickly, and soon only Elver could see clearly where they were going.

'We should stop for the night,' said Sunay. She was trying to extricate herself from a particularly clingy holly bush. 'If we can find a patch of ground that isn't covered in pointy little bastards.'

Lucian turned to look for Elver, who was some distance ahead of them, but instead found his eye caught by something on the leaf litter. It looked like a smudge of light, followed by another, and another. It was easily the brightest thing in that place, and as he got closer he realized it was in the shape of a boot print. He looked up and followed the trail straight to Elver, who had turned round and spotted them too. Every time her boot had sunk into the soil, it had left behind a little patch of glowing light.

'Is this a weird ancient-forest thing?' asked Sunay, who had caught up.

'I don't know what it is,' said Elver. 'And, look, there's another set. Those look like pawprints.'

'They're Fleet's,' said Lucian. He turned back to look the way they had come, but neither Sunay nor himself had glowing footprints. 'What does it mean?'

The keltraxia cub had returned from his scouting and was sniffing madly at the glowing marks. He pushed his snout into the glowing leaf litter and then leapt back yelping. He shook his head briskly, as though a bee had stung him. Elver frowned.

'What is it?' asked Lucian.

'According to Fleet,' said Elver, 'we're being hunted.'

CHAPTER 27

Elver waited in the dark, listening. Around her, the ancient wood was a dark, unsettling presence. She was familiar with forests, had largely grown up in one, and had always thought there'd be little in a wood that could ever make her uneasy, yet this place felt watchful – even unfriendly. The new senses the Queen of Serpents had gifted her with were prickling, a swirling inner darkness that made her feel on edge, and by her feet Fleet was standing to attention, his feathers all bushed up. His eyes were glowing pale green, lending an eldritch light to the inside of the hollow tree.

I don't see why we're hiding, he said, tail lashing back and forth. *I am not prey. Look at my teeth! My teeth are big!*

'We're being hunted. You said so yourself,' said Elver. She bent to ruffle the feathers on the back of his head, but he pulled away from her. She told herself that Fleet was too big to be treated like a cub any more, but it still hurt a little. 'We have to be careful.'

The others are out there, said Fleet. *They are doing what we should be doing. We are hiding inside a tree, like a squirrel. Like a little baby squirrel.*

'That's because they can move around without their footprints lighting up the bloody forest. I told you, Lucian and Sunay are following our tracks and covering them over, so that whoever is looking for us will lose our trail. Hopefully.' She tried to find a more comfortable spot to sit, but the bottom of the broken tree was lumpy with roots. 'Barleycorn's mage told us that we should get a head start on anyone coming after us, but it seems they caught up with us straight away.' She looked at Fleet's wide green eyes. 'Maybe this is a mage of the Pack. Who else would find us so quickly?'

No, said Fleet immediately. *It's not them. Doesn't smell like them. The Pack smells like . . . blood, heartbeat, dawn, chase. The Pack smells like hunger, paw-striking-earth, like moving-as-one. This . . .* Fleet scratched at his nose with one paw. *The smell is cold. Empty. And also hot.*

'Fleet, that makes no sense. How can it smell cold and hot?'

It does, he insisted. *Smells like hate. I don't like it.*

Elver frowned. She suspected that Fleet was showing off a little, but his description of what was hunting them wasn't making her feel better about hiding in a tree. Her instinct was the same as his, in truth: get out there, find what was after them, and stop it. She thought of the way the patch of glowing ground had burned Fleet's snout. That worried her.

'When the others get back, we'll come up with a new plan,' she told him. 'You and me, we know how to get around a forest, right? Better than anyone who might be following us.' She leaned down and slung her arm round the animal's shoulders. This time he didn't pull away from her, and she felt very glad of that. 'We'll find whoever this is and you can bite them. Maybe we both will.'

They lapsed into silence after that. Elver was worried about her friends. Artair was reasonably practical and had survived on his own in the Jih Forest, but Lucian had spent much of his life studying in a temple. And although Sunay had come a long way from the mage who wanted to take a coach everywhere, she wasn't at home in a wood like this. Someone out there was hunting them, and the two most capable members of their party were hiding in a tree. The thought agitated her so much that she stood up, suddenly sure that they had made a mistake. Fleet, who had started to nod off, sat up.

'They've been gone too long,' she said. She opened her mouth to say more, and a terrible shriek shattered the quiet, then was just as swiftly silenced. Elver didn't stop to discuss it further; she climbed out of the gap in the trunk and jumped down to the ground, listening. The scream had sounded somewhere between a human cry and the noises foxes made in the night. A noise Sunay might make if she were in trouble.

Fleet brushed past her, his eyes dimmed. There was something new in the way he moved; he was more alert, wilder, and more focused.

The noise came from the south, he said.

'Can you find it?'

Yes.

He streaked away into the gloom, and Elver set off after him at a pace, letting her eyes adjust to the dark. His pawprints still left behind a faint glow, so he wasn't hard to follow, and even through the thick undergrowth Elver moved easily, darting around trees or simply crashing through the smaller shrubs. Despite the foreboding atmosphere of the forest, she almost felt at home: a wild creature, running through the night, human concerns left behind.

We are close, said Fleet. *There's more of the bad scent up ahead.*

'Be careful.'

She glanced over her shoulder once. Her own footprints shone with a pearly white glow, and above them, glimpsed in tiny shards, the night sky was turning from black to purple. Dawn was on its way.

It's here. Fleet skidded to a stop. They were near a small ring of boulders, the space between them the largest piece of flat ground Elver had seen in the forest so far. Fleet pressed his nose to the ground and sniffed. *Something was here.* He trotted from one rock to the next.

'Sunay?' Elver raised her voice. 'Sunay!'

Fleet gave a strangled yelp, and, to Elver's shock, he shot up into the air, suspended in a net of thick black threads.

'Fleet!'

They had run straight into a trap.

Elver jumped up onto the closest boulder and reached for Fleet, but as she did so a rain of short spears crashed down around them. Several clattered against the boulders, but one sliced through her left arm, tearing open the skin and sending a bolt of pain through her entire body. She cried out, stumbling off the boulder, while Fleet thrashed inside the net, getting himself even more tangled.

'Shit.' Ignoring the pain in her arm, Elver scrambled back onto the boulder and reached for the place where the net met the rope. She grabbed it and yanked with all of her strength. It snapped, and she fell back onto the ground, Fleet's not inconsiderable weight on her chest. Suddenly, the whole forest felt hostile. Every shadow could hold an enemy, an army of enemies.

One of the shadows peeled away from the others. It was tall, and carried a crossbow. When she scrambled to her feet, Fleet dropping to the ground, a crossbow bolt thudded into the ground between his paws. And then another, an inch closer.

'Run!'

They pelted into the trees, running in almost a blind panic. Elver knew that she was tough and difficult to kill – that she could heal faster than any human. But she was also fairly certain that a crossbow bolt to the heart or neck would be enough to knock her down permanently, and Fleet was even more vulnerable. Behind them, she heard the sounds of someone else moving through the undergrowth – not as fast as them, but hardly slow, either. Another bolt shuddered into a tree trunk just next to her head.

'Keep moving!'

The problem was the footprints. The hunter could follow them all night and all day easily enough, without even having to track them as a wolf might. Desperately, Elver grasped after her sense of the world around her, and specifically the watery places. Most of them were just too far away, but there was a small river somewhere ahead of them. If they could get into that, perhaps the glowing marks would be washed away as they moved, and they could lose the hunter. She trained her focus on that thin line of cold, and called to Fleet to follow her lead.

Where are we going? We should turn and fight!

Elver thought of the two bolts striking the dirt in front of Fleet. A few inches further, and they would have pinned him to the ground.

'Just watch where I go.'

They ran on, and the hunter followed. Whoever they were, they didn't seem to tire, and they apparently had a large supply of bolts and spears because whenever the pair of them slowed, even a touch, a fresh volley would fire down on them. Fleet was panting freely, and Elver could feel herself tiring too. She longed to turn and fight the hunter, to grab hold of the human's bare skin and kill them. Inside her, the poison heart pulsed. Perhaps it wasn't enough to poison them, the heart seemed to whisper. Perhaps she could pull the human to pieces – there would be no question of whether they deserved it or not, after all – and wasn't she tired of being hunted? A being like her, hunted like a prey animal . . . Elver blinked these instincts away, aware they came from a part of her she barely understood. To stand and face the hunter was too risky. The hunter could shoot them from a distance, and Fleet had none of her healing power. They just had to hope the river was the place they could lose them.

And it was close now, somewhere just ahead. Elver gathered her last pieces of strength, running as fast as she could, already anticipating the cold shock of plunging into the water. She leaned forward, ready to follow the course of the river to the east, when Fleet gave a sharp, warning bark.

Stop! Elver, stop!

She skidded to a halt around half a foot away from the edge of a sudden drop. Beyond it, far below, she could just glimpse a trickle of movement – the river she had been running towards.

'Ah, *shit!*'

The cliff face was steep, and the drop was considerable.

From out of the trees behind them, a shadow moved. They were too far away to make out much about them, but Elver could still see the crossbow. She backed away towards the edge. Inadvertently, she had provided her own trap; they couldn't retreat any further, and the drop framed them against the rest of the forest. They were an easy target.

'Fleet, come here.' She crouched briefly and he leapt into her arms. Then she raised her voice. 'Stay back!'

The hunter didn't reply, although she thought she heard a low chuckle. There was a flash as a piece of metal caught the first of the dawn light, and a crossbow bolt whizzed past her cheek. Distantly, her arm throbbed.

'You'll need to trust me, Fleet.'

What are we going to do?

'Just hold on.'

She squeezed the keltraxia cub tight to her chest, and jumped.

The fall was bad, but the landing was worse. Elver rolled as best as she could, trying to use her body to shield Fleet, and in doing so she felt her head and her back take heavy blows, almost knocking her unconscious. When she finally came to a stop, she could just about hear the murmur of the river under the ringing in her own ears.

Elver? Elver?

Fleet was licking at her face.

Elver, you are bleeding.

She raised her head and touched it gingerly. There was a gash just above her temple, and it hurt to blink. Carefully, she looked back up towards the top of the cliff. There was a figure there, looking down at her. He wore a mask of white clay that covered the top half of his face.

'Trilot . . .?'

The figure gave her a lazy salute, as if promising he would see her soon, and then he vanished back beyond the cliff's edge.

Elver closed her eyes, and let darkness overtake her.

CHAPTER 28

For the third time, Lucian felt his foot slide into an unseen hole in the forest floor, filling his boot with cold muddy water.

'Curse this shithole forest!'

'You know,' said Sunay, from somewhere in the gloom ahead of him, 'if there is a hunter around here somewhere, arrows trained on our sweet little heads, you're practically giving him a cheery wave.'

'You're hardly the stealthy type yourself,' snapped Lucian. He extracted his foot, and then used it to kick earth over one of Elver's glowing footprints. Making sure every last bit of magical light was covered, when some of it was smeared on twigs and stones and leaves, was slow work. More aggravatingly, he felt especially clumsy in this dark, crowded forest. He was constantly catching his hair or his clothes on branches, or blundering into a bush full of prickles. He felt cold, wet, covered in scratches and, worst of all, increasingly tired.

Let me take over.

Artair was close – he had been since they'd realized that something was hunting them. Lucian ignored him.

'How long do we have to do this for?' asked Sunay. Like Lucian, she was struggling to navigate the ancient forest, and some of the usual cheer was missing from her voice.

'Until we're thoroughly sick of it? I don't know.'

If you are tiring, let me take over.

'Shut up.'

'What?' asked Sunay.

'I wasn't talking to you.'

'Oh!' Sunay's tone brightened. 'Hi, Artair! Say hello to him for me, won't you, Lucian?'

'Absolutely not. What is that noise?'

There was a crunching sound in the undergrowth, loud and fast, as though something sizeable were running towards them. Lucian felt his heart sink. If he had to use magic, he'd have to ask Artair to help, and after his revelation about kissing Elver the monk was even brusquer than usual.

But the noise turned out to be the keltraxia cub. The small monster appeared quite suddenly, nearly colliding with Sunay's legs, then began to run round them in circles, making small, gruff yapping noises.

'What are you doing here, idiot? You're supposed to be hiding with Elver.'

Fleet continued his odd display, his green eyes flashing with anxiety.

'He's trying to tell us something,' said Sunay. She crouched to address the creature directly. 'We can't understand you like Elver can, Fleet. You'll have to show us.'

At the mention of Elver's name, the animal grew much more agitated, his gruff yaps becoming full-on barks. He lunged at Lucian's trouser cuff and, taking it in his teeth, began to yank at it.

'Hey, get off me, you mangy creature!'

Something's happened to Elver, said Artair, speaking very clearly in Lucian's head. *Let me through. Now.*

'I think Elver's in trouble,' said Sunay, inadvertently echoing Artair. 'Look at his feathers. There's black blood on them. We should go back.'

Lucian, let me through.

'What can you do that I can't? We might need the magic, and I can control it better.'

I will move through the wood faster than you. Get to her faster, said Artair.

'We have the same body, idiot. As much as I fervently wish we did not.'

You know that it works better for me. That I'm stronger than you.

'Nonsense.' Lucian reached down to bodily shove Fleet off his trousers, and the monster cub deftly avoided him, instead jumping forward to nip at his ankle. It wasn't a hard bite, and it certainly didn't break the skin, but it was enough that Lucian abruptly found the idea of Artair having to navigate the shithole forest much more attractive.

'Ow! Fine, take over, monk. But when you come through, do me a favour and give this little turd a kick.'

It was strange to come back into his body while he was standing, with no sense of coming out of sleep. Artair shook himself once, taking in the dark wood and Sunay's face, grey in the predawn light. He crouched, and gently took hold of Fleet's shoulders.

'Where is she, Fleet?' He could sense Lucian scoffing in the back of his head: how was Fleet supposed to answer? But he realized there was only really one question that mattered anyway. 'Did you come straight from her?'

Fleet hopped around excitedly, then trotted over to the place in the bush from which he had emerged. From here it was possible to see his glowing white tracks, leading away into the wood.

'Alright. Fleet, stay here with Sunay and guard her. Can you do that?' The animal hopped around excitedly again.

'You go,' said Sunay, standing up straight. 'I've no doubt you can move through this murk faster than I can. Fleet and I will follow on at a less breakneck pace.'

Artair nodded once, and then headed off into the dark, his heart full of worry.

The gardens at the monastery had been extensive, and he had spent much of his time running around them – the novices would run races sometimes; sometimes even the brothers and sisters would join in. This wood was much harder to run through, with roots and branches promising at every step a broken ankle or a poked-out eye, yet he found a rhythm quickly, and he let his body concentrate solely on the task ahead of him: follow the tracks, keep moving, find Elver. Underneath this there were other concerns waiting: what had happened to Elver? Had the person hunting them caught her? And deeper, somehow more persistent than even those, had she really kissed *Lucian*?

Eventually, as the sky began to turn the burnished peach of dawn, he came to a steep incline swarming with rocks and scree. Here, Fleet's pawprints took a winding route round the obstacles and sometimes over them, and he found that he had to pick his way down very carefully to avoid losing his footing. Once or twice, the ground under his feet shifted dangerously, sliding him faster than he intended towards the base of the incline. When he eventually made it down onto firmer ground, he found that his body was prickling with sweat, but he barely noticed: Fleet's pawprints led directly to a crumpled shape on the ground, a bright smudge of white hair giving away its identity.

'Elver!'

She was curled on her side, her eyes closed. There was a dark patch of dried blood on her hair and her sleeve was soaked with it, but when he touched her arm her eyelids flickered.

'Where's Fleet?' she asked thickly.

'He's with Sunay. He found us. Can you sit up?'

'Ow. Yes, I think so.' He put his arm round her and helped her to sit forward. There was leaf litter stuck to her cheek, so he gently brushed it off with his fingers. 'My head feels like something took a shit in it. He caught my arm with a spear too. It hasn't quite healed yet.'

'What happened?'

'It was the hunter. He drew us out into the open, and I took the bait, like an idiot. He's a mage of Trilot, Lucian. A monster hunter. And I think he's toying with us. Where is Sunay? Is she safe?'

'I'm Artair,' he said shortly, and she winced. He reminded himself she'd just taken a big knock to the head, and Lucian had been in charge the last time she'd seen him. 'Sunay is at the moment, but we aren't. We have to get under cover somewhere. Can you walk?'

He helped her to her feet, and although she seemed a little wobbly, she managed a few steps . . . And then they both stopped. Her footprints were as bright as ever.

'Ah. I forgot about that,' she said.

'I'll carry you.'

'What?'

'My footprints aren't glowing. If I carry you, it'll be harder for him to track us.' Even as he said the words, Artair felt his face growing hot. When they'd been on top of the tower, he had held her to keep her from falling, and he could remember all too clearly how that had made him feel. 'If we can get under cover somewhere, we can keep a lookout while you heal.'

'Alright.' Elver looked uncertain, and he thought of how it hadn't been that long ago that Elver's only experience of touching another human was to poison them.

Yet when he scooped her up, one arm under her back and the other under the crook of her knees, she settled next to his chest easily enough, and even looped her own arm round his neck. She was light in his arms, and warm. Lucian's presence had ebbed away, and suddenly it seemed it was just them alone in the forest together as the birds and plants began to wake up. He reminded himself firmly that they were in grave danger still, and that Elver herself had been badly hurt. They needed to look for shelter. He did not need to be, for example, wondering what her hair smelled like.

'Fleet will be able to find us,' she said quietly. He could feel her breath tickling his chest as she spoke. 'The Pack taught him a lot.'

'You think it was a Trilot mage?'

'I know it was.' Her voice grew a little sharper, and he was glad. She sounded more like herself. 'He was wearing a mask. And he was smug. They're always bloody smug. Some Trilot mages specialize in eradicating jih spirits. He probably spends his life chasing anything that has escaped the Jih Forest. He'll know exactly how to hunt things like me and Fleet.'

'But not me? Not Lucian?'

She gave him a rueful look.

'Perhaps the Sleepless aren't monstrous enough to be worth his attention. You need to get some scales, yellow eyes, something like that before this flavour of turd will look at you.'

They came to a narrow, fast-flowing river, through which Artair waded, and on the other side was a pile of grey stones that he initially took to be a random collection of boulders until he saw part of an old iron gate, rusted on the ground. It was a ruin, so old that it had mostly been taken over by the living green things of the forest, but it meant there was a place to hide. He took Elver into the portion that still had something like a roof – although it was mainly made of vines and dead leaves now – and set her on the ground. From where they were they had a reasonable view of the little river.

'Does this mean that Trilot is helping Maura?'

Elver laughed bitterly. 'That would make sense, wouldn't it? I'm sure he's happy to have any excuse to hunt down a couple more jih spirits. And maybe he knows we're trying to find his son.' She grimaced. 'I still can't believe the Queen of Serpents never thought to mention that she was married to the god who keeps trying to kill us. Why, by the Twelve, would she ever have been interested in that pompous, hateful turd stain? He doesn't even have a real body. He's a floating mask.'

'Perhaps he looked different once. Like she did.' Artair sat on a low wall, looking out at the brightening day. 'And love is complicated. I mean, I imagine it is, anyway.' He glanced over at her. 'Do you remember all those couples at the Temple of Threshold? There was that boy who had come there with his girlfriend, only he really wanted to be with her sister. When she found out, she was heartbroken.'

Elver snorted. 'She should have been relieved.'

'People fall in love with the wrong person sometimes,' he said, and all at once the question was on his lips. He took a breath, trying to force it back down again, but he realized he had to know. However painful the answer would be, not knowing for sure was worse. 'Did you kiss Lucian?'

Somewhere over their heads, a blackbird began singing into the silence that fell between them. Elver looked thunderstruck, her golden eyes very wide. In his chest, Artair felt a slow trickle of despair. He knew from the expression on her face that it was true. He turned away. At least Lucian felt distant, so he wouldn't have to endure his gloating.

'Don't answer that,' he said quickly. 'I shouldn't have asked. It's none of my business. I mean, you could say it's my business because he's using my body to kiss you. And I don't know that he really cares about you. Not like . . . But it really isn't my business.' He looked down at the ground between his feet. 'Gods damn it. Let's pretend I didn't say anything. Please.'

There was more silence, and then a gentle hand touched his shoulder. He looked up to see Elver standing over him; she had moved silently across the space, her footprints still glowing with faint light.

'Artair, it's true. I did kiss him. I had died, and been brought back, and everything was very confusing . . .' She shook her head. 'But the important bit is I, uh, I thought it was you. I thought I was kissing you.'

'You did?'

Her cheeks were very pink. 'In truth, I only recently realized it *wasn't* you.' She cleared her throat. 'I thought you'd decided you'd made a mistake, and were trying to pretend it hadn't happened. I don't know. It just seemed more likely that you were upset that I had died, and were so relieved to see me back you did something you'd never normally do. Like kiss a monster girl.'

'Elver.' He stood up, and brushed her hair away from her cheek. The rest of the world seemed to have fallen into silence. He felt as though he were standing on the edge of the dream cliff again, about to jump off into the void. He'd either fall, or he would soar. 'I could never, ever regret a thing like that.' He bent his head to hers, hesitated for half a second, and then very gently pressed his lips to hers. Her mouth was soft, and tasted like clear spring water. 'Elver . . . I could do that forever, and never feel bad about it.'

'Forever?' The corner of her mouth quirked into a half-smile. 'You should probably try again, just to be sure.'

He obliged, his heart thundering in his chest, and this time when he went to pull away she looped her arm round his neck again, keeping her mouth in contact with his. Dimly, Artair was aware that they were no longer watching out for danger, that the mage of Trilot could turn up at any time and finish them off. But as she pressed closer to him and his hand found the small of her back, it all felt very far away indeed. Her fingers tugged at the bottom of his shirt, pulling it loose from his trousers, and Artair swallowed hard.

'Are you sure?' He murmured the question into her ear, afraid that speaking too loudly would scare the moment away. He felt her smile into his shoulder in answer.

CHAPTER 29

Kissing Artair was, somehow, very different from kissing Lucian.

There were the same lips, and the same arms, but he moved differently, just as he did in everyday life. The hand that stroked the bare skin of her back was gentle, and his kisses were softer, as though he were afraid of hurting her. When Elver looked into his eyes, there was none of Lucian's fury and uncertainty. Instead, there was a kind of unshakeable tenderness that made her feel light. Artair carried with him a solidity and a stillness that was apparent in the strength in his arms, the long planes of his body, the easy confidence of his size. At some point he had picked her up again, and now they were curled together under a small apple tree that was growing up through the ruins. She knew that there were urgent problems they should be thinking about: when would Sunay and Fleet join them? Had the Trilot mage lost track of them? But her hands almost seemed to move of their own accord, exploring the hair growing across his chest, the broad shape of his shoulders. She was running her fingers over his knee, tracing the muscle that started there, when he suddenly jerked.

For a second, she wondered if she had managed to burn him through his clothes, that somehow Trilot's magic had broken that one small gift, and she drew away.

'Are you alright?'

Artair laughed. 'Yes. Sorry – a beetle just landed on my arm.' He held it up for her to see. It was a bright green beetle with pink stripes on its back, and as they watched it turned in a sharp circle, antennae wiggling, before lifting off from Artair's arm. The creature moved slowly, wings whirring loudly beneath its thick wing casings, and Elver watched it fly to a nearby section of broken wall. There, it joined scores of other identical beetles, who were teeming together across the brickwork.

'Were they there a moment ago?'

Artair looked where she pointed and, as they watched, the beetles began to form patterns together, lining up into rows and curves.

'I don't think they were. What are they doing?'

Gradually, the patterns began to form words. They were shaky and initially difficult to read, as though someone were writing with a pen that was much too big for their hands, but in the end there were only three words to read:

HE IS CLOSE

The pair of them stood up. Beyond the ruin, the river looked undisturbed, and she could see no one lurking there, yet still, something wasn't right. It made her think of the Jih Forest when a human had foolishly decided to travel through it: everything around them was knocked slightly out of its own rhythm, like ripples in a pond. The sun was fully up, yet in this old forest the light took longer to reach the ground, and there were still plenty of shadows.

Elver shrugged her shirt back on and stepped out of the ruin, no longer caring if her footprints glowed.

'Show yourself!' she shouted. 'I know you're there.'

The scene around them did not change, but a voice floated to them over the river.

'My, what a treat it is to hunt you, little jih creature. The things I hunt are never normally so clever. How did you know I was here?'

'The stink,' she said. Artair appeared at her shoulder. 'Are you just going to hide from me, you coward?'

'Oh, you'll see me eventually. Probably your best look at me will come when I'm bending over you to cut your throat. I was the last thing your feathery little friend saw – he made quite a noise when I ran him through. I'm surprised you didn't hear it. But then, uh, it seems you were busy.'

The voice chuckled even as Elver felt her skin turned cold all over. Next to her, Artair had drawn in a sharp breath.

'What are you talking about?' It was hard to keep the panic out of her voice.

'He shouldn't have left the Jih Forest,' continued the voice. 'One day, my lord will get access to that place and we'll cleanse the whole thing. Trilot's purifying light will burn every last scrap of monster from Tlevrae.'

'I'll kill you,' said Elver. 'If you've touched a feather on his head, I'll pull your guts out with my teeth.'

The hunter laughed, and it sounded as though he had moved, although she had heard nothing.

'I'm sure you would, little monster. But I'm afraid that, for you, the chase is over.'

An arrow shot up from the canopy, far to the left of where Elver thought the hunter was. It arched into the sky, shimmering with a pearly light, and Artair took hold of her arm, meaning to pull her back into the relative safety of the ruin. But the arrow disintegrated in the sky in a shower of sparks, and where it had been was a large glowing rune, made of many interlacing lines. Looking at it, Elver felt a sudden terror that she couldn't name, and then it vanished. A second later, she felt a burning sensation across her chest, and when she tugged at her shirt she saw the rune again, in miniature now, and traced across her breastbone.

'What is this? What have you done to me?'

The hunter did not reply.

Elver rubbed a hand across the mark, which was glowing faintly, just like her footprints. Other than a prickling feeling of heat, it didn't appear to be doing anything.

'Come on,' said Artair. 'Let's get under cover, before he—'

But before he could finish the sentence, another arrow pierced the roof of the canopy, glowing with Trilot's light. They ran back to the ruin, getting underneath the makeshift roof of vines and rotted wood, but when they turned back it was to see the first arrow turning in midair as though an unseen hand had twisted it.

'Watch out!'

Faster than Elver could follow, the arrow spiralled down out of the sky as though it were going to hit the ground, and then it turned away, straightening itself so that it was pointed directly at her – at the rune on her chest. She had a bare second to realize what was about to happen, and then it struck her.

The faint burning sensation increased tenfold and she gritted her teeth. The stem of the arrow, which was sticking out of her chest, shimmered and then vanished. Elver dropped to one knee, waves of pain moving through her. The thought that Fleet might be dead was another arrow in her heart.

'I had been told that you would be hard to kill, but I'm not sure I believed it,' called the hunter in a conversational tone. 'Not to worry, I've plenty where that came from. I want you to feel the full wrath of my lord, and then I will have a few questions for you.'

Two more arrows zipped up into the sky, turning as the first one had to find her. Artair stood in front of her, motioning her to stay down.

She yanked on the back of his trouser leg.

'Get out of the way, you idiot,' she hissed. 'If these arrows hit you, they *will* kill you. At least I have a chance.'

'Lucian's with me,' he said, and as he raised his arms she saw a faint aura of red magic around his fists.

When the next arrow flew under the ruins, he struck at it with the flat of his hand and it vanished. The following two arrows went the same way, and she distinctly heard a noise of annoyance from across the river – the mage wasn't sounding so smug now. Elver got to her feet, rubbing the spot on her chest where the arrow had hit her.

'I have to get out there and find him.'

'Wait. He'll run out of arrows eventually.'

Just as Artair said this, a vast glowing cloud of arrows rose up from the canopy opposite the river. There had to be a hundred arrows, all shining like stars, and they all twisted in the air together like a murmuration of starlings. It would be impossible for Artair to stop them all, she realized, and some of them would hit him. He would never survive it.

Without thinking too closely about what she was about to do, Elver shoved Artair to one side, hard enough that he hit the ground, and then she jumped over him and ran out of the ruin. Here, the arrows would have no difficulty finding the rune on her chest.

'Elver, no!'

The arrows swarmed, funnelling down to meet her. She had a second or so to brace herself, planting her feet in the mud, and then they struck, so many at once it became one giant blow. The pain was immense, a scouring of every part of her body that seemed to wipe her mind entirely clean. For one long moment, there was nothing save for pain and light. When that had passed, she distantly heard the hunter laughing, his voice much closer than it had been. There was cold mud underneath her – at some point she had collapsed, she realized.

'Never seen that happen before,' he said. 'A bit overkill, if I do say so myself. Still, my lord was very clear that you would be especially difficult to handle, so I don't mind taking it extra careful.'

Inside Elver, something else was rising up. She still felt blinded with pain, but her poison heart was pulsing with fury, and her black blood was boiling. Almost without realizing, she was back on her feet, balanced on the tips of her toes as though something else were holding her up. Through slitted eyes, she saw the hunter, who had been in the process of wading through the river. He was dressed as any hunter might be – brown and green travelling clothes, mud on his exposed skin, a bow across his back – but his face still wore the simple clay mask. Seeing that she wasn't dead after all, he stumbled.

'What stinking monster magic is this?' he asked sharply.

'This,' Elver murmured, 'is *my* stinking monster magic.'

Her eyes opened fully, and a new power surged through her. She felt bigger, stronger, and when she glanced down she saw a sheen of golden scales on her forearms. The shape of her head felt different, and when she darted towards the hunter he shrieked and fell over in the water. Artair was calling her, but she ignored him.

'What are you?' screamed the hunter.

'*I am your end*,' said Elver, and it didn't sound like her voice. She raised her hand, and the grass on the bank nearest the hunter began to twist and writhe, becoming longer, thicker and stranger, until vines with yellow thorns on them were twisting their way around the hunter's shoulders, trying to hold him in place. He took a knife from his belt and cut at them savagely, freeing himself enough to be able to scramble up the bank. Elver moved forward again, meaning perhaps to change the forest itself into something else, but Artair called her again, and she paused. The hunter made it to the treeline, and she watched him go, still full of that strange, churning power.

She looked down into the waters of the river, and saw the ways in which she had changed reflected there: long golden horns sprouted from the top of her head, similar to the Queen of Serpents', and her hair was now a nest of white snakes, writhing and hissing with outrage. Her eyes were gold from lid to lid, and when she smiled – pleased, somehow, to see this transformation – her teeth were sharp.

'Elver!'

And then she came back to herself. The horns and the snakes and the scales vanished, and she was just Elver, the poison child. She dropped to her knees on the edge of the river, shaking. This was what the queen had done to her.

This was the price of her new heart.

CHAPTER 30

'What . . . what *was* that?'

The alarm in Artair's voice was like a shard of ice in Elver's heart. Dreading what she would see on his face, she stood up and turned to him. He looked paler than he had a moment ago.

'You changed,' he continued. 'I thought all those arrows had killed you, but then you became . . . something else.'

Elver smiled bitterly. 'I am very hard to kill, thanks to my god. And what you just saw was thanks to her too. When the Queen of Serpents sent me back from the shadowed lands, she told me that I would be changed, that I would be more monstrous. I knew that she had given me a new heart.' Her hand floated up to touch her breastbone. The rune had disappeared. 'But I suppose I didn't know the full extent of it. That'll teach you to go kissing strange girls in forests.'

'Elver . . .'

Not so long ago, they had been in each other's arms – she could still feel an echo of the warmth of his body on her skin – but now Artair stood apart from her, and he didn't move towards her. She thought she could see a new wariness on his face, and who could blame him, really? When you kissed a girl for the first time you didn't expect to see her grow snakes out of the top of her head. She ran her hands through her hair, reassuring herself it was back to normal, and looked over to where the hunter had disappeared into the wood.

'Fleet. If that bastard has hurt him . . .' She thought of returning to the Jih Forest without the keltraxia cub, how much she'd miss his wild confidence and puppyish mischief. Fleet had grown so much, changed so much, only to be hunted down by a mage of Trilot when he should have been safe in the Jih Forest, where the Queen of Serpents could protect him. All because he had wanted to follow her. 'If he's hurt Fleet, I'll eat him alive.'

As it happened, they didn't have to wait long to find out what had happened to Fleet. They were gathering themselves as best they could; Artair's movements were slow, and when she gave him a questioning look, he mentioned that using the magic in tandem with Lucian made him feel wrung out. He sat down on the low wall of the ruin, his hair in disarray, and Elver took half a step towards him, uncertain what to do – should she kiss him again? Would he even allow it now that he had seen what she truly was? – when a blue-and-red shape shot out of the thick foliage to their right. Fleet ran up to her and then away again, before coming back. All his feathers were standing on end.

I found you! I tracked you! No one else could do that.

'Fleet!' She reached down to hug him and he shied away, still bristling with energy. A moment later, Sunay climbed down through the thicket. Her long black hair was plastered to her cheeks with sweat.

'There you are,' she said, sounding greatly relieved. 'I swear I've been running after this scamp for days. Or that's what my feet insist, anyway. What happened? Where's this hunter?'

Elver glanced at Artair. He still looked shaken.

'We scared him off. Hopefully it's the last we'll see of him.'

No, Fleet came skittering back towards her. *We have to stop him. He thinks we're prey and that's wrong! The Pack said we are never prey. We are the spirit of the hunt!*

'Goodness, I hope so,' said Sunay, who was picking burs and leaves off her jacket. She was oblivious to Fleet's agitation. 'I'd be very glad to get out of this old forest, which I have to say seems to have more mud and thorns than I think is entirely reasonable. I miss my old conker trees. And the animals in this forest are weird too. I swear we were followed by squirrels much of the way here. Every time I looked up, a bushy little tail was just disappearing out of sight.' She swished her own fox tail. 'And I see enough of those, as you can imagine.'

Elver wasn't really listening. She was looking at Fleet, who was still talking about predators and prey.

We ran, and we shouldn't have run, he was saying. His eyes flashed with light, brighter than Elver had ever seen. *The Pack would laugh at me. No, the Pack doesn't laugh, but the Pack would be disappointed. They would say, oh, so Fleet is still a cub after all, that he must run away like a small thing that squeaks.* He trotted up to Elver and tugged at her trouser leg with his sharp little teeth. *You are no prey creature, Elver of the Jih Forest.*

'No,' she said to him quietly, thinking of the horns that had sprouted from her head, how her teeth had grown sharp. 'I'm not.'

Then we must track him, and kill him. Fleet sat then, tucking his paws neatly in front of him, his eyes trained on her. All at once he reminded her of the wolves in Bawric's cave; there was a focus and an attentiveness there that made him look bigger, older. *This human hunts not for food, or survival, but to satisfy a dark thing in him. To satisfy hate. We can't let him do that, Elver. We shall track him, and I will bite him.*

The power that had bloomed inside her by the river felt very close. Fleet was right, she realized. They weren't prey, and running from the hunter had been a mistake. The hunter couldn't be allowed to do this to any other jih spirit.

'Can you track him, Fleet?'

She felt the other two look at her curiously, but she ignored them.

'I thought you'd said you two scared him off,' said Sunay. 'Surely we can just leave, right? Leave this awful forest and be on our way? Yes? Please? We have to find the First of Monsters before Maura finds us.'

I can track him, said Fleet. *I can smell his blood.*

The keltraxia cub trotted over to the river, sniffing madly.

Yes. The thorns caught his skin, and he has leaked, like a weak prey animal. I can follow this. And when we find him, Elver, we will bite his flesh and his legs and arms and then he'll die. We'll kill him.

'Yes,' said Elver. 'That's what we'll do, Fleet.'

'What are we doing?' asked Artair, that wariness still on his face.

She turned to look at him, being careful to hide the murder in her heart.

'We all know that a mage of Trilot will never stop coming after us,' she said. 'We need to stop him long enough that we can get far away. So we'll find him, tie him up. Leave him in a camp or something. And then we can go.' She glanced at Fleet. 'Then we'll be safe.'

They tracked the hunter rapidly, Fleet running ahead with his snout a few inches off the forest floor. Sunay and Artair followed on behind as best they could. Elver could sense their reluctance, but she pushed their concerns to one side. In some ways, this was familiar to her. She was the guardian of the Jih Forest, and it was her job to keep the monsters safe.

Fleet's right, she thought. *I'm the predator here. Time to hunt the hunter.*

The morning became the afternoon, and the sky clouded over, sending the ancient forest into an even darker murk. At around this time, they briefly lost the trail. Elver thought it likely that the hunter had paused to bind up his wound at this point; even if he thought himself safe from them, there was always the risk that a bear or a wolf could decide they liked the taste of it. Fleet stomped around, pushing his nose into the leaf litter and huffing, and she began to wonder if they'd have to give up the hunt after all, when Sunay gave a little shriek.

'I told you this forest was weird.' She was running her hands rapidly over her clothes, as though trying to brush something off. 'I just looked down and there were four or five beetles in a circle on my jacket. Can you believe it?'

Artair pointed at a nearby tree trunk. 'It's the same ones from before,' he said. 'Why are they helping us?'

'I don't know,' said Elver. 'But I'll take it.'

The green beetles had formed a simple arrow on the tree. When they followed it, they came to a creek so small it had been easily hidden from them by a cloud of blackberry bushes. On the other side of this, Fleet found the man's scent, and they were off again, racing against the setting sun.

When they eventually found him, the Trilot mage was clearly setting up some kind of new trap. In the centre of a small clearing, he had placed a large, white crystal, and round it, their points pushed into the dirt, were ten arrows. They looked like normal arrows to Elver, their only unusual feature was a lack of fletching feathers – instead they had strips of white silk tied round each end. Fleet flattened himself to the ground, and Elver copied him, watching the movements of the man in the mask. Sunay and Artair had hung back, although she could still sense them trying not to make any noise.

The prey animal is building a nest, Fleet said with slightly too much confidence. *They do this. They hide in nests.*

'So does your mum,' Elver murmured. Despite herself, she enjoyed the way Fleet's ears twitched with annoyance. 'You were hatched in one.'

Be quiet, I am watching, he replied. *When you are hunting, you have to watch a lot. You're distracting me.*

The Trilot mage approached the crystal. He was murmuring something to himself, and then he leaned down and touched his hand to the crystal, which had started to glow. The horrible white light filled the small clearing, and Elver felt her blood teem in response to it. Trilot, or an aspect of him, was close. One by one, the arrows began to fill with the light too, and she realized what they were seeing: the hunter was crafting his magical arrows, the ones that could be commanded to fly at any creature marked with the magical rune. They were meant for her, those arrows, and Fleet, and any other jih creature this mage of Trilot happened to come across. He might not be wearing the full silver mask of Faceless Isnere or the white robes of Kantor Witt, but this hunter was just as dangerous to her kind – and her kind included Artair and Lucian too. Perhaps if he saw Sunay with her fox tail, he would shoot her as well. She suspected he wasn't picky. There was only one thing she could do, really.

In the clearing, the light from the crystal faded, leaving the arrows standing like eerie shards of light in the ground. The hunter began to gather them up, putting them in the quiver slung across his back.

'You've done well, Fleet.' She placed her hand on the cub's head. 'The Pack would be proud. Now, I want you to stay here and let me do the rest.'

She expected him to protest, but instead he raised his feathery eyebrows.

Rend him with your teeth!

Elver stepped out of cover. The hunter was instantly aware of her presence, and he quickly notched one of his glowing arrows to his bow, aiming it at her heart. This close, he didn't need a rune to aim true.

'Stay back, beast,' he said. He had lost some of his easy confidence. 'This arrow might not kill you, but it'll stun you long enough to get my knife to your throat.'

'Try it,' said Elver, and she changed.

Golden horns like a crown reached up to the sky. A garland of ivory snakes framed her cheeks. She saw terror flicker across the hunter's face, and she grinned her sharp grin at him.

'You're not just a monster – you're an abomination.' He fired the arrow and she caught it, holding it in her fist while it burned against her golden scales. When he loosed the second one, she let it hit her, then watched his face as it dissolved into nothing.

'I'm too strong for your little tricks, magpie,' she said pleasantly. 'You won't be hunting any more jih spirits. Not in this forest. Not in any forest.'

His resolve broke then, and he turned to run. Elver reached out for the wood itself, encouraging the foliage to grow and change and *grasp*. A wall of green surged into life, cutting off the hunter's escape, and when he tried to run round it more vines and brambles whipped out like snakes, curling round his ankles and legs, holding him in place. The hunter pulled the knife from his belt and began hacking away at the strands, but every one he cut was immediately replaced with another. He grunted with effort, and then glanced at the inert crystal in the middle of the clearing. Elver kicked it over as she passed it. She felt powerful. She felt *wonderful*.

'Don't worry. I'll be sure to bury that where no one else can find it.' She smiled. 'I'm sure Trilot will love that, one of his crystals lying in the mud and the muck.'

When she reached him, she gestured again, and the newly created vines whipped round his arms and hands.

'Get away from me,' he said, anger mixing with the fear. 'Don't touch me!'

'Is that the worst thing you can imagine, little man?' She pressed one clawed fingertip to his exposed chin. 'Because I've got bad news for you. This is where you die, mage of Trilot.'

'Elver, don't. Please.'

Artair appeared at her side. She found she was surprised to see him. She'd almost forgotten he and Sunay were there. And, even more surprising, he was looking at her directly, as though the horns and the snakes weren't his biggest concern. He put his hand on her shoulder.

'There's no need to kill him. Lucian and I can send him through a portal. I'm not sure where he'll go, but he won't be here, and that's enough.'

'He was going to kill *you*. He was going to kill all of us.'

Artair shrugged. 'That hardly makes him unique. You don't have to be as bad as him, Elver. It's not who you are.'

She paused, thinking. Behind her, she could hear Sunay picking her way through the bushes towards them, and in front of her the hunter was sweating freely. His mask was slightly askew.

'Maybe you're right,' she said eventually. 'That's not who I am. *This* is who I am.'

It was harder than the others, but not by much. Perhaps this man's monstrous nature was simply closer to the surface. When she caressed his cheek, he screamed, and his skin turned green. From his neck, webbed ridges erupted, standing up like the frills of a strange lizard. His eyes changed too, his pupils becoming slitted like a cat's, and when the vines dropped away and he scrambled to his feet, she saw that there were webs between all his fingers. *That'll make it much harder to use a bow*, she thought.

'What have you done to me?' The hunter's voice was different too – garbled somehow, as though he were talking from under the water. 'What have you done?'

'I thought you should know what it's like to be hated by Trilot,' she said mildly. The horns were receding now. The snakes had turned back into hair. 'I want you to know what it's like to be hunted for being different. That's all.'

When she did nothing further, the hunter monster got up and ran, disappearing quickly into the darker shadows of the forest. She turned back to Artair and she saw that he was looking at her with horror.

'I didn't kill him,' she said simply. 'And he won't be bothering us again.'

'Elver . . .' He looked full of sorrow, which only made her angrier. 'What you just did was possibly even worse than killing him. What will he do now? If he has a family, he can't go home to them. Does he just live out here, in the forest, forever?'

'Is that the worst thing you can think of, Artair? Being a monster in a forest?' He winced, and she laughed bitterly. 'I see how it is. That man tried to kill me, as I'm sure he has ended the lives of countless jih spirits – all kin of mine – and the worst punishment you can think of is to make him *exactly like me*? Am I so horrifying to you?'

'No,' he said firmly. 'Never. You could never be horrifying to me, Elver. I care more about you than . . . I can't even tell you . . .' He shook his head, frustrated with his own words. 'But this feels wrong. Can't you feel how wrong it is?'

'Oh, just the opposite. It feels *right*.' And this was true, she realized; it felt like the most natural thing in the world, to reach out and change what was in front of her. When she had turned the hunter into a monster, the impulse had come from deep within her chest – from within her poison heart. Changing the duck had felt like an instinct she couldn't disobey, and it had frightened her. This, though: she had seen what was terrible beneath the man's skin and simply brought it forward. 'When she changed me, the Queen of

Serpents told me that humans would not accept me. I never thought that would mean you, Artair.'

'No, you don't understand—'

At that moment, Sunay crashed out of the undergrowth. When she saw the two of them glaring at each other, she stopped, her hair hanging in her face.

'What's going on? You two look like you're about to go for each other, and not in the good way.'

'Nothing is going on. It's nothing.' Elver turned away from them both. It seemed impossible that a short time ago she had been in Artair's arms; in those moments, she had felt cherished, and safe, and like anything was possible. Now, despite the possibilities of her new powers, it felt as though her life had become one narrow line again: a monster girl, alone. 'The hunter is dealt with – that's what we should focus on.' She brushed herself down, resisting the urge to look at Artair. 'This forest is safer than it was. Let's go before Trilot finds another masked turd to send our way.'

CHAPTER 31

'It's funny, Lucian. When you told me you and Elver kissed, you failed to mention it was because she thought she was kissing me.'

The dreamworld in which they found themselves this time had changed. They were still sitting on a cliff's edge, but the world beneath them was stranger. Undulating waves of grey-blue sand stretched out of sight, marked here and there by what looked like the wrecks of ships. Lucian had been studying them, trying to decide if he had seen anything like them before, but Artair's words made him scowl. The monk sat down next to him, his legs hanging over the edge.

'I suppose I didn't think it was important,' he replied, attempting to sound casual. 'It was me that kissed her, and I'm fairly certain she enjoyed it.'

'Well, I suppose now she has something to compare it to.'

Lucian looked up at Artair sharply, and was annoyed to see that the monk's cheeks were pink. Yet, even so, he did not look happy.

'Did she kiss you to cheer you up?' Despite himself, Lucian was curious. He would have expected Artair to be incredibly smug, or rubbing it in his face, but instead the monk was looking off into the distance, a troubled expression on his bland, handsome face. 'If you've finally had this moment of passion with the monster girl, why do you look like you've been ordered back to your monastery for a hundred years?'

Artair shook his head. 'I don't understand what's going on with Elver. She's changed.' He turned to meet Lucian's eyes. 'I mean, she actually changed. Into something else. And then she turned the hunter into a monster.'

Lucian laughed. 'That really happened? I thought I'd been blessed with an especially odd dream while I was waiting for my turn. How interesting.' He had seen Elver in glimpses, great golden horns growing from her head, hissing serpents where her hair should be. She had looked powerful; she had looked like a thing made of magic. 'This is down to the Queen of Serpents, no doubt. And this is exactly why you'll never understand her like I do, monk. She is god-touched, and so am I.'

'I don't care about the snakes, or the horns, or the scales,' said Artair quietly. 'I mean, it was a bit of a surprise, but then she's always been surprising. And her anger has always been a part of her too. I just don't know how I feel about her using monstrousness as a punishment.'

Somewhere below them, a cloud of white birds flew out of one of the ruined ships where they'd been roosting. Lucian could feel wakefulness tugging at him, and his sense of the dreamworld disintegrating.

'You've never known how to use what you have,' Lucian said to Artair before he woke up. 'If you can't handle how she uses her power, step aside for someone who can.'

When Lucian woke up, he found that they had camped for the night. There was a small, smoky fire that smelled powerfully of pine needles, and Fleet was stretched on the other side of it, snoring faintly. Sunay had her pack open and was pawing through it.

'We're pretty much out of everything, I'm afraid,' she said. 'Even the tea. The boys have steamed through my supply of kopi, the scamps. Elver, I'm really not sure what we're going to eat for breakfast. Or supper, come to that.'

'This forest is strange, and getting stranger,' said Elver. She looked almost as she always did – her hair wasn't hissing or biting. Yet there was a new sadness in the cast of her face that made Lucian wonder what the monk had said to her, exactly. 'In the Jih Forest there's always something to eat – berries, nuts, these hard little tubers you can dig out of the ground—'

'Sounds delightful,' put in Sunay.

'But here . . . There's so much vegetation around us, and hardly any of it edible. The whole place has a . . . a deadness to it.'

Lucian cleared his throat, and they both looked at him.

'You missed some excitement, Lucian,' said Sunay. 'Unless you didn't? I am never sure how *present* you are these days.'

'I saw some of it,' he said, looking at Elver. She stared down at her feet. 'I'm glad you got rid of the hunter,' he said pointedly. 'A mage of Trilot is no laughing matter, and I'm sure we'll have to endure more from that tedious god of piousness before this is all over. How close are we to the First of Monsters?'

'We're close,' said Elver. 'Another day or so, maybe.'

'Good.' Lucian got up and stretched his legs. Any day he woke up without ropes round his wrists and ankles was a good day. 'When I have everything I need, we won't have any more trouble from *lesser* gods.'

When Sunay went to sleep, Elver seemed to relax a little, although she was still quieter than normal. It made for an eerie night, as the forest itself seemed caught in its own silence; no owls called, and the wind had dropped to nothing.

'I thought it was magnificent, for what it's worth.'

She looked at Lucian warily. 'What are you talking about?'

'This new form you have.' He spread his fingers and held his hands above his head, imitating the horns and snakes. 'Of course, any mage of a lesser god would piss himself at the sight of it, but I know power when I see it. I can also tell that you're worried about it, and I'm guessing the reaction of a certain monk has displeased you.'

Elver snorted. 'Artair thinks it was wrong to make the hunter into a monster. He would have preferred we send him somewhere else, with your magic. But he doesn't understand. People like the hunter will always hate us. We're nothing to them.'

'Naturally, Artair doesn't understand.' Lucian went and sat next to her, stretching his legs out towards the fire. 'He isn't god-touched like you and me. This is something your god has given you, right? Why shouldn't you use it?'

'The Queen of Serpents gave me a new heart.' Her fingers rubbed at a spot on her chest. 'And she did tell me I would change. I just didn't know how much.'

'Can you summon this new form whenever you like?' he asked.

'I'm not sure. It feels closer when I'm angry. When I'm angry, it's almost hard *not* to change.'

'This is a great gift, monster girl. Do you know why she gave it to you?'

'To stop me from dying. Or, well, stop me from staying dead, I suppose. She sent me back, but she had to remake me again.' Elver stretched her legs out too, and her boot knocked into his lightly.

'Yes, but what is the real reason? The actions of gods always carry another meaning – they never give you anything for nothing, and they all carry knives up their sleeves.' Lucian retrieved the leather tie from his pocket and pulled his hair back into its braid; it was getting longer all the time and he hated it hanging in his face. 'The Queen of Serpents hasn't brought you back to life twice out of the goodness of her heart, Elver.'

'She told me that my life was hers to weave,' she said quietly. The light from the fire danced in her eyes, turning them into a molten gold. 'That she had a purpose for me, and that eventually I'd know what it was.'

'Well, I am only sorry I wasn't here to see you in the flesh,' he said. He turned to her slightly, so that he could see her face. The wariness there had gone, to be replaced with a speculative look that he much preferred. 'You are fierce, and powerful, and extraordinary, Elver,' he said. 'Do not waste your time on anyone who thinks otherwise.'

That surprised a laugh out of her. 'You are full of shit, Lucian.'

He laughed with her. 'I mean it, though. I know I've given you no reason to believe what I say, but in this you can trust me.'

Their eyes met, and the moment shivered between them, as fragile as glass. Lucian reached out and took her hand, and leaned a little closer. This would be it, he decided. His own kiss, one that was unambiguously the two of them – he and Elver. He saw her glance at his lips, and knew that she was thinking the same thing too.

'Elver . . .'

Sunay snorted and turned over, shaking one arm briskly in the air.

'There's a beetle on my arm! Can you see it? It's huge!' When she'd dislodged the creature, she sat up, her hair in disarray. Elver leaned back a little, and let go of Lucian's hand. 'These things are everywhere, I swear. Ugh, my skin is crawling all over, I may never sleep again.'

'Join the club,' said Lucian, a touch sourly.

In the morning, when the orange light of dawn had just brushed the tops of the trees, a giant walked into their camp.

The others were asleep – even Fleet was still snoring – but Lucian had been trying to brew a tea out of pine needles. When the man initially appeared, he thought he must have been dreaming again, but a second later he leapt to his feet. Elver and Sunay woke with a start, and Fleet began barking.

'Peace, peace.' The enormous man held up his hands to show there was nothing in them. He had to be at least seven feet tall, and he had the same heavy solidity as the ancient trees that stood around them. His beard was black, and knotted into a variety of plaits; it reached down to the centre of his considerable chest. He wore a hooded cloak of dark green, which had a finely stitched border around the hem, and he carried a staff of oak that was as tall as he was.

'Who are you?' Lucian reached for the magic, and felt Artair suddenly close, ready to help him. 'Were you following us?'

'Peace,' the giant man said again. 'I am a mage of Milik the Small.'

Sunay looked him up and down. 'Are you quite sure?'

The man chuckled, and gave a brief, sharp whistle. Apparently in response to this signal, the foliage surrounding their camp began to rustle.

'My name is Gus,' he said, 'and my lady has asked me to help you. She tells me she swore to give you assistance.'

From the bushes, all manner of creature began to emerge. Lucian saw mice, squirrels, beetles, rabbits, pine martens, wrens – even slowworms, their bronze scales the colour of coins in the early-morning light.

'Another magpie,' said Elver. 'I think we've had enough of mages for the time being. Uh, no offence, Sunay. We should keep moving by ourselves for a while.'

'Ah, let's not be hasty.' Sunay bent to look at one of the beetles crawling over her boot. 'Am I right in thinking you've been helping us for a while now, Gus?'

Incredibly, the huge man blushed – or, at least, the parts of his face that Lucian could see beyond the beard turned faintly pink.

'When my lady allows it, I can see through the eyes of all the tiny living things,' he said. Gus had a quiet way of speaking, as though afraid to make too much noise. 'They have showed me things, so I showed you things. When it was needed.'

'You warned us about the hunter,' said Elver. 'With the beetles.'

Gus nodded shyly.

'Then you have our thanks, Gus, mage of Milik the Small,' said Sunay, sketching him a brief bow. 'We'd invite you for breakfast, but I'm afraid we're out of anything interesting to eat or drink.'

'Ah, that's why I came to see you,' said Gus. He shuffled where he stood, one hand worrying at the stitching on the edge of his cloak. 'Normally, I wouldn't. People . . . make me nervous. But I thought you'd probably want this bit explained. Or you might not eat it.'

He whistled again, and more animals emerged from the bushes around them. This time, they were all carrying pieces of food; there were nuts and blackberries and fat grey mushrooms. A few of them had little blue eggs, which were laid carefully at Sunay's feet. Very quickly, the makeshift camp was full of scraps of food. Elver began building up the fire, so that they could cook the mushrooms and eggs.

'While you're here, my friends will forage for you.' Despite Sunay's many invitations, Gus would not sit with them. Instead, he stood off to one side awkwardly, his breath misting in the cold air. 'It is a way that my lady can help.'

'Do you live out here all alone, Gus?' asked Sunay. The small animals had vanished back into the forest.

'It's how I prefer it,' he replied. 'There's enough space for me here. Around other people, I get in the way.'

'But it's so quiet here!' exclaimed Sunay. 'Don't you get lonely?'

'I have all the company I could ask for,' he said, smiling a little. 'But this is a quiet forest, it is true. The animals are wary of it. They have only come this far east because I have asked them to. They believe that it is haunted, this place.'

'Why?' asked Elver. 'Why would they think that?'

Gus bowed his head. 'Because of what you seek, my lady. The forest is dark, because it hides a darkness at the heart of it. There is a place, further east from here, where none of my lady's creatures will tread, and even she cannot convince them. Darkness makes its home there.'

When they had eaten, Gus bade them goodbye, although Lucian suspected that the mage was still watching them via the many tiny eyes of the forest animals. Together, they set off again through the trees, and the land around them grew steeper, and wilder. Sometimes they would see large birds flying overhead, and these would call to each other, harsh mournful cries that made Lucian uneasy, but otherwise they heard very little. Even Elver seemed to retreat into a silence, and when he asked her if she was quite well she gave him a slightly pained look.

'He's close,' she said. 'The First of Monsters. And Gus was right. It makes everything . . . darker.'

As the sun set on that brief, wintery day, they breached the top of the hill, and an even greater section of forest spread out below them. They were so high up that there were little wisps of misty cloud below them, and Lucian had to suppress a superstitious shiver. It reminded him of the dream place he had shared with Artair. In the middle of the dark trees below, there was a vast lake, covered in black ice. Elver pointed at it, but Lucian knew the significance of it before she spoke.

This was where they would find the First of Monsters.

CHAPTER 32

Trilot's realm was a cold, desolate place. Maura found herself thinking of the shifting white space that lay beyond the fences in her own realm, but somehow this was worse. There was a landscape of blue-grey sand, stretching as far as she could see in all directions, without a single tree or plant or building to break it up, and above them there was only a blank, white space, as plain and unadorned as a sheet of paper. To look at either one for too long was to invite a strange sensation of vertigo, as though her feet might lose touch with the gritty sand and she could just float up into that terrible nothingness, never to find her way back.

The god himself wasn't any more reassuring. In his own realm, he was even more abstract, and she had the sense that the vaguely human shape he had worn in Lady Dusk's forest was something he had constructed out of chilly courtesy for those who had to converse with him. Here, he was a confusing vortex of white light and strips of white silk, a simple mask hanging at the centre of it all. Sometimes, he would form a hand or a foot out of the silk, in some kind of reflexive action.

'How long will we have to wait?' she asked.

The strips of white material made a glove, which drew one finger across the sand. The grains it disturbed clumped together in familiar shapes: trees, hills, tiny human figures. They were moving.

It is difficult to see, said Trilot. **I suspect this is because the place where Brishta hid Tython is shielded from me. She will have woven many magics to hide the abomination from the only**

being that can save him.

'Brishta is who the Queen of Serpents used to be,' said Maura.

Yes. Once, she was the god of all bright things, of dawn and of balance. No living thing, god or mortal, could match her beauty, and I loved her above everything.

Maura looked at the silver mask. The voice was as expressionless as the mask, and it was hard to imagine such a thing ever loving anyone.

I imagine, Mother, that you know what it is like to love a being so completely.

'I do.' Maura thought of the bone fragments hidden in the secret chamber at Prideful Leap.

But Tython became ill. When Brishta changed him, she changed his nature so drastically he became anathema to gods. A curse on them. He has the power to kill us, Mother. That is why they seek him.

In front of Maura's boots, the grains of sand were still moving, although they were difficult to follow. She had the sense that some of them were running, or hiding. Tiny points of light moved back and forth.

'What are you going to do with your child when you find him again? Can he be changed back?'

For a long moment, Trilot did not answer. The silk ribbons curled and moved as though they were being blown back and forth by a wind Maura could not feel, and the white light at the centre of the god flickered.

No, he said eventually. **I am not the god of change, and she who is would never do it.**

'Because Tython would just die?'

Yes. But I can cleanse the monstrousness from him and give him peace.

Kill him, in other words, thought Maura. She expected to feel something then, a pang of guilt, perhaps – they were talking about the death of a child, after all. But she found she was as empty as Trilot's realm. Who cared if the ancient child of a pair of gods was wiped from the face of Tlevrae? She only cared about her own children, and to get them back she needed the last of the Bloody Claw's power, and to get that she needed to kill Lucian.

'What is happening down there?' she asked sharply, annoyed that she had been distracted. 'Has your mage caught them yet?'

The glove re-formed and drew another line in the sand. More tiny figures came to life, and Trilot's mask tilted, peering at them more closely. One of the clumps of sand began to convulse, moving rapidly through a variety of shapes. Trilot jerked back as though something had burned him.

The poison child dares?

'What is it? What has Elver done?'

Trilot rose up in a swirl of silk and light. At the centre of the maelstrom, the silver mask had not changed, yet the blank eye holes radiated fury.

She has tainted my mage, turned him monstrous just as Brishta did our son.

'She can do that?' Maura shook her head. 'It doesn't matter. Have your mage kill her and let's get on with it.'

But Trilot was still rising. He barely seemed to be listening to her.

The mage has been cast out of my light, he said. **He begs for my mercy, and wishes only to die. He tells me that he knows now where they are heading. I will go to him, receive my son's location and put an end to the wretched creature.**

'What are you doing? You said you would help me!'

The mask twitched towards her. **I know where Tython has been hiding all these centuries. Your problems are no concern of mine,**

Mother. The jih spirits will be cleansed in time, but there is one who has waited aeons for the purity of my light.

With that, Trilot vanished.

Maura stood, breathing hard, the nothingness of another god's realm stretching out around her.

'That useless, pompous, thick-headed son of a turd . . .'

'Yes, he was never my favourite either. Terrible dress sense too.'

Maura whirled to face the voice and was met with a fox standing just behind her, the blue sand making his orange fur stand out like a flame. Tisk shook himself, turning his tail bushy.

'Ugh. Always hated this place too,' he said. 'Trilot truly has no imagination.'

'What are you doing here? What do you want?'

'I knew them, of course, when they were both young. And, honestly, he used to be a lot more interesting. Still not what you would call a charmer, but he loved his wife and child. It's shocking, isn't it, what tragedy can do to you. If you're not careful, it can turn you into something bitter and broken.'

Maura ignored this pointed comment. 'I see more of you now than when I was your bloody mage. Get out of my sight, Tisk.'

Tisk the Trickster shrugged, and abruptly he was wearing his human shape. He twirled his silver fox-headed cane.

'I'm just here to remind you, Mother, that there is a way out of this. Take back your humanity, give up the power you stole from the Bloody Claw and walk away from all this.' He gestured at the vast desert. 'Are you having a good time? Because it doesn't look like it.'

'Why do you care?'

Tisk nodded slowly. 'That is a great question. I wish I knew. But it seems to me that you were always a loose end, Maura, and I suppose I have an urge to tidy you away.'

'Enough.' She flapped a hand at him dismissively. 'What is the point of any of you? The Bloody Claw couldn't help me, Enos was worse than useless and Trilot is a fool.' She pushed her hands into her hair, grasping hold of it and tugging lightly. 'I should have killed you all.'

'You'll never be a god, Maura,' Tisk said quietly. 'Instead, you will exist in this halfway state, bleeding away your power until you cease to exist. Half human, half god and entirely nothing.'

She turned back to him and grinned. He flinched away from it, and that only made her grin all the wider.

'All the nonsense that comes out of your mouth, and you finally say something useful. You're right. I am not quite a god yet, and maybe that means I don't have to obey the rules that govern gods. I have been trying to do things your way, and when has that ever worked for me?' She laughed.

'Mother, what are you talking about?' Tisk looked worried, which made her so happy she laughed again.

'Oh, you'll see,' she said. 'You'll see.'

CHAPTER 33

They made their way down the hill in the last scraps of light and made a new camp at the base of it. Darkness fell thickly, and the fire that Elver built felt too small somehow, as though the flames were struggling against the cold. She kept adding twigs to it, old leaves, poking the embers to stir it to life, but the light it gave off was meagre and the warmth almost non-existent. Fleet seemed particularly unsettled by it and sat with his back to the fire, looking out into the dark. His ears were pricked, all his feathers bristling.

'What is it?' she asked him, as the others were bedding down for the night.

There are things out there, in the dark, he said, with none of his usual bravado. *Their eyes are big. They are watching us.*

'What do you mean? Are we in danger?'

Fleet didn't answer immediately. When he did, he seemed distracted.

I don't like to be watched by things I can't see. I am the hunter. I should be the one watching.

'Try to get some sleep,' she told him. 'We'll be on the move again soon.'

When Elver woke up, she was surprised to find that it was still dark. Their little fire had dwindled down to embers, casting a faint ruddy light over their camp, and when she sat up her body felt stiff, as though she had been lying down for hours. Yet judging from the darkness around her, they were still some distance from the dawn.

'Elver?' It was Artair. She glanced at Sunay and Fleet, who were both still asleep. 'Something is wrong here.'

'What do you mean?' Her words came out stiffly, with a chill she didn't quite intend. The argument over the hunter still felt like a fresh wound.

'I've been awake for hours, and it's still dark. It's hard to keep track of time in the middle of this forest, but I feel like it should have been dawn at least two hours ago.'

She stood up and stretched. 'The nights are longer in winter, Artair. You're confused.'

'Doesn't it feel like it should be dawn to you?'

The sky above them was black, no sign of stars or the moon. Which simply meant it was cloudy, she told herself. She remembered Fleet's concern that something was watching them from the dark, then shook it off. The cub had been rattled by the hunter – that was all.

'I'm going back to sleep,' she said, ignoring his question. But when she settled back down on the hard earth, sleep wouldn't come.

Artair got up and began moving around, and eventually she heard Sunay wake up too. The mage rolled over and began poking at the fire with a stick.

'Artair, I know it's the middle of the night, but I am absolutely famished. What do you say to an early breakfast? If I can get this dubious campfire to cook anything, of course.'

Predictably, Fleet woke up at the word 'breakfast', but rather than dashing around he made a high-pitched whining noise.

'I don't think it is the middle of the night,' said Artair.

Elver sighed and sat up.

'Fine. If we're all awake, we may as well get moving. Let's eat and go.'

Sunay cooked some more of the food that Gus had foraged

for them, and then they packed away their bedrolls. Elver made a torch from wood and a scrap of Artair's old robes and lit it from the campfire before kicking earth over it, and all during this time the light around them did not change. The torch, like the campfire, was weak, barely painting a glow across Elver's face, and beyond that the forest was still in absolute darkness. Fleet pressed himself to her leg.

'I don't like this,' said Sunay. 'We're liable to snap an ankle in a hole we can't see. Perhaps we should wait a little longer for the sun to come up.'

Elver felt a surge of irritation. She could see perfectly fine; they were the ones who had decided to wake up and be noisy. Memories of the Jih Forest returned. There, she could go days without talking to anyone. Her new monstrous form would be welcomed, and she could do as she wished. The great serpent lake was waiting for her there, cold and dark and silent. Humans were so . . . small.

'It won't be much longer,' she said shortly. 'We'll go slowly, and the sun has to be rising soon.' When the other two looked at her sceptically, she scowled at them. 'We just narrowly avoided being murdered by a hunter full of Trilot's magic, right on the heels of a toddler mage trying to trap us in dreams. All of which is Maura's doing, right? Do we really want to hang around to let her have another chance? Or do we want to get to the First of Monsters and end this thing?'

Artair simply watched her in that careful way he had, as though she were some sort of priceless object about to fall off a shelf, but Sunay nodded once.

'You're right,' she said. 'The longer we take, the more danger we're in.'

Elver held up the torch. 'Good. Follow me.'

★

The darkness persisted, and Artair found he wasn't surprised.

He had known as soon as he'd opened his eyes onto the dark that there was something wrong with it and, sitting there waiting for the others to wake up, he'd only grown more certain. Now, walking through the forest, it even seemed, somehow, to be getting darker. Just ahead he could make out the lithe form of Elver, the torch giving her more shape and definition than anything else in the wood. To one side, he could sense more than see Sunay; certainly he could hear her, crunching through leaves and bracken and keeping up an almost constant stream of quiet swear words as she did so. He couldn't see Fleet at all – he assumed that he was ahead, with Elver.

There was a splash, and Sunay's swearing suddenly increased in volume.

'Curse the Twelve to the stars and back, there's a bloody hole here full of freezing water. My boot is full of it and it's splashed all up my leg . . .' She sounded annoyed, but underneath it she sounded frightened too. 'I can't see my own hand in front of my face. Can you . . . Elver, can you stop for a moment? Can you bring the light over here?' Sunay laughed, a slightly shrill sound in the silence of the forest. 'I just want to check I have hands.'

Elver turned towards them. To Artair, it was as though she were the only real thing in the world, a sketch of her face hanging in the dark, made of faint smudges of orange light.

'The sun should have been up by now,' said Artair. 'Elver, this is bad. Where has the morning gone? We're essentially blind here.'

'I can see,' she said, although she sounded less sure about that than she had before.

'There's magic behind this,' said Sunay. 'I'll bet my sodden boots on it.'

He half expected Elver to disagree – she had been disagreeable since she had woken up, and distant from him since the incident with the hunter – but instead she nodded.

'I think it's him. The First of Monsters. Or . . . No, that's not quite right. I think it's the Queen of Serpents. This is all to hide her son. Somehow, she's caught this place in an eternal night.'

'It's more than that,' said Artair. 'Even in the darkest nights in the Jih Forest, was it ever this dark, Elver? This is like . . . swimming through ink.'

'What if it never gets light again?' asked Sunay. There was an edge of panic in her voice.

'I can still see,' said Elver. 'But it is getting harder. And there's a pressure here too, a heaviness.' Artair saw the torch flicker as she shook her head slightly. 'It's like being underwater, almost. But we can't turn back. The only way out is ahead. We're so close now. I can feel him, just ahead.'

The torchlight flickered again, guttering as though it were about to go out. Sunay gasped.

'We should tie ourselves together,' said Artair. 'If we're going forward, we have to be careful not to lose anyone.' He reached out blindly to one side and found Sunay's shoulder. He squeezed it. 'There are some strips left from my old robes. We can tie them to each other's belts.'

Elver held the torch as close as she dared while Artair tore the last of the yellow fabric into long pieces and then set about tying them to each of their belts. Even as they did that, the darkness grew thicker, almost suffocating, and the thin torchlight grew dimmer. Artair just caught a glimpse of the worried expression on Elver's face in the last of the light.

They'd been walking for another hour when they saw the first of the creatures. There was a jerk on the piece of fabric tethering Artair to Sunay, and when he turned in her direction he saw it too.

'What is that?' asked Sunay. 'Please tell me you see it too? If I've started hallucinating monsters, I think I am done.'

'No, I see it,' he said quietly. Somewhere around their feet, Fleet gave a single low bark. 'What is it, Elver?'

It looked like a salamander, or a lizard with a soft, wide head. It was about the size of a cat and it was perched halfway up a tree. Huge black eyes, full of shifting purple reflections, watched them carefully; the rest of it was white, and glowing faintly. After so long in the deep black, looking at it hurt Artair's eyes.

'Jih of some kind,' Elver replied, her voice floating to them out of the dark. 'I've never seen it before. But—'

'Leave this place. Only death here for you. Leave this place.'

When the creature spoke, little flickers of greenish flames played around its mouth. Fleet immediately began barking, loud, angry yips of protest.

'Well, that's not very friendly, is it,' said Sunay, her voice tight. 'I swear this place gets better and better by the moment.'

'It's just one of the queen's creatures,' said Elver. 'It's just like the dark. It's trying to keep people out. Come on.'

'Death for you. Leave. This place is not a place of honour.'

The creature was still speaking to their backs as they left it behind, and then, very shortly, they saw another one. It was very similar to the first, only smaller. Black eyes winked at them in the dark.

'What is here is dangerous. It will wound you. Kill you. Nothing of value here.'

'Ignore them.' Elver stomped past the jih spirit, her angry movements tugging on the tether between the three of them. 'These are designed to keep wandering humans out, but we don't have to pay attention to it. Could have done with a few of these in the Jih Forest, would have saved me a lot of work.'

Time was slippery in the lightless forest, but Artair could feel his body tiring. They had to have been walking for much of the day, or night, or whatever it was, and he could tell from the way Sunay's footsteps were faltering that she was close to dropping too. Eventually he called to Elver that they should stop.

'But we're so close . . .'

'Are we? You said that when we set out, Elver. We can't keep walking indefinitely.' He took a deep breath. *Here and now, in this moment, I am safe.* 'Enough, Elver. We need to rest.'

They stopped where they stood, laying out their bedrolls as best they could, passing around the last of the food from hand to hand. Elver attempted to build another fire, but the flames just wouldn't come, and while they were doing that, the torch winked out. Sunay gave a low moan, and Artair felt his stomach turn over. Surely, without light, they were entirely lost. He felt a rising panic in the back of his throat, and once again he reached for the words of his mantra. *Here and now, in this moment, we are safe.* It felt hollow.

'Go to sleep, Sunay,' Elver said, not unkindly. 'Close your eyes, and we'll get going again when we've rested.'

'How can I even tell if I've closed my eyes?' said Sunay. But she did, and she slept remarkably quickly. Listening to her snores, Artair felt his own exhaustion rise up. He swallowed it down.

'Elver. Could the magic be keeping us from finding the lake? The Queen of Serpents is a god, after all. If she really doesn't want anyone to find the First of Monsters . . .' He kept his voice soft, not wanting to wake the mage. 'Maybe this is a lost cause.'

'We're not just anyone,' Elver said firmly. Her voice was closer than he was expecting, and when he reached a hand out into the dark, she took it. 'I can find him. I know I can, Artair. You just have to trust me.'

'I do,' he said quickly. 'I trust you more than anyone.' Somehow, being in the dark made it easier. He couldn't see how she would react to his words. 'Since I first met you in the basement of that tavern, I knew you were extraordinary. You helped me when anyone else would have driven me away. You defended me, fought for me. You have been my dearest friend, Elver. I can't do without you.' It wasn't quite what he wanted to say, but even in the inky darkness of the forest, those particular words would not pass his lips. 'Please tell me, when all this is done, that I won't have to do without you.'

She didn't answer immediately. She squeezed his hand. Around them, it seemed to Artair that the world held its breath.

'Artair, you taught me what caring is. I'd been looking through a lens that only showed me all the ways the world had hurt me, and you showed me what the world *could* be, if I let it in. When you touch me . . .' She paused, and he heard the click in her throat as she swallowed past some strong emotion. 'When you touch me, I feel complete. But this isn't all I am. I haven't finished changing yet, and I'm afraid that when that happens, it'll change everything between us. You deserve something better. Something that isn't filled with poison.'

'What? I don't care about—'

'Please.' She squeezed his hand again, and then he felt her mouth against his; the kiss felt like both a promise and an apology. 'We should rest as much as we can. I don't know when this will end, but I am determined I'll get us through.'

With that, she let go of his hand, and he felt her move away.

CHAPTER 34

In her dream, Elver was standing on a high road looking down over the distant city of Addersport, the strip of blue sea beyond it glittering like a river of sapphires.

Behind her she knew the Jih Forest was waiting, a vast green space full of her kin; comforting, safe. A gentle cage. The path forked ahead of her. Down one road she could see Artair. He was wearing the jacket he had worn to the Temple of Threshold, and his dark brown hair fell loose to his collar. The shirt he wore was buttercup yellow, like the robes of his old order, and he had a bow slung over his back, the bow he had taken from the monastery and used to wound the keltraxia vixen.

In the way of dreams, when she looked at him, she felt the stirrings of a potential future. With Artair, there would be long meandering journeys across Tlevrae, visiting all the places she'd heard mentioned on the streets of Addersport, or noted in the old books she had collected. They would look out for each other, talk into the early hours of every morning about all the things they had seen and experienced, always grateful that they had both escaped their respective prisons. Her poison heart would be cherished by him, and she would keep him safe. It would be a love she both craved and yet felt she didn't deserve.

Artair caught her eye, and smiled. He raised a hand to greet her.

Down the other road, stood another figure, someone she found she knew instantly. Lucian was shorter, slighter, sharper. His hair was black and cut brutally short at the sides, only allowed to be long and untidy on top. He wore a gold torc at his throat, and although his clothes were simple, they were finely made. An aura of magic crested behind his head like a small, bloody sun, and his eyes were alight with it: magic, and power. When Elver looked at Lucian she saw competition and fire, the pair of them constantly striving to beat the other, to come out on top, and reach the next level. It was a future that embraced being god-touched, a future of passion and wildness. But there was also a peace in the acceptance of someone who saw power in her horns and snakes and wildness.

Lucian, catching her eye, grinned and held out his hand.

Elver looked beyond them both. On the distant horizon, the broken mountains were a purple jumble, storm clouds banked behind them like a curtain about to be raised.

'This is ridiculous.'

Elver turned away from the fork in the road and looked behind her. There was the Jih Forest, as expected, but it had the look of something hastily painted. The details were off.

'I know you're there,' she said, raising her voice. 'Come out. Now.'

The lush green foliage of the trees shimmered, then parted, and Enos the god of dreams stepped into view. She brushed down her gown with three of her arms and gave Elver a rueful look.

'I still do not understand how you can do that,' she said. 'There's something strange about you, girl.'

'You've only just noticed?' said Elver drily. She gestured behind her to the fork in the road. 'What's all this about? What are you up to?'

Enos came forward. As she drew closer, Elver realized that the god was much taller here than she had initially thought. And had she believed her to only have six arms? There were more arms than she could count, fanning out behind the blue-skinned woman like the feathers of a peacock. Here, in this realm, Enos was changeable and hard to look at. Elver glared at her.

'Well, I thought it might help you decide,' said the god. 'It's something you're wrestling with, isn't it? The pure-hearted boy who cares about everything, or the fractured mage who lives for power. It's a fascinating problem. I'm only sorry you've stopped the dream before it really began! I had all sorts planned. I think you would have enjoyed it a great deal.'

'This *problem* is none of your business,' said Elver. 'It wasn't long ago that we narrowly escaped having our throats cut because a mage of yours had put us into a magical sleep. What's going on?'

'Ah, Plinko.' Enos stepped onto the road, arms weaving and flickering behind her. Just above her head, a tiny moon floated. 'He was over three hundred years old. Did you know that? One of my longest-serving mages. I didn't expect him to be so reckless, but even humans who've been around for three centuries can make mistakes. And now he is lost to me forever, journeying through a realm I cannot reach.' A crease appeared in three identical foreheads. 'Another thing the Mother will pay for.'

'Is that what this is about? Pissing off Maura?'

'Of course.' All three heads grinned, their teeth very neat and very sharp. 'She insulted me, when I had offered her my help out of the goodness of my hearts. And I thought, well, one way to rile her would be to help you, Elver of the Jih Forest. You intend to kill her, do you not?'

'I do.'

'Then,' Enos gestured down the road to where the dream versions of Lucian and Artair waited, 'why not enjoy yourself? It's my treat.'

'They're not real,' said Elver, not looking at them. 'What use are they to me? If you really want to help me, Enos, then *help* me. We're trapped in a forest where the night never ends. The others can't see at all, and it's only getting darker. What if you did something about that, instead of poking around in my love life?'

'Ah,' said Enos, 'so you admit that you love them. Both of them? One of them?'

'I'm warning you . . .' Elver felt her hair turn into snakes, a thunderous hissing in her ears.

Enos sighed. 'Very well. A light in the darkness is something I can help with, after all.' She reached up above her head and plucked the small moon from its orbit, before turning it over and over in her hands. To Elver it looked as though she were folding it like a piece of paper. 'Come here.'

When she approached, Enos grabbed her hand and pressed something tiny and cold into it.

'Use this to find your way,' she said. All around them, the sunny road to Addersport was growing dark. 'And bring about the end of the Mother. Let her know that it is not wise to insult the night.'

When Elver woke, her fist was clasped tightly round something so cold that it stung. She opened it, and the black forest around her lit up with silvery moonlight, bright enough that it woke up Sunay and startled Artair. In the palm of her hand there was a tiny fragment of the moon, a piece of burning silver.

'Finally,' Elver said aloud, 'a god does something useful.'

CHAPTER 35

With the light of the moon gifted to Elver by Enos, the eerie inky darkness of the forest was driven back, and the grip of dread that had been closing around them all loosened. They saw one more of the strange pale creatures with big eyes, but it didn't speak to them, and it scurried away from the silvery glow. After that, the day itself began to return. Sunay spotted it first: a faint pink hue to the edges of the sky.

'I've never been happier to see the dawn,' she said, before blowing a kiss directly upwards. 'Morning, I will never curse you again, not even when hungover, I swear.'

In daylight, the tiny piece of moon looked like nothing more than a white pebble, small and ordinary in Elver's hand. She whispered a quick thank you to it before slipping it back into her pocket: the magic might have been temporary, but she suspected her gratitude would last some time.

It took them another full day of hiking to get to the black lake, moving down through a forest that still seemed quieter than usual, if not actively hostile. When they finally stood at the edge of it, breath misting in the air, cold seemed to radiate from the water itself, beating against Elver's skin like a freezing mirror of the sun's warmth. Fleet ventured out onto the black ice, and then quickly came skittering back.

Too cold, he said. *It hurts my paws. Don't like it. Shall we go somewhere else?*

'We need what's under it,' she said. 'Which raises another

question. How do we get down there? The ice looks too thick to break with a stone.'

'You're not going to go under the water, are you?' asked Sunay. 'Look at it! It would be like walking into death itself.'

'I've got that bit covered, I think.' Elver remembered the lake under the hill where she had called out for the Queen of Serpents. Even then, she had sensed that the water meant her no harm. Now, since she had gained her new form, she was sure it wouldn't be a problem at all.

'I have an idea,' said Artair. 'If Lucian will help me.'

He knelt at the edge of the ice and placed the flats of his hands against it. A red glow blossomed around his fingers, and a ring of light traced across the ice. There was a flicker of magic, and the ice vanished, leaving just water as black as ink. The two of them had made a portal together.

'Thank you.' Elver stepped forward, resting her hand on his shoulder as she stepped into the water.

'Is this safe?' he asked, looking up at her. She remembered the way he had looked at her after she had turned the hunter into a jih spirit. She remembered the kiss she had given him in the dark, half suspecting it was a kiss goodbye.

'Nothing is ever safe,' she said. 'Keep this portal open for me, if you can.'

As the water closed over her head, she felt the change come over her automatically, as though the lake had washed away her human form. It was not as dark as she'd been expecting, and a faint greenish light played across the golden skin on her hands and arms. All at once she could feel the swishing of the snakes that sprouted from her head and, like her, they could breathe underwater. Curious, she held up a hand to them, and one of them curled round her fingers fondly.

I suppose my hair was always untidy, she thought.

The bottom of the lake was silty and littered with the occasional boulder. Some of them, she saw as she passed, contained the bones of creatures that had to be jih, although she recognized none of them. The way became steep, and soon she was sinking as much as she was walking, forcing herself down into the darkest depths of the lake. Eventually, she spotted something huge and pale in the murk ahead. At first, she thought it must be some kind of giant net, but as she drew closer she saw it was a vast structure of white coral, except it was covered all over with long, vicious-looking thorns, some at least the length of her forearm. It was a barrier, like a great white thorn bush, the final protection built by the Queen of Serpents to keep her dangerous son safe, and to keep the world safe from him. She waded over to it, and placed her hands on its surface. It felt like old bone under her fingers.

I told you to stay away.

The coral of thorns shivered threateningly.

'Well, tough.' Water flowed into her mouth, icy and mineral. 'I think we're connected, Tython, and there aren't many people in the world I can say that about. So I want to see your face, at least.'

When the voice spoke again, it sounded less angry and more afraid.

I warned you, it said. *If you get hurt, it's your fault.*

Elver slipped into the vast coral of thorns, searching for a way through. Instantly, the structure tightened around her like a carnivorous plant, trying to trap her in place. A thorn with a wickedly sharp point pressed into her stomach, attempting to skewer her, but she reached down and snapped it off in her hands. It was uncomfortable, and somewhere deep inside she could feel the remnants of her human self panicking: black icy water, the surface far above her head and a trap crushing her in place. But her new form was unconcerned. The snakes hissed at the thorns, and, with some effort, she began to push her way through, bending the constricting bone-coral away from herself. After a few minutes, she got into a kind of rhythm, until it was not so different from making her way through a particularly dense part of the Jih Forest. After a while, she heard the voice again, sounding terser than it had.

You really will persist in this? When I have told you not to?

'Tython, it's a forgivable mistake, because you don't know me,' said Elver through gritted teeth, 'but I don't like being told what I can or can't do. It makes me very . . .' she paused to snap another thorn away from her, '. . . contrary.'

Why? Why not just leave me in peace? I have done nothing to you.

'Because my friends need your help.' Down here, deep under the water, it was easier to say out loud. 'And, unfortunately for you, I would do anything for them. They are like my family, Tython. I suspect you remember what it's like to have family.'

There was an answering silence from the voice, and then abruptly the bone-coral gave up its attempts to crush her to death, releasing its grip and falling away. Elver picked her way through the last of it and finally stepped free. The snakes stretched out to their full lengths, enjoying the space.

'Thank you,' she said, no longer sure Tython was listening.

Just ahead of her, the ground dropped away entirely, and after a moment to contemplate the wisdom of what she was doing, she stepped off the edge into the deeper dark. Here, she felt herself pass into another world: this was the realm of Tython, the First of Monsters.

It looked a little like a ruined castle sitting on the bottom of the lake, or, at least, a castle that had been deconstructed into its separate parts and then placed in a haphazard fashion on a wide stretch of greenish-grey sand. Walls meandered, and winding stairs led up to rooms that stood open on two sides. Towers stood alone, or sprouted from the edge of a path. The castle was wrought from oddly prickly stone: like the bone-coral, the outside surface of each stone was covered in thorns. It reminded Elver of a conker casing. The rooms that she could see looked remarkably cosy, with chairs and cushions and broad, overstuffed sofas, and almost every room contained bookcases that were bowed under the weight of hundreds of books. All of it was encased in a green bubble of light, through which the occasional fish swam, like silver motes of dust.

Elver made her way over to it, watching closely to see if the First of Monsters was about to appear, but she could see no living creatures aside from the fish. When she got to the boundary of the bubble, she paused, then stepped through.

All at once the water was gone, and she was standing in a light, airy space. It smelled of old books, a scent that made her think of her own shack back in the Jih Forest, where her precious collection of scavenged books took up a single shelf. She wondered, briefly, if it were still there, or if the forest had eaten up her shack. The First of Monsters had apparently been collecting books for much, much longer than her.

'Hello?'

There was no answer.

Elver walked slowly across the green sand, which was perfectly dry, and made her way round the other side of a spiral staircase. There, with one wall missing, was a reading room, complete with a blue velvet armchair and a low table stacked with books. The First of Monsters was sitting on the chair with a large book across his lap. When she appeared, he looked up, although he didn't appear startled. If anything, his expression was resigned.

'It's you,' was all he said.

Elver didn't know exactly what she had been expecting, but it wasn't this, she realized. The First of Monsters was a humanoid about her size, with a reptilian head not unlike the Queen of Serpents, except his was broader, with smaller horns that ran along his forehead ridges like eyebrows. He was covered in pearly white scales, and his expressive eyes had bright red irises. The First of Monsters was wearing a simple pair of trousers and a tunic, both of which reminded Elver of what Artair had been wearing when she first met him. He put the book aside, and stood up slowly.

'You know me?' asked Elver.

He tipped his head to one side and sniffed, his scaled nostrils flaring.

'I know your smell,' he said. He sounded young, Elver realized. Hardly older than her, certainly, yet he had to be thousands of years old. 'You smell like my mother. And me. You are her other child, aren't you?'

'I suppose I am.' It was an odd thought, but who else did she belong to, with her snake hair and her golden eyes? She'd never known who her human mother was. 'My name is Elver.' She stuck out her hand for him to shake, feeling awkward, but he looked at it as though she'd waved a hot poker.

'I can't,' he said quickly. 'My touch is poisonous. It'd kill you.'

'Oh!' Elver laughed. 'Me too. I mean, my skin is poisonous too. I think we probably cancel each other out.'

'Even so.' He looked down at his clawed hands. The tip of each finger was topped with a sharp, golden claw. 'I've spent thousands of years with the knowledge that to touch is to kill. It's not something I can just push aside.'

She nodded once. His words had brought back a memory for her: being squashed into a carriage with Sunay and a bunch of other humans, terrified that she might accidentally brush a hand against theirs.

'I know something of what that is like.'

He sat back down on the edge of the chair, and Elver sat in another opposite him. Above them she could sense the heavy, dark waters of the lake, but Tython's sanctum was cosy.

'Do you live here alone, Tython?'

The First of Monsters nodded. 'I have to, Elver. I can never leave here, because I am an abomination. Father said so.'

For a second or so, Elver was too angry to speak. She swallowed it down, aware that, despite the connection she felt between them, she did not know Tython, and did not know how he'd react to her unvarnished fury.

'Trilot is wrong,' she said with feeling. 'The Queen of Serpents changed your nature to save your life, and what she made was no abomination. We're just different, Tython, and there's nothing wrong with that.'

Tython shook his head. 'My father is a god, Elver. He is not wrong about these things. He *can't* be wrong about them.'

Elver snorted. 'Your father is unwell,' she continued. 'He wants everything to be pure and clean and lifeless, and that is not what the world is like. That's not what life is like.' She took a deep breath. 'The world is brilliant, colourful, strange. It's full of odd things, and funny humans, and all sorts of sights you could never guess at. I used to live alone too, Tython. I hid away in the Jih Forest, and it is a wonderful place, but it's only one place. Outside of it, I have met so many interesting people, and have learned so much. I have friends now, Tython. You could have friends too.'

'I have books,' said the First of Monsters. He leaned forward to touch the books stacked on the little table. There was a conker on top of them. 'I've learned a lot from them. And no one needs to suffer for it.'

'It's not the same. Have you ever been outside, since the Queen of Serpents made this place for you?'

He shook his head. 'Humans will hate me. They will try to kill me. And I might accidentally kill them.'

'Not all humans will. My friends won't. And we need your help, Tython.'

She told him then their own story, of her and Artair and the keltraxia cub leaving the Jih Forest, of Lucian's imprisonment and the rise of Maura the half-god. She told him how Tisk had said that the First of Monsters was capable of killing a god, although with every word she felt something inside her shrink. They needed his help, this was true – without it Lucian might be hunted forever, and that meant that Artair would never know peace either – but the thought of Tython raising a clawed hand to anyone felt wrong. And asking him to do it felt even worse.

When she finished, Tython went very quiet, as though chewing over every word she had said. She had expected to find something powerful and terrifying under this lake, she realized, but what she had found was something altogether different. The poison within him must be very powerful indeed, to threaten the gods, but Tython himself was thoughtful, sheltered even. And of all the jih, this was the one that felt the most like kin: she knew what it was to be dangerous, to be feared and to fear even the smallest, simplest connection.

'Father was right,' he said eventually. 'I am a truly terrible creature, to be able to kill anyone, let alone a god. I must never leave here.'

'Don't you see?' Impulsively, Elver leaned across the table and took hold of his scaled hand. He jumped with surprise. 'Tython, none of this is your fault, and you deserve better. Whether you decide to help us or not, will you come up to the surface with me, and meet my friends? I want you to see the sky at least, breath the winter air, see the birds. Don't make the same mistake I did.

The world is up there for the taking.'

'My touch did not kill you . . .'

'Because we are kin. Because you are not the abomination that Trilot is trying to make you into. Will you come with me, Tython? See the sky, just for a day?'

He blinked his red eyes at her slowly.

'Will there be conker trees?'

CHAPTER 36

Artair wasn't sure what he was expecting to see when Elver returned. Would the First of Monsters be a gigantic beast, a creature like the Queen of Serpents, or an oversized version of the monsters they had seen at Booster Barnham's circus? Would it crash its way out of the ice and eat them all, tearing them to pieces with giant serrated teeth? A glance at Sunay's face confirmed that she'd been having similar thoughts.

What he didn't expect was to see a slight figure emerging behind Elver as she waded out of the lake, every angle of its body suggesting that it felt it had made a poor decision. The child of the Queen of Serpents had a white reptilian head with red eyes, and thorny scales covering him, but otherwise had a roughly human shape, meaning he did not look like the other jih creatures – at least, the ones that weren't Elver. The boy shook himself, water droplets flying everywhere.

'Sunay, Artair, Lucian, Fleet – this is Tython.' Elver stood aside so that he could reach the shore. Fleet trotted over to sniff at his feet. 'I suppose he is my brother.'

'Greetings.' Tython glanced down at Fleet. 'Be careful, I am poisonous.'

'We're used to that sort of thing,' said Sunay. 'It's a great honour to meet the child of two gods. Would you like some nettle tea?'

Tython looked at Elver and then back to Sunay. He shrugged.

They made a small fire on the shore of the black lake, Sunay brewing her dubious tea and Artair serving up the last of the foraged food provided by Milik the Small, and as they began to talk, a strange thing happened. The deep cold of the lake seemed to recede, so that their breath no longer appeared in white clouds, and the thick black ice began to melt. They could hear it shifting and cracking all the time, and little runnels of ice water trickled onto the shore. Even the trees seemed to grow less ominous, and the quiet chatter of birdsong, so ubiquitous in every other place they had travelled, could be heard in all directions again. Almost as an afterthought, the sun came out.

Tython told them about his early life in the realm that his mother and father once shared, a place of endless sunrises and warm afternoons, how they'd all been happy then, in the land of light and purity and balance. He spoke of his mother with genuine fondness: how she was quick, and laughed often, and taught him how to play games. And then, on one particular sunrise, Tython had felt too weak to greet the dawn, and his easy strength had rapidly dwindled. He told them a little of his life in the lake watching the silver fish drifting past, or reading the thousands and thousands of books he kept down there. He didn't seem to be aware that he'd been down there for a very long time, or, at least, wasn't very concerned about it – Artair thought it likely he didn't have much of a sense of time. Perhaps time didn't matter too much to gods.

'What was it like, when the Queen of Serpents changed you?' asked Elver. She had seated herself next to Tython and would occasionally pat his arm in a reassuring way. Artair felt a little flare of jealousy at that, and realized in that moment that Lucian was close by; he could feel his jealousy too.

'It was agonizing,' Tython said in a matter-of-fact way. 'Like everything about me was taken apart and put back together again. But when it was over, all the old sickness was gone.' Despite his lizard-like face, Artair found he could see quite clearly the downcast expression that passed over it. 'Father was furious. He was so angry that he changed shape too. He said that I was an abomination, that my mother had ruined what I was. They fought. It was my fault.'

'Now then,' said Sunay, her voice almost stern. 'I won't hear anything like that from you, young man. It seems to me that you haven't had much choice about any of this. For what it's worth, I am very glad that you decided to come up here and meet us, and see the sun for a little while. Fish and books are all very well and good, but you need a bit of variety.'

Is he going to help us kill Maura or not? We're not opening a nursery for wayward monster-gods here. Lucian's voice was loud enough to make Artair wince. Elver noticed and raised an eyebrow.

'What does Lucian have to say?' she asked.

'He's wondering if you told Tython why we came to see him.'

'I don't know if I can help you.' The First of Monsters looked pained. 'I had Mother create my home so that I could stay a safe distance from everyone. I'm too dangerous to be outside. Even here, with you, the idea that I might cause terrible harm at any moment hangs over me. I might be an abomination, but I know that to kill someone deliberately is an even worse abomination.'

The First of Monsters is a child, said Lucian, disgust dripping from each word. *He'll have to get over his squeamishness pretty sharply or we're all in trouble.*

Artair ignored him. He was thinking of his own years in the Golden Tower, his constant terror that the dark spirit inside him would get out and hurt innocent people. He remembered the fear and the responsibility as a physical weight, like carrying a heavy chain slung around his shoulders every waking hour, and as he thought about it, he realized that the weight had gone. Had been gone for some time, in fact.

'Tython, I don't know if you will fight for us. I don't even know if you should.' Lucian made an angry noise of disbelief; Artair ignored that too. 'But I do know that nothing in life is truly safe. You have to take risks, or you're not really living at all. Whatever your parents think about it, I think you should have your own life.'

Elver smiled, meeting Artair's eyes, and he felt a flare of warmth.

'Maybe,' said Tython. 'It *is* good to see the trees. Pictures of them in books just aren't as good.'

Quite abruptly, Fleet began to bark, short little yips of fright that made Elver frown.

'What is it?' she asked him, but Fleet went on yipping.

Artair felt his skin prickle with alarm, and then realized it was more than that; a faint steam was rising off his bare arms, and when he looked at Elver and Fleet, he saw that the same was true of them.

Something is coming, said Lucian. *And it means us harm.*

The warm, yellow glow of the sun was drowned out by a cold, clinical white light that drained all the colour from the day and burned his eyes. It seemed to be coalescing over the lake, a piercing star that gradually grew, and grew, until it was a jagged crystal like a starburst. Elver had jumped to her feet, and was trying to shield Tython, who had his hands over his face.

'I shouldn't have left,' he said miserably. 'I knew it would make him angry.'

The crystal cracked, and then its pieces slowly moved apart, an explosion in slow motion, and from within it came a violent storm of white silk and silver light.

'Is that Trilot himself?' Sunay laughed weakly. 'Oh, this isn't going to be any fun *at all*.'

A long silver mask, pointed like a dagger, drifted out of the crystal towards them. The silk ribbons began forming a shape below it, something like a human, although it seemed a little confused about how many arms and legs it should have. Elver changed too, her golden horns and snakes making her taller, more imposing.

'Leave him alone!' she shouted. 'Come near Tython, or any of us, and I'll find a way to hurt you.'

Trilot's mask twitched in her direction. Artair had a moment to hear Lucian shout – *Let me take over, monk* – and then it was already too late. He was encased in a crystal, his body held perfectly still. He could see that Sunay, Fleet and Elver had been similarly caught, each trapped as though frozen in ice. Miraculously, he could still breathe, but the magic that surged inside him had no route out, and the presence of Trilot's power so close was agonizing. Lucian reeled off a list of colourful oaths that Artair suspected even Elver didn't know, and Artair braced himself against the pain. He called to mind his old mantra, the one he had relied on when he was at the monastery.

Here and now, in this moment, I am safe.

He didn't feel especially safe, but he was aware that the burning touch of the crystal could easily overwhelm him and Lucian, so he took hold of that pain and held it, containing it within the cage of his own body.

Meanwhile, Trilot had drifted closer to Tython, who was still crouched by their campfire.

I will deal with the jih and those tainted by them later. The god's voice was flat, a note struck on a broken bell. **My son. My son. I never thought to see you again. Your mother hid you well.**

'I'm sorry, Father.' Tython bowed his head. 'I wanted to see the sky again for a little while. And the trees.'

Do not concern yourself. Everything will be good now. Everything will be pure. Trilot was now a figure with two arms and two legs, and he stood over Tython, silvery light pouring through the eye holes of his mask. Artair strained against the crystal holding him in place, causing the burning pain to flare and sting, but there was no give in it at all. **Your pain, and mine, will finally come to an end.**

The god reached out a hand to his son, and stopped.

You always loved the trees. And all growing things.

An odd thing was happening, Artair realized. The light that animated Trilot, that was so difficult to look at directly, was dimming, and his feet were in contact with the ground. The ribbons of white silk stopped their ceaseless movement and hung loosely from his body.

Tython lifted his head. 'Father?'

I planted rows and rows of trees for you, and you named every one, said Trilot. **Do you remember? I would look for new seeds, just to see the delight on your face when a tree you did not know began to grow.**

'I remember,' said Tython. 'When they got very tall, you carried me on your shoulders so that I could reach the branches.'

Yes.

There was a loud crack, and Artair saw that Elver's crystal had broken, freeing up part of her head. She had clearly been straining against it with her new strength; there was a sheen of sweat on her golden forehead.

'All those memories are still there, Trilot,' she said through clenched teeth. 'Do you know why, you idiot turd? Because, whatever his shape, *Tython is still your son.*'

The god stood on the shores of the lake, broken ice around his bandaged feet.

I . . . I don't know. It's wrong. He's tainted, and strange to me. She ruined him.

'His heart is still the same. You know I'm right.'

Trilot turned slowly to look at Elver. Inside Artair, Lucian boiled with a fear and anger that matched his own, but the magic was as trapped by the crystal as they were.

The jih are a plague on this world, said Trilot. Curiously, Artair thought he could see a head wearing the mask now. It looked as if it was made from liquid silver, but it also looked like a man's head – he could see an ear, and a suggestion of a hairline. **Taking good, normal things, and making them different. Your poison is something that must be burned away for the greater good. But Tython is different. He is pure, at heart.**

'Father.' Tython stood up. He wasn't short, but next to his father he still looked small somehow. 'Elver is my sister. Please—'

Behind them all, there was a huge twinkling smash, as though the large plane of glass had just been shattered, and a great wave of black water surged over the banks of the lake, putting out their meagre fire and lapping around the bottom of the crystals. A vast golden coil rose out of the lake, the Queen of Serpents' jaws agape with fury.

YOU WILL LEAVE MY CHILDREN BE, HUSBAND!

The human shape that Trilot had gradually been building dropped away from him as though it were a cloak he could discard, and the god rose up into the air again, streamers of white silk in a storm of light.

Brishta, you are the root of this evil, he thundered. **I will cleanse you, and the poison you have spread will finally leave Tython. He'll be himself again, pure and good. Perhaps he will live, perhaps he won't. But I see now what must be done. The age of jih ends here.**

CHAPTER 37

No, husband. You will die here.

Elver watched as the Queen of Serpents rose out of the black waters of the lake, Trilot's stark glow turning each of her golden scales into a tiny flame. Her giant jaws gaped, revealing her long black tongue, and then the god lunged directly at the figure of silver and white silk. As fast as she was, Trilot was faster; a silver trident appeared in his hand and a beam of light flew from it, striking the Queen of Serpents in the exposed portion of her underbelly.

'No!' cried Elver.

There was a terrible sound, taking her back in an instant to Addersport: the serpents who screamed all day and all night, the noise so persistent that the people paid a mage to sacrifice a child to the Bloody Claw in hopes of ending it – a hundred thousand serpents, crying out in agony. The Queen of Serpents fell to the shore, and the instant her body struck the ground her serpent-self fell away. Instead, there was a woman lying there, her hair shining like the sun. She was larger than a normal human, and her skin was gold, as Elver's was, and she was beautiful. But she was dying.

'Mother!' cried Tython.

The anger made Elver feel lighter, and stronger. It suddenly seemed ridiculous that the crystal could hold her at all, and when she flexed her body this time, every piece of it shattered. She shrugged off the fragments and ran to the Queen of Serpents.

Trilot, meanwhile, had drifted back to the ground. The silver mask was turned towards Tython.

Son. You have not changed.

Tython had gone to his mother's side too. Even now, he hesitated to touch her, but the Queen of Serpents raised one hand to his cheek fondly.

My poison children, she said.

'I should never have left the lake!' Tython bowed his head. Tears coursed down his scaled face. 'I've ruined everything, just like Father said I would.'

Your father is a fool, replied the Queen of Serpents, her voice taking on its more familiar edge. *A man who threw away his own family and his own nature for the sake of pride.*

Why has Tython not changed? I can feel your death approaching, your monstrousness has been burned from you, and you are the root and heart of all this poison. Usually so emotionless, the voice of Trilot wavered with fury and panic. **Why is he still tainted?**

'You're a god,' said Elver, looking at the Queen of Serpents' face. Somehow it was still familiar despite its new shape: something in her cheekbones, the way she rarely blinked. 'You can't die.' Although even as she said it, she remembered the Bloody Claw. Maura had killed him, and she hadn't even been a god at the time.

I am no longer the heart of poison, said the Queen of Serpents. She pressed her other hand against Elver's chest. *The heart of poison rests here now. Elver will be the next god of change. And I can finally rest.*

'I'm sorry, what?' asked Elver. Inside her chest, her heart pulsed as though reacting to the words.

I am tired, said the Queen of Serpents. *I want to rest. But my work goes on, poison child. This is the fate I wove for you, and you accepted it when you accepted your new heart.*

'That can't be right.' Elver stood up. Tython was looking at her curiously, and she backed away from them both. 'I didn't agree to that. I'm no god. I'm just me.'

The process has already started, replied the Queen of Serpents, a touch impatiently. *Look at your hair, child. Is that a normal human's hair?*

Elver raised her hand to her head, and felt a snake coil around it.

Enough! The billowing white threads of Trilot were expanding, ribbons of light and silver and silk all interlacing to create a vast tessellating shape that hung over them. The silver mask had elongated again, becoming as long and as sharp as a sword. He swung over towards Elver, and she felt his light searing across her scales. On her head, every one of the snakes hissed with pain. **If you are the heart of the poison now, I shall kill you too, before your godhood comes to fruition. You have danced away from purification once too often, child.**

Elver reached for the earth and grass around her and summoned the change within it, entreating it to protect her. A shield of mud and thorny vines leapt up over her head, but Trilot's light cast it into dust in an instant and she was left exposed again. He lifted the silver trident in the air, holding it over her as if he intended to pin her to the ground.

I will pierce your heart, monster, he said. **And my child will be free.**

Smoke was rising from her skin, and with it Elver felt her strength beginning to leak away. Somewhere deep inside her, she felt the child she had once been shiver in recognition – the monster would be burned away, and she would be left in her original form – an orphan, her lungs full of water, dead at the bottom of the sea. This would be it: she would die here, on the shores of the black lake.

The arm holding the trident flexed, and then . . . stopped.

The strange oscillating shape that was Trilot stayed fixed in place as though stunned, and then Elver saw suddenly that part of him had changed. One of the white ribbons of silk that cascaded from his form had turned black. And then the one next to it darkened too, and then the next. Tython, she realized, was standing with his hand raised, one golden claw touching the end of the trident. As Elver watched, that tarnished too, turning black and orange with rust.

'No, Father,' said Tython. 'Elver is my sister.'

The silver mask elongated further, and began to drip onto the ground, a pattering of silver droplets. All the parts of Trilot that had been a bright, shining white, were turning grey and brown and green, yellow and orange and black and blue, all manner of colours, all of them more interesting than white.

Tython . . . what have you done?

The boy didn't answer. Instead, he drew his hand away, and watched as the last parts of Trilot discoloured and shrank, drifting down onto the mud. The mask itself had liquefied, becoming a little pool of silver that dripped onto the dirt with a hissing noise. In a handful of heartbeats, it was all over. The light that had once inhabited Trilot, god of purity and truth, was extinguished.

Elver went back to the Queen of Serpents, eager to tell her that their old enemy was dead, that in the end he had failed to kill her or Tython, when she saw the light had left her hair too. The Queen of Serpents was dead.

CHAPTER 38

'What happened?'

'The pain was too much.' Artair was already sitting on the edge of the cliff, his head down. His shoulders were rising and falling as though he'd just run up a mountain. Beyond them, the landscape had changed again; the blue sands had been replaced by a green sea, rills of white edging the top of each wave. On the horizon, hazy with distance, was the top half of a great statue, rising from the ocean. 'I held it off as long as I could.'

'You mean you passed out?' Lucian glared at him. 'Two gods just died in front of us, and you have a nap.'

Artair didn't reply. When Lucian went and sat on the cliff edge next to him, he saw that the monk was pale and sweating.

'I didn't feel any pain,' Lucian said reluctantly.

'No,' agreed Artair.

'Why did you do that?' asked Lucian. 'I didn't ask you to do that.' He was remembering the trap Plinko had sprung for them, how Artair had fought the Maura-spider to save him.

'If the pain overwhelmed me straight away and I passed out, you would have taken over.' The monk gave him a rueful look. 'I didn't think you'd last as long as me, somehow.'

'Yes, alright, you are very tough. It's all very impressive, I'm sure.' Lucian shook his head. 'The Queen of Serpents dead, Trilot dead. And Elver a new god? This is all excellent news. We just need Tython to send Maura on her merry way so that I can attain the full power of the Bloody Claw and all will be well.'

'I'm not sure that Elver wants to be a god,' said Artair. Below them, the sea was crashing against the cliffs with a roar, growing louder all the time, and Lucian could feel the waking world pulling him back.

'Nonsense. The power she could wield . . .' *That we could wield together*, he thought. Lucian wasn't sure what would happen when he received the last of the Bloody Claw's power, but he suspected it would make him close to a god, at least. He had an image of himself and Elver, taking their place in the Twelve. Together. As a god, he'd no longer need Artair's body. 'Now that the Queen of Serpents is dead, it won't be long before she's a god in her own right.'

Artair looked troubled. Lucian clapped him on the shoulder in what he imagined was a friendly manner.

'Don't worry, monk. I'm sure she won't forget the small people like yourself.' He grinned. 'I might, though.'

Artair narrowed his eyes and opened his mouth, but Lucian was already gone.

When Lucian awoke, it was to find Elver kneeling over him, looking worried. She was back in her human form, her white hair falling forward to frame her face. He grinned up at her.

'Oh good, you're all right.' She stood up, and he got to his feet. 'I think Trilot was keeping us in those crystals so he could deal with us later, but just being close to his power is painful for jih. Fleet had a very rough time.'

Sunay was sitting with the keltraxia cub in her lap, although really he was much too big for it. She was stroking his feathers and talking to him in a soft voice.

'And you, Queen of Poison?' Lucian grinned at her again. 'How does it feel to find out you are the heir to a god?'

'Don't call me that.' She crossed her arms over her chest. 'And we have other problems.'

She nodded towards Tython. The First of Monsters was sitting on the shore of the lake, his head bowed. As if in response to his mood, the water in front of him was choppy and unsettled. Despite all that had happened it was still the middle of the day, and the weak winter sun was doing a slow job of melting the last chunks of black ice.

'I know you're looking at me,' said Tython, without turning around. 'I'd rather you didn't.'

'You shouldn't blame yourself,' said Elver. She walked over to Tython and placed her hand lightly on his shoulder. 'You saved me, Tython. You saved all of us. Once Trilot had killed our mother, he would have killed me, and Fleet, and my friends. I doubt he would have spared Sunay even. He said she had been tainted by us too. So don't be sorry.'

'Indeed, you have done us a remarkable service,' said Lucian. 'We'll forever be in your debt. And there is just one more thing to ask of you . . .'

'Lucian . . .' Elver's voice held a tone of warning to it, which he put down to shock.

'First of Monsters, we've told you about Maura, and how she now styles herself as the Mother. A false god operating with stolen power. I am the rightful heir of the Bloody Claw's power, he meant it to come to *me*, just as your mother means for Elver to take over in her place. As you've just demonstrated, you have the ability to kill gods and—'

'*Lucian.*' This time, Elver kicked him smartly on the ankle.

'What?'

'Tython just saw both his parents die.'

'And? Yes, it's terrible, Elver, I agree, but Maura remains a pressing matter! At any moment, she could send a fresh round of mages to deal with us, and our fate will be just the same as if Trilot had triumphed.' He pointed at the young monster. 'He's the key to defeating her. You know it as well as I do.'

'Will you just give him a moment?'

'We don't have the time!'

Tython stood up, and they both stopped talking. When he turned to them, he looked older somehow, as though in the last few hours some of the thousands of years he'd spent under the lake had caught up with him.

'My parents died,' he said, his voice barely more than a whisper. 'And in a way I killed them both. My mother only came here because I was in danger. Father was full of misery, and gave me no choice.' He walked past both of them to what was left of the campfire; it was a smudge of soot on the ground now, but on the spot where Trilot had died there was a new plant growing. It had tiny white flowers. Where the Queen of Serpents had taken her last breath, there was a splash of gold lichen across the stones. 'I know you're all in trouble, and I'm sorry. I wish I could help. But I cannot raise my hand against another being. Not after today. I think it would be the end of me.'

The old fury, hot and suffocating, filled Lucian's throat. 'This is ridiculous. You barely even need do anything. Just a touch, as you did your father.' He took a step towards Tython. 'If we can figure out where she is, I could open a portal now and push you through it to meet her . . .'

Elver took hold of his arm. The grip was firm. 'Do that, Lucian, and you'll have more than one angry god to deal with.'

'I'm sorry,' Tython said again. 'I really am. But I need to be alone for a while.'

'Where will you go?' asked Sunay. She had been very quiet, and her face was unusually sombre. 'Surely not back down into the lake?'

'No,' said Tython. 'I want to see more trees, I think. I'll go out into the world and see it properly, for myself.' He hesitated. 'I will be careful. I won't let anyone get hurt.'

'Oh, you should come by my temple in the autumn,' said Sunay. 'The leaves are all colours. You'd love it.'

'And the Jih Forest,' said Elver, smiling. 'I think your mother would want you to see it.'

'I'm sorry, have we all lost our minds?' Lucian threw his arms up in the air. 'This boy is our one chance of getting rid of Maura for good and we're recommending places for him to visit! Tython, why not visit the spot on the shattered mountain where Maura expelled my soul from my body? I'm sure that there are a few interesting plants for you to look at there. You might even find my scattered bones.' He took a breath. 'Have you forgotten, Elver, that she threw you in the sea? That she sacrificed you to the Bloody Claw? That she's been hunting our every step since Prideful Leap?'

Elver sighed and, to his surprise, took hold of his hand.

'Come with me,' she said. 'Let's talk.'

They went to a place some distance beyond the treeline, where rocks formed around a spring that was feeding into the lake. There was a pool there filled with clear water, and the stones at the bottom of it were covered with golden algae. Lucian wondered if this was more of the Queen of Serpents' influence, the last parts of her essence creeping out into the wider world.

Elver sat on one of the rocks, and then patted the one next to her without looking at him. When he sat, she began to speak.

'Tython is no longer an option. I don't know what I expected when we came here, Lucian, but it wasn't a brother. A brother who is confused and lonely, at that. One who has suffered enough, I think. He's no weapon. And we shouldn't ask him to be one. I reckon you know that well enough, actually.'

Lucian leaned down and put his fingers into the water. It was icy cold, and somehow it seemed to soothe some of the anger inside him. For a long time, neither of them spoke.

'All right,' he said eventually. 'Then what do we do?'

'I think it has to be me,' said Elver. 'What the Queen of Serpents did to me, I don't think it's completely finished yet, but I can feel the power building. When Maura comes for us, I will fight her. I think this is what I was made for.'

She looked down at her hands, and Lucian realized that despite her confident words she was troubled.

'What is it?' he asked her.

'I never wanted to leave the Jih Forest. I wanted nothing to do with humans – all they'd ever given me was pain, and misery, and disappointment. And then I went after Fleet, and I got to know them better. I was still glad to be who I was, and what I was, but my human shape started to feel like a good thing – that I could walk among them and not be noticed.' She curled her hands into fists. 'Now, though, I think my time of looking like a human is coming to an end. I'm not sure how I feel about it.'

'I've seen your god form,' said Lucian. 'And it was magnificent. You looked powerful, and fierce. You looked like *you*. Don't shy away from it.'

'Easy for you to say,' she said, the corner of her mouth crooking into a half-smile. 'No snakes growing out of your head.'

'Elver, you are beautiful. In either form.' He cleared his throat. He wasn't sure where these feelings had come from. Artair was distant, likely sleeping off his ordeal, so it couldn't have been the monk. They surged up to the surface. 'You trusted me when no one else would. You treated me like a person when I'd almost forgotten what that was like. I think you're remarkable, Elver.'

She shook her head. 'Did you hit your head when the crystal broke?'

'No, oh no, don't do that. I might have lied in the past, I might have bent the truth, but I'm being absolutely serious here, and it's killing me.' He took her hand and kissed it, relishing the lake-water scent of her. 'Elver . . . We kissed once before, monster girl, in the Jih Forest, and it's been driving me mad since. In fact, I'm not sure I can go another minute without doing it again.'

He expected to get pushed into the pool of water, but instead Elver put her hand on his arm, and when he bent to kiss her she kissed him back just as firmly. After a few moments, it seemed that they weren't close enough, and he pulled her into his lap. A sudden golden light pushed at his eyelids, and when he opened his eyes he saw that she had taken on her monster form. This close, he could see the tiny delicate scales across her cheeks and forehead, and the snakes were watching him attentively with eyes like dots of blood.

'Oh.' Elver looked mortified and tried to turn away. 'I don't know why that happened . . .'

Lucian grinned. 'Like I said, Elver, your godly form is beautiful.' He pulled her back and kissed her again. 'So let me worship you.'

She smiled, and then something else passed over her face, a fleeting darkness like the shadow of a cloud.

'What is it?'

'Nothing.' She didn't quite meet his eyes.

'He'll never love you as much as I do,' said Lucian, and then, 'He'll never love you *the way* that I love you, at least. And that's what really matters, isn't it?'

The sorrow on her face drew into focus for a moment, and then he saw her push it away. When she kissed him again it was with purpose, and her cold hands slid up the back of his shirt, making him shiver. Making all sorts of things happen.

'Let's stay here for a little while longer,' he said. 'My goddess.'

CHAPTER 39

When they returned to their bedraggled camp, Tython was saying his goodbyes. Sunay had been giving him detailed instructions on how to find the temple of Tisk, but she looked up when they arrived, a raised eyebrow suggesting she knew the direction their talk had taken. Elver smoothed down her tunic while her snakes attempted to look anywhere but at the mage. Lucian did not mention his previous concerns about Tython leaving, and Elver had to suppress a smile at the way he swaggered into the camp, his cheeks flushed. Kissing him had felt so different from kissing Artair; it had been wild and heated, full of hunger. With Artair there had been so much sweetness, and a feeling of being complete. At the thought of Artair, a wave of guilt moved through her, so strong it made her dizzy.

I am poison, she reminded herself. *I don't even know what I am any more. I can't ask him to love that.*

'There you are,' said Sunay. 'Our friend is setting off shortly. I imagine there are things you want to say to him, Elver?'

'You'll visit me, won't you?' she asked.

Tython nodded once, looking serious, and then he awkwardly put his arms round her. After a moment, Elver embraced him back, smiling. Family wasn't something she had been expecting to find when she'd left the Jih Forest, but it seemed the world was full of unexpected things.

'It's a long way out of this misbegotten forest,' said Sunay. 'Are you sure you don't want to travel with us a little longer? Fleet only snores a little, and if you put a blanket over his head it's more or less bearable.'

'Thank you, Sunay Tiskertalia,' said Tython. 'But I have an idea of how to travel.'

He stepped back from them, and after a final nod, his form dissolved into a flock of noisy white birds. They flew up into the sky, turned a circle and then headed off to the west. In a handful of seconds, they were gone.

'Huh,' said Lucian. 'Can you do that, Elver?'

'Not as far as I'm aware.' When she looked at him, the memory of their time alone felt very close. Her monstrous form hadn't concerned him at all. 'Let's get away from this lake, shall we? Being close to the place where two gods have died feels too much like tempting fate.'

With the First of Monsters released from his self-imposed prison, the forest seemed less gloomy and oppressive, but it still took them some time to find a place open enough to rest and talk. Eventually, they settled on a spot between a clutch of towering oak trees, because the ground there was covered in a thick green moss, and by this time it was already dark. Elver began building the fire, although the place was too damp for it to take properly. Lucian came and crouched near her while Sunay searched the nearby bushes for anything edible.

'Elver.' He seemed less certain of himself than usual. 'Can we talk?'

'Sure. What is it?'

He glanced at Sunay, checking she wasn't in earshot. 'I know that the monk has feelings for you too. It's all over his mind when I am with him, although he tries to hide it from me.' He picked up a small stick and threw it into the beginnings of her fire, smothering the flame she had been building up.

'Can you not do that?' She had a sense of where this conversation was going, and she would rather talk about the difficulty of making fires in damp forests. 'There's only so much dry kindling here.'

'I know that you and he have kissed too.' He snorted. 'I doubt it was anything like our time together, but certainly it appears to have meant a lot to him. What I'm saying, I suppose, is that I'm not willing to share you. And I doubt he is either.'

Elver stood up, abruptly annoyed. 'I am not a portion of dried meat to be shared around.'

'Of course not.' Lucian stood up rapidly too. He looked faintly alarmed. 'That is not what I meant to suggest. I just . . .' He pushed some loose hair back from his forehead. 'Gods, I am not good at this stuff. I just mean that . . . Elver, I think you have to choose. For all our sakes.'

Elver looked down into the embers of the fire. Smoke was rising from it in sooty trails, and the light it gave off was minimal.

'Listen,' she said quietly. 'Artair is *good*. He's good down to his bones, right? And that's not what I am. He deserves better.'

'You love him, don't you?'

A dead leaf in the fire curled inward, giving itself up to the beginnings of a flame.

'It doesn't matter. I am poison, and I'll only ruin him.'

She expected Lucian to look pleased at this comment, but instead he looked sad.

'Do you truly believe that? Artair saved me, but so did you, Elver. You are better than—'

There was a gentle cough from ground level. They both looked over to see a fox sitting on the other side of the fire, its eyes winking with orange light.

'Oh, don't mind me,' said Tisk. 'Please continue. All these human dramatics are so fascinating.'

'My lord?' Sunay appeared, with Fleet at her heels. 'We are honoured by your visit.'

'Your timing could be better,' muttered Lucian.

'Naturally,' said Tisk. 'I trust that the allies I provided have been helpful?'

'Oh, extremely, my lord,' said Sunay with enthusiasm. 'A mage of Barleycorn gave us entry to the Inn at the End of All Worlds, which was marvellous and full of exciting things, and Gus – he's a mage of Milik the Small – has been instructing his little friends to bring us the most remarkable provisions, which has been wonderful.'

'Yes, wonderful if you like to eat food that has been handled by rodents,' said Lucian.

'I see you are as charming as ever,' said Tisk. 'I am gratified that I have been able to provide assistance in this, your time of great need, and so on. But I'm afraid the situation has changed.' He trotted over to Sunay and transformed into his human shape. 'Being the exemplary mage that you are, Sunay, I believe you took something from the Inn at the End of All Worlds, which I assume you were intending to give to me at some point as part of a tithe?'

'I . . . Yes, I did,' said Sunay. A crease had appeared in her forehead, and she glanced at Elver, who shrugged.

'Well?' Tisk held out his hand.

'What is this about?' asked Lucian. 'What do you mean, the situation has changed?'

Sunay reached into her pocket and brought out a tiny blue glass bottle about two inches long. She handed it over to Tisk, who weighed it in his hand for a moment, and then nodded.

'This is satisfactory. I'm going to do you a favour, Sunay.'

'Is it taking away this fox tail?' she asked hopefully.

'I'll take away more than that,' he said. 'I'll take away your whole self – that is, I'll take it away from this miserable forest and deposit it somewhere significantly safer.' He turned to the others. 'Don't let it get around, but I have a certain fondness for my own mages, and I prefer them not to get involved in anything too dangerous. And I've done what I can for you, Lucian.' He paused, his green eyes taking in Elver.

'Nice snakes. I don't know, no new gods for aeons and suddenly we are inundated with them. It hasn't escaped my notice, as you can imagine, that two of my sibling gods are dead, the spiritual remains of their bodies infiltrating the woods just south of here, and that is, frankly, the last straw. Not to mention, the great killer of gods is now loose in the world. This game has become much too dangerous.' He sniffed. 'The hard truth is that your old friend Maura has decided the rules don't apply to her, and I'm no longer sure what she's going to try.'

'Wait,' said Elver. 'You can't just take Sunay away against her will. And you promised you'd help us!'

'And I am the god of lies.' He stepped up to Sunay and placed a hand on her shoulder. Elver had time to see Sunay open her mouth, about to protest, and then the pair of them vanished in a flash of orange light. In the silence that followed, Fleet gave a single, outraged bark.

'That hardly bodes well,' said Lucian. 'If the god of lies and tricks is running scared, we may be in serious trouble.'

Elver looked at the spot where Sunay had been standing. It seemed impossible that the mage had just vanished, and she felt a keen sense of loss.

Where did she go? demanded Fleet. *I liked that human. She fed me. And she told me I was a good boy. I ate her socks and she didn't mind.*

'Maura isn't obeying the rules any more. What are the rules of gods, exactly?' Elver walked over to Sunay's pack, which had been left on the ground. When she opened it up, she got a whiff of her scent, which only made her sadder.

Lucian shrugged. 'They aren't to interfere directly in mortal affairs – if they want to do that, they have to act through their mages. Except, of course, that they are all partial to flouting that rule – Tisk himself being one of the biggest offenders. Even the Queen of Serpents catching you when you were thrown into the sea was flirting with breaking that rule, although no doubt she would have argued that you were already dead, and therefore already outside the mortal realm. Not that I imagine she has much time for obeying rules anyway. *Had* much time, I mean. Sorry.'

Elver nodded. They kept losing people. The Queen of Serpents, Tython and now Sunay.

'But Maura wouldn't dare turn up here to confront me,' continued Lucian. 'If she did, I could attempt to draw the Bloody Claw's power from her directly. No, I don't know what Tisk is alluding to, but I don't think it could be that. There are other rules – no possession of mortal beings, no fighting each other in their own realms, no keeping the mage of another god from attaining their rightful tithes, that sort of thing.'

Elver took some crumpled paper from Sunay's pack and gently pushed it into the smoky fire. This fed the flames much better than the old leaves she'd found, and the fire flared up, filling the space under the oak trees with red light before dying down again. She frowned.

'Did you hear that?'

There was a crunching noise, like the sound of something walking across the leaf litter. It was a quiet noise, and she wondered if it could be Gus; perhaps the mage had come to check on them again – despite his size, he was good at moving through the forest silently. A gift, he had explained, from Milik herself.

Lucian turned to the direction of the noise just as a small figure emerged from the shadows. It was a girl, perhaps no more than nine years old. She was slight, and she was wearing a white robe over dark clothes, and the expression on her face was blank. There was a white circle painted on her forehead, and Elver felt a shiver of recognition.

'Oh, great,' said Lucian. 'Thank you, but we've learned our lesson with regards to creepy children. Go and bother someone else.'

'That's a kid from Maura's temple,' Elver said quickly. 'From the orphanage. What are you doing out here?' she asked the child directly. 'Did someone send you here to find us?'

The child looked in her direction, her eyes swivelling wetly in her head in a way that suggested she wasn't entirely in control of them. Elver had the distinct impression that she hadn't understood her words at all, but was instead reacting to the sound of her voice. There was another flash of red light from somewhere behind them – it hadn't been the fire that lit up the trees, Elver realized too late – and the girl in front of them produced a dagger from her belt. It looked a little too big for her, but it also looked wickedly sharp.

'Wait, stop!' Elver glanced behind her to see a portal of red fire hanging in the air, and another child stepping through it. This one was a boy, perhaps twelve years old; he also had a circle on his head and a dagger in his hand. Both the children advanced on them, daggers held up. 'Keep away from us,' she said. 'I don't want to hurt you.'

'There are more,' said Lucian tersely, and she saw that he was right. Everywhere she looked, suddenly, portals were flaring into life, and through them more and more of Maura's orphans poured, blades flashing in the light.

'Can any of you hear me?' shouted Elver.

The boy who had appeared behind her lunged forward, his dagger swinging, and she knocked his arm to one side. He dropped the dagger, but her hand brushed his skin, instantly bringing up a searing red burn. The boy cried out and dropped to the ground, and Elver felt a rush of horror move through her. Maura had sent them an army of children armed with simple weapons – children from an orphanage, just as she had been. Children that were considered expendable, and all Elver had for them was poison and pain.

High above them in the trees, a new star blazed into life, and a familiar voice floated down.

'This game has gone on long enough, my wayward children,' said Mother Maura. 'Nothing has changed, Lucian – everything comes down to knives and murder in the end.'

CHAPTER 40

Lucian knew very quickly that he was in trouble.

Children with knives were rushing at him out of the dark, the portals that were bringing them appearing and disappearing quicker than he could follow, and Maura was above them somewhere, out of reach.

'Artair, I need you!'

The monk stepped forward, his presence suddenly close, and Lucian felt his body begin to move with a new grace and strength. As the next child reached him, Artair knocked the dagger from their hands and pushed them away, just in time to catch the next kid. But more and more were appearing all the time.

When the first child returned, throwing herself at their legs and trying to drag them to the ground, Lucian summoned the magic into a burning red flame nestled in their hands.

What are you doing? cried Artair.

'I don't know if you've noticed, monk, but these delightful children are trying to stab us to death! I'm sure being set on fire will put them off. I can fill this whole wood with fire, wipe them all out at once . . .'

Look at them, Lucian! Don't they remind you of anyone?

Small blank faces in the dark, their minds intent only on one thing: serving their god, even if that meant pain, or death. Lucian remembered the dream in which Plinko had attempted to trap them, the underground chamber where younger versions of himself ran back and forth with buckets of blood, trying to satisfy a god that was all appetite. The memory lasted less than a moment, but it was enough to turn his blood to ice.

You were as innocent as them, once. Until the Bloody Claw got hold of you, said the monk. *Did you deserve to burn to death?*

'Not then, maybe,' said Lucian, a black wave of despair filling his gut.

And not now, either, said Artair firmly. *We'll use the portal magic, together. Send them out of harm's way.*

'It'll take too long. I have to get to Maura and take the magic from her. It's the only way to end this.' But, even as he spoke, another child ran at them, and this time when Artair struck the child's arm – little more than a tap, really – Lucian summoned his own portal, letting the child fall through it to safety.

The children were not strong, or even smart. All they did was rush them, knives held up, with no regard for their own safety, but they kept coming and coming. Artair moved faster and faster, spinning from one to the next, his arms moving through a complicated series of strikes that Lucian could barely follow; it was all he could do to keep forming the portals, one after the other, until he began to feel dizzy. At one point they caught sight of Fleet, his teeth buried in the robe of one child, and together they reached out for the cub and sent him through a portal too.

Where's Elver?

Lucian looked and spotted the monster girl in the midst of her own crowd of children. There were around a dozen on the floor around her, unconscious or dead, he couldn't say. Her eyes were wide with panic, and the snakes on her head were weaving and spitting with distress. He saw a dagger cut through the air too close to her throat.

'Gods damn it all!' He lunged towards a portal that had just appeared, meaning to siphon Maura's magic through it if he could, but it vanished before he could reach it. Instead, he brought himself too close to the boy who had just appeared, and the dagger slashed at the top of his thigh, tearing open the fabric of his trousers and slicing a shallow cut in his leg. The pain flared, and then vanished.

In this moment, in this place, we are safe.

'What are you talking about?'

Lucian went back to concentrating on the portal magic. While all these daggers were flying about, he could barely think about anything else. Meanwhile, the number of children appearing in the wood was increasing, and somewhere above them, Maura was laughing. An old, dark hatred rose up in him.

How many of these children will she send against us? asked Artair.

'As many as it takes,' Lucian grunted. 'She'd see them all die to get what she wants. Get me closer to one of these portals. If I'm next to it for long enough, I can take her power. Weaken her.'

Artair moved them even faster, his breathing still slow and calm despite the exertion and the danger, but Lucian thought he could feel their body tiring, all the same. Another child managed to get close, but the edge of their dagger slipped across their tunic, tumbling to the ground. A portal flared into life only an arm's length away, and they both leapt for it.

Quick!

Lucian reached for the magic, felt his fingers brush the outer edges of the power, and something pierced his lower back. For a moment the pain was so terrible, so overwhelming, that he couldn't move at all. The power flickered away, and he felt Artair struggling to contain the agony of what had just happened.

In this moment, in this . . . Ah, it's too much. In this moment . . . this place . . .

The world turned grey.

'What . . . what is happening . . .?'

The trees around them shivered, as insubstantial as a reflection in a pond. Initially, Lucian took this to be the result of blood loss – the pain was such that he felt close to passing out – but when he looked up, it was to see a tall, dark shape standing over them. A long beak the colour of bone poked from a deeply hooded cowl.

'I promised my aid,' said the Hooded Crow. 'So I grant you a single boon.'

Some of the strength had left their legs. Distantly, Lucian was aware of blood soaking their shirt, but his eye was caught by a more extraordinary sight: all around them, the world had stopped moving. The children advancing out of the dark were stilled, their glazed eyes trained on them but unmoving. Even Elver, half glimpsed through a crowd of young assassins, was as still as a statue out of myth, her snake-garlanded head caught mid hiss, although there was a golden aura flickering around her, suggesting this magic would not hold her for long.

'What have you done?'

'This is only the briefest pause, I'm afraid. You have been mortally wounded, Lucian and Artair. Your fate is inevitable. But I will not take what is due to me just yet. I will give you enough time to do what needs to be done.' The Hooded Crow paused. 'The Mother must pay for her transgression, child of the claw.'

Deep in the hood, Lucian caught a glimpse of an eye, black and wet.

'What do you mean?'

'Time enough,' the Hooded Crow said again. 'That is all I can give you. Use it wisely, and quickly.'

With that, the old god vanished and the world leapt into motion again. The pain of the wound surged back too, and Artair reached round and pulled the dagger free from their back. For a second, Lucian was sure they would both pass out, but Artair took a deep breath.

In this moment, in this place, we are safe.

The pain faded, held within the monk's resolve.

'Thank you,' said Lucian, and he found he truly meant it.

What do we do?

As they spoke, their arms were moving again; portals opened and children vanished, and still they came on and on. He knew that Artair was thinking the same thing he was: they were dying. The monk's sorrow was a chill wind moving through both their souls, but the knowledge only made Lucian angry. After all this time, Maura had got him. And Artair would pay the price too, when as far as Lucian could tell he had done nothing wrong.

'Like the old bird said, we do what needs to be done – end Maura, and save Elver. I have an idea, although I will be honest with you, monk, it's a terrible one.' He paused, glancing around the scrum. 'Speaking of which, where *is* Elver?'

CHAPTER 41

This was a nightmare.

Everywhere she looked, children were stumbling towards her out of the dark, blades flashing, their eyes somehow both lifeless and intent. Two or three had got close enough to strike her, but the golden scales had turned their knives aside; her problem was being swarmed by them, when all she could do was risk touching them and hope it was a brief enough contact that they would only pass out.

She shoved a few of them away, but even that was risky with her new strength. Fleet had positioned himself at her feet and was snarling and nipping at those that came close; none of the children, however, had the natural fear of an angry monster that they should. Maura had to be controlling them, some kind of godly version of the magic she had used on Elver all those years ago. She remembered reaching the top of the Tumble Stone – the mage had grasped her wrist and all her strength had fled from her in that moment.

'Fleet!' The cub had hold of one of the children's ankles and was trying to drag them away. 'Don't hurt them.'

They started it! Fleet sounded outraged. *It is forbidden for one pack to attack another. They use their claws and I bite them!*

'They don't know what they are doing, Fleet.'

On the other side of the small clearing, she could see Lucian, and from the way he was moving she knew that Artair was with him. They were knocking children back through new portals, although it was like trying to hold back a flood with a single bucket. As fast as they worked, more possessed children appeared. There was a wink of red fire and Fleet himself vanished through a portal, out of harm's way, but, before she could even register the relief of that, one of the children got too close and a dagger sailed through the air inches from her neck. Elver drew away rapidly and the girl, who looked to be around twelve years old, stumbled to the ground. When the crowd of children briefly parted, she looked up again only to see one of the small assassins strike Artair across the leg, drawing blood. Something shifted inside her.

I am the poison child, she thought. *I have the heart of a god, and it's in my power to end this. I haven't finished changing yet.*

She could see the potential within herself still, a further level of monstrousness that hadn't yet been breached. Elver reached out for it, and it reached back eagerly. There was a sensation of expansion and relief, like having a good long stretch, and she felt two wings unfurl from her back. She glanced at them long enough to see that they were golden webbed things, not unlike the wings of the moth-bat she had met weeks ago, and then she put them to use. The children surrounding her were thrown back by the force of them, and in seconds she was flying up through the canopy, branches and leaves whipping against her skin and clothes, and then out, into the dark above the trees. What she saw there made her pause.

Mother Maura hung in space, her bone-white hair cascading down her back and beyond her feet, like a cloak. Her face looked sharper than it had done when she was a mortal, the bones more prominent, and she was muttering something under her breath, her eyes trained on the ground below them. All around her there was an aura of magic, a white glow threaded with fiery red that flickered and surged; Elver was put in mind of a guttering candle. Every now and then Maura would twitch violently, and grin, and Elver realized that their old enemy was very close to completely losing her mind.

'Maura.' Elver let herself hang in the air, wings beating to keep herself aloft. It was remarkably easy, as though she'd been waiting all her life to fly.

The Mother's head snapped up and a wide smile split her face. 'Is that you, Elver? Time has not been kind, I see.'

'I could say the same about you.' She raised her voice. 'There are kids down there in harm's way. They're from your temples, right? Kids with no one to look out for them, and you're willing to throw their lives away. Just like you did with me. And you've the cheek to call yourself Mother.'

'Yes. Tell me, poison child, how many have you killed yourself? How many have you burned and poisoned? All in the name of love.' Maura laughed. 'Although, how does that boy feel now that you've got scales and snakes for hair? I imagine he's no longer so keen.'

'You're a monster.'

'Have you looked in the mirror lately, child?'

Elver lunged forward, her wings carrying her like an arrow. She wanted to get her hands on Maura's exposed skin, but the older woman threw up a shield of white and red light, and when Elver struck it she felt her whole body jerk with pain. She turned and leapt, moving with ease thanks to her new wings, but the shield just reappeared, and this time Maura put force behind the blow, throwing her back. Elver tumbled for a few seconds, her body alight with pain.

'Get away from me, you little shit.' All of the brittle humour had dropped from the older woman's face. Now she looked furious, two hectic points of colour high on her cheeks. Her eyes looked glassy, and there was spittle on her thin lips. It occurred to Elver that all this magic was costing Maura greatly. 'Don't you *touch* me, filthy monster.'

'Tisk said that you could have asked the Queen of Serpents to bring your children back.' Elver was breathing hard, still reeling from the pain. 'But you couldn't do it, could you? Couldn't risk what they might be. How much do you really love them, Maura? Or do you just love the idea of them? The idea of being a mother?' She pointed to the clearing below them. She could hear Fleet barking. 'You don't care about children at all. You never have. You are a *terrible* mother.'

Maura flew at her, screaming, her white hair streaming behind her like the tail of a comet. Elver had barely a second before the god was on her, the shield of white and red light having transformed into a huge grasping hand with long hooked claws. It caught hold of her and squeezed, passing an electric pain through her body. There wasn't even breath enough to scream. Instead, Elver passed all her strength to her wings, willing them to open and push the hand apart. It didn't budge.

'Get . . . off.'

'Oh no.' Maura's face was very close. Elver could feel the heat coming off her, could smell the rank scent of madness. 'I am going to show you a mother's love, my poor little orphan.'

The giant hand of magic squeezed. Elver gasped, still trying to push against it with her new wings, but she could feel her bones being ground against each other. The air in her lungs was being crushed out of her.

No. It can't end here, after all this. I've changed so much.

Her arms were pinned at her sides, and one of her hands was pressed against her pocket. Through the material, pressed against her palm, she could feel the conker she had taken from trees around Sunay's cottage, all that time ago. It had shrunk in the way that conkers did, and lost its shininess, but she'd never quite been able to throw it away. It had been her link to her home, a reminder that the Jih Forest was something she carried with her: in her pocket, and in her heart. She thought of Tython sitting alone in his sanctum, a conker sitting on top of a pile of books.

At least he's free now, she thought. *He'll grow and change and see the world, just like I did.*

The heart of the serpent queen pulsed in her chest, full of bright anger and curiosity.

And I haven't finished growing yet, either.

The last shreds of her human self protested weakly. She knew that to change again would be to leave that behind entirely; she'd never be able to walk the human world again – not without causing a lot of trouble, at least. But this was who she'd always been, she realized. When Lucian had picked her out from the other orphans to be sacrificed, he had said she was bold, and clever, and full of the need to fight. He'd said she had the potential to do something great with her life, and he'd been right. All that potential was still in her, waiting to turn into something extraordinary. She just had to let her form catch up with it.

The change, when it came, was as easy as shrugging off a cloak. Quite suddenly, she was bigger than the hand that held her, and the fingers split apart. Maura gave a choked cry and fell back, the corona of power that surrounded her flickering and dipping. Elver rose up and spread her wings.

'What are you?' Maura's voice was barely more than a whisper, but Elver heard it well enough.

'I am a god,' said Elver. Everything human about her form had left her. She wasn't quite the Queen of Serpents, despite the golden scales and the long head; she had arms and legs, a long tail, and wings sprouting from her back. The horns on her head marched down a long, flexible neck, and in her mouth she could feel rows and rows of lethal fangs. 'I am the Ever-Changing Dragon, Maura. It's time for all this to end. Or become something else.'

From deep within her chest, Elver felt a boiling heat come rushing up her throat, and when she opened her mouth a gout of bright green flame shot across the space between them, lighting up the night with an emerald glow. Maura threw up her shield of power just in time and the green flames curled across it, peeling harmlessly away into nothing. Elver flew up into the sky above the woman, and threw more fire down on her, but Maura flung up her shield again.

'I've got him!' Maura shrieked suddenly. 'One of my children has done as asked and stuck a knife in that duplicitous little shit. The power will all be mine soon, and it doesn't matter what you claim to be!'

A cold hand clutched at Elver's heart, but there was no time. More green fire boiled out of her, lighting up the canopy below as bright as a summer's day. Maura deflected it again, her power now being thrown entirely into escaping Elver's attacks. If Lucian and Artair had been badly hurt, it could mean that Maura was about to grow a lot more powerful. Despite everything, they could still fail.

And then, just above Maura, a new portal flared into life. Elver had a second to wonder if Maura was about to start throwing children at them from the sky, when Lucian dropped through the portal, his arms spread. In that brief second Elver recognized both Lucian's anger and Artair's determination in his face, and then he landed directly on Maura, avoiding the shield that was aimed at her. The Mother shrieked again, attempting to throw him off, but already the power was leaving her and streaming to him, a boiling line of red fire. After a handful of seconds, the shield that had been hovering in place flickered and went out.

Lucian and Artair let go, and dropped back into the canopy. Elver heard them crashing through the branches, her heart in her mouth.

'No!' Maura grasped at her own throat, as though trying to keep in what had already escaped. In that second, she looked so much older, almost skeletal, her green eyes sinking into her head. Elver felt a stirring of something almost like pity.

And then she opened her jaws and blasted the woman from the sky.

CHAPTER 42

When Artair opened his eyes, the sight that met him wasn't the dark crowded forest full of murderous children. He was standing on a bleak shoreline of grey sand, a sea the colour of sadness stretching away towards the horizon. A bone-coloured sun hung in the sky, giving off no warmth. There were objects in the sea, strange ones, but his attention went to the young man standing next to him – Lucian, his pale face sharp in the dull light – and Elver, who was no longer a golden dragon, yet still had serpents for hair. Around ten feet away, lying on the sand, was Maura. She was dragging herself to her feet, although she no longer looked like a god; she barely looked like a living thing.

'Attend me!' she screamed. 'Attend me, brother and sister gods!' She appeared to be addressing the objects in the sea.

Elver glanced at the old woman once and then seemed to dismiss her, turning instead to them. They stood together, the three of them, for the first time. Artair grasped Lucian's arm, and then Elver's. After a moment, they both did the same, and Elver laughed.

'You're all right,' she said, her snakes weaving and bobbing.

'Well –' Lucian glanced at Artair, a rueful expression on his face that was tinged with sorrow – 'not quite.'

Artair realized that they were dressed identically, and both their shirts were soaked with blood.

'Elver,' Artair said quickly, 'whatever happens, it's okay. We defeated Maura. This has been the best time of my life, knowing the both of you . . .'

'What are you talking about? You're here.' She squeezed his arm; he saw her squeeze Lucian's. 'You're both here. You're fine.'

Maura was on her feet, although she was staggering. She screamed again, her voice breaking.

'You will attend me, or so help me . . .'

Figures began walking out of the sea. Some of them were difficult to look at, their forms too strange or too shifting. Artair saw a cloud of floating wolf heads, their jaws hanging open and ready to snap. He saw a woman with blue skin and three heads, her long dark hair braided with silver. He recognized Tisk in his human form, and Barleycorn, and Milik the Small. There were others too, although he didn't see the Hooded Crow there, a fact that gave him a crumb of hope.

'What do you want, Mother?' asked Tisk when his boots met the sand. He was twirling his walking stick and, although his tone was light, there was a mixture of triumph and cruelty on his foxy face that was frightening to behold. 'You've no business here any more.'

'I am one of you.' Maura was breathing hard, her bony chest rising and falling. She appeared to be growing more skeletal by the moment, her heavily embroidered dress hanging on her like a shroud. This, Artair supposed, was the result of Lucian absorbing her power and Elver's terrible flames. 'I am one of the Twelve. You have to help me.' She raised her arm and pointed a twig-like finger at the three of them. 'What does it say of the gods if they allow a bunch of children to murder one of their own? Are the gods so weak they can be thrown down by mortals such as these? Restore me. Restore the sanctity of the Twelve.'

'Sanctity?' This was Milik the Small. Her mousy form looked especially incongruous amongst all the mighty figures, but she radiated a kind of quiet power all the same. 'You know nothing of that. Wasn't it you who threw down our brother? Wasn't it you who broke all our rules?'

'And now you crawl to us for favours,' Barleycorn laughed. 'Know when you are beaten, Mother.'

'My small sister has a good point,' said Tisk. 'You decided our rules were not for you, isn't that right? You attacked mortals directly, you possessed them. And now you come back asking to be restored, as though you were truly one of us? Oh no, Maura. Whether it's the god you serve as a mage, or the rules you obey as a god – *you cannot pick and choose.*'

'So you'll strike me down yourselves?' Maura bared her teeth at them. Her skin was so thin now that Artair wasn't sure if it were a grin or a grimace. 'Isn't that breaking your own rules?'

The god with the many heads and arms stepped up onto the sand. She looked a little like the carving that had sat atop the inn where they had rested once, and Artair had to assume this was Enos, god of sleep and dreams. Her three heads smiled grimly and one arm gestured to a spot in the sky over their heads. Artair was surprised to see the moon appear there, a solemn white disc, looking washed out and strange in that colourless sky.

'No, no,' said Enos. 'Luckily, in this instance, we don't have to do our own dirty work.'

The moon shimmered, and suddenly it wasn't a moon – it was a hole – and small white shapes were climbing out of it and dropping to the sand. They were laughing, the cheerful high-pitched laughter of children.

Maura began to scream.

The ghostly children fell on her, little hands and mouths grasping and tearing. Very quickly, Maura was overwhelmed, falling down onto the sand and becoming lost underneath them all. Artair lost sight of her, and she stopped screaming, and then it was all over. The ghostly children drifted away like smoke, and there was nothing left of the half-god who had chased them across Tlevrae.

'Well, I don't know what she was expecting,' said Tisk. 'As you said, Elver, she was a *terrible* Mother. What of you, poison child? You're a god now, and a true one, elected and blessed by the Queen of Serpents. See?'

He pointed to the grey waters, and standing in the waves there was a small golden tree that hadn't been there a moment before. There were spiky golden casings growing in the branches. The other gods, Artair realized, were drifting away, heading back to the other objects in the surf and vanishing. Clearly, they were done with this business. Only Tisk remained, his sharp eyes glinting with amusement.

'What will you do, Ever-Changing Dragon?' he asked her.

Elver glared back at him steadily. 'What did you do with Sunay?'

Tisk laughed and made a dismissive gesture with his free hand. 'That's what you're worried about? She is absolutely fine. I asked a favour of Barleycorn and popped her back in the Inn at the End of All Worlds, since she was so taken with it. You know, Elver, now that you are a god, you'll have to let go of these ties to the living. Speaking of which . . .'

A tall, hooded figure stepped out of the surf. Next to him, Artair heard Lucian sigh. It seemed he had been hoping the Hooded Crow had forgotten about them too.

'Brother,' said Tisk. 'You missed the family reunion. And it's so rare for us all to be in one place these days.'

'No one wants me at gatherings,' said the Hooded Crow. 'I spoil the mood.'

'What's going on?' Elver stepped up to face them both, her snakes agitated. 'It's all done with now. *You* don't have to be here, crow.'

'I'm afraid I do, sister.' It was hard to tell, given his face was little more than a long bony beak, but Artair sensed he was looking at

Elver with kindness. 'I gave your friends a boon, but the span of its influence is over, and it is time for them to go.'

Elver spun on them both, fury and panic making her eyes wide.

'What is he talking about?'

'One of Maura's little assassins got us,' said Lucian. He was smiling faintly, as though he'd always expected it to come to this. 'The Hooded Crow granted us enough time to help you, but that's it.'

'No.' Her skin might be golden and her hair might be snakes, but Artair found he very much recognized the stubborn line that appeared on her forehead. She was getting angry.

'We're dying, Elver,' he said gently. 'Or, I suppose, we died already.' Looking at where they were, he thought that was likely.

'And I have come to shepherd their souls onwards,' added the Hooded Crow.

'*No,*' she said again, a dangerous glint in her eye. Artair had the idea they were about to see the dragon again. She pointed at Lucian. 'He has the power of the Bloody Claw. That must mean something. It means you can't take them, at least.'

The Hooded Crow shook his head slowly. 'They took the fatal wound before they absorbed the rest of the Bloody Claw's power, I'm afraid. They should have died then and there on the forest floor. It was only my boon that kept them from my realm for a time, but the reality is they are already dead.'

'I will fight you,' said Elver. The air around her shimmered with gold, as though she were about to transform. 'I will *make* you leave them.'

'Ever-Changing Dragon, please.' There was a note of genuine sorrow in the Hooded Crow's voice. 'You cannot fight me. I am death itself, child.'

'I could change them . . .'

'They are already jih,' said Tisk. Even he sounded regretful. 'You cannot change them more than they have already been changed.'

'But I have! I've been changed!'

'Elver.' Artair put his hand on her shoulder. 'It's alright.' When she turned to him, he gathered her into his arms. 'We knew that this was coming. I meant what I said: this has been the best time of my life.' She squeezed him back fiercely, then let go. There were tears in her eyes.

Lucian stepped forward with one hand held out, almost as though he were formally asking her for a dance. When she hung her head, he took her hand and kissed it.

'It's certainly been interesting, monster girl,' he said. 'I know I have been a source of trouble for you for some time, but still I dare to hope that you might miss me.'

'I can't lose you both. I can't.'

When Lucian held her, Artair put his arms around them both. He knew that he loved Elver and he wasn't surprised at the sorrow he felt at leaving her. He was, however, surprised at his own sadness at Lucian's loss too. Despite everything, Lucian was perhaps the person to whom he had been closest – no one else had ever shared his body and his mind, had seen his past and the landscape of his dreams.

'I love you,' said Elver.

Tisk cleared his throat. 'You know, she has a point, brother.' When Artair looked up, he saw that the god of lies was stroking his little carroty beard in a thoughtful manner. 'There's one body. Perhaps you only need to take one soul? Taking two seems greedy, and I never thought of you as such.'

The Hooded Crow looked mildly put out.

'Tisk, you know that one of these souls has been evading me for years . . .'

'Oh, what does that *really* matter? I know that there's a heart underneath that cowl somewhere.'

Artair felt his own heart turn over in his chest. Now that the moment was upon him, a terrible cold sorrow was filling him up like icy river water. He didn't want to go. There was so much of Tlevrae he hadn't seen, so many people he had never met. If he had lived, he could have travelled south, perhaps; he could have tried to find what was left of his people in the land of the long grasses. He could have gone to the coast Sunay had told him about, where the people ate fried potatoes out of paper bags; he could have walked the Jih Forest again, unafraid this time. He loved Elver, and hadn't told her.

'Very well,' said the Hooded Crow. He gestured to the sand next to him, and a hole opened up in the ground. Through it, Artair could see a land of endless hawthorn trees, the sky busy with birds. 'Which of you is it to be? You need only step forward. The way is open for you.'

'What do you mean?' asked Elver.

The Hooded Crow sighed. 'I will take only one soul. Consider it a welcoming gift for my new sister.'

Artair was startled to find Lucian suddenly standing very close, his hand wrapped round the top of his arm. When Lucian spoke into his ear, he could hear laughter in his voice.

'I'm sorry, monk,' he said. 'This is just the way it has to be.'

EPILOGUE

Three months later

'Now you aim at mine and try to hit it. As hard as you can. You want to try to break it.'

Tython leaned forward, one eye closed, the tip of his tongue poking out of the corner of his mouth. He held the end of the string, and in his other hand the conker. Elver watched him with amusement. He was concentrating fiercely, with the same quiet intensity he brought to everything. When he swung the conker, it missed.

'This is harder than it looks,' he said.

They were sitting in the Jih Forest, the finery of spring all around them. It had been hard to find new conkers at this time of the year, but Elver had simply encouraged a horse chestnut tree to give up its wares early, and now they each had a little pile. When it was her turn, she gave Tython's conker the lightest tap, being careful not to obliterate it. Getting used to the strength of a god had taken some time.

'You're good at this!' His simple pleasure in her success reminded her of Artair, which caused a pang of sadness. She decided to distract herself from it.

'How are you finding the world?' she asked. 'Where have you been since I saw you last?'

'I have been all over,' said Tython, lining up his next shot. 'I've been to the mountains, and the sea. I've walked through the hills. I saw them tearing down temples.' His red eyes darted towards her. 'The ones for the false god you threw down. And some of my father's too, although I heard people say that the Faceless priests are trying to keep them open. I haven't seen any temples for our mother at all.'

'No,' said Elver, smiling faintly. 'She wasn't really the temple type. Did you speak to any of the humans you saw, Tython?'

This time he hit her conker, sending it whizzing around on its string. They grinned at each other.

'I didn't,' he said eventually. 'I hid from them, and watched. I think they'll be frightened of me.'

'Probably.' Elver shrugged. 'But now Trilot is gone, I think that might start to change. I intend to make it change. Humans have nothing to fear from jih.'

They played for much of the afternoon, laughing and working their way through the conkers. Occasionally, they would be visited by a jih spirit wandering through. The monsters of the forest had been alarmed by the loss of the Queen of Serpents, and initially confused by Elver's new form, but ultimately had accepted that she occupied the queen's role now, and to them she hadn't changed all that much; she just looked a bit more like them.

At one point, Fleet came by, running with his siblings. He was a touch bigger than the rest of them, and they were shy, hanging back just beyond the trees while he trotted up to her directly, eyes flashing.

I am teaching them to hunt, he explained. *They are bad at it. But eventually they might get better, if they watch me all the time.*

'Will you see the Pack again, Fleet?' asked Elver. 'It seemed like you enjoyed your time with them. Like you found a purpose, or something.'

Fleet sniffed. *The Pack are good, but I do not think so. I serve a more important god, because I am very important.*

'Is it me? Are you talking about me?' She reached down and gathered the cub into her arms, burying her face in his feathers. Tython laughed. 'Do you serve the Ever-Changing Dragon, Fleet? Are you a good boy?'

Fleet scrambled to get down, casting looks at the trees where his siblings were hiding. *Get off. Your snakes are getting tangled. Get off.* When she put him down, though, he jumped around in a circle as if he were a very young cub again. *I am the Ever-Changing Dragon's chief hunter!* he shouted, before running back into the wood.

Eventually, Tython got up to leave. He'd decided he was travelling to the south of the Jih Forest, to the place where the trees gave way to wide, endless plains of grass. It pained him to leave behind the trees, he told her, but there had to be interesting things to see in all that grass. Elver made him promise to tell her all about it when he next passed by the Jih Forest, and he agreed, although she sensed his mind was already on his future travels. She remembered how she'd felt when she'd left the forest for the first time since becoming jih, looking out on the long white road that led down to Addersport, seeing a tiny figure in the distance that she had to chase. The world beyond the forest had seemed dangerous, unfair and full of cruelty, while the trees held everything that was dear to her. It was fair to say she had been less than enthusiastic. But she had done it, and everything had changed.

'Are you going to see him today?' asked Tython before he left.

'Oh . . . maybe.' She shrugged, not quite meeting his eye. 'I've got a lot to do this afternoon . . .'

'Say hello to him for me,' said Tython, grinning. 'Tell him I said hello.'

There was a small pool of spring water at the monastery, and technically Elver could simply appear there, travelling through the connection she felt to all ponds, lakes, seas and rivers. But for some reason she preferred to walk up the mountain path, letting it lead her out of the trees and into the higher, colder places. The colours of spring were vivid in the trees and bushes, and the air clamoured with birdsong and the shrill calls of tiny frogs, all new to the world. White clouds floated in the vast blue bowl of the sky, like petals in a pond. When she reached the gates, she found them standing open – as they always were, these days – and the first thing she saw was a group of small children sitting on the grass, all watching attentively as Sunay made a silver coin dance across her knuckles. Sunay spotted her immediately. The mage turned the coin into a mouse, which she gave to the nearest child, before coming over to Elver. Her fox tail still swished from side to side.

'It's good to see you, Sunay.' The children peered at Elver curiously. They'd got used to her strange appearance very quickly and, from what Sunay told her, none of them remembered very clearly the fight in the wood, or even their time at Maura's temples.

'Always pleased to see those snakes waving at me as they come through the gate,' said Sunay warmly. 'He's up in the dorms, by the way.'

Elver felt her cheeks grow warm. 'Maybe I am here to see you. Did you think of that?'

'Give over,' Sunay scoffed. 'You forget how good I am at spotting a lie. Get out of here.'

The hallways of the monastery were bright and full of the scent of the mountains, all the shutters thrown open, and here and there she spotted evidence of the new occupants: a toy horse left on a windowsill, a paintbrush staining a sheet of paper, sticky sweet wrappers under a table. When she found him, he was in one of the long rooms full of small beds, his arms full of fresh laundry.

'Artair,' she said.

He dropped the sheets.

Some time later, when they had finished kissing, they sat on one of the small beds together. Artair held her hand in his, absently stroking her palm with his fingers.

'They can have their own rooms if they want them,' he was saying. 'But most of them prefer to be in here. They never have to be alone, if they don't want to be.' A shadow seemed to pass over his face, and she knew he was remembering all the mornings he woke up locked inside his own small cell. 'A few of them have the odd nightmare still. I think deep down part of them does remember that night in the wood, and some of it comes back when they dream. But I'm always here if they need me. I give them sandwiches and kopi when they can't sleep.'

Elver laughed. 'How does that help?'

He smiled at her. 'It makes them happy.'

'What about the acolytes?'

His face grew more serious again. When Artair had arrived back at the monastery, most of the novices they had saved from Prideful Leap had left, disappearing back out into the world. The ones who had remained were still frightened, and it took some time for Artair to convince them of the true nature of the Sleepless. Knowing what they were didn't entirely solve the problem, of course, but it was a start – he had spoken to their 'other' spirits too, and some bridges had been built between them. A few had stayed to make the monastery fit for Maura's orphans.

'They're doing well, I think. We have been writing letters to Addersport, and other towns, telling them what the Sleepless really are. It might make a difference.' He paused, and cleared his throat. His cheeks had turned a little pink. 'Reah asked me the other day if

I would go walking with her down to the river. I thought she meant to go fishing or something, but . . . that's not what she meant.' He rubbed the back of his neck with his free hand. 'She said she didn't believe that I was really in a relationship with a god. I told her that I love you. I love you, Elver.'

She smiled. He said that a lot these days, as though making up for not saying it sooner. 'Then come with me, Artair. There's so much of the world still to see. Let's go and look at it, together.'

'We will,' he said gently. 'I just want to make sure these children are settled. They've had no one else to look out for them for such a long time. And I want to make this a different sort of place.'

She squeezed his hand. 'A place where the gates are always open.'

'Yes,' he agreed. 'And one day, soon, I'll walk back out of them again.'

Tisk the god of lies and tricks waited in the midst of a storm of hawthorn trees. There were crows in the distance somewhere, making a racket, but the spot he had chosen was quiet, and he heard the young man coming long before he saw him. He walked with a confidence and an impatience that amused Tisk. Only a soul such as this could be impatient in the realm of the god of death.

'Do you have it?'

Lucian Prideson startled a little, but he did his best to hide it. He looked much as he had done in life: the same sharp cheekbones, the same hazel eyes. With a flourish, he took something from his pocket and held it out to the fox.

'Will this do?' asked Lucian. 'There's very little in that castle of his, you know. I can hardly drag out one of those giant bone statues under my tunic. I'm fairly sure he'd notice.'

The object in his hand was a cat's skull, its eye sockets filled with teeming lilac light. Tisk had no idea what its purpose was, but then that hardly mattered. It belonged to the Hooded Crow – that was all he needed to know. Tisk turned into his human form and took the skull from Lucian's palm, nodding his thanks.

'It will do,' said Tisk. 'Although I am less than sure about this deal. You are not even my mage. I'm not quite sure *what* you are, Lucian Prideson, with the Bloody Claw's power churning around inside you.' He sniffed. 'You can't go back, you realize. If there is one thing that is truly beyond me, it is turning back the magic of the god of death.'

'I know that,' said Lucian, a touch too casually. 'I'm done with that world. But there are other places I could see. I caught a glimpse of them at the Inn at the End of All Worlds. In those places, anything is possible, right?'

Tisk snorted. He had to admire the mortal's gumption. 'Very well. You're not going back, but you're going *somewhere*.' He paused. 'Are you sure about this? It will annoy my brother greatly, and it isn't wise to antagonize the god of death.'

'Oh yes.' Lucian grinned. 'I've not finished causing trouble just yet.'

ACKNOWLEDGEMENTS

As the Sleepless duology draws to a close, it is time to thank all the people who helped to sing this particular spell into being. Thanks to my wonderful editors, Emma Jones in the UK and Sara Goodman in the US, who knew how to make *The Dreamless* into the ending these characters deserved. Special thanks as ever to my agent and friend Juliet Mushens, the human whirlwind of energy and belief that makes all things possible.

The usual rogue's gallery kept me mostly sane throughout the writing process. Gratitude must go to Andrew Reid and Den Patrick-Mushens for the weekly Monday podcasts – sometimes you just need to hear your chums chatting nonsense for fifteen minutes, you know? Thanks also to Adam Christopher and Michaela Ellis for continued support and spirited bitching, and more generally to my family for occasionally feeding me a roast dinner whenever I wander back to London. Parades and giant inflatable cartoon characters please in honour of my dearest and oldest friend Jenni, whose fortnightly discord chats have been a real highlight of the last couple of years.

Lastly, the biggest and probably soppiest thank you (picture me with hearts in my eyes as I type this) goes to Peter Newman, who I am now thrilled to call my fiancé. Not only am I fortunate enough to be madly in love while I write these books about love, I also get to live with (and learn from) an extraordinary writer. What a lucky little goblin I am.

ABOUT THE AUTHOR

Jen Williams is a writer from London currently living in Bristol. A fan of witches and dark folklore from an early age, these days she writes character-driven fantasy novels with plenty of banter and magic, as well as horror-tinged crime thrillers with strong female leads. She was nominated for Best Newcomer in the British Fantasy Awards and her books *The Ninth Rain* and *The Bitter Twins* both went on to win Best Fantasy Novel, which she won again in 2024 for *Talonsister*. *The Sleepless* was her first novel for YA readers.